To Craig –
May these futures
not come true.
Shayne

VANISHING ACTS

VANISHING ACTS

A SCIENCE FICTION ANTHOLOGY

Edited by

ELLEN DATLOW

TOR®

A TOM DOHERTY ASSOCIATES BOOK / NEW YORK

VANISHING ACTS

A Tor Book
Published by Tom Doherty Associates, LLC
175 Fifth Avenue
New York, NY 10010

www.tor.com

Tor® is a registered trademark of Tom Doherty Associates, LLC.

Design by Lisa Pifher

Library of Congress Cataloging-in-Publication Data

Vanishing acts : a science fiction anthology / edited by Ellen Datlow.—1st ed.
    p.   cm.
    "A Tom Doherty Associates book."
    ISBN 0-312-86962-2
    1. Science fiction, American. I. Datlow, Ellen.

  PS648.S3 V365 2000
  813'.0876208—dc21

                            00-026512

First Edition: June 2000

Printed in the United States of America

0 9 8 7 6 5 4 3 2 1

To my friends in Albuquerque, who lit the fire

CONTENTS

ACKNOWLEDGMENTS

I'd like to thank David Hartwell and Jim Minz
for being behind this book.

INTRODUCTION

Several of the anthologies I've edited have had their origins during conversations with friends about overlooked stories—stories that we felt should have attracted more attention upon their first publication or that deserved reprinting. *Vanishing Acts* began that way. A few years ago, while in Albuquerque, New Mexico, some friends and I were discussing Suzy McKee Charnas's work and I mentioned one of my favorite of her stories, "Listening to Brahms"— originally published in *Omni* and a subsequent Nebula nominee, but rarely reprinted. The story is about a lizard race that takes in the few survivors of the late great planet Earth and how those humans influence an entire culture. It's also about the healing power of music. It is one of very few stories that gives me a lump in my throat no matter how many times I read it. It prompted me to bring up two other stories I consider underappreciated classics— Bruce McAllister's "The Girl Who Loved Animals," about a woman who chooses to act as birth mother for an embryo of an endangered species and the emotions and ethical considerations this selfless act engenders. The other was Avram Davidson's "Now Let Us Sleep," about the last natives of a colonized planet. I decided then and there that I wanted to create a mostly original anthology that would emanate from these three stories. As I was unaware of any other recent science fiction anthology with the theme of endangered species, I hoped the theme would spark author enthusiasm—it did.

One might assume that an anthology about extinction would be depressing. Of course, some of the stories are heartbreaking and some are downbeat but there are also healthy doses of exuberance, adventure, and even twinges of humor in this book. I hope that the stories, rather than creating a feeling of hopelessness in the reader, will instead stir a sense of anger and indignation and responsibility. And even more, perhaps spur at least a few readers into doing something to prevent endangered species from becoming extinct species like some of those in this book.

I find polemic in fiction boring. The stories that most influence are the gentle persuaders. I don't mean gentle stories, but those that are so engrossing and well-told that the reader doesn't realize they've been poleaxed until after the story is done. I've tried to present a variety of stories; most are science fiction, but each goes at the subject from different angles, different tones, different points of view. Some are not meant to be taken seriously. You'll know them when you read them.

The range of species written about by the contributors runs the gamut from insects and buffalo and humans to aliens and plants and creatures that have never existed in our universe—and imaginary genetically-engineered creatures that perhaps shouldn't.

For information contact: The Endangered Species Coalition, http://www.stopextinction.org or write to: esc@stopextinction.org or 1101 14th Street, NW, Suite 1200, Washington, D.C. 20005. (202) 682-9400, fax: (202) 682-1331

Suzy McKee Charnas, a born and bred New Yorker, has lived with her husband in New Mexico for the past thirty years. She has taught high school and university classes and still gladly does teaching or speaking engagements in the areas of writing and SF. Her first novel, *Walk to the End of the World* (1974), was a John W. Campbell Award finalist. *The Conqueror's Child*, the fourth book of the series begun with *Walk*, completed that extensive fiction project in 1999. Various SF and fantasy books and stories have won her the Hugo Award, the Nebula Award, and the Mythopoeic Society's Award for young-adult fantasy. She ventured into theater by turning her prize-winning novella "Unicorn Tapestry" into a play, first staged at the Magic Theatre in San Francisco in 1991. She has recently revised the lyrics and written several new songs for the musical *Nosferatu*, by British composer Bernard J. Taylor.

She says of "Listening to Brahms" that "this is the only story I have written that was first told to me in a dream on the sunny terrace of a seaside restaurant by a human-sized lizard sitting across the table from me. I did not remember a word this creature had said when I woke up, but a few days later I sat down and wrote this story in a sustained burst of clear energy. The original germ of 'Brahms' had been a scrap of conversation overheard at a concert in Santa Fe; unable to come up with the fictional context that I knew lurked behind this brief dialog, I had written down the lines and stuck them in a drawer to ripen. It was months later that the lizard-person narrated the story itself to me in my sleep. I do not know what all this means with regard to a) the creative process, b) astral travel to alien planets and/or restaurants, or c) the actual future of the human species. Maybe when you've read the story, you can tell me."

LISTENING TO BRAHMS

Suzy McKee Charnas

Entry 1: They had already woken up Chandler and Ross. They did me third. I was supposed to be up first so I could check the data on the rest of our crew during their cold sleep, but how would a bunch of aliens know that?

Our ship is full of creatures with peculiar eyes and wrinkled skin covered with tiny scales, a lot like lizards walking around on their hind legs. Their skins are grayish or greenish or even bluish sometimes. They have naked-looking faces—no hair—with features that seem polished smooth. The first ones I met had wigs on, and they wore evening clothes and watered-silk sashes with medals. I was too numb-brained to laugh, and now I don't feel like it. They all switched to jumpsuits once the formalities were over. I keep waiting for them to unzip their jumpsuits and then their lizard suits and climb out, regular human beings. I keep waiting for the joke to be over.

They speak English, some with accents, some not. They have breathy voices and talk very softly to us. That may be because of what they have to say. They say Earth burned itself up, which is why we never got our wake-up signal and were still in the freezer when they found us. Chandler believes them. Ross doesn't. I won't know what the others think until they're unfrozen.

I sit looking through the view plate at Earth, such as it is. I know what the lizards say is true, but I don't think I really believe it. I think mostly that I'm dead or having a terrible dream.

Entry 2: Steinbrunner killed himself (despite their best efforts to prevent anything like that, the lizards say). Sue Anne Beamish, fifth to be thawed, won't talk to anybody. She grits her teeth all the time. I can hear them grinding whenever she's around. It's very annoying.

The lead lizard's name is Captain Midnight. He says he knows it's not the most appropriate name for a space-flight commander, but he likes the sound of it.

It seems that on their home planet the lizards have been fielding our various Earth transmissions, both radio and TV, and they borrow freely from what they've found there. They are given native names, but if they feel like it later they take Earth-type names instead. Those on Captain Midnight's ship all have Earth-type names. Luckily the names are pretty memorable, because I can't tell one alien from another except by the name badges they wear on their jumpsuits. I look at them sometimes and I wonder if I'm crazy. Can't afford to be, not if I've got to deal on a daily basis with things that look as if they walked out of a Walt Disney cartoon feature.

They revive us one by one and try to make sure nobody else cuts their wrists like Steinbrunner. He cut the only way that can't be fixed.

I look out the viewplate at what's left of the earth and let the talk slide over me. We can't raise anything from down there. I can't raise anything inside me either. I can only look and look and let the talk slide over me. Could I be dead after all? I feel dead.

Entry 3: Captain Midnight says now that we're all up he would be honored beyond expression if we would consent to come back to Kondra with him and his crew in their ship. *Kondra* is their name for their world. Chu says she's worked out where and what it is in our terms, and she keeps trying to show me on the star charts. I don't look; I don't care. I came up here to do studies on cryogenic nutrition in space, not to look at star charts.

It doesn't matter what I came up here to do. Earth is a moon with a moon now. *Nutrition* doesn't mean anything, not in connection with anything human. There's nothing to nourish. There's just this airless rock, like all the other airless rocks rolling around in space.

I took the data the machines recorded about us while we slept, and I junked it. Chu says I did a lot of damage to some of our equipment in the process. I didn't set out to do that, but it felt good, or something like good, to go on from wiping out information to smashing metal. I've assured everybody that I won't freak out like that again. It doesn't accomplish anything, and I felt foolish afterward. I'm not sure they believe me. I'm not sure I believe my own promise.

Morris and Myers say they won't go with the Kondrai. They say they want to stay here in our vessel just in case something happens down there or in case some other space mission survived and shows up looking for whatever's left, which is probably only us.

Captain Midnight says they can rig a beacon system on our craft to attract anybody who does come around and let them know where we've gone. I can tell the lizards are not going to let Morris and Myers stay here and die.

They say, the Kondrai do, that they didn't actually come here for us. After several generations of receiving and enjoying Earth's transmissions, Kondran authorities decided to borrow a ship from a neighboring world and send Earth an embassy from Kondra, a mission of goodwill.

First contact at last, and there's nobody here but the seven of us. Tough on the Kondrai. They expected to find a whole worldful of us, glued to our screens and speakers. Tough shit all around.

I have dreams so terrible there are no words.

Entry 4: There's nothing for us to do on the Kondran ship, which is soft and leathery inside its alloy shell. I have long talks with Walter Drake, who is head of the mission. Walter Drake is female, I think. Walter Duck.

If I can make a joke, does that mean I'm crazy?

It took me a while to figure out what was wrong with the name. Then I said, "Look, it's Sir Walter *Raleigh* or Sir *Francis* Drake."

She said, "But we don't always just copy. I have chosen to com-
memorate two great voyagers."

I said, "And they were both males."

She said, "That's why I dropped the *Sir*."

Afterward I can't believe these conversations. I resent the end
of the world—my world, going on as a bad joke with Edgar Rice
Burroughs aliens.

Myers and Morris play chess with each other all day and won't
talk to anybody. Most of us don't like to talk to each other right
now. We can't look in each other's eyes, for some reason. There's an
excuse in the case of not looking the lizards in the eyes. They have
this nictitating membrane. It's unsettling to look at that.

All the lizards speak English and at least one other Earth language. Walter Drake says there are several native languages on
Kondra, but they aren't spoken in the population centers anymore.
Kondran culture, in its several major branches, is very old. It was
once greater and more complex than our own, she says, but then it
got simple again, and the population began to drop. The whole
species was, in effect, beginning to close down. When our signals
were first picked up, something else began to happen: a growing
trend toward population increase and a young generation fascinated by Earth culture. The older Kondrai, who had gone back to
living like their ancestors in the desert, didn't object. They said fine,
let the youngsters do as they choose as long as they let the oldsters
do likewise.

I had to walk away when Walter Drake told me about this. It
started me thinking about my own people I left back on Earth, all
dead now. I won't put their names down. I was crying. Now I've
stopped, and I don't want to start again. It makes my eyes hurt.

Walter Drake brought me some tapes of music that they've
recorded from our broadcasts. They collect our signals, everything
they can, through something they call the Retrieval Project. They
reconstruct the broadcasts and record them and store the record-

ings in a huge library for study. Our classical music has a great following there.

I've been listening to some Bach partitas. My mother played
the piano. She sometimes played Bach.

Entry 5: Sibelius, Symphony No. 2 in D, Op. 43; Tchaikovsky,
Variations on a Rococo Theme, Op. 33; Rachmaninoff, Symphonic
Dances, Op. 45; Mozart, Clarinet Quintet in A major, K581;
Sibelius, Symphony No. 2 in D, Op. 43; Sibelius, Symphony No. 2
in D, Op. 43.

Entry 6: Chandler is alive, Ross is alive, Beamish is alive, Chu
is alive, Morris is alive, Myers is alive, and I am alive. But that
doesn't count. I mean I can't count it. Up. To mean anything. *Why*
are we alive?

Entry 7: Myers swallowed a chess piece. The lizards operated
on him somehow and saved his life.

Entry 8: Woke up from a dream wondering if maybe we did die
in our ship and my "waking life" in the Kondran ship is really just
some kind of after-death hallucination. Suppose I died, suppose we
all actually died at the same moment Earth died? It wouldn't make
any difference. Earth's people are all dead and someplace else or
nowhere, but we are *here*. We are separate.

They're in contact with their home planet all the time. Chu is
fascinated by their communications technology, which is wild, she
says. Skips over time or folds up space—I don't know, I'm just a
nutrition expert. Apparently on Kondra now they are making up
their own human-style names instead of lifting them ready-made.
(Walter Drake was a pioneer in this, I might point out.) Captain
Midnight has changed his name. He is henceforth to be known as
Vernon Zeno Ellerman.

Bruckner and Mahler symphonies, over and over, fill a lot of
time. Walter Drake says she is going to get me some fresh music,
though I haven't asked for any.

Entry 9: Beamish came and had a talk with me. She looked
fierce.

"Listen, Flynn," she said, "we're not going to give up."

"Give up what?" I said.

"Don't be so obtuse," she said between her teeth. "The human race isn't ended as long as even a handful of us are still alive and kicking."

I am alive, though I don't know why (I now honestly do not recall the exact nature of the experiments I was onboard our craft to conduct). I'm not sure I'm kicking, and I told her so.

She grinned and patted my knee. "Don't worry about it, Flynn. I don't mean you should take up where you left off with Lily Chu." That happened back in training. I didn't even remember it until Beamish said this. "Nobody's capable right now, which is just as well. Besides, the women in this group are not going to be anybody's goddamn brood mares, science-fiction traditions to the contrary."

"Oh," I said. I think.

She went on to say that the Kondrai have or can borrow the technology to develop children for us in vitro. All we have to do is furnish the raw materials.

I said fine. I had developed another terrible headache. I've been having headaches lately.

After she left I tried some music. Walter Drake got me *Boris Godunov*, but I can't listen to it. I can't listen to anything with people's voices. I don't know how to tell this to Walter Drake. Don't want to tell her. It's none of her business anyhow.

Entry 10: Chu and Morris are sleeping together. So much for Beamish's theory that nobody is capable. With Myers not up to playing chess yet, I guess Morris had to find something to do.

Chu said to me, "I'm sorry, Michael."

I felt this little, far-off sputtering like anger somewhere deep down, and then it went out. "That's okay," I said. And it is.

Chandler has been spending all his time in the communications cell of the ship with another lizard, one with a French name that I can't remember. Chandler tells us he's learning a lot about

Kondran life. I tune him out when he talks like this. I never go to the communications cell. The whole thing gives me a headache. Everything gives me a headache except music.

Entry 11: I was sure it would be like landing in some kind of imitation world, a hodgepodge of phony bits and pieces copied from Earth. That's why I wouldn't go out for two K-days after we landed.

Everybody was very understanding. Walter Drake stayed on board with me.

"We have fixed up a nice hotel where you can all be together," she told me, "like the honored guests that you are."

I finally got off and went with the others when she gave me the music recordings to take with me. She got me a playback machine. I left the Mozart clarinet quintet behind, and she found it and brought it after me. But I won't listen to it. The clarinet sound was made by somebody's living breath, somebody who's dead now, like all of them. I can't stand to hear that sound.

The hotel was in a suburb of a city, which looked a little like LA, though not as much as I had expected. Later sometime I should try to describe the city. There's a hilly part, something like San Francisco, by the sea. We asked to go over there instead. They found us a sort of rooming house of painted wood with a basement. Morris and Chu have taken the top floor, though I don't think they sleep together anymore.

Ross has the apartment next door to me. She's got her own problems. She threw up when she first set foot on Kondra. She throws up almost every day, says she can't help it.

There are invitations for us to go meet the locals and participate in this and that, but the lizards do not push. They are so damned considerate and respectful. I don't go anywhere. I stay in my room and listen to music. Handel helps me sleep.

Entry 12: Four and a half K-years have passed. I stopped doing this log because Chandler showed me his. He was keeping a detailed record of what was happening to us, what had happened, what he thought was going to happen. Then Beamish circulated her version, and Dr. Birgit Nilson, the lizard in charge of our mental health, started encouraging us all to contribute what we could to a "living history" project.

I was embarrassed to show anybody my comments. I am not a writer or an artist like Myers has turned out to be. (His pictures are in huge demand here, and he has a whole flock of Kondran students.) If Chandler and Beamish were writing everything down, why should I waste my time doing the same thing?

Living history of what, for whom?

Also I didn't like what Chandler wrote about me and Walter Drake. Yes, I slept with her. One of us would have tried it, sooner or later, with one lizard or another. I just happened to be the one who did. I had better reasons than any of the others. Walter Drake had been very kind to me.

I was capable all right (still am). But the thought of going to bed with Lily or Sue Anne made my skin creep, though I couldn't have said why. On the Kondran ship I used to jerk off and look at the stuff in my hand and wonder what the hell it was doing there: Didn't my body know that my world is gone, my race, my species?

Sex with Walter Drake is different from sex with a woman. That's part of what I like about it. And another thing. Walter Drake doesn't cry in her sleep.

Walter and I did all right. For a couple of years I went traveling alone, at the government's expense—like everything we do here— all over Kondra. Walter was waiting when I got back. So we went to live together away from the rooming house. The time passed like a story or a dream. Not much sticks in my head now from that period. We listened to a lot of music together. Nothing with flutes or clarinet, though. String music, percussion, piano music, horns only if they're blended with other sounds—that's what I like. Lots of light stuff, Dukas and Vivaldi and Milhaud.

Anyway, that period is over. After all this time Chu and Morris have committed suicide together. They used a huge old pistol one of them must have smuggled all this way. Morris, probably. He always had a macho hang-up.

Beamish goes around saying, "Why? Why?" At first I thought this was the stupidest question I'd ever heard. I was seriously worried that maybe these years on Kondran food and water had addled her mind through some weird allergic reaction.

Then she said, "We're so close, Flynn. Why couldn't they have waited? I wouldn't have let them down."

I keep forgetting about her in vitro project. It's going well, she says. She works very hard with a whole team of Kondrai under Dr. Boleslav Singh, preparing a cultural surround for the babies she's developing. She comes in exhausted from long discussions with Dr. Boleslav Singh and Dr. Birgit Nilson and others about the balance of Earth information and Kondran information to be given to the human babies. Beamish wants to make little visitors out of the babies. She says it's providential that we were found by the Kondrai—a race that has neatly caught and preserved everything transmitted by us about our own culture and our past. So now all that stuff is just waiting to be used, she says, to bridge the gap in our race's history. "The gap," that's what she calls it. She has a long-range plan of getting a ship for the in vitros to use when they grow up and want to go find a planet they can turn into another Earth. This seems crazy to me. But she is entitled. We all are.

I've moved back into the rooming house. I feel it's my duty, now that we're so few. Walter has come with me.

Entry 13: Mozart's piano concertos, especially Alfred Brendel's renditions, all afternoon. I have carried out my mission after all— to answer the question: What does a frozen Earthman eat for breakfast? The answer is music. For lunch? Music. Dinner? Music. This frozen Earthman stays alive on music.

Entry 14: A year and a half together in the rooming house, and Walter Drake and I have split up. Maybe it has nothing to do with being in the rooming house with the other humans. Divorce is becoming very common among young Kondrai. So is something like hair. They used to wear wigs. Now they have developed a means of growing featherlike down on their heads and in their armpits, etc.

When Walter came in with a fine dusting of pale fuzz on her pate, I told her to pack up and get out. She says she understands, she's not bitter. She doesn't understand one goddamned thing.

Entry 15: Beamish's babies, which I never went to see, have died of an infection that whipped through the whole lot of them in three days. The Kondran medical team taking care of them caught it, too, though none of them died. A few are blind from it, perhaps permanently.

Myers took pictures of the little corpses. He is making paintings from his photos. Did I put it in here that swallowing a chess piece did not kill Myers? Maybe it should have, but it seems nothing can kill Myers. He is as tough as rawhide. But he doesn't play chess, not since Morris killed himself. There are Kondrai who play very well, but Myers refuses their invitations. You can say that for him at least.

He just takes photographs and paints.

I'm not really too sorry about the babies. I don't know which would be worse, seeing them grow up as a little clutch of homeless aliens among the lizards or seeing them adapt and become pseudo-Kondrai. I don't like to think about explaining to them how the world they really belong to blew itself to hell. (Lily Chu is the one who went over the signals the Kondrai salvaged about that and sorted out the sequence of events. That was right before she killed herself.) We slept through the end of our world. Bad enough to do it, worse to have to talk about it. I never talk about it now, not even with the Kondrai. With Dr. Birgit Nilson I discuss food, of course, and health. I find these boring and absurd subjects, though I cooperate out of politeness. I also don't want to get stuck on health problems, like Chandler, who has gone through one hypochondriacal frenzy after another in the past few years.

Beamish says she will try again. Nothing will stop her. She

confided to Ross that she thinks the Kondrai deliberately let the babies die, maybe even infected them on purpose. "They don't want us to revive our race," she said to Ross. "They're trying to take our place. Why should they encourage the return of the real thing?"

Ross told me Beamish wants her to help arrange some kind of escape from Kondra, God knows to where. Ross is worried about Beamish. "What," she says, "if she goes off the deep end and knifes some innocent lizard medico? They might lock us all up permanently."

Ross does not want to be locked up. She plays the cello all the time, which used to be a hobby of hers. The lizards were only too pleased to furnish her an instrument. A damn good one, too, she says. What's more, she now has three Kondrai studying with her.

I don't care what she does. I walk around watching the Kondrai behave like us.

I have terrible dreams, still.

Symphonic music doesn't do it for me anymore, not even Sibelius. I can't hear enough of the music itself; there are too many voices. I listen to chamber pieces. There you can hear each sound, everything that happens between each sound and each other sound near it.

They gave me a free pass to the Library of the Retrieval Project. I spend a lot of time there, listening.

Entry 16: Fourteen K-years later. Beamish eventually did get three viable Earth-style children out of her last lot. Two of them drowned in a freak accident at the beach a week ago. The third one, a girl named Melissa, ran away. They haven't been able to find her.

Our tissue contributions no longer respond, though Beamish keeps trying. She calls the Kondrai "Snakefaces" behind their backs.

Her hair is gray. So is mine.

Kondran news is all about the growing tensions between Kondra and the neighbor world it does most of its trading with. I don't know how that used to work in economic terms, but apparently it's begun to break down. I never saw any of the inhabitants of that world, called Chadondal, except in pictures and Kondran TV news reports. Now I guess I never will. I don't care.

Something funny happened with the flu that killed all of Beamish's first babies. It seems to have mutated into something that afflicts the Kondrai the way cancer used to afflict human beings. This disease doesn't respond to the cure human researchers developed once they figured out that our cancer was actually a set of symptoms of an underlying disease. Kondran cancer is something all their own.

They are welcome to it.

Entry 17: I went up into the sandhills to have a look at a few of the Old Kondrai, the ones who never did buy into imitation Earth ways. Most of them don't talk English (they don't even talk much Kondran to each other), but they don't seem to mind if you hang around and watch them a while.

They live alone or else in very small settlements on a very primitive level, pared down to basics. Your individual Old Kondran will have a small, roundish stone house or even a burrow or cave and will go fetch water every day and cook on a little cell-powered stove or a wood fire. They usually don't even have TV. They walk around looking at things or sit and meditate or dig in their flower gardens or carve things out of the local wood. Once in a while they'll get together for a dance or a sort of mass bask in the sun or to put on plays and skits and so on. These performances can go on for days. They have a sort of swap economy, which is honored elsewhere when they travel. You sometimes see these pilgrims in the city streets, just wandering around. They never stay long.

Some of the younger Kondrai have begun harking back to this sort of life, trying to create the same conditions in the cities, which is ridiculous. These youngsters act as if it's something absolutely basic they have to try to hang on to in the face of an invasion of alien ways. Earth ways.

This is obviously a backlash against the effects of the Retrieval Project. I keep an eye on developments. It's all fascinating and actually creepy. To me the backlash is uncannily reminiscent of those fundamentalist-nationalist movements—Christian American or Middle-Eastern Muslim or whatever—that made life such hell for so many people toward the end of our planet's life. But if you point this resemblance out, the anti-Retrieval Kondrai get furious because, after all, anything Earth-like is what they're reacting against.

I sometimes bring this up in conversation just to get a rise out of them.

If I'm talking to Kondrai who are part of the backlash, they invariably get furious. "No," they say, "we're just trying to turn back to our old, native ways!" They don't recognize this passion itself as something that humans, not Kondrai, were prone to. From what I can gather and observe, fervor, either reactionary or progressive, is something alien to native Kondran culture as it was before they started retrieving our signals. Their life was very quiet and individualized and pretty dull, as a matter of fact.

Sometimes I wish we'd found it like that instead of the way it had already become by the time we got here. Of course the Old Kondrai never would have sent us an embassy in the first place.

I talk to Dr. Birgit Nilson about all this a lot. We aren't exactly friends, but we communicate pretty well for a man and a lizard.

She says they have simply used human culture to revitalize themselves.

I think about the Old Kondrai I saw poking around, growing the kind of flowers that attract the flying grazers they eat, or just sitting. I like that better. If they were a dying culture, they should have just gone ahead and died.

Entry 18: Ross has roped Chandler into her music making. Turns out he played the violin as a kid. They practice a lot in the rooming house. Sometimes Ross plays the piano, too. She's better on the cello. I sit on my porch, looking at the bay, and I sit.

Ross says the Kondrai as a group are fascinated by performance. Certainly they perform being human better and better all the time. They think of Earth's twentieth century as the Golden Age of Human Performance. How would they know? It's all secondhand here, everything.

I've been asked to join a nutritional-study team heading for Kondra-South, where some trouble spots are developing. I have declined. I don't care if they starve or why they starve. I had enough of looking at images of starvation on Earth, where we did it on a terrific scale. What a performance that was!

Also I don't want to leave here because then I wouldn't get to hear Ross and Chandler play. They do sonatas and duets and they experiment, not always very successfully, with adapting music written for other instruments. It's very interesting. Now that Ross is working on playing the piano as well as the cello, their repertoire has been greatly expanded.

They aren't nearly as good as the great musical performers of the Golden Age, of course. But I listen to them anyway whenever I can. There's something about live music. You get a hunger for it.

Entry 19: Myers has gone on a world tour. He is so famous as an artist that he has rivals, and there are rival schools led by artists he himself has trained. He spends all his time with the snakes now, the ones masquerading as artists and critics and aesthetes. He hardly ever stops at the rooming house or comes by here to visit.

Sue Anne Beamish and I have set up house together across the bay from the rooming house. She's needed somebody around her ever since they found the desiccated corpse of little Melissa in the rubbish dump and worked out what had been done to her.

The Kondran authorities say they think some of the Kondrachalikipon (as the anti-Retrieval-backlash members call themselves now, meaning "return to Kondran essence") were responsible. The idea is that these Kondracha meant what they did as a symbolic rejection of everything the Retrieval Project has retrieved and a warning that Kondra will not be turned into an imitation Earth without a fight.

When Dr. Birgit Nilson and I talked about this, I pointed out that the Kondracha, if it was them, didn't get it right. They should have dumped the kid's body on the Center House steps and then called a press conference. Next time they'll do it better, though, being such devoted students of our ways.

"I know that," she said. "What is becoming of us?"

Us meant "us Kondrai," of course, not her and me. She likes to think that we Earth guests have a special wisdom that comes from our loss and from a mystical blood connection with the culture that the Kondrai are absorbing. As if I spend my time thinking about that kind of thing. Dr. Birgit Nilson is a romantic.

I don't talk to Sue Anne about Melissa's death. I don't feel it enough, and she would know that. So many died before, what's one more kid's death now? A kid who could never have been human anyway because a human being is born on Earth and raised in a human society, like Sue Anne and me.

"We should have blown their ship up and us with it," she says, "on the way here."

She won't come with me to the rooming house to listen to Ross and Chandler play. They give informal concert evenings now. I go, even though the audience is 98 percent lizard, because by now I know every recording of chamber music in the Retrieval Library down to the last scrape of somebody's chair during a live recital. The recordings are too faithful. I can just about tolerate the breath intake you hear sometimes when the first violinist cues a phrase. It's different with Ross and Chandler. Their live music makes the live sounds all right. Concerts are given by Kondran "artists" all the time, but I won't go to those.

For one thing, I know perfectly well that we don't hear sounds, we human beings, not sounds from outside. Our inner ear vibrates to the sound from outside, and we hear the sound that our own ear creates inside the head in response to that vibration. Now, how can the Kondran ear be exactly the same as ours? No matter how closely they've learned to mimic the sounds that our musicians produced, Kondran ears can't be hearing what human ears do when human music is played. A Kondran concert of human music is a farce.

Poor Myers. He missed the chance to take pictures of Melissa's dead body so he could make paintings of it later.

Entry 20: They are saying that the reason there's so much crime and violence now on Kondra isn't because of the population explosion at all. Some snake who calls himself Swami Nanda has worked out how the demographic growth is only a sign of the underlying situation.

According to him Kondra made an "astral agreement" to take in not only us living human survivors but the souls of all the dead of Earth. Earth souls on the astral plane, seeing that there were soon going to be no more human bodies on Earth to get born into, sent out a call for new bodies and a new world to inhabit. The Kondran souls on the astral plane, having pretty much finished their work on the material world of Kondra, agreed to let human souls take over the physical plant here, as it were. Now the younger generation is all Earth souls reborn as Kondrai on this planet, and they're re-creating conditions familiar to them from Earth.

I have sent this "Swami" four furious letters. He answered the last one very politely and at great length, explaining it all very clearly with the words he has stolen for his stolen metaphysical concepts.

Oh, yes: Another dozen K-years have passed. I might as well just say *years*. Kondran years are only a few days off our own, and Chandler has stopped keeping his Earth-time calendar since he's gotten so deep into music.

Chandler is now doing some composing, Ross tells me.

Ross rebukes me when I call the Kondrai snakes, talking to me as gently and reasonably as the Kondrai themselves always talk to us. That makes me sick, which is pretty funny when I recall how she used to vomit every day when we first came here. So she can stop telling me how to talk and warning me that it's no good to be a recluse. No good for what? And what would be better?

Nobody ever taught me to play any instrument. My parents said I had no talent, and they were right. I'm a listener, so I listen. I'm doing my job. I wouldn't go to the rooming house and talk to Ross at all except for the music. They are getting really good. It's amazing. Once in a while I spend a week at the Retrieval Library listening to the really great performances that are recorded there, to make sure my taste hasn't become degraded.

It hasn't. My two crewmates are converting themselves, by some miracle of dedication, into fine performers.

Last night I had to walk out in the middle of a Beethoven sonata to be alone.

Entry 21: Sue Anne had a stroke last week. She is paralyzed down her left side. I am staying with her almost constantly because I know she can't stand having the snakes around her anymore.

She blames me, I know, for having cooperated with them. We all spent hours and hours with their researchers, filling out their information about our dead planet. How could we have refused? In the face of their courtesy and considering how worried we all were about forgetting Earth ourselves, how could we? Besides, we really had nothing else to do.

She blames me anyhow, but I don't mind.

A wave of self-immolation is going on among young Kondrai. They find themselves an audience and set themselves afire, and the watching Kondrai generally stand there as if hypnotized by the flames and do nothing.

Dr. Birgit Nilson told me, "Your entire population died out; many of them burnt up in an instant. This created much karma, and those who are responsible must be allowed to pay."

"You're a Nandist, then," I said. "Swami Nanda and his reincarnation crap."

"I see no other explanation," she said.

"It all makes sense to you?" I said.

"Yes." She stroked her cheek with her orange-polished talons. "It's a loan: We have lent our beautiful material world and our species's bodies in exchange for your energetic souls and your rich, passionate culture."

They are the crazy ones, not us.

Entry 22: Some wild-eyed young snake with his top feathers dyed blue took a shot at the swami this morning with an old-fashioned thorn gun.

They caught him. We watched on the news. The would-be assassin sneers at the camera like a real Earth punk. Sue Anne glares back and snorts derisively.

Entry 23: Dreamed of my mother at her piano, but her hands were Kondran hands. The fingers were too long, and the nails were set like claws, and her skin was covered in minute, grayish scales.

I think she was playing Chopin.

Entry 24: Sometimes I wish I were a writer, to do all this justice. I might have some function as a survivor.

Look at Sue Anne: Except for some terrible luck, she would have created out of us a new posterity.

Myers is doing prints these days, but not on Earth themes anymore, though the Kondrai beg him to concentrate on what's "native" to him. He says his memory of Earth is no longer trustworthy, and besides, images of Kondra are native to the eyes of reborn Earth souls now. He accepts Nandism openly and goes around doing Kondran landscapes and portraits and so on. Well, nobody will have to miss any of that in my account, then. They can always look at Myers's pictures.

Walter Drake died last winter of Kondran cancer. I went to the funeral. For the first time I wore makeup.

Myers, the arrogant son of a bitch, condescended to share a secret with me. He used this face paint, plus a close haircut or a feathered cap, to go out incognito among the snakes so he can observe them undisturbed. Age has smoothed his features and made him thin, like most Kondrai, and he's been getting away with it for years. Well, good for him. Look at what *they're* trying to get away with along those lines!

Being disguised has its advantages. I hadn't realized the pressure of being stared at all the time in public until I moved around without it.

They said, "Ashes to ashes and dust to dust," and I got dizzy and had to sit down on a bench.

Entry 25: Four more years. My heart still checks out, Dr. Birgit Nilson tells me. I put on makeup and hang out in the bars, watching TV with the Kondrai, but not too often. Sometimes they make me so damn nervous, even after so long here. I forget what they are and what I am. I forget myself. I get scared that I'm turning senile.

When I get home Sue Anne gives me this cynical look, and my perspective is restored. I play copy-tapes of Dvořák for her. Also Schubert. She likes the French, though. I find them superficial.

To hear Brahms and Beethoven and Mozart, I go to the rooming house. I go whenever Ross and Chandler play. While the music sounds the constant crying inside me gets so big and so painful and beautiful that I can't contain it. So it moves outside me for a while, and I feel rested and changed. This is only an illusion, but wonderful.

Entry 26: Poor Myers got caught in a religious riot on the other side of the world. He was beaten to death by a Kondracha mob. I guess his makeup job was careless. Dr. Birgit Nilson, much aged and using a cane, came to make a personal apology, which I accepted for old times' sake.

"We caught two of them," she said. "The ringleaders of the Kondracha group that killed your poor Mr. Myers."

"Kondrachalations," I said. Couldn't help myself.

Dr. Birgit looked at me. "Forgive me," she said. "I shouldn't have come."

When I told Sue Anne about this, she slapped my face. She

hasn't much strength even in her good arm these days. But I resented being hit and asked her why she did it.

"Because you were smiling, Michael."

"You can't cry all the time," I said.

"No," she said. "I wish we could."

Dr. Birgit Nilson says that Kondrai are now composing music in classical, popular, and "primitive" styles, all modeled on Earth music. I have not heard any of this new music. I do not want to.

Entry 27: At least Sue Anne didn't live to see this: They are now grafting lobes onto their ugly ear holes.

No, that's not the real news. The real news is about Kondra-South, where a splinter group of Kondracha extremists set up a sort of purist, Ur-Kondran state some years ago. They use only their version of Old Kondran farming methods, which is apparently not an accurate version. Their topsoil has been rapidly washing away in the summer floods.

Now they are killing newborns down there to have fewer mouths to feed. The pretext is that these newborns look like humans and are part of the great taint that everything Earthish represents to the pure. The official Kondrachalikipon line is that they are feeding themselves just fine, thank you. The truth seems to be mass starvation and infanticide.

After Sue Anne died, I moved back into the rooming house. I have a whole floor to myself and scarcely ever go out. I watch Kondran TV a lot, which is how I keep track of their politics and so on. I stop looking for false notes that would reveal to any intelligent observer the hollowness of their performance of humanity. There isn't much except for my gut reaction. The Kondran claim to have preserved human culture by making it their own would be very convincing to anyone who didn't know better. Even their game shows look familiar. Young Kondrai go mad for music videos and deafening concerts by their own groups like the Bear Minimum and Dead Boring. I stare and stare at the screen, looking for slip-ups. I am not sure that I would recognize one now if I saw one.

I hate the lizards. I miss her. I hate them.

Entry 28: Ross and Chandler have done the unthinkable. At last night's musicale they sprang one hell of a surprise.

They have trained two young Kondrai to a degree that satisfies them (particularly Gillokan Chukchonturanfis, who plays both violin and viola).

Now the four of them are planning to go out and perform in public together as the Retrieval String Quartet.

The Lost Earth String Quartet I could stomach, maybe. Or the Ghost String Quartet, or the Remnant String Quartet. But then, of course, how could Kondran musicians be in it?

I walked out in protest.

Ross says I am being unreasonable and cutting off my nose to spite my face, since as a quartet they have so much more music they can play. To hell with Ross. The traitress. Chandler, too.

Entry 29: I cut my hair and put on my makeup and managed to get myself one ticket, not as Michael Flynn the Earthman but as a nameless Kondran. The debut concert of the Retrieval String Quartet is the event of the year in the city: a symbol of the passing of the torch of human culture, they say. An outrage, the Kondracha scream. I keep my thoughts to myself and lay my plans.

Lizards are pouring into the city for the event. Two bombings have already occurred, credit for them claimed by the Kondracha-likipon, of course.

As long as the scaly bastards don't blow me up before I do my job.

The gun is in my pocket, Morris's gun that I took after he and Chu killed themselves. I was a good shot once. My seat is close to the stage and on the aisle, leaving my right hand free. I have had too much bitterness in my life. I will not be mocked and betrayed in the one place where I find some comfort.

Entry 30: Now I know who I wrote all this for. Dear Dr. Herbert Akonditichilka: You do not know me. Until a little while ago I didn't know you either. I am the man who sat next to you in

Carnegie Hall last night. Your Kondran version of Carnegie Hall, that is: constructed from TV pictures; all sparkling in crystal and cream and red velvet—handsomer than the real place was, but in my judgment slightly inferior acoustically.

You didn't notice me, Doctor, because of my makeup. I noticed you. All evening I noticed everything, starting with the police and the Kondracha demonstration outside the hall. But you I noticed in particular. You managed to wreck my concentration during the last piece of fine music I expected to hear in my life.

It was the Haydn String Quartet Number One in G, Opus 77. I sat trying to hear the effect of having two Kondrai among the players, but your damned fidgeting distracted me. *Just my luck*, I thought. *A Kondran who came for a historic event, though he has no feeling for classical Earth music at all.* All through the Haydn you sat locked tight except for these tiny, spasmodic movements of your head, arms, and hands. It was a great relief to me when the music ended and you joined the crashing applause. I was so busy glaring at you that I missed seeing the musicians leave the stage.

I watched you all through the interval. I needed something to fix my attention on while I waited. The second piece was to be one of my favorites, the Brahms String Quartet Number Two in A minor, Opus 51. I had chosen the opening of that quartet as my signal. I meant to see to it that the Brahms would never be played by the traitors Ross and Chandler and the two snakes they had trained. In fact, no one was ever going to hear Ross and Chandler play anything again.

What would happen to me afterward I didn't know or care (though it crossed my mind in a farcical moment that I might be rescued as a hero by the Kondracha).

I wondered if you would be a problem—an effective interference, once the first note of the Brahms piece sounded and I began to make my move. I thought not.

You were small and thin, Dr. Akonditichilka, neatly dressed in your fake blazer with the fake gold buttons; a thick thatch of white top feathers; a round face, for a lizard; and glasses that made your eyes enormous. I wondered if you had ruined your eyesight studying facsimile texts taken from Earth transmissions. I could see by the grayed-off skin color that you were elderly, like so many in this audience, though probably not as old as I am.

You fell into conversation with the Kondran on your left. I realized from what I could overhear that the two of you had met for the first time earlier that same day. She was now exploring the contact. "Oh," she said, "you're a doctor?"

"Retired," you said.

"You must meet Mischa Two Hawks," she said, "my escort tonight. He's a retired doctor, too."

The seat to her left was empty. Retired doctor Mischa Two Hawks may have withdrawn to the men's room or gone out in the lobby for a smoke.

You must understand; my mind made automatic translations as fast as the thought finished: Imitation retired, imitation doctor Mischa S. (for Stolen names) Two Hawks was in the imitation men's room or smoking an imitation cigarette.

His companion, an imitation woman in a green, imitation wool dress, wore a white wig with a blue-rinse tint. God, how Beamish used to rage over the tendency of Kondran females to choose the most traditional women's styles as models! Beamish would have been proud of my work tonight, I thought.

Green Wool Dress, whose name I had not caught, said to you, "The lady with you this afternoon at the gallery—is she your wife? And where is she tonight?"

You shook your head, and your glasses flashed. It pleases me that the nictitating membrane prevents you snakes from wearing contact lenses.

"We used to go to every concert in the city together," you said. "We both love good music, and there is no replacement for hearing it live. But she's been losing her hearing. She doesn't go anymore; it's too painful for her."

"What a pity," Green Wool Dress said. "To miss such a great event! Wasn't the first violinist wonderful just now? And, so young, too. It was amazing to hear him."

Damned right it was. Chandler had literally played second fiddle to his own student, Chukchonturanfis. For that alone I could have killed my old crewmate.

I shut my eyes and thought about the gun in my pocket. It was a heavy goddamned thing. I thought about the danger of getting it caught in the cloth as I pulled it out, of missing my aim, of my elderly self being jumped by you two elderly aliens before I could complete my job. I thought of Chandler and Ross, no spring chickens themselves anymore, soon to die and leave me alone among you. The whole thing was a sort of doddering comedy.

Another Kondran, heavyset for a lizard and bald, worked his way along the row of seats. He hovered next to Green Wool Dress, clearly wanting to sit down. She wouldn't let him until she had made introductions. This was, of course, retired doctor Mischa Two Hawks.

"Akonditichilka," you said with a little bow. "Herbert." And the two of you shook hands across Green Wool Dress. All three of you settled back to chat.

Suddenly I heard your voices as music. You, Doctor, were the first violin, with your clear, light tenor. Dr. Two Hawks's lower register made a reasonable cello. Green Wool Dress, who scarcely spoke, was second violin, of course, noodling busily along among her own thoughts. And I was the viola, hidden and dark.

If this didn't stop I knew I would use the gun right now, on you and then on myself. I listened to the words you were saying instead of your voices. I grabbed onto the words to keep control.

"A beautiful piece, the Haydn," you were saying. "I have played it. Oh, not like these musicians, of course. But I used to belong to an amateur chamber group." (How like you thieving snakes, to mimic our own medical doctors' affinity for music-making as a hobby!) You went on to explain how it was that you no longer

played. Some slow, crippling Kondran bone disease. Of course—
your lizard claws were never meant to handle a bow and strings.
What was your instrument? I missed that. You said you had not
played for six or seven years now. No wonder you had twitched all
through the Haydn, remembering.

Some snake in a velvet suit pushed past, managing to step on
both my feet. We traded insincere apologies, and he went on to
trample past you and your companions. They were all hurrying
back in now. My moment was coming. The row was fully occupied,
so I sat down and pretended to skim the program notes for the next
piece.

On you went, in the clear, distantly regretful tone. I couldn't
stop hearing. "It's been a terrible season for me," you said. "My
only grandchild died last month. He was fifteen."

Your voice was not music. It was just a voice, taking a tone I
remembered from when I and my crewmates first began to be able
to say to each other, "Well, it's all gone, blown up—mankind and
womankind and whalekind and everykind smashed to smithereens
while we were sleeping." It's how you sound instead of screaming.
You have no more acute screaming left in your throat, but you
can't stop talking about what is making you scream, because the
screaming of your spirit is going on and on.

My eyes locked on the page in front of me. Had you really
spoken this way, to two strangers, at a concert? The other two were
making sounds of shock and sympathy.

"Cancer," you said, though of course you meant not our kind
of cancer but Kondran cancer, and of course even if you were
screaming inside it wasn't the same as the spirit of a human being
screaming that way.

You leaned forward in your seat to talk across Green Wool
Dress to Dr. Two Hawks. "It was terrible," you said. "It started in
his right leg. None of the therapy even slowed it down. They did
three operations."

I sneaked a look at you to see what kind of expression you wore on your imitation human face while you recited your afflictions. But you were leaning outward to address your fellow doctor, and the back of your narrow lizard shoulders was turned toward me.

Between you two, Green Wool Dress sat with a blank social smile, completely withdrawn into herself. I tried to follow what you were saying, but you got into technical terms, one doctor to another.

The musicians were tuning up their instruments backstage. The gun felt like a battleship in my pocket. Under the dimming lights I could make out the face of Dr. Two Hawks, sympathetic and earnest. Amazing, I thought, how they've learned to produce the effect of expressions like our own with their alien musculature and their alien skin.

"But it's better now than it was at first," Dr. Two Hawks protested (I thought of Beamish's babies and the death of Walter Drake). "I can remember when there was nothing to do but cut and cut, and even then—there was a young patient I remember, we removed the entire hip—oh, we were desperate. Dreadful things were done. It's better now."

All around, oblivious, members of the audience settled expectantly into their seats, whispering to each other, rustling program pages. Apparently I was your only involuntary eavesdropper, and soon that ordeal would be over.

The audience quieted, and here they came: Ross first, then Chandler (the Kondran players didn't matter). Ross first: You wouldn't see the blood on her red dress. No one would understand exactly what was happening, and that would give me time to get Chandler, too. I needed my concentration. My moment was here.

On you went, inexorably, in your quiet, melancholy tone: "As a last resort they castrated him. He lost most of his skin at the end, and he was too weak to sip fluids through a tube. I think now it was all a mistake. We should never have fought so hard. We should have let him die at the start."

"But we can't just give up!" cried Dr. Two Hawks over the applause for the returning musicians. "We must do *something*!"

And you sighed, Dr. Akonditichilka. "Aaah," you said softly, a long curve of sounded breath in the silence before the players began. You leaned there an instant longer, looking across at him.

Then you said gently (and how clearly your voice still sounds in my mind)—each word a steep, sweet fall in pitch from the one before—"Let's listen to Brahms."

And you sat back slowly in your seat as the first notes rippled into the hall. After a little I managed to uncramp my fingers from around the gun and take my empty hand out of my pocket. We sat there together in the dimness, our eyes stinging with tears past shedding, and we listened.

Paul J. McAuley, a native of the UK, has worked as a researcher in biology in various universities, including Oxford and UCLA, and for six years was a lecturer in botany at St. Andrews University. When he was twenty, the first short story he ever finished was accepted by the American magazine *Worlds of If*, but the magazine went bankrupt before publishing it and McAuley took this as a hint to concentrate on an academic career instead. He started writing again after a period as a resident alien in Los Angeles, and is now a full time writer, living in London.

His first novel, *Four Hundred Billion Stars*, won the Philip K. Dick Memorial Award, and *Fairyland* won the 1995 Arthur C. Clarke Award for best SF novel published in Britain, as well as the 1996 John W. Campbell Award. In 1995, his short story "The Temptation of Dr. Stein" won the British Fantasy Award. Although McAuley is best known for his hard science fiction, he seems just as comfortable writing soft SF, alternative history, fantasy, and the occasional horror story. A collaboration with Kim Newman, "Residuals," was reprinted in *The Year's Best Fantasy and Horror*, and his stories have been reprinted in *The Year's Best Science Fiction* and *Best New Horror*.

He writes a regular review column for the British SF magazine *Interzone*, and also contributes reviews to *Foundation* and *Event Horizon*. He recently completed a very long novel, *Confluence*, set ten million years in the future—the third and final volume of which, *Shrine of Stars*, has been published in the UK—and a near future novel, *The Secret of Life*.

THE RIFT

PAUL J. MCAULEY

1. Ron Vignone

He was standing at the very edge of the Rift, bare chested in only shorts and hiking boots, kicking loose rocks down the steep slope. They clattered away, gaining speed as they rolled, beginning to bounce, bounding along until hitting a snag or outcrop and sailing out into the air, dwindling until they smashed into ledges or dry slopes of scrub far below, and Ron turned and looked at Ty Brown's video camera and yelled, "Virgin no more!" and danced along the edge and kicked down more rocks, feeling terrifically keyed up, the way he always did before a climb, like the anticipation of sex. He was slim and wiry, sweat glittering in the black hair which matted his chest, in the beard he'd started growing in the week it had taken them to get here, by light plane, by boat up a wide tributary of the Amazon, finally by helicopter from a loggers' camp.

The deep, narrow Rift stretched away for miles in either direction, the bluffs of its western edge overhung by forest, slopes and terraces and cliffs dropping away toward the perpetual mists which hid its bottom. There were plenty of loose rocks along the rim-slope, dangerous to anyone climbing below them, and it took most of the day to get it clear and safe so they could think of beginning the first pitch. Ron and a couple of the other climbers wanted to do it right then, even though the light was going, but the Old Man, Ralph Read, said no, they had plenty of time to do this right. He made a little speech about the Rift, saying that it was one of the last wildernesses, speaking to Ty Brown's camera with the sun going down in glory over the Serra Parima mountains.

Ron, who was really looking forward to penetrating this baby all the way to the bottom, told Matt Johnson in disgust, "The Old Man's just realized he's too old for this, I reckon. He fucked up on the first expedition, and he's lost his nerve. We'll be carrying him down."

Matt, who spared a word only when he really had to, so that most days you thought he'd been struck dumb, just shrugged.

They camped out on bare rimrock, with the two helicopters tied down against wind which started to pick up after sunset, tents and piles of supplies and rope bags scattered on the stony ground and Coleman lanterns hissing out white glare here and there. It was the last time they would all be together.

In the middle of the night, Ron woke with a full bladder and moonlight shining through the fabric of the tent he shared with Matt Johnson. He went out and crabbed up a knob of rock that overhung the edge of the Rift. Far out and far below, the mist glowed faintly in the moonlight, looking like radioactive milk. Ron pissed into the void, and saw as he picked his way back to his tent that the science-geek woman, the botanist, was watching him from the open flap of her tent. He grinned to himself. Maybe she'd loosen up before the trip was over.

The next day didn't start well: more rock kicking after the first easy pitch had been made, hard sweaty work crabbing along the sixty degree slope with the sun burning down and a hot wind blowing up from the Rift, while Barry Lowe and the Danes worked out the route. The Old Man had determined that the Danes would set the pace; the others would set up a relay for bringing down the supplies. And that was the way it went for the next three days as they descended into the Rift—the Danes forging ahead while Ron and the others worked like slaves moving supplies down to each new base camp, following pitches the Danes had made. The Old Man stayed up at the rim, keeping in radio contact with his number two, Barry Lowe; Ty Brown spent most of his time with the Danes, because that was where the action was, coming back up to the supply team's base camp each night breathless and elated.

The Danes were moving fast, Ron had to give them that, but they were using up rope, pitons and rock bolts at a terrific rate and outstripping all efforts to keep up with them. Even the two science geeks started to complain. On the third night, Amy Burton got on the radio and, with Ty Brown filming her, told the Old Man that she couldn't do any work because she was too busy humping supplies.

They were camped on a wide dry ledge more than a mile into the Rift, having spent most of the day following traverses that zigzagged down a huge bluff, and then sliding down steep smooth chutes where temporary rivers of floodwater poured down into the Rift during the rainy season. The bluff loomed above, blocking out half the sky; below, a forested forty-degree slope stretched away to its own edge.

"You told him right," Ron said to Amy Burton afterward, as they all sat around the campfire. "Everyone should get their turn."

Burton pushed a lock of lank blond hair from her eyes. A stout, sunburnt woman in khaki shorts and a T-shirt and hiking boots. Like everyone else she smelt strongly of sweat and woodsmoke. She said wearily, "He got money from the UN because he claimed this was a potential world heritage park, but all I can do is sight surveys while I'm working as a Sherpa."

"Maybe I can help," Ron said, thinking of an assignation off in the bush. A couple of the guys were staring at him, and he gave them the finger surreptitiously, then saw, shit, that Ty Brown was filming, and Barry Lowe was watching him too.

"We're all caught up in this mad scramble," Amy Burton said. "Like the most important thing is to get to the bottom."

"Well," Ron said, turning his head to give the camera his best profile, "that's the point, isn't it? This is about the last place we can go without finding someone else's camp litter. Don't you think that's important?"

He was trying to be reasonable, but she stared at him with disgust. She said, "Maybe there should be places where no one ever goes."

Ron said, needled, "Then what's the point of them?"

"Because," she said, "what happens when everything's used up?"

Barry Lowe chipped in then, with bullshit about how much the scientific work was appreciated and how time would certainly be found for it once routes had been opened up, speaking for the record, and Alex Wilson, the TV guy who was looking for some kind of extinct sloth, said he certainly hoped so or else the expedition was a pointless show of macho bravado. It became a fierce argument, with Ty Brown's camera capturing everything. Ron, sidelined and silent, felt anger tighten in his chest, kinking like a twisted rope until he could hardly breathe, and he got up and walked away to the far end of the ledge. This wasn't what he had signed up for, carrying supplies and nursemaiding a couple of science geeks, and as they all hiked along a narrow trail through the steep little forest the next day he tried to tell Lowe that, tried to explain that he wanted some of what the Danes were getting, the pure stuff of establishing new routes. Lowe told him that his turn would come, but Ron knew now that the Rift was fucked forever in his head, and that some kind of payback was due.

2. Ty Brown

He was exhausted every moment of the day, but exhilarated too, because he knew that he was getting something good here, a real drama unfolding in front of his lens. The expedition was slowly pulling itself apart. The Danes were moving too fast and the rest could barely keep up with them, and now Barry Lowe was worried that the rope would run out; none of the routes were as straightforward as the limited aerial surveys had suggested, making it necessary to establish many traverse pitches. Lowe had pleaded with Read over the radio to have more rope flown in, but Read wanted to press on because the rainy season was drawing near and he knew from the bitter experience of his first failed expedition that the Rift would be unclimbable then. And because the secret of the Rift was out, someone else, probably the Brazilian Army, would want to have a go next year. Meanwhile, the other climbers resented the fact that the Danes were the advance party and they did nothing but resupply, the two scientists resented the fact that they had had to virtually give up their work and pitch in to help, and the Old Man, Ralph Read, the grizzled charismatic climber who'd conquered every famous peak in the world, was reduced to an impotent god lost somewhere above, trying to run things through a bad radio link.

Communication was getting worse as they descended, the granite walls bouncing signals or simply swallowing them; no one knew what was below the perpetual mists because radar was bounced around the same way. The best guess was that the Rift was more than four miles deep. It had been completely unknown until Read had discovered it five years ago, although there were rumors of an expedition to this area a hundred years before, and the Indians who had lived in the forests below the massif before logging had displaced them told stories of the monsters which lived there.

Ty had always thought that there wasn't much chance of getting an undiscovered beast on tape, although that was how he had got the commission; he was supposed to be filming Alex Wilson's search for giant sloths, and had hours of material of the crypto-zoologist talking to Indians, examining tufts of greenish hair they produced, squatting with them to examine animal tracks, or staring meaningfully into the darkness beneath the giant forest trees. But now things were definitely taking on a human angle, which was what audiences loved. Finding some animal previously thought

extinct was a two-day thrill, but human conflict was an eternal
story.

Ty had cut his teeth as a second unit cameraman on nature
documentaries. He'd spent more than a decade camping out in
remote areas, spending days waiting to get just the right thirty-
second shot of a bower bird's mating display or a baboon caught by
a leopard (that one, filmed on the fly and shaky as hell, had won an
award). He'd started up his own company, accumulating library
shots and filler work for films that would go out on *National Geographic* or PBS to decreasingly small audiences, but he knew it
wouldn't last. Most people lived in cities; the only animals they
saw in real life were roaches and pigeons (someone had won an
award a couple of years ago with a documentary on urban pigeons;
there was a joke in the trade that soon vermin would be the only
species left to film). Nature documentaries were wallpaper, something to pass the time before the ball game started. And it was getting harder to find an animal species which hadn't already been
filmed and which was sexy enough to get some attention. There
had been three documentaries last year about the last remaining
Galapagos tortoise, for Christ's sake.

But now he'd lucked out: His first real independent feature,
which had started out as a pretty straightforward quest-for-a-living-
fossil twenty-three minute filler, was turning into something different. Just as well, because so far there had been no trace of any
animals at all in the Rift, and it was just too big, too inhuman in
scale, to film properly. You could descend all day, and when you
looked back all you'd see was the last fifty meters of overhang
you'd abseiled down, hiding the bluff you'd spent most of the day
traversing and the forest above that you'd spent the previous day
hiking through. Right now, for instance, he was following Barry
Lowe and one of the climbers, a vain little Brooklyn Italian,
through a stunted forest which wasn't much different from the
understorey growth at the edge of what remained of the true forest, and you couldn't see that this was clinging to the side of a huge

cliff because the skinny little trees were packed too closely together. He'd have to get some aerial shots afterwards, but it wasn't the Rift that mattered anyway.

They were carrying a load of rope and following some kind of animal track which had been enlarged by the Danes (who weren't Danish) and marked here and there with red paint sprayed on a boulder or a tree bole; the rest of the party had returned to the previous base camp, to retrieve more supplies. It was mid-morning, the sun beginning to break through the canopy. They'd been descending for more than two hours when at last they came out of the edge of the forest. They abseiled a smooth dry chute to another ledge, then abseiled again, this time down a vertical cliff to more stunted forest, taking a lot of time to get all the rope bags down. And then they hiked for an hour through the forest to where the Danes had made camp yesterday afternoon, by a boulder field and a series of pools; Ty had taken some good footage of Kerry Dane unselfconsciously swimming in her underwear in the biggest pool.

But the Danes weren't there, although they had told Ty they'd wait.

The climber, Ron Vignone, dumped the three big blue nylon bags of rope in disgust and flopped back on them and stared up at the sky; Lowe switched on his radio and tried to contact the Danes. He got through after a couple of minutes of switching channels, but had scarcely established contact when the radio squealed and went dead. He couldn't get through to Read or to the supply team either, although he tried every one of the channels, and at last said they'd rest up and unpacked his Coleman stove and brewed some tea. He was big and blond, a strong, capable climber, affable in a baffled, English way and not too bright, very much Read's right-hand man. He was drenched in sweat, and his face was badly sunburnt despite the fluorescent orange sunblock he had smeared over his nose and cheeks. He thought it might be best to wait until the rest of the party brought down the supplies, and then press on and catch up with the Danes the next day, but Ron Vignone said they would have gotten even farther ahead by then.

"Well," Lowe said, "they'll have to stop sometime. They'll run out of rope."

"Yeah," Vignone said angrily, "and then they'll start free-climbing and where'll we be? They'll run off with this fucking expedition if someone doesn't do something. I'll tell Read that if you haven't got the balls."

"The Old Man knows about it," Lowe said. He was trying to calm Vignone down, but his bland affability only riled the climber more.

The two men tossed it back and forth for a few more minutes, with Ty filming. Lowe tried the radio again, but succeeded only in running down his batteries. So they decided to go on while it was still light, and picked up the baggage and went on down through the boulder field, following the red splotches the Danes had helpfully sprayed here and there.

Half an hour into this, they saw the bird.

They were following a trail between two stands of forest towards a drop-off half a mile ahead. The bird flew straight across their path, so low that Vignone, who had the lead, threw himself flat. Ty managed to swing his camera on it: vaguely pigeon-shaped but bigger than a pigeon, dusty black plumage and a naked red head. It flew clumsily, crashing into the nearest trees and scrambling away through tangled branches. Ty thought he saw claws at the angles of its wings; then it was gone. A black feather floated down and he picked it from the air.

Vignone jumped up. "Did you see that fucking vulture go for me?"

"It was only a crow," Lowe said.

"They don't have crows in the Amazon basin," Ty said.

"A fucking vulture," Vignone said, and dusted himself down and went on, jumping from boulder to boulder with a careless agility.

It hadn't been a vulture either.

A couple of hours later, they caught up with the Danes. There was a short drop at the end of the long boulder field, which obviously was a stream in the rainy season, and then a series of pools stepping down between huge water-carved rocks, strange tree-ferns growing in pockets of soil on top of the rocks and shading the pools so that it was like descending through a green water chute. Most of the pools could be waded; the water was warm, and it was very humid. The only really deep pool could be crossed by clinging to a blue nylon rope bolted to the curved flank of a huge boulder while using a second rope as a kind of tightrope, and then swinging around the corner onto a knife-edge of slippery black rock that lipped the pool (Ty, made clumsy because he had to hold his camera away from the rock, scraped his arm badly). Then there was an easy descent over cobbled boulders to a forest of fern trees, the air hot and humid under their stiff green fronds, their scaly trunks covered in creepers and bromeliads, blackflies and sweat bees a torment. They came out of this, and there were the Danes camped at the edge of a wide apron of rock.

The Danes weren't Danish; they were an Australian family who spent their lives adventuring. They'd sailed a yacht around the world, trekked through the Himalayas, spent two years trying to save one of the last coral reefs off Belize. Ken, who had a bit of Aborigine blood and never let you forget it, and his wife Kerry, were both in their early forties, super-fit and very competent. Their son, Sky, was seventeen, the youngest member of the expedition, but one of the best climbers. He and his parents worked together in a close knit team.

Vignone started in on them almost straight away, of course. He'd been working himself up to it on the descent. He told them that they were taking the best of the climb and turning everyone else into their bearers, that they were being selfish and wrecking the spirit of the expedition.

"Now hold on, mate," Ken said, "don't you think that's a bit harsh?"

"We're doing what we were asked to do," Kerry said. She put a hand on her husband's shoulder. She was taller than him. Her blond hair was tied back from her tanned, lined face.

"I'd say we're doing a fair job," Ken said to Lowe, who shrugged uncomfortably, his face turning redder under its sunburn, and mumbled that there was a bit of feeling amongst the others, and maybe it would be a good idea to make a camp here and wait.

"And not rip on?" Ken said. "That's crazy. You can see what comes next. This beauty could be twenty miles deep for all we know."

They were at the top of a cliff that dropped into a narrow band of forest growing along the edge of another cliff, and so on, a series of cliffs and forested set-backs that stepped away toward the permanent mist cover, the banded bluffs on the far side of the Rift only half a mile away. Ty had taken a panoramic shot of it in the last light; now he had switched on the camera's floodlight and was filming the argument, swinging from face to face and hoping the microphone caught it all.

Vignone wanted the Danes to go back and join the resupply team while some of his climbing friends took their places; the Danes didn't see what was wrong with pressing on; both parties wanted Lowe to make a decision, and Lowe didn't want to. He tried using the Danes' radio to contact Read, but without any success, then said it would be best to wait, they'd done fantastically well and it was time to rest up and plan the next part of the descent.

"We've hardly begun to crack it," Ken Dane said.

"If you hadn't set up so many traverses," Vignone said, "we'd be much farther down and we wouldn't be so short of rope."

Which started another argument as the air darkened around them, until at last Vignone said that he was making the next pitch right now and would camp out alone, glaring at Lowe when the Englishman said mildly that it wasn't a very good idea.

"I want some fucking climbing," Vignone said. He was already sorting through one of the rope bags, paying out blue nylon cord in neat loops.

Sky said that he'd go with Vignone, but Vignone said he would solo it; the rock was dry and craggy. So after the wiry little man had put on his harness and climbing shoes and fixed the rope to the edge of the cliff, Ty filmed the first stage of his descent in the dusk, with Sky watching beside him. Sky was taller than his parents, his blond hair shaved close to his skull. When Vignone disappeared into a chimney and Ty turned off the camera, Sky said thoughtfully, "There are all sorts of weird things out here. I hope that guy doesn't run into any of them."

"I saw a bird today," Ty said, "A very strange bird."

Ken Dane said that there might be anything down here, there were hundreds of kilometers of forest after all, and his wife said, "This kind of place would make a fine reserve, don't you think? That's partly why we're here. You people make so much noise you've scared off all the wildlife—even we can hear you, sometimes. But we've seen a few things, moving away from us. There are some big animals down here. Ron has let his pride overrule his caution."

Ty knew that a jaguar could crush your skull in its jaws while you slept, or an anaconda could ease you into its gullet without waking you. Wild pigs could knock you down and strip your bones in a couple of minutes. There were dozens of species of poisonous spiders and snakes and scorpions. The campfire seemed very small in the huge darkness of the Rift.

Sky said, "I should go down there maybe."

"It's too dark now," Ken said. "We'll check him out first thing."

Ty told the Danes about the bird, and showed them the black feather he'd caught. It was greasy, and had a pungent, musky odor.

"Dr. Wilson will be pleased," Kerry Dane said.

They all woke a little after dawn. Ken and Sky Dane abseiled down the cliff to check on Ron Vignone; Ty and Kerry Dane and Lowe were eating breakfast when they came back and said that there was no sign of him but his torn sleeping bag.

3. Dr. Alex Wilson

There was so much fuss about the missing climber that Ty Brown forgot to tell Alex about the bird until the evening after the search.

Alex wasn't too worried about the climber. It was well known that the man had been pretty pissed at the way the Danes had charged ahead of everyone else, and he'd probably gone off to get some glory of his own. Foolish and selfish, yes, but that was all it was. He'd left his sleeping bag behind and it had been torn up by animals. There was no blood, no trail; any animal dragging away a human body would have left both. No one would listen to Alex's opinions though, and Lowe insisted on wasting the day by searching the long narrow forest.

Ever since they had begun the descent into the Rift, Alex had been possessed by a kind of smouldering fury mixed with anxiety—the whole expedition had been turned into a circus, a race for the bottom at all costs, and he had been helpless to stop it. The search for the missing climber was finally a chance to look around, but Alex was paired up with a taciturn climber who took the search seriously and the noise the others made probably scared off every animal in the Rift: He saw nothing and returned in a bad temper made worse because the botanist woman, Amy Burton, was brimful of enthusiasm. The forest was a relic community, she said, full of cycads, gnetophyte vines and ancient species of pines; even something she was pretty sure might be a species of cycadeoid, a group which was thought to have died out tens of millions of years ago, although she couldn't be sure because it had not been bearing any cones. She wanted Alex to help her do some quadrats right there so that she could attempt to determine species diversity, but he refused of course, and tried to explain that diversity best correlated with the number of bird species—what was the point of counting plants or insects when it was easier to look for birds?

"At least we can count plants," Amy Burton said. She was a defiant, dumpy woman, her T-shirt sweat stained and her dishwater blond hair ratty around her face. Alex pointed out that when it came to preserving ecosystems, rare animals were essential in raising a media profile, and she walked away, flushed with anger.

Alex turned to Ty, who had been filming them, and said, "I hope you got all that."

He was pissed with Ty, too. The cameraman had become obsessed with silly little spats and disputes when he should have been concentrating on Alex's work; after all, the bulk of the sponsorship had been raised to look for rare or previously unknown animals. But like most naturalists Ty was contemptuous of cryptozoology. He saw it as monster hunting, searching for Bigfoot or the Loch Ness Monster or dinosaurs in the Congo when really it was nothing of the sort—well, it was true that Alex *had* collaborated with Read in a search for Bigfoot in the Sierras a couple of years ago, but that had just been to raise his profile so he could get money to do some real scientific work, something a snobby academic like Amy Burton, with her university sinecure couldn't understand. No, cryptozoology was just what it meant: the study of hidden animals. Even today, with ecosystems all over the world in poor shape and even the most remote forests being cut down, new species were turning up all the time: an ungulate in Vietnam, a parrot in Venezuela; a big flame-kneed tarantula in the Sonoran Desert. It was quite possible that some of the large mammals which had been wiped out by human invasion of North America had survived in remote areas of the South American rain forest; there had been indisputable sightings of giant sloths by loggers and Alex was pretty sure that the hair samples he had obtained from the local Indians would yield DNA for testing.

He was so riled by the dumb argument with the Burton woman that at first he ignored Ty when the cameraman said he'd seen an odd bird the day before, but then Ty produced the feather and described what he'd seen, and Alex's anger melted away because even before he saw the brief blurred video clip on the camera's tiny screen he knew what it had to be, and that this would make his name and end forever the hard scrabble for funds and the contempt of lab-bound scientists.

On the other side of the camp, Lowe shouted and clapped his hands for attention, saying that he'd finally made contact with the Old Man, and he was already on his way down.

4. Ralph Read

It was all falling apart, and the injury to his knee was almost the final blow. He'd come here to prove that he was still who they all thought he was, Ralph Read, the Old Man, Himalayan veteran back when Katmandu hadn't been full of bad German cooking and American hippies, before the real explorers had run out of world to explore, before it had become so small and used up. Last time he'd been up Everest, escorting some film actor and a documentary crew, he had been horrified by what had happened to the beautiful mountain: the queues of fee-paying novice climbers waiting their turn to strike for the summit, the litter, the piles of shit, the toilet paper and food wrappers blowing around, the discarded oxygen and propane cylinders, the dead bodies lying in the ice, everyone too preoccupied with getting to the top or too exhausted to bury them properly, let alone bring them down. He had helped do that to her, he realized—the horde had followed in his footsteps. She was ruined. And now his life in ruins too. It was the Rift, the bitch of the Rift. All mountains were women to Ralph; he had seduced them—*ravished* them—with the same inexhaustible energy with which he had pursued real women. And the Rift was no different, except they had to conquer her from the top down, but she was hard, the bitch, too hard for him. The Old Man: old and fucked up.

Perhaps it was because of the dirty secret, he thought, the thing no one else but he knew, the way he'd found out about her and then pretended she was his discovery when all along she'd been someone else's. Like many of the old style mountaineers, Ralph was a deeply superstitious man. Back then you relied on yourself and your own good luck, not on piton guns and free-running carabineers and nylon rope, on oxygen and lightweight sleeping bags and radios—good Christ, people even took portable phones up mountains now, to call up the rescue services when they got in trouble or ran out of soup. No, you had needed skill and luck in the glory days of climbing, before technology all but factored luck out of the equation, and luck was an intangible gift that had to be carefully cultivated.

But now he'd blown it; he should have known on his first expedition into the Rift, when he had tried to follow the route of the Victorian explorers and had been caught by an early start to the rainy season and had almost drowned. And now this, a man lost and his knee fucked and Alex Wilson babbling in his face about some stupid bird—Wilson had never understood that at the heart of the expedition was the need to conquer, to claim, to show that the Rift's wilderness could be matched and overcome by the human spirit.

It was all just too bad: bad luck.

It took Ralph a day to descend to where the expedition had stalled, far longer than he had expected. He had always known that he wasn't up to forging the path all the way down, but he thought that he could make the last mile or so, wherever it was below the perpetual mists, be the first to the bottom. So he waited at the rim, ostensibly to coordinate the supply lines and the advance party, but even that went wrong very quickly—the Rift's granite walls scrambled radio signals, and the helicopter pilots refused to descend within her walls because of unpredictable updrafts and katabatic winds dropping over the edge. So in the end he'd decided to go down early, and just as well, because halfway down, when he finally made contact with Lowe, he learnt that one of the young climbers had gone missing and Lowe was in a panic about it, a good second-in-command but without the backbone to make decisions in the pinch.

Ralph had trained rigorously, but he was too old; no amount of training could get him fit enough. His arms were still strong and he could bench press twice his weight, but his lung capacity was half what it was and his legs were giving out. Even though he was helped by two climbers, the descent took far too long, and then he banged up his knee.

He had been all right abseiling down the easy pitches—the equipment and gravity took care of that—but there were far too many traverses and far too much walking, and then there was a tricky move around a big boulder at the edge of a pool, something that in his prime he would have managed easily. But he hurt his knee badly making the move, and hurt it again when he landed half in water, half on the pool's rocky rim, and it quickly swelled even though one of his helpers put a pressure bandage on it. He insisted on going on, although every step jammed a red-hot needle under his tender kneecap, at last having to be supported on either side by his helpers down the boulder field, then lowered in a sling down the cliff like a sack of meal, sweating like a pig and itching with prickly heat, the muggy air like gruel in his lungs.

So when he finally arrived at the camp, he was exhausted and almost in tears, from the pain of his injury and from the shame of his failure, not at all ready to deal with the pandemonium which erupted around him almost at once. Lowe was desperate for advice while at the same time pretending that he'd done everything he could; the other climbers all wanted to give their opinion; and Alex Wilson was babbling about some bird someone had spotted.

Ralph waved them all off, demanding in his stentorian voice that he be given some hot chocolate and perhaps something to eat and certainly somewhere comfortable so that he could put up his knee. That gave him a breathing space, at last he was seated on a pile of rope sacks like a monarch, turning his good profile to the glare of the light clipped to Ty Brown's video camera, one big hand wrapped around a steaming tin mug, the other stroking his bristling beard, for all the world like a monarch and the climbers his supplicants, Wilson skulking with the botanist woman, the two of them exchanging furious whispers like plotters at the edge of his court. He got the story out of Lowe, silencing with glare anyone who tried to chip in, and knew it was bad. The expedition had been strung out too thinly—he'd let the Danes set the pace and they had gone off without any regard for the difficulties of resupply. Despite the money they'd brought, bamboozled from some long-haired bleeding-heart pop-singer millionaire, it had been a mistake taking them on: They weren't team material. And it was clear that his guesses about what supplies would be needed had been hopelessly inadequate. At this rate they'd run out of rope in two or three days, and they were nowhere near the bottom yet. But he had to try and salvage what he could.

Ralph asked for silence and made a pretense of thinking, but he had decided what to do almost at once. Divide and rule, the only way. So he told them that the climbers would be divided into two teams, taking turns to forge new pitches or work on resupply, scavenging rope if necessary. The Danes, who had already done so much good work, would have the important job of looking for the missing climber . . . for a moment he couldn't remember his name. Vignone, that was it, Ron Vignone.

"He's probably gone off on his own, but we need to make sure he isn't lying up somewhere with a broken ankle, eh?" He looked around at them all, beaming: patriarchal but stern.

Lowe objected of course, because Ralph had undermined his authority, such as it was. He especially didn't like the idea of scavenging rope from pitches higher up. "What if we need to ascend quickly? If someone gets hurt or the rains start early?"

"We've plenty of good climbers," Ralph said. "I'm sure they can re-establish the routes quickly enough, especially as the pitons are already emplaced."

"I don't know," Lowe said. "Some of those overhangs are rather—"

"I chose my climbers well I hope," Ralph said. "I'm sure they're up to the challenge."

And of course they all nodded, either because they were as full of piss and vinegar as he had been at their age, or because they didn't want to admit their fear; once you let your fear show you're finished as a climber.

"Well then," Ralph said, and smiled at them all and lit a cigar, even though he was still short of breath in the soupy air, and asked Ty Brown, "I hope you got all that, young man. It's a pivotal point in our little adventure."

Alex Wilson came forward, stepping amongst the climbers, and said, "What about the bird?"

Ralph had forgotten about that detail. He blew a plume of cigar smoke and said, "You and the young lady there can help look for Ron, and perhaps you'll find this bird, too."

In his opinion the whole thing would go faster without having to nursemaid a couple of scientists. Perhaps this really would work out after all. Of course, losing a team member was lamentable, but it was excusable as long as they reached their goal. A necessary sacrifice.

Wilson wanted more, of course—he wanted everyone to look for the confounded bird, and the botanist woman backed him up even though the two of them had previously been like cat and dog. Wilson babbled about relic populations, about the importance of a living fossil which might resolve the debate about whether or not birds had evolved from dinosaurs. "If I can find a fertile egg, I can determine whether its digits are reduced according to the theropod pattern or that of modern birds. And dissection will show whether the lungs are bellow-like or flow-through. It will be the discovery of the century, believe me," and so on, playing to Ty Brown's camera until Ralph cut him off.

"We still need to get to the bottom of the Rift, so we must push on."

Wilson was so wound up he was actually quivering with indignation. "But the science—"

"Science and exploration go hand in hand here," Ralph told him. "Now, I think we've had enough talk. I'm sure we all need some rest. We have a lot of work to do, but I'm confident you are all up to it."

But later, he was unable to sleep. The expedition was falling apart, a man missing and almost certainly dead, and he had staked everything on a last throw, a desperate race for the bottom which would only succeed if his luck held. He lay awake a long time, thinking of the notebook he had discovered, the diary of a member of a Victorian expedition which had penetrated several miles into the Rift before being chased off by a fierce tribe of Indians. The notebook he had kept secret, the clues it provided enough to pinpoint the Rift on photographs taken by a Russian landsat so that he could claim it for himself, and himself alone. Read's Rift. It had a certain ring. He had never told anyone about the notebook; no one but him knew about the indigenous tribe or the other things. The relic bird was nothing compared with the claims of the Rift's first explorers, but of course he couldn't tell Wilson about that, just as he couldn't reveal that he knew that a lost tribe of Indians lived here.

And so no one was armed except for him. He had brought his ex-army Wembley .45. He hoped upon hope he wouldn't have to use it. That his luck would hold.

5. Amy Burton

"At least we can get some work done," Alex Wilson said *sotto voce* to Amy the next morning, as the two parts of the expedition got ready, one to descend further, the other to retrieve ropes from higher up. A sentiment which managed to shock her even though she had already decided that, this side of snake oil sellers, dieticians and shampoo manufacturers, Wilson was quite the most amoral person masquerading as a scientist she'd ever come across. A man had gone missing, for God's sake; he might be dead. Well, perhaps she shouldn't be surprised. It was common gossip that Wilson's Ph.D. was nothing of the sort, merely an honorary doctorate from a Midwest college dazzled by his series of lost world TV documentaries, and it seemed to Amy that he was both horribly arrogant and desperately insecure. She'd kept away from him as much as possible, given that he kept trying to pick fights with her on specious grounds, and fortunately he'd spent more and more time arguing with the cameraman, who proposed following the new lead team rather than filming Wilson searching for his bird.

Meanwhile, Ralph Read sat on his throne of rope bags saying nothing yet trying to look as if he was still in command. He was pale under his tan, sweating heavily, and massaging his bandaged knee when he thought no one was looking. When Amy saw him take a swig of something from a silver flask, she assumed her best no-nonsense voice and told him she'd take a look at that knee, and he gave in after a token protest.

"I've no objection to be administered to by a comely young woman," he said.

"Bullshit," Amy said, for she harbored no illusions about herself—she was a dumpy, pear-shaped thirty-five, a handmaiden to science with a poor career profile because she loved field expeditions far more than the publication mill or the petty rivalries of university departmental politics. Her father had worked for the

CIA in Central America in the sixties, when half the governments had been in the pay of the United Fruit Company, and although she was irredeemably left wing in the classic pattern of anti-parental rebellion, she loved her father for the camping expeditions on which he'd taken her and her brother—it was where she had developed her passion for botany, and where her life had been shaped.

She got rid of the poorly knotted bandages by using her Swiss Army knife; Read winced as she probed his knee with expert fingers. It was in bad shape, misshapen and swollen with internal bleeding, the skin a shiny black. She treated it with Novocaine cream and splinted it, and told Read that he should really be taken back up.

"The expedition needs me," he said. "I'm quite comfortable, and I'm sure the radio will work better down here. Thank you," he added. "It does feel better."

"In this climate it'll get gangrenous if you don't get proper treatment," she warned him.

"Oh, a little gangrene is nothing," he said, with a ghost of his usual braggadocio. "I lost two toes on my first assault on K2."

Before they left, Amy had two of the climbers rig up a sunshade for the silly, vain old man, and then the expedition divided with noisy banter. The Danes got up from where they had been squatting and drifted into the forest—a strange secretive bunch, but Amy quite liked them, despite Ken's aggressive assertion of his one-eighth Aboriginal ancestry. Ty Brown went down the cliff with the lead party; Alex Wilson ascended with the rope scavengers to search for his bird where Ty had seen it yesterday. Amy shouldered her backpack and made herself scarce before the old man tried to persuade her to stay and keep him company rather than wandering off into a dangerous forest by herself.

Amy didn't think the forest dangerous at all, although it *was* spectacularly strange. With cycads as the primary growth, it really was the kind of place where you expected to be confronted by a dinosaur, and she was certain that several of the species she saw were new to science—either relic species or genuinely unknown. If she could have her way, the expedition would abandon all efforts to get to the bottom and concentrate on doing some real science, but there was no chance of that while Read was still its leader. He was interested in nothing but climbing. He'd even called this place a rift for God's sake, when it was nothing at all like a rift valley: it was a canyon, probably formed on a fault line and deepened by irregular uplift and water erosion, perhaps even the collapse of an underground water course.

The narrow belt of forest stretched for more than a mile to either side of the camp, slashed by smooth rock flood channels. It was like the cliff forests which had been discovered in Canada, a refuge for dozens of species which could obtain precarious footholds in its diverse range of microhabitats; and it was also an island population, its environment both geographically isolated and physically distinct from the rain forests around the massif which the Rift bisected, an evolutionary laboratory where species could explosively radiate to fill empty niches.

Amy passed through the forest which had been searched yesterday, descended a long gentle grade of tumbled rocks, an old rockfall overgrown by creepers and ferns and moss, and rambled on through the unexplored lower terrace of the forest. She sketched and took meticulous photographs with a scale always in the foreground, took samples of leaves and cones and flowers and placed them in plastic bags with a dusting of camphor powder to kill bugs, carefully documented each photograph and specimen. She took species counts of gridded areas too, and assessed growth habits as best she could.

And always she was filled with wonder at the treasure house through which she wandered, a last wilderness that even now was being despoiled by the expedition. Wilson was right about the bird, of course; if it was a living fossil, a close relative of the ancestral species of modern birds, surviving as coelacanths had survived in the deep waters off East Africa before they had been fished out, then it really was a fantastically important scientific discovery. Yet the forests were important too, although he couldn't see it—that was the problem with zoologists. They were so focused on their big mammal star species—pandas or tigers or blue whales—that they often didn't see the importance of the infrastructure of plants and fungi and insects and even bacteria which made up the habitats where the mammals lived. The primary mistake of zoos and many conservation bodies was to believe that by saving a rare animal they had somehow preserved the most important member of a vanishing habitat, but without the thousands of unacknowledged species which coexisted with it, it was no more than a trophy living out the last of its days in sterile captivity. More enlightened programs held that everything in a habitat was important; they took cores or sweep samples, tried to calculate and define biodiversity. That was why Amy's work was so important.

In this way, the day passed quickly, until she discovered the standing stone.

In fact, she walked right past it without really seeing it. It was only when she was taking a photograph a little way off that she really saw what it was, and went back with her heart hammering, suddenly full of apprehension.

It was a columnar piece of native granite a dozen feet high, perhaps originally flaked from the cliff by weathering, but someone had set it upright in the thin laterite soil and shaped its base into the crude likeness of a pregnant woman. It reminded Amy of the ancient clay figures discovered in prehistoric cave dwellings. She walked around it, noting brown, wilted flowers at the base, and a pile of rotten figs, and started to take photographs, the click of the camera shutter and the whine of the motor suddenly very loud and obtrusive in the watchful green of the forest. She was just putting the camera back in her pack when she heard a faint crackle far off, as if someone had stepped on one of the dried cycad fronds which everywhere littered the ground. Heart in mouth, she lifted the pack and backed into a stand of feathery mimosa, settling down on her haunches, her eyes skittering back and forth as they tried to distinguish movement in the green shadows.

There! A tall figure drifting silently down the path she had followed. Amy almost burst out laughing, for she saw at once who it was. He was quite naked, and carried something before him—a bright wreath of orchids, which he placed with awkward yet touching reverence at the foot of the standing stone.

When Amy stood up and stepped from her hiding place, he jumped almost a foot in the air and then she did laugh, and after a few seconds he did, too.

"Well, you caught me I guess," Sky Dane said, with a rueful grin.

"I didn't mean to." Amy wanted to ask where his parents where, and where his clothes were, too (although he was so unselfconsciously naked that he was clad, as it were, in his dignity). Instead, she asked him about the standing stone, and who might have carved it.

"I mean," she said, "no Indian tribes would work something like this in stone. It isn't in their tradition."

"Not in their tradition, I guess, no."

"But there is a tribe living here."

"Sort of."

"And you know about them, you and your parents."

"Sort of." She stared at him and he did blush then, and added, "We've seen signs here and there. We travel fast, faster than the others suspect, so we've had time for a bit of exploring. We saw one or two things. There's an old cliff dwelling half a mile up, made in a cave under an overhang. They must have lived there a fair old time because the ashes from their fires are more than ten feet deep, but my dad reckons that no one has lived there for thousands of years. We found some glyphs carved in the rocks, too, although you have to have the eye to see them."

"Who are they? Do you think they took the climber?"

For a moment Amy had the horrible thought that perhaps the Danes had murdered him—but no, Ty Brown and Alex Wilson had been with them.

Sky said, "They killed him most like. It's what Indians do with intruders on their patch. Look, are you going to tell about this?"

Amy said carefully, "Is it important that I don't?"

"Not when you get back. In fact, it's important you tell people, because of the government rules about undiscovered tribes. We can give you stuff about what we found, photos and the like. But I mean, you won't tell the others now."

"I don't see why—"Amy started to say, but got no further because that was when the shots rang out in the distance.

Two shots, close-spaced, echoing off the cliff above. A third rang out just after Amy started to run, chasing after Sky's fleet figure, his buttocks glimmering in the green gloom as he raced away from her.

It was a long run, across the old rockfall and through another mile of forest. She arrived at the camp covered in sweat and out of breath, mouth parched with fear. Sky, now wearing shorts and a T-shirt, was tending to a man who lay on the ground clutching his thigh—there was blood running between his hands, soaking his shorts. Ralph Read stood at the edge of the drop, propping himself up with a tent pole and menacing the air with a huge antique revolver.

"They ran, by God," he shouted to Amy, fierce and exultant. "By God how they ran!"

"Here," Amy told Sky, "let me look," and knelt by the wounded man.

It was one of the young climbers, Matt Johnson. His face was grey, and slick with sweat. He told Amy, his voice tight with pain, "They came at us while we were hacking through forest a couple of terraces below. I don't know where the others are."

Amy glanced at Sky and said, "Tell me later," and pried his fingers away from his thigh and saw the slim arrow shaft which stood up from it, fletched with dyed red feathers. She probed around it, determined that the head wasn't in the bone, and told Matt Johnson what she was going to do. "It will hurt," she said.

"It already hurts."

"You had better hurry there," Read shouted. "The buggers will be back."

Amy twisted up her handkerchief and gave it to Matt Johnson to bite down on, then cut the shaft in half with her knife and with one quick hard motion pushed the remainder of the arrow through the meat of his thigh. Blood gushed as the arrowhead broke through the skin on the far side. Its point was flaked stone, neatly socketed in the shaft. She got a grip on blood-slick stone and drew the rest of the shaft from the wound.

Matt Johnson looked at it and shuddered and said, "Jesus fuck."

"Don't faint on me now," Amy told him, hoping he wasn't going into shock.

"It isn't so bad."

"You're lucky it wasn't poisoned," Sky said.

Amy washed blood from the young climber's wounds, sprinkled antibiotic powder in them and packed them, and wound a bandage tightly around his thigh. A little blood soaked through, but the arrow seemed to have missed the major vessels.

Ralph Read had been hobbling up and down at the edge of the cliff, yelling into the radio, cursing, switching frequencies and yelling some more. Now he threw the radio aside and drew his revolver and fired three times at something below the cliff edge, each shot a tremendous shocking noise. "Here they come!" he shouted into the echoing silence, and broke the revolver open and thumbed brass cartridges into its chamber, closed it, and started to fire again.

Amy reached the edge of the cliff and looked down just as the arrows started to fly up, dozens of them twinkling at the peak of their ascent and then slipping back down the air. Ralph Read began

to shoot into the trees from which they came, the revolver bucking
in his hand. Amy thought she saw shadows slipping through shadows beneath the cycads along the edge of the talus slope at the bottom of the cliff, and then Sky pulled her away.

"You must go!" Sky yelled, but she hardly heard him, half-
deafened by the revolver and the hammering of her heart. He tried
to drag her across the rock apron towards the cliff and the fixed
ropes, but she pulled back.

Ralph Read was leaning on the tent pole and reloading his
revolver, a wild and grim expression on his face. He glanced at
them and said, "I'll keep them off until you reach the top of the
cliff. I can't climb with this blasted knee, but you can lower a sling
and get me up that way. Go on now!"

Sky said, "He's right. I'll stay and help him. You go. And
remember to tell the authorities that there are Indians living
here!"

Matt Johnson had already climbed into his harness, and now
he helped Amy get into hers. She hadn't realized how scared she
was until she tried to do up the buckles, all thumbs. She said to
Matt Johnson, "Can you climb?"

"I can always climb. I got back, didn't I?"

His face was still grey with shock, and his hands were trembling, but he got her harness fastened and roped her to him and
they started the climb, leaning out more or less horizontally and
walking up the face of the vertical cliff of hard red-black granite.
The harnesses were fixed to the ropes with jumars, metal clasps
which slid up the rope but not down, and although these made the
climb easier, Amy's arms and shoulders were soon burning. There
was a traverse thirty feet up, along a narrow ledge to the chimney
that led up through a big overhang. Matt Johnson started to spider
along it; he had to use his legs as much as his arms, and she heard
his gasps of pain. Then he was at the chimney and paid out the
belay rope, and it was her turn. Just as she started the traverse, her
clumsy hiking boots slipping on the ledge, her hands cramping

around the rope, the greasy granite an inch from her nose, something clattered beside her. An arrow. More lofted towards her, small deadly things that struck the rock on either side and dropped away. Then she was at the chimney and hauled herself up with Matt Johnson yelling encouragement. When she was lodged safely in it, rock on either side, she dared look back.

Below, Ralph Read was standing by the piled equipment in the center of the rock apron, firing first to one side and then the other. Arrow shafts stuck out from his torso. Figures were dancing at the edge of the cycads, seemingly dressed in shaggy hides. She could not see Sky. Then the belay rope tightened. Matt Johnson was climbing on and she turned and followed him and saw no more.

6. *The Danes*

What can you say about the Danes? They are not Danish but Australian. They are a tightly bound unit, mother and father and son. They have their own rituals, their own body language. They are bonded together so tightly that nothing can pry them apart—not Ken's occasional infidelities, not Sky's occasional moony girlfriends, whom he mostly ignores because he needs nothing more than his family and their way of life.

They had a long palaver after Ralph Read's speech, realizing that they had reached the crux of their private mission. "We'll look for this cludger," Ken said, "but they certainly murdered him, and they don't want us to find his body or they would have just left it."

Sky, who loved horror movies, said, "Ate him, I reckon."

"Now we don't know that," Kerry said. "The evidence of cannibalism was only found in grave sites, and it was probably ritual."

"It's what they do in the New Hebrides," Sky said.

"These people aren't anything like that," Kerry said.

"They murdered him and stuffed his body somewhere," Ken said. "And they'll probably kill the rest of the climbers, too. It's a

72   PAUL J. MCAULEY

shame, but there it is. It isn't their fault these bastards came blundering in."

"That's just why we should tell Read what we know," Kerry said, but Ken vetoed that. "That bugger Wilson would chase after them," he said, "and so would Read. The two of them went looking for Bigfoot together, remember. So we can't let them know what's here; the poor people would be turned into circus freaks."

They talked some more, but it was decided. The next day they went their separate ways into the forest, and when the inevitable happened, Read's revolver shots ringing out into the Rift and finally ceasing, they met up in a prearranged spot several miles south of the campsite.

Even when part of other expeditions, the Danes always had their own agenda. It added spice, as Ken liked to say, and spice was everything in life. He didn't mind that people said they were hippies, relics from a lost age, that he was trying to keep his youth alive through adventure. It was all part of the cover of the half-world they inhabited. There were others like them, keeping the secrets of the world safe, a disorganized conspiracy which somehow worked most of the time.

They had been allowed to join the expedition because they had wangled money from a pop star to look for new tribes of Indians. There were still plenty to be found in the Amazonian basin, even at this late stage in its exploitation. The forests really were very extensive and very close grown. A hundred people, the size of most Indian tribes, living off the land in a small area, could stay hidden until some prospector or logger stumbled into them by accident. Just a couple of years ago, a jaguar hunter had been murdered, shot with an arrow, when he had encountered a hunting party of a previously unknown tribe, and a subsequent aerial survey had spotted the tribe's huts, almost invisible beneath the close-knit forest canopy. Like all recently discovered tribes, it had been left alone; the late twentieth century was as toxic to these Stone Age indigens as poison gas. The whole area had been declared off-limits.

That was what the Danes hoped for here, and they were pretty certain now that this was a very special tribe indeed.

They met at the standing stone. Sky was naked again, as were his mother and father. Sky had smeared the green juice of berries on his face and bare chest. He had knotted a black T-shirt around his head to hide his blond hair. He told his parents what had happened, and Ken nodded and asked what the botanist woman had seen.

"They didn't come into the open until she was halfway up the cliff," Sky said. "I reckon she didn't see too much. But one of the climbers got away too, and I don't know what he saw."

Ken scratched at the pelt on his chest. He was a stocky man, with a broad nose and a shock of wiry hair. "Well, it's a risk," he said, "but not a bad one. The others will be too scared to look around much."

Sky thought about how Amy had found him, and her questions, but kept silent. He trusted her; she had been the only one who had tried to understand this place.

"They'll think it's just Indians," his wife said. "They don't have the imagination for anything else."

"We'll wait here a while I reckon," Ken said. "When the fuss has died down we'll see what's left of the supplies, and then we can begin."

They sat in green shadow a little way from the standing stone. "They ran from everyone," Kerry said dreamily, leaning against her husband.

"It was the first great extinction," Ken said. "They were killed just like my people were killed when the Europeans came to Australia. They were hunted for sport because it was easier to think of them as animals than accept that people come in many different forms. *Homo sapiens* has done a lot of harm in its time, but that was the beginning of it all."

"Some got away," Kerry said. "Think how far they came! They were pushed further and further from Africa."

"Or Java," Ken said.

"They must have been the first to cross from Asia to Alaska," Kerry said, "but the modern humans followed and pushed them farther. Until they ended up here, with the other relic species."

"Something's coming," Sky said, and at the same moment the first of them stepped out of the darkness between the cycads.

"Steady," Ken said. "Remember we're not like the others."

The figure which confronted them was small and stooped yet muscularly broad, and covered in a reddish pelt. Its feet clutched the earth; one leathery hand clutched a sapling whittled into a spear. Little eyes glinted under the shelf of its brow; its nose was broad and bridgeless; there was no chin beneath its wide mouth. It made no signal, but suddenly there were others behind it.

Sky and Ken and Kerry slowly got to their feet. Naked, they held out their hands to show that they had no weapons, that they were no threat, and waited for judgment.

Bruce McAllister was a regular contributor to *Omni* magazine and its related anthologies in the eighties and early nineties. His science fiction and fantasy has appeared in magazines, original anthologies, year's best reprint anthologies, and college textbooks since the sixties. His 1988 novel *Dream Baby* is slated for a Vietnamese edition both in the U.S. and in Southeast Asia in 2000, and is available in English from Tor Books' Orb trade paperback line.

After two decades of teaching writing at a small university in southern California and moonlighting in fields as diverse as advertising, seismic policy, and the behavioral sciences, he now makes his living as a writer and "editorial consultant" to new and established writers of novels, nonfiction books, and screenplays. He is married to the choreographer Amelie Hunter.

"The Girl Who Loved Animals" is one of several stories written by McAllister in the mid-eighties about an all too plausible near-future in which most animals are extinct and as a last ditch effort at preservation some have been put into "arks." McAllister's best work is imbued with passion and compassion. It's a loss to the field that he has written so little fiction in the past decade.

THE GIRL WHO LOVED ANIMALS

BRUCE MCALLISTER

They had her on the seventeenth floor in their new hi-security unit on Figueroa and weren't going to let me up. Captain Mendoza, the one who thinks I'm the ugliest woman he's ever laid eyes on and somehow manages to take it personally, was up there with her, and no one else was allowed. Or so this young lieutenant with a fresh academy tattoo on his left thumb tries to tell me. I get up real close so the kid can hear me over the screaming media crowd in the lobby and see this infamous face of mine, and I tell him I don't think Chief Stracher will like getting a call at 0200 hours just because some desk cadet can't tell a privileged soc worker from a media rep, and how good friends really shouldn't bother each other at that time of the day anyway, am I right? It's a lie, sure, but he looks worried, and I remember why I haven't had anything done about the face I was born with. He gives me two escorts—a sleek young swatter with an infrared Ruger, and a lady in fatigues who's almost as tall as I am—and up we go. They're efficient kids. They frisk me in the elevator.

Mendoza wasn't with her. Two P.D. medics with sidearms were. The girl was sitting on a sensor cot in the middle of their new glass observation room—closed-air, antiballistic Plexi, and the rest—and was a mess. The video footage, which four million people had seen at ten, hadn't been pixeled at all.

Their hi-sec floor cost them thirty-three million dollars, I told myself, took them three years of legislation to get, and had everything you'd ever want to keep your witness or assassin or jihad dignitary alive—CCTV, microwave eyes, pressure mats, blast doors, laser blinds, eight different kinds of gas, and, of course, Vulcan minicannons from the helipad three floors up.

I knew that Mendoza would have preferred someone more exciting than a twenty-year-old girl with a V Rating of nine point six and something strange growing inside her, but he was going to have to settle for this christening.

I asked the medics to let me in. They told me to talk into their wall grid so the new computer could hear me. The computer said something like, "Yeah, she's okay," and they opened the door and frisked me again.

I asked them to leave, citing Welfare & Institutions Statute Thirty-eight. They wouldn't, citing hi-sec orders under Penal Code

Seven-A. I told them to go find Mendoza and tell him I wanted privacy for the official interview.

Very nicely they said that neither of them could leave and that if I kept asking I could be held for obstruction, despite the same statute's cooperation clause. That sounded right to me. I smiled and got to work.

Her name was Lissy Tomer. She was twenty-one, not twenty. According to Records, she'd been born in the East Valley, been abused as a child by both sets of parents, and, as the old story goes, hooked up with a man who would oblige her the same way. What had kept County out of her life, I knew, was the fact that early on, someone in W&I had set her up with an easy spousal-abuse complaint and felony restraining-order option that needed only a phone call to trigger. But she'd never exercised it, though the older bruises said she should have.

She was pale and underweight and wouldn't have looked very good even without the contusions, the bloody nose and lip, the belly, and the shivering. The bloody clothes didn't help either. Neither did the wires and contact gel they had all over her for their beautiful new cot.

But there was a fragility to her—princess-in-the-fairy-tale kind—that almost made her pretty.

She flinched when I said hello, just as if I'd hit her. I wondered which had been worse—the beating or the media. He'd done it in a park and had been screaming at her when Mendoza's finest arrived, and two uniforms had picked up a couple of C's by calling it in to the networks.

She was going to get hit with a beautiful post-traumatic stress disorder sometime down the road even if things didn't get worse for her—which they would. The press wanted her badly. She was bloody, showing, and *very* visual.

"Has the fetus been checked?" I asked the sidearms. If they were going to listen, they could help.

The shorter one said yes, a portable sonogram from County, and the baby looked okay.

I turned back to the girl. She was looking up at me from the cot, looking hopeful, and I couldn't for the life of me imagine what she thought I could do for her.

"I'm your new V.R. advocate, Lissy."

She nodded, keeping her hands in her lap like a good girl.

"I'm going to ask you some questions, if that's all right. The more I know, the more help I can be, Lissy. But you know that, don't you." I grinned.

She nodded again and smiled, but the lip hurt.

I identified myself, badge and department and appellation, then read her her rights under Protective Services provisions, as amended—what we in the trade call the Nhat Hanh Act. What you get and what you don't.

"First question, Lissy: Why'd you do it?"

I asked it as gently as I could, flicking the hand recorder on. It was the law.

I wondered if she knew what a law was.

Her I.Q. was eighty-four, congenital, and she was a Collins psychotype, class three dependent. She'd had six years of school and had once worked for five months for a custodial service in Monterey Park. Her Vulnerability Rating, all factors factored, was a whopping nine point six. It was the rating that had gotten her a felony restraint complaint option on the marital bond, and County had assumed that was enough to protect her . . . from him.

As far as the provisions on low-I.Q. cases went, the husband had been fixed, she had a second-degree dependency on him, and an abortion in event of rape by another was standard. As far as County was concerned, she was protected, and society had exer-

cised proper conscience. I really couldn't blame her last V.R. advocate. I'd have assumed the same.

And missed one thing.

"I like animals a lot," she said, and it made her smile. In the
middle of a glass room, two armed medics beside her, the media
screaming downstairs to get at her, her husband somewhere wishing he'd killed her, it was the one thing that could make her smile.

She told me about a kitten she'd once had at the housing project on Crenshaw. She'd named it Lissy and had kept it alive "all by
herself." It was her job, she said, like her mother and fathers had
jobs. Her second stepfather—or was it her mother's brother? I
couldn't tell, and it didn't matter—had taken it away one day, but
she'd had it for a month or two.

When she started living with the man who'd eventually beat
her up in a park for the ten o'clock news, he let her have a little
dog. He would have killed it out of jealousy in the end, but it died
because she didn't know about shots. He wouldn't have paid for
them anyway, and she seemed to know that. He hadn't been like
that when they first met. It sounded like neurotransmitter blocks,
MPHG metabolism. The new bromaine that was on the streets
would do it; all the fentanyl analogs would, too. There were a
dozen substances on the street that would. You saw it all the time.

She told me how she'd slept with the kitten and the little dog
and, when she didn't have them anymore, with the two or three
toys she'd had so long that most of their fur was worn off. How
she could smell the kitten for months in her room just as if it were
still there. How the dog had died in the shower. How her husband
had gotten mad, hit her, and taken the thing away. But you could
tell she was glad when the body wasn't there in the shower anymore.

"This man was watching me in the park," she said. "He always
watched me."

"Why were you in the park, Lissy?"

She looked at me out of the corner of her eye and gave me a smile, the conspiratorial kind. "There's more than one squirrel in those trees. Maybe a whole family. I like to watch them."

I was surprised there were any animals at all in the park. You don't see them anymore, except for the domesticates.

"Did you talk to this man?"

She seemed to know what I was asking. She said, "I wasn't scared of him. He smiled a lot." She laughed at something, and we all jumped. "I knew he wanted to talk to me, so I pretended there was a squirrel over by him, and I fed it. He said, Did I like animals and how I could make a lot of money and help the animals of the world."

It wasn't important. A dollar. A thousand. But I had to ask.

"How much money did he tell you?"

"Nine thousand dollars. That's how much I'm going to get, and I'll be able to see it when it's born, and visit it."

She told me how they entered her, how they did it gently while she watched, the instrument clean and bright.

The fertilized egg would affix to the wall of her uterus, they'd told her, and together they would make a placenta. What the fetus needed nutritionally would pass through the placental barrier, and her body wouldn't reject it.

Her eyes looked worried now. She was remembering things— a beating, men in uniforms with guns, a man with a microphone pushed against her belly. *Had her husband hit her there? If so, how many times?* I wondered.

"Will the baby be okay?" she asked, and I realized I'd never seen eyes so colorless, a face so trusting.

"That's what the doctors say," I said, looking up at the side arms, putting it on them.

Nine thousand. More than a man like her husband would ever see stacked in his life, but he'd beaten her anyway, furious that she could get it in her own way when he'd failed again and again, furious that she'd managed to get it with the one thing he thought he owned—her body.

Paranoid somatopaths are that way.

I ought to know. I married one.

I'm thinking of the mess we've made of it, Lissy. I'm thinking of the three hundred thousand grown children of the walking wounded of an old war in Asia who walk the same way.

I'm thinking of the four hundred thousand walljackers, our living dead. I'm thinking of the zoos, the ones we don't have anymore, and what they must have been like, what little girls like Lissy Tomer must have done there on summer days.

I'm thinking of a father who went to war, came back, but was never the same again, of a mother who somehow carried us all, of how cars and smog and cement can make a childhood and leave you thinking you can change it all.

I wasn't sure, but I could guess. The man in the park was a body broker for pharmaceuticals and nonprofits, and behind him somewhere was a species resurrection group that somehow had the money. He'd gotten a hefty three hundred percent, which meant the investment was already thirty-six grand. He'd spent some of his twenty-seven paying off a few W&I people in the biggest counties, gotten a couple dozen names on high-V.R. searches, watched the best bets himself, and finally made his selection.

The group behind him didn't know how such things worked or didn't particularly care; they simply wanted consenting women of childbearing age, good health, no substance abuse, no walljackers, no suicidal inclinations; and the broker's reputation was good, and he did his job.

Somehow he'd missed the husband.

As I found out later, she was one of ten. Surrogates for human babies were a dime a dozen, had been for years. This was something else.

In a nation of two hundred eighty million, Lissy Tomer was one of ten—but in her heart of hearts she was the only one. Because a man who said he loved animals had talked to her in a park once. Because he'd said she would get a lot of money—money that ought to make a husband who was never happy, happy. Because she would get to see it when it was born and get to visit it wherever it was kept.

The odd thing was, I could understand how she felt.

I called Antalou at three A.M., got her mad but at least awake, and got her to agree we should try to get the girl out that same night— out of that room, away from the press, and into a County unit for a complete fetal check. Antalou is the kind of boss you only get in heaven. She tried, but Mendoza stonewalled her under P.C. Twenty-two, the Jorgenson clause—he was getting all the publicity he and his new unit needed with the press screaming downstairs—and we gave up at five, and I went home for a couple hours of sleep before the paperwork began.

I knew that sitting there in the middle of all that glass with two armed medics was almost as bad as the press, but what could I do, Lissy, what could I do?

I should have gone to the hotel room that night, but the apartment was closer. I slept on the sofa. I didn't look at the bedroom door, which is always locked from the outside. The nurse has a key. Some days it's easier not to think about what's in there. Some days it's harder.

I thought about daughters.

We got her checked again, this time at County Medical, and the word came back okay. Echomytic bruises with some placental bleeding, but the fetal signs were fine. I went ahead and asked whether the fetus was a threat to the mother in any case, and they laughed. No more than any human child would be, they said. All you're doing is borrowing the womb, they said. "Sure," this cocky young resident says to me, "it's low-tech all the way." I had a lot of homework to do, I realized.

Security at the hospital reported a visit by a man who was not her husband, and they didn't let him through. The same man called me an hour later. He was all smiles and wore a suit.

I told him we'd have to abort if County, under the Victims' Rights Act, decided it was best or the girl wanted it. He pointed out with a smile that the thing she was carrying was worth a lot of money to the people he represented, and they could make her life more comfortable, and we ought to protect the girl's interests.

I told him what I thought of him, and he laughed. "You've got it all wrong, Doctor."

I let it pass. He knows I'm an MPS-V.R., no Ph.D., no M.D. He probably even knows I got the degree under duress, years late, because Antalou said we needed all the paper we could get if the department was going to survive. I know what he's doing, and he knows I know.

"The people I represent are caring people, Doctor. Their cause is a good one. They're not what you're accustomed to working with, and they've retained me simply as a program consultant, a 'resource locator.' It's all aboveboard, Doctor, completely legal, I assure you. But I really don't need to tell you any of this, do I?"

"No, you don't."

I added that, legal or not, if he tried to see her again I would have him for harassment under the D.A.'s cooperation clause.

He laughed, and I knew then he had a law degree from one of the local universities. The suit was right. I could imagine him in it at the park that day.

"You may be able to pull that with the mopes and 5150's you work with on the street, Doctor, but I know the law. I'll make you a deal. I'll stay away for the next three months, as long as you look after the girl's best interests, how's that?"

I knew there was more, so I waited.

"My people will go on paying for weekly visits up to the eighth month, then daily through to term, the clinic to be designated by them. They want ultrasound, CVS, and amniotic antiabort treatments, and the diet and abstinence programs the girl's already agreed to. All you have to do is get her to her appointments, and we pay for it. Save the county some money."

I waited.

His voice changed as I'd known it would. The way they do in the courtrooms. I'd heard it change like that a hundred times before, years of it, both sides of the aisle.

"If County can't oblige," he said, "we'll just have to try Forty-A, right?"

I told him to take a flying something.

Maybe I didn't know the law, but I knew Forty-A. In certain circles it's known simply as Fucker-Forty. Under it—the state's own legislation—he'd be able to sue the county and this V.R. advocate in particular for loss of livelihood—his and hers—and probably win after appeals.

This was the last thing Antalou or any of us needed.

The guy was still smiling.

"You've kept that face for a reason, Doctor. What do young girls think of it?"

I hung up on him.

With Antalou's help I got her into the Huntington on Normandy, a maternal unit for sedated Ward B types. Some of the other women had seen her on the news two evenings before; some hadn't. *It didn't matter,* I thought. *It was about as good a place for her to hide as possible,* I told myself. I was wrong. Everything's on computer these days, and some information's as cheap as a needle.

I get a call the next morning from the unit saying a man had gotten in and tried to kill her, and she was gone.

I'm thinking of the ones I've lost, Lissy. The tenth-generation maggot casings on the one in Koreatown, the door locked for days. The one named Consejo, the one I went with to the morgue, where they cut up babies, looking for hers. The skinny one I thought I'd saved, the way I was supposed to, but he's lying in a pool of O-positive in a room covered with the beautiful pink dust they used for prints.

Or the ones when I was a kid, East LA, Fontana, the drugs taking them like some big machine, the snipings that always killed the ones that had nothing to do with it—the chubby ones, the ones who liked to read—the man who took Karenna and wasn't gentle, the uncle who killed his own nephews and blamed it on coyotes, which weren't there anymore, hadn't been for years.

I'm thinking of the ones I've lost, Lissy.

I looked for her all day, glad to be out of the apartment, glad to be away from a phone that might ring with a slick lawyer's face on it.

When I went back to the apartment that night to pick up another change of clothes for the hotel room, she was sitting cross-legged by the door.

"Lissy," I said, wondering how she'd gotten the address.

"I'm sorry," she said.

She had her hand on her belly, holding it not out of pain but as if it were the most comforting thing in the world.

"He wants to kill me. He says that anybody who has an animal growing in her is a devil and's got to die. He fell down the stairs. I didn't push him, I didn't."

She was crying, and the only thing I could think to do was get down and put my arms around her and try not to cry myself.

"I know, I know," I said. The symptoms were like Parkinson's, I remembered. You tripped easily.

I wasn't thinking clearly. I hadn't had more than two or three hours of sleep for three nights running, and all I could think of was getting us both inside, away from the steps, the world.

.   .   .

Maybe it was fatigue. Or maybe something else. I should have gotten her to a hospital. I should have called Mendoza for an escort back to his unit. What I did was get her some clothes from the bedroom, keep my eyes on the rug while I was in there, and lock the door again when I came out. She didn't ask why neither of us were going to sleep in the bedroom. She didn't ask about the lock. She just held her belly, and smiled like some Madonna.

I took two Dalmanes from the medicine cabinet, thinking they might be enough to get the pictures of what was in that room out of my head.

I don't know whether they did or not. Lissy was beside me, her shoulder pressing against me, as I got the futon and the sofa ready.

Her stomach growled, and we laughed. I said, "Who's growling? Who's growling?" and we laughed again. I asked her if she was hungry and if she could eat sandwiches. She laughed again, and I got her a fresh one from the kitchen.

She took the futon, lying on her side to keep the weight off. I took the sofa because of my long legs.

I felt something beside me in the dark. She kissed me, said "Good night," and I heard her nightgown whisper back into the darkness. I held it in for a while and then couldn't anymore. It didn't last long. Dalmane's a knockout.

The next day I took her to the designated clinic and waited outside for her. She was happy. The big amnio needle they stuck her with didn't bother her, she said. She liked how much bigger her breasts were, she said, like a mother's should be. She didn't mind being careful about what she ate and drank. She even liked the strange V of hair growing on her abdomen, because—because it was hairy, she said, just like the thing inside her. She liked how she felt, and she wanted to know if I could see it, the glow, the one expectant mothers are supposed to have. I told her I could.

I'm thinking of a ten-year-old, the one that used to tag along with me on the median train every Saturday when I went in for caseloads while most mothers had their faces changed, or played, or mothered. We talked a lot back then, and I miss it. She wasn't going to need a lot of work on that face, I knew—maybe the ears, just a little, if she was picky. She'd gotten her father's genes. But she talked like me—like a kid from East LA—tough, with a smile, and I thought she was going to end up a D.A. or a showy defense type or at least an exec. That's how stupid we get. In four years she was into molecular opiates and trillazines and whose fault was that? The top brokers roll over two billion a year in this city alone; the local *capi* net a twentieth of that, their street dealers a fourth; and God knows what the guys in the labs bring home to their families.

It's six years later, and I hear her letting herself in one morning. She's fumbling and stumbling at the front door. I get up, dreading it. What I see tells me that the drugs are nothing, nothing at all. She's running with a strange group of kids, a lot of them older. *This new thing's a fad,* I tell myself. It's like not having your face fixed—like not getting the nasal ramification modified, the mandibular thrust attended to—when you could do it easily, anytime, and cheaply, just because you want to make a point, and it's fun to goose the ones who need goosing. *That's all she's really doing,* you tell yourself.

You've seen her a couple of times like this, but you still don't recognize her. She's heavy around the chest and shoulders, which makes her breasts seem a lot smaller. Her face is heavy; her eyes are puffy, almost closed. She walks with a limp because something hurts down low. Her shoulders are bare, and they've got tattoos now, the new metallic kind, glittery and painful. She's wearing expensive pants, but they're dirty.

So you have a daughter now who's not a daughter, or she's both, boy and girl. The operation cost four grand, and you don't want to think how she got the money. Everyone's doing it, you tell yourself. But the operation doesn't take. She gets an infection, and the thing stops being fun, and six months later she's got no neurological response to some of the tissues the doctors have slapped on her, and pain in the others. It costs money to reverse. She doesn't have it. She spends it on other things, she says.

She wants money for the operation, she says, standing in front of you. You owe it to her, she says.

You try to find the ten-year-old in those eyes, and you can't.

Did you ever?

The call came through at six, and I knew it was County.

A full jacket—ward status, medical action, all of it—had been put through. The fetus would be aborted—"for the mother's safety . . . to prevent further exploitation by private interests . . . and physical endangerment by spouse."

Had Antalou been there, she'd have told me how County had already gotten flack from the board of supervisors, state W&I, and the attorney general's office over a V.R. like this slipping through and getting this much press. They wanted it over, done with. If the fetus were aborted, County's position would be clear—to state, the feds, and the religious groups that were starting to scream bloody murder.

It would be an abortion no one would ever complain about.

The husband was down at County holding with a pretty fibercast on his left tibia, but they weren't taking any chances. Word on two interstate conspiracies to kill the ten women had reached the D.A., and they were, they said, taking it seriously. I was, I said, glad to hear it.

Mendoza said he liked sassy women as much as the next guy, but he wanted her back in custody, and the new D.A. was screaming jurisdiction, too. Everyone wanted a piece of the ten o'clock news before the cameras lost interest and rolled on.

Society wasn't ready for it. The atavistic fears were there. You could be on trillazines, you could have an operation to be both a boy and a girl for the thrill of it, you could be a walljacker, but a mother like this, no, not yet.

I should have told someone but didn't. I took her to the zoo instead. We stood in front of the cages watching the holograms of the big cats, the tropical birds, the grass eaters of Africa—the ones that are gone. She wasn't interested in the real ones, she said—the pigeons, sparrows, coyotes, the dull hardy ones that will outlast us all. She never came here as a child, she said, and I believe it. A boyfriend at her one and only job took her once, and later, because she asked her to, so did a woman who wanted the same thing from her.

We watched the lions, the ibex, the white bears. We watched the long-legged wolf, the harp seals, the rheas. We watched the tapes stop and repeat, stop and repeat; and then she said, "Let's go," pulled at my hand, and we moved on to the most important cage of all.

There, the hologram walked back and forth looking out at us, looking through us, its red sagittal crest and furrowed brow so convincing. Alive, its name had been Mark Anthony, the plaque said. It had weighed two hundred kilos. It had lived to be ten. It wasn't one of the two whose child was growing inside her, but she seemed to know this, and it didn't matter.

"They all died the same way," she said to me. "That's what counts, Jo." *Inbred depression,* I remembered reading. *Petechial hemorrhages, cirrhosis, renal failure.*

Somewhere in the nation the remaining fertilized ova were sitting frozen in a lab, as they had for thirty years. A few dozen had been removed, thawed, encouraged to divide to sixteen cells, and finally implanted that day seven months ago. Ten had taken. As they should have, naturally, apes that we are. "Sure, it could've been done back then," the cocky young resident with insubordina-

tion written all over him had said. "All you'd have needed was an
egg and a little plastic tube. And, of course"—I didn't like the way
he smiled—"a woman who was willing. . . ."

I stopped her. I asked her if she knew what The Arks were, and
she said no. I started to tell her about the intensive-care zoos where
for twenty years the best and brightest of them, ten thousand
species in all, had been kept while two hundred thousand others
disappeared—the toxics, the new diseases, the land-use policies of a
new world taking them one by one—how The Arks hadn't worked,
how two-thirds of the macrokingdom were gone now, and how the
thing she carried inside her was one of them and one of the best.

She wasn't listening. She didn't need to hear it, and I knew the
man in the suit had gotten his yes without having to say these
things. The idea of having it inside her, hers for a little while, had
been enough.

She told me what she was going to buy with the money. She
asked me whether I thought the baby would end up at this zoo. I
told her I didn't know but could check, and hated the lie. She said
she might have to move to another city to be near it. I nodded and
didn't say a thing.

I couldn't stand it. I sat her down on a bench and told her what
the County was going to do to her.

When I was through she looked at me and said she'd known it
would happen, it always happened. She didn't cry. I thought maybe
she wanted to leave, but she shook her head.

We went through the zoo one more time. We didn't leave until
dark.

"Are you out of your mind, Jo?" Antalou said.

"It's not permanent," I said.

"*Of course* it's not permanent. Everyone's been looking everywhere for her. What the hell do you think you're doing?"

I said it didn't matter, did it? The County homes and units weren't safe, and we didn't want her with Mendoza, and who'd think of a soc worker's house—a P.D. safe house maybe, but not a soc worker's because that's against policy, and everyone knows that soc workers are spineless, right?

"Sure," Antalou said. "But you didn't *tell* anybody, Jo."

"I've had some thinking to do."

Suddenly Antalou got gentle, and I knew what she was thinking. I needed downtime, maybe some psychiatric profiling done. She's a friend of mine, but she's a professional, too. The two of us go back all the way to corrections, Antalou and I, and lying isn't easy.

"Get her over to County holding immediately—that's the best we can do for her," she said finally. "And let's have lunch soon, Jo. I want to know what's going on in that head of yours."

It took me the night and the morning. They put her in the nicest hole they had and doubled the security, and when I left she cried for a long time, they told me. I didn't want to leave, but I had to get some thinking done.

When it was done, I called Antalou.

She swore at me when I was through but said she'd give it a try. It was crazy, but what isn't these days?

The County bit, but with stipulations. Postpartum wipe. New I.D. Fine, but also a fund set up out of *our* money. Antalou groaned. I said, Why not.

Someone at County had a heart, but it was our mention of Statute Forty-A, I found out later, that clinched it. They saw the thing dragging on through the courts, cameras rolling forever, and that was worse than any temporary heat from state or the feds.

.   .   .

So they let her have the baby. I slept in the waiting room of the maternity unit, and it took local troops as well as hospital security to keep the press away. We used a teaching hospital down south— approved by the group that was funding her—but even then the media found out and came by the droves.

We promised full access at a medically approved moment if they cooled it, which they did. The four that didn't were taken bodily from the building under one penal code section or another.

At the beginning of the second stage of labor, the infant abruptly rotates from occiput-posterior to right occiput-anterior position; descent is rapid, and a viable two-thousand-gram female is delivered without episiotomy. Interspecific Apgar scores are nine and ten at one and five minutes, respectively.

The report would sound like all the others I'd read. The only difference would be how the thing looked, and even that wasn't much.

The little head, hairless face, broad nose, black hair sticking up like some old movie comic's. Human eyes, hairless chest, skinny arms. The feet would look like hands, sure, and the skin would be a little gray, but how much was that? To the girl in the bed it wasn't anything at all.

She said she wanted me to be there, and I said sure but didn't know the real reason.

When her water broke, they told me, and I got scrubbed up, put on the green throwaways like they said, and got back to her room quickly. The contractions had started up like a hammer.

It didn't go smoothly. The cord got hung up on the baby's neck inside, and the fetal monitor started screaming. She got scared; I got scared. They put her up on all fours to shift the baby, but it didn't work. They wheeled her to the O.R. for a C-section, which they really didn't want to do; and for two hours it was fetal signs getting better, then worse, doctors preparing for a section, then the signs somehow getting better again. Epidural block, episiotomy, some concerted forceps work, and the little head finally starts to show.

Lissy was exhausted, making little sounds. More deep breaths, a few encouraging shouts from the doctors, more pushing from Lissy, and the head was through, then the body, white as a ghost from the vernix, and someone was saying something to me in a weak voice.

"Will you cut the cord, please?"

It was Lissy.

I couldn't move. She said it again.

The doctor was waiting, the baby slick in his hands. Lissy was white as a sheet, her forehead shiny with the sweat, and she couldn't see it from where she was. "It would be special to me, Jo," she said.

One of the nurses was beside me saying how it's done all the time—by husbands and lovers, sisters and mothers and friends—but that if I was going to do it I needed to do it now, please.

I tried to remember who had cut the cord when Meg was born, and I couldn't. I could remember a doctor, that was all.

I don't remember taking the surgical steel snips, but I did. I remember not wanting to cut it—flesh and blood, the first of its kind in a long, long time—and when I finally did, it was tough, the cutting made a noise, and then it was over, the mother had the baby in her arms, and everyone was smiling.

A woman could have carried a *Gorilla gorilla beringei* to term without a care in the world a hundred, a thousand, a million years ago. The placenta would have known what to do; the blood would never have mixed. The gestation was the same nine months. The only thing stopping anyone that winter day in '97 when Cleo, the last of her kind on the face of this earth, died of renal failure in the National Zoo in DC, was the thought of carrying it.

It had taken three decades, a well-endowed resurrection group, a slick body broker, and a skinny twenty-one-year-old girl who didn't mind the thought of it.

She wants money for the operation, my daughter says to me that day in the doorway, shoulders heavy, face puffy, slurring it, the throat a throat I don't know, the voice deeper. I tell her again I don't have it, that perhaps her friends—the ones she's helped out so often when she had the money and they didn't—could help her. I say it nicely, with no sarcasm, trying not to look at where she hurts, but she knows exactly what I'm saying.

She goes for my eyes, as if she's had practice, and I don't fight back. She gets my cheek and the corner of my eye, screams something about never loving me and me never loving her—which isn't true.

She knows I know how she'll spend the money, and it makes her mad.

I don't remember the ten-year-old ever wanting to get even with anyone, but this one always does. She hurts. She wants to hurt back. If she knew, if she only knew what I'd carry for her.

I'll find her, I know—tonight, tomorrow morning, the next day or two—sitting at a walljack somewhere in the apartment, her body plugged in, the little unit with its Medusa wires sitting in her lap, her heavy shoulders hunched as if she were praying, and I'll unplug her—to show I care.

But she'll have gotten even with me, and that's what counts, and no matter how much I plead with her, promise her anything she wants, she won't try a program, she won't go with me to County—both of us, together—for help.

Her body doesn't hurt at all when she's on the wall. When you're a walljacker you don't care what kind of tissue's hanging off you, you don't care what you look like—what anyone looks like. The universe is inside. The juice is from the wall, the little unit translates, and the right places in your skull—the medulla all the way to the cerebellum, all the right centers—get played like the keys of the most beautiful synthesizer in the world. You see blue skies that make you cry. You see young men and women who make you come in your pants without your even needing to touch them. You see loving mothers. You see fathers that never leave you.

I'll know what to do. I'll flip the circuit breakers and sit in the darkness with a hand light until she comes out of it, cold-turkeying, screaming mad, and I'll say nothing. I'll tell myself once again that it's the drugs, it's the jacking, it's not her. She's dead and gone and hasn't been the little girl on that train with her hair tucked behind her ears for a long time, that this one's a lie but one I've got to keep playing.

So I walk into the bedroom, and she's there, in the chair, like always. She's got clothes off for a change and doesn't smell, and I find myself thinking how neat she looks—chic even. I don't feel a thing.

As I take a step toward the kitchen and the breaker box, I see what she's done.

I see the wires doubling back to the walljack, and I remember hearing about this from someone. It's getting common, a fad.

There are two ways to do it. You can rig it so that anyone who touches you gets ripped with a treble wall dose in a bypass. Or so that anyone who kills the electricity, even touches the wires, kills you.

Both are tamperproof. The M.E. has twenty bodies to prove it, and the guys stuck with the job downtown don't see a breakthrough for months.

She's opted for the second. Because it hurts the most.

She's starving to death in the chair, cells drying out, unless someone I.V.'s her—carefully. Even then the average expectancy is two months, I remember.

I get out. I go to a cheap hotel downtown. I dream about black-outs in big cities and bodies that move but aren't alive and about daughters. The next morning I get a glucose drip into her arm, and I don't need any help with the needle.

That's what's behind the door, Lissy.

We gave them their press conference. The doctors gave her a mild shot of pergisthan to perk her up, since she wouldn't be nursing, and she did it, held the baby in her arms like a pro, smiled though she was pale as a sheet, and the conference lasted two whole hours. Most of the press went away happy, and two of Mendoza's girls roughed up the three that tried to hide out on the floor that night. "Mendoza says hello," they said, grinning.

The floor returned to normal. I went in.

The mother was asleep. The baby was in the incubator. Three nurses were watching over them.

The body broker came with his team two days later and looked happy. Six of his ten babies had made it.

Her name is Mary McLoughlin. I chose it. Her hair is dark, and she wears it short. She lives in Chula Vista, just south of San Diego, and I get down there as often as I can, and we go out.

She doesn't remember a thing, so I was the one who had to suggest it. We go to the zoo, the San Diego Zoo, one of the biggest once. We go to the primates. We stand in front of the new exhibit, and she tells me how the real thing is so much better than the holograms, which she thinks she's seen before but isn't sure.

The baby is a year old now. They've named her Cleo, and they keep her behind glass—two or three vets in gauze masks with her at all times—safe from the air and diseases. But we get to stand there, watching her like the rest, up close, while she looks at us and clowns.

No one recognizes the dark-haired girl I'm with. The other one, the one who'd have good reason to be here, disappeared long ago, the media says. Sometimes the spotlight is just too great, they said.

"I can almost smell her, Jo," she says, remembering a dream, a vague thing, a kitten slept with. "She's not full-grown, you know."

I tell her, yes, I know.

"She's sure funny looking, isn't she."

I nod.

"Hey, I think she knows me!" She says it with a laugh, doesn't know what she's said. "Look at how she's looking at me!"

The creature is looking at her—it's looking at all of us and with eyes that aren't dumb. Looking at us, not through us.

"Can we come back tomorrow, Jo?" she asks when the crowd gets too heavy to see through.

Of course, I say. We'll come a lot, I say.

I've filed for guardianship under Statute Twenty-seven, the old W&I provisions, and if it goes through, Lissy will be moving back to LA with me. *I'm hetero, so it won't get kicked for exploitation, and I'm in the right field,* I think. I can't move myself, but we'll go down to the zoo every weekend. It'll be good to get away. Mendoza has asked me out, and who knows, I may say yes.

But I still have to have that lunch with Antalou, and I have no idea what I'm going to tell her.

Ian McDowell is the author of *Mordred's Curse* and *Merlin's Gift*, two dark anti-heroic fantasies. His short fiction has appeared in *The Magazine of Fantasy and Science Fiction*, *Asimov's Science Fiction*, *Deathrealm*, and anthologies such as *Love in Vein*, *Camelot Fantastic*, and *Borderlands 2*. His short fiction has also been chosen for reprint in Karl Edward Wagner's *The Year's Best Horror Stories*. He is a graduate of the MFA Writing Program of the University at North Carolina, and lives in Greensboro, NC. His work has been banned in Canada and at Kmart.

He says of his story, " 'The Piedmont prairie' is real, although there's not much of it left, but this story is as much about psychological ecosystems as physical ones. My apologies to the three long-suffering friends who unknowingly 'lent' me small distorted pieces of themselves."

SUNFLOWERS

IAN MCDOWELL

Kelly spotted Jesse while the bus was still pulling into the tiny station. Her cousin wasn't the only white girl waiting there, but she sure was the skinniest, not to mention the only henna-haired one in a black trenchcoat. Kelly winced at the garment. Besides looking damned uncomfortable on the hottest day of a September that felt like late July (maybe goths are born without sweat glands, she thought, not for the first time), it could target a teenager for vicious abuse in more cosmopolitan places than Sherwood, North Carolina. At least she was a girl, and not quite as likely to get her ass kicked by rednecks. Putting her Powerbook back in its stained case, Kelly brushed pork rinds off her black jeans and white Heroic

Trio T-shirt, pulled her bag down from the overhead rack and waited for the door to open.

There was an awkward moment before they hugged; Kelly suspected that the gesture came no more naturally to Jesse than it did to her, but they were still Southern and family, and certain protocols had to be kept. "God, you're tall," said Jesse, shaking dyed bangs out of her eyes. "I don't remember you being tall. Maybe because everybody was when I was little. And I wish my hair was naturally that color."

"It was purple when I was your age," said Kelly. Seeing her cousin in the flesh confirmed what the photos on Jesse's webpage had suggested; the troll-like little girl with the braces and Pippi Longstocking hair that she vaguely remembered from her late grandmother's Christmas dinners had turned into a babe. Oh, there was more than a hint of acne, and her makeup was applied with about as much finesse as one would expect from a high school kooky-spook, but those were cheekbones to die for, and wonderful green eyes. Was that a shiner fading under her left one?

Yes, it was. Kelly remembered what the results of a punch to the face looked like, having given and received a few in those days when she lived with four other punk wannabes in Carrborro's Crack Alley after dropping out of Carolina. That was before she got an American Skin boyfriend who taught her that the throat, the eyes and the instep made better targets.

"Somebody hit you." She didn't say it as a question.

Jesse's response was just as blunt, and Kelly immediately decided her e-mail impressions had been correct and that she really, really liked this girl. "It wasn't Dad. He's a drunk sometimes, but a nice one."

Kelly felt the old familiar anger. Every dangerous encounter in the old days had begun when she was taking up for somebody else, usually somebody who'd been stupid and shot off his mouth, but sometimes someone who'd been guilty of nothing but looking like an easy victim. Getting tired of being all her squatmates' street-mom was one thing that had driven her back into mainstream society. That and Aaron getting himself shot in a meth deal. "Who did it, then?"

Jesse twitched and twirled hair protectively over the bruised eye. "Just this guy at school."

"All he do was hit you?" Kelly immediately wanted to bite her tongue; it wasn't her business, not yet, and the platform of the Greyhound station was no place to talk about it.

"Damn straight that's all he did," said Jesse, sticking her chin out and looking for a moment like the pugfaced little girl that Kelly remembered. "This is a small town, and guys around here only rape their dates. He didn't want to date me. Hell, he hit me because he thought I wanted to date his sister. That and because of me kicking him after he called me a carpet muncher." She looked down at the scuffed toe of her Redwing. "Even with these, kicking a guy in the balls doesn't work as well as it does in the movies. Especially if he's a jock."

"Not if he's already angry and full of adrenaline, it doesn't," said Kelly, ruefully remembering her own lessons in the subject. "Later maybe I can show you some things that will." Oh, great, she thought, I've been here less than five minutes and I'm offering to be the kid's streetfighting sifu. Six years of respectability and yet it all comes back like that.

For the first time, Kelly noticed the paperback that Jesse was holding. It was a tattered copy of *Night Wings*, closed over the stem of a bright yellow flower. Somebody had blackened the teeth on the silly back cover photo.

Jesse's gaze followed Kelly's. "I didn't do that," she said, looking abashed. "I got it out of the stack of used books at the Lock and Key shop. Didn't think to look for it when it was new."

"I expect not," said Kelly dryly. "You're the one whose website has that hilarious rant about vampire novels and the trendigoths who buy them."

Jesse flushed. "Yeah, but I didn't know my cousin had written one, not till Mouse told me about this book she'd read by a lady with the same last name as me. Good thing it isn't something regular like Smith, else I wouldn't have thought to look you up on the net and find out if you were you. I'd never have recognized you from that photo, even if I'd been older than five when I saw you last."

"The name's the reason I allowed them to doll me up like that," said Kelly with a laugh. "The publisher really wanted me to call myself something like Raven Bloodfire, or just about anything other than Kelly Gooch, and only let me keep the name if I agreed to a 'sexy' photo shoot, saying they were going to make me the next Poppy Z. Brite. I took enough shit about being a Gooch when I was in grade school and wasn't about to change it on account of some dildoes in New York. You got a car waiting?"

Kelly had started to walk towards the station doors, but Jesse pointed her in the other direction, towards a path that ran through the grass behind the building and into the alley beside it. "Dad's got the car with him at work. This way's a short cut. You want me to carry your bag?"

"That's all right, I've got it," said Kelly as she followed. "Anyway, don't sweat what you said about vampire novels. I only thought I never wanted to read another one until I actually wrote one of the damned things; then I *knew* I didn't."

The building next door was a KFC. A scrawny raccoon scrambled out of a trashcan and down a storm drain, trailing chicken bones in its wake. As they passed the drain, Kelly saw its mask peering up at them from the gloom and wondered if it preferred Traditional or Extra Crispy. She always preferred Church's herself, and had been the only white person she knew who ate there when she lived in Carrborro.

Then they were on Sherwood's main street, three blocks of shops and dogwood trees, with the courthouse circle at one end and the exit to the highway at the other. They passed a shoeshine parlor, the first she'd seen in years, and a pawnshop and a Rexall drugs. "Oh, shit," said Jesse, stiffening.

The big, blond-stubbled broad-shouldered kid came ambling towards them with a tomcat's arrogance, flanked by two equally Aryan-looking cornfed mutants. He had bright blue eyes and brighter white teeth and even without the letter sweatshirt, which must have been nearly as uncomfortable in this weather as Jesse's overcoat, he would have looked straight from jock central casting. "Hey, Jesse, that your new girlfriend?"

"Fuck off, Jake," said Jesse, placing herself between the guys and Kelly, a gesture Kelly found touching but impractical.

The kid's laugh was predictably ugly "Hey, it's not like I give a shit whose muff you're diving, as long as you stay away from my sister."

Kelly strode around Jesse and right into the kid's face. He blinked before she did, and she got the feeling he was really looking at her for the first time. "This the guy who hit you?" she said quietly. Five years ago, she could have put him on the pavement fast. Maybe not now, though.

Apparently, she wouldn't need to, because he gave an audible swallow, always a sign of submission. "Don't listen to what she says, lady," he mumbled, that last word indicating that he'd suddenly realized that Kelly was a decade older and above him in the social pecking order. She knew his type all too well, the kind of "good" kid whose sadism and aggression were only turned towards "acceptable" targets. "I only socked her because she kicked me."

Kelly leaned in close, and was gratified to see him flinch back. Yeah, she still had The Glare, and far more dangerous guys than this one had withered under it. "You lay a hand on my cousin again and I'll hurt you worse than you can imagine."

His lip quivered, and she flattered herself that he would have actually said "yes Ma'am" if his buddies hadn't been present. Instead, he turned around and stalked off with studied cool, his friends following. At the next curb, they paused and exchanged a few snickers, with him shooting a rather theatrical and not entirely convincing leer in her direction. She made out the words "nice tits for a skinny girl," but then he looked quickly away, and he'd said it low enough that she could pretend she hadn't heard.

"Wow," said Jesse. "I think he was scared of you. I think I would have been, too, if you'd looked at me like that."

Kelly chuckled. "Yeah, it's amazing the guys who'll back down from one hundred and twenty-six pound me." She should have weighed at least ten pounds more than that, but had gotten positively gawky since things went bad with Rob. There's a weight loss plan for you; your boyfriend dumps you for his research assistant, you lose your cushy day job *and* your apartment and have no place to go. Well, maybe the kindness of relatives she hadn't spoken to in over a decade, plus some good southern cooking, would put more of the old curves back on her five-eleven frame and make her hips feel less like edged weapons. To hell with the idea that starving fueled creativity.

"Here it is," said Jesse.

BUFFALO BILLIARDS, said the sign on the dusty glass, above a picture of something that looked more like a cow in a Beatles wig. Inside, the ceiling fan purred like a lazy porch cat and dustmotes floated like beer bubbles in the amber air. There were half a dozen pool tables, but no sign of the football or pinball machines that college towns had taught her to expect. The chipped and scuffed oak bar was lined with jars of pig's feet and pickled eggs and fishbowls full of boiled green peanuts. Above the tabs, a huge mounted buffalo head glared down from the gloom, dust clouding its glass eyes. "Where on earth did you get that?" asked Kelly.

A big, slope-shouldered man with a boiled-ham face and a ridiculous island of salt-and-pepper hair combed down over his forehead came ambling round the bar, holding out a surprisingly delicate hand. *Just like Dad's,* thought Kelly as she took it, remembering a grip she'd not felt in over a decade. *I guess the big hands and feet come from Mom's side of the family.*

Bob Gooch gestured at the buffalo head with his free hand. "My grandpappy shot that sucker in our back acre. Hello, Kelly, it's been too long. How's your momma?"

Kelly found the old formality coming back to her. "I wouldn't know, sir. I don't talk to her much."

Her uncle's face turned impassive. "Me neither, not since your dad passed away. I don't think she ever had much use for his family. And call me Bob, not sir."

Kelly nodded. "I don't think she ever had much use for most people."

Bob smiled again, and she finally imagined she saw a bit of her father in that froggy grin "I'm glad you got use for us, and that you looked us up."

Kelly reached out and chucked Jesse on the shoulder. "It was your daughter who looked me up. I appreciate the invitation."

Bob nodded. "What else could we do, once we heard you was a published writer who needed a place to hole up and work on her next book? I've been meaning to crack your first one, but Jesse here won't let go of it."

"You wouldn't like it, Dad," said Jesse. "It begins with a blow job."

Bob surprised her by chuckling. "Guess you ain't sent a copy to your momma, then."

Kelly smiled back. "Damn straight I did."

Bob's grin became a guffaw. "Sit down, girl, and let me pour you a beer on the house."

Kelly put her bag down and hoisted herself onto a barstool. "Draft usually gives me a headache, but a bottle of Rolling Rock would be very nice." She hoped she wasn't being offensive by implying he had dirty taps, but it was true, she could drink four bottled beers without feeling the effects of one piddling draft.

Jesse sat on the stool beside her and gave herself a half-spin. "I'll have one, too, Dad."

"You most certainly will not. I'm not even really supposed to be letting you in here." He poured her a Coke, which she accepted with sullen grace.

Kelly sipped the longneck and looked up at the glowering buffalo head. "My great-great-uncle shot that here? But there aren't any buffalo in North Carolina."

"Not any east of the Rockies, is what the books will tell you, not since Colonial days," said Bob. "But my grandpappy shot one, just the same."

Jesse gave her stool another half-spin and flipped an ice cube out across the unmopped floor. "The last buffalo in the Carolinas were killed in 1794. A farmer came home one winter to find a small starving herd pawing at the snow in front of his farmhouse. The idiot walked up behind the lead bull and shot it in the ass with his musket. It went right through his front door and all the cows and calves followed, knocking out the inside walls and packing themselves in like sardines. He had to get men from the next farm to help him take one of the walls off, just so he could drive the buffalo out and scrape up what was left of his kinfolk. It's the only case of death by indoor buffalo stampede on record."

"She knows her history," said Bob approvingly. "Paleontology, too. You wouldn't expect that in a high school junior who dresses like Elvira's kid sister."

Kelly was actually more surprised to hear Bob use the word paleontology. "My favorite writer used to be a vertebrate paleontologist, and she's more goth than I am," declared Jesse. She spun her stool back to face Kelly, looking suddenly abashed. "I mean, one of my favorite writers; I liked your book, too, really!"

Kelly laughed, wondering if Jesse had actually been able to finish it. "It's okay, hon; lots of novels are better than mine, especially those by authors whose agents didn't insist they write about vampires." *Of course, now you don't have an agent at all, smart girl;*

maybe you could have listened more politely when he said that your next book should be A New Orleans Vampire in King Arthur's Court.

Jesse stopped twirling herself and started twirling the pressed bloom she'd been using as a bookmark. Kelly saw that it was a sunflower, about two inches wide. "Lots of botanists will tell you this came close to being extinct as the Carolina bison. It's one of the rarest wildflowers in the world and federally recognized as an endangered species."

"Not on Gooch land, it's not," said Bob, pouring himself a Bud draft.

Kelly recognized the broad leaves from some of Jesse's paintings, the ones she'd mentally labeled "Vincent Van Goth" when she first looked at her cousin's website. "It's an *Helianthus schweinitzii* or Schweinitz's sunflower," said Jesse, making Kelly wonder how many class presentations she'd done on the subject. "It only grows in ninety populations, most of them under powerlines or beside railroad tracks, all within sixty miles of Charlotte. Once almost the whole Piedmont was rolling prairie, just like out west, and covered in these flowers, growing up to fifteen feet high. Now there are only a few patches of that prairie left, and the clearing Dad calls our back acre is the largest one, other than the two restored preserves that the Fish and Wildlife people are starting up in Mecklenburg County. Ours is the only privately owned one, and the only one its size that's naturally survived rather than being re-created."

Bob burped loudly, making Jesse wince. "You see, my grandpappy married into our land when he wed my grandmomma. She was a Bushyhead, and part Cherokee, like so many backcountry folk used to be between here and the mountains—this isn't backcountry now, but it was then. Her family had looked after the land in these parts, before most of it was given over to farms, burning off the grass every so often to keep the prairie growing and the forest from coming back. When my grandpappy got that land, he had to promise he wouldn't farm it, that he would just let it sit, except for burning if off every so often, just like it had been before the white man came. We've looked after the land and it's looked after us."

He's already finished his beer, and Kelly thought his face looked redder, even in the gloom. "My daddy hunted that land regular, and fed his family off what he shot, back during the Depression. It was twice as large then as it is now, because he ended up selling off some of it when my momma took sick, but even so, he shot more critters there than you'd ever expect to find in a few acres. No buffalo, but some elk." He burped again. "That's right, elk, not whitetail deer."

"The Fish and Wildlife people want to buy our land and make another preserve out of it," said Jesse, "but Dad won't sell. Like so many folks around here, he doesn't trust the government. He'll be babbling about black helicopters next."

Bob snorted. "Girl, don't make me sound like one of those Klan assholes who call the radio shows." He poured himself another beer, and Kelly wondered how much of his own profits he'd drunk before they'd arrived. "I'm no paranoid redneck, and no fool, neither. I know the Fish and Game people will do a better job of taking care of that land than my daughter will be interested in doing, once I'm gone to join her mother. I'm just holding out for a good price, is all. Get me a real bar in Charlotte, some place where folks like to drink and watch football."

Jesse stood up. "Yeah, Dad, that's the ticket, a Charlotte sports bar," she said wearily. She turned to Kelly. "I better drive you out to the place; I still need to get my paintings out of the guest house, so you can get settled in."

Kelly reached across the bar and shook hands again. "Thanks for everything, Uncle Bob. We'll talk more later."

He burped again, but his voice wasn't slurred. "You know it, girl. Maybe you can tend bar some nights. This place might actually make money if I had a pretty girl at the taps."

. . .

The guest "house" was a boxy little brick structure with a tin roof, containing a shower bath, kitchenette and combination living room and bedroom. Still, the main room had French doors that opened out on an oakwood deck, and Kelly imagined it would be very nice to sit out there in the early evening and write, while bats and swallows chased moths through the porchlight and cicadas sang in the sheltering branches.

Beyond the small stand of trees that half-surrounded the building was an oval clearing about eighty yards across at its widest point, framed by a horseshoe of blackjack oaks, red cedars and pine, the open end of the semicircle blocked off from the neighboring property by a dilapidated stretch of chainlink fence where honeysuckle bloomed and scurrying green anoles blinked in the late afternoon sun. Kelly followed Jesse out into the open meadow, her initial wariness of thistles and sandspurs proving unfounded, and marveled at the thick dark green and purple stalks that towered above the russet waves of Indian grass and little bluestem and the comparatively small golden blooms that swayed as high as eight feet above their heads. Here and there amongst the clumps of sunflowers, Jesse pointed out other nearly extinct species with names like gray-headed coneflower and prairie rosin-weed. At one point, she stuck her hand down a chipmunk hole, making Kelly wince at the thought of snakes, and produced a palmful of bright red clay. "It's called Iredell soil," she said, once again sounding more like a high school teacher than student. "It dries brick-hard, and can break the roots of young trees. It's one reason the prairie stayed prairie when things started getting cooler and wetter around six thousand years ago and the forests began to eat up the grasslands. That and the fires that lightning or the Indians started, to keep the pastureland clear so the buffalo could graze."

Flies buzzed on a large gray-green disk of dried, digested plant matter a couple of feet from the hole. "Something's been grazing here," said Kelly. "Your neighbors let their cows run loose?"

Jesse picked it up, made a comical face and threw it like a turd Frisbee, then brushed off her dusty hands. "Too big for a cow; must be buffalo." Kelly couldn't tell if she was joking, but smiled anyway. "You're not exactly my idea of a nature girl," she said, amused by how out of place Jesse's black overcoat, dress and boots looked against such a pallet of floral yellows, lavenders and blues. She wished she had a camera.

It happened with no warning. One moment the sky was robin's egg blue and sheep's wool white and very far away, the next it was a dark rushing canopy of wings, close overhead and beating so loudly it sounded like everyone who'd ever lived applauding all at once. Kelly stared, open-mouthed until the splatter of droppings suggested that was a bad idea, and Jesse laughed and clapped her hands and danced a little jig, like some spritely hippie girl in funeral lace, until she noticed that those clothes were in danger of turning more white than black, and grabbed Kelly's hand and dragged her towards the guest house.

Overhead, the birds still passed in a billowing stormfront of feathers, more of them than Kelly would have ever thought there were flying things on earth. She had no idea what species they might be, ducks or buzzards or parrots or crows or archaeopteryxes, their sheer numbers denied them any particular identity. Standing under the porch roof, she held Jesse's small rough hand in her big smooth one and watched bird shit fall like hail on the open meadow. Jesse said something, but Kelly couldn't hear her. She pulled her cousin inside and shut the glass door, muting the thunderous flapping.

"Passenger pigeons," said Jesse, her face unreadable.

Kelly just stared at her. Oddly, there was no sound of bird shit splattering on the small out-building's tin roof, even though a dozen yards away and through the closed glass door, she could still hear it pelting the stalks. "They're passing overhead," she said at last, "they must be, so why can't I hear the noise of their droppings on the roof?"

"Come look," said Jesse, leading her back to the creaky old bed, where she crawled across the fluffy sheep-embroidered comforter to open a window, affording a view of the main house twenty yards away, with cornfields and a winding stretch of road visible through the tree, and over everything the blue and white arch of empty sky, touched with bloody red where the sun was setting behind the distant foothills and free of any birds but a couple of wheeling hawks.

"They're only flying over that patch of prairie," said Jesse. "I mean, they're flying through miles and miles of prairie sky hundreds of years ago, but we can only see a small patch of it here. If you stood outside and looked up, you'd see them disappear as they reached the treeline. What, did you think Iredell County still had passenger pigeons, and no biologist had ever noticed?"

Kelly, who'd been kneeling on the bed, rose and shook herself, running her fingers through her fouled hair and exploring the reassuring solidity of her own skull. She looked at the cream-colored wall, the smiling sheep on the comforter, the plaster ceiling, the scuffed hardwood floor, her own Doc Martens, the left one splattered with a large toothpaste-colored dropping. She'd always been a mechanistic rationalist; writing about the weird had never entailed believing in it. Hell, she even read *The Skeptical Inquirer* and used to sneer at Rob's obsession with Forteana.

"I think I need a drink," she said at last. "I wish we'd brought some of your father's beer."

"I have pot," said Jesse in the tone of a grade-schooler coaxing a straitlaced friend into playing truant. "We can sit on the porch and get high and see how long it takes them passing overhead."

It took maybe twenty minutes, although the pot buzz made time elastic. Normally, Kelly would have declined the opportunity to get stoned, as it reminded her too much of her days with Aaron. She'd never really been all that fond of getting high; the euphoria was always undercut by a creeping sense of guilt at having willfully made herself stupid, of being a hypocrite for slowing down part of her brain when she was always railing at other people for not properly using theirs. These, however, were special circumstances. Two joints later, the pigeons were gone, the darkening air overhead empty of anything but sunset-stained clouds, the silence sharp as the blade of the knife she'd carried in her left boot when she was still street. Neither of them spoke for a long time, and gradually the normal nightfall bird and bug sounds came back, although not so loudly that Kelly couldn't still hear her own heartbeat.

"You okay?" asked Jesse, squeezing her shoulder and looking at her with big did-I-do-wrong eyes.

"Umm, I don't think I want to talk about this, not right now," said Kelly, killing the joint. *Am I so dead to wonder?* she thought. *All I feel is numb, and what I just saw deserves something more than numb.*

Maybe so, but it wasn't getting it now. Now, mundanity was needed, a sense of things being like they'd been before, the impossible extinct pigeons nothing more remarkable than the sight of a redtailed hawk or bobcat. Jesse seemed to understand this. "Want to help me get my paintings back up to the house?"

Kelly stood, stretched, reached out a hand to help Jesse to her feet, gripping the younger girl's palm tightly for a moment. "Sure."

Fireflies started to dance above the meadow, tiny stars among the battered blooms. Kelly wondered in what year they'd hatched.

They did talk about it a bit the next day, over a delightfully cold chocolate ice cream soda at Rexall Drugs, one in which the smooth sweetness of the syrup and the bitter fizz of the soda had reached that ineffable balance that's the grail of those lucky few who've had a perfect soda once in their lives and have been searching for another one since.

Jesse tapped a black fingernail on the chipped Formica counter.

"I was hoping you'd see something that spectacular while you were here. Most of the time, it's just like any other field. I've never even seen a buffalo in it, although I've found paths where they've flattened the sunflowers. It would be cool to go out back one day and see Indians or settlers, but I think it's just animals that come unstuck in time like that. I wish the Piedmont prairie was even older than it is—that maybe someday I'd see a smilodon or a woolly mammoth, or dinosaurs—wouldn't dinosaurs be great? God, am I hard to satisfy or what? There's something magical in my backyard and I'm so used to it that all I do is bitch about the limits of the magic."

Kelly removed her straw from the soda, reversed it, and sucked out the ice cream that had clotted it. "How many people know about this?

"Still living? There's me and Dad and Mouse. You need to meet Mouse, she was the girl in some of those paintings." Kelly remembered a spikey-haired waif with even bigger eyes than Jesse's, who'd been naked in a couple of them, her thin pale tattooed body as incongruous against a background of sunflowers as Jesse's black clothing. "Lots of folks in town have a vague idea, I guess, but they've always seemed as blasé as the citizens in *The Circus of Dr. Lao*. You live with something long enough, you get used to it. There were some kids I used to hang with, my little coven, the assholes at school called them—well, the assholes who knew what 'coven' meant—and I'd take them back there on summer nights and show them how the stars looked five thousand years ago, and wait for the elk to come drifting by, bigger than any moose in Canada. Some of them thought it was cool at first, but even they got bored, and the main thing any of them were interested in was that I usually had good weed. Except for Mouse, they were all trendoids, babybats and vampire role-players, you know the type, and after the media made things rough on kids who wore black coats, most of them changed their wardrobes and even stopped hanging out with each other. Fuckers."

Kelly recognized the sentiment, even though her high school hangers-on had been punks who affected to sneer at goths and got violent when mistaken for them. "Anybody in your family ever tried to make money from it?"

Jesse slurped the soda's thick sweet dregs, then held the straw above her head and dripped ice cream into her open mouth. "Dad talks about it, but it's just talk. He's not really going to sell that land to Fish and Wildlife, or call the TV people or open a theme park or do any of the other schemes he keeps going on about. We've talked about writing a book, though." She paused a beat and smiled disarmingly. "Or maybe seeing if you wanted to write one."

Kelly looked into her cousin's cat eyes. *Did I seem this smart and assured when I was her age?* "A book?" She picked up a napkin and wiped off Jesse's whipped cream mustache. "You think there's money in *books*?"

Her laughter had been fond rather than mocking, but Jesse still looked hurt. "I wasn't thinking about money, even though it would be cool to get Dad out of debt. I just thought, y'know, you could write it, if you were interested, and I could take the pictures. I'd rather do paintings, but I'm not technically good enough to be a wildlife illustrator. The photography class I took as a junior was crap, but once I graduate, I can sign up for a real one at Mecklenburg Community College."

Kelly very much wanted a cigarette, but no, she'd quit, dammit, turned over a new leaf, even if coming south meant she was back in the heart of tobacco country. "I've never really tried to write anything but fiction. Well, there was some technical writing for the educational publisher I used to work for, back before they hired a highly-paid vice-president away from a competitor and cut expenses by getting rid of half the editorial staff, but that was just captions in catalogs and directions for grade school bulletin board projects. I was never a journalist, never even worked on a school paper. I tried doing some reviews for a webzine once, but realized I sucked before I'd finished my first one, and quit."

Jesse stuck out her lower lip, looking much more like a high school kid than usual. "You're a good writer, Kelly. C'mon, wouldn't this be more *fun* than a vampire book?" Her face suddenly seemed ten years older. "Don't be scared."

Kelly realized she was actually flushing. *Stop it*, she thought, *and if you're going to get mad, do it at yourself for letting her play you.* "Dammit, girl," she said, relieved to feel her anger turn to amusement, "you called that one right. It *is* scary, the idea of wrestling down something like this and pinning it to the page, of either trying to make sense of it or just making sense of the fact that it doesn't. Mystery, wonder, the sublime, all that stuff—it's okay when we create it in our heads, when it's not real and staring back at us—but turning the flesh of its impossible reality into word, that's one tall order."

"But you'll try it?" said Jesse, her face back in pleading kid mode.

Kelly wondered if Buffalo Billiards was open yet, for a Rolling Rock or five seemed very inviting right now. "Let me think about it a couple of days, okay?"

Before Jesse could answer, something caught her eye over Kelly's shoulder. "Over here, sweetie."

Kelly recognized the spiky little raccoon-eyed waif girl who sidled in beside Jesse from her paintings. Her hair was dyed green and she was wearing a Nick Cave T-shirt. She looked at Kelly as impassively as a cat, if one could imagine a cat chewing bubble gum.

"This is Mouse," said Jesse. "She doesn't talk much."

"Do too," said Mouse.

"Hi, Mouse," said Kelly, extending a hand. "My name's Kelly."

"Meet'cha," said Mouse, squeezing her hand more than shaking it.

"I'm Jesse's cousin, come down to visit."

Mouse blew a bubble. "I know."

"I like the paintings that Jesse did of you."

Mouse smiled, exposing a gold tooth, and scrunched her thin shoulders. "Me too."

Kelly noticed the pigment splattered on her hands. "Do you paint also?"

Mouse bobbed her head from side to side. "A little."

"She's very good," said Jesse. "Not very verbal, but good."

Mouse blew another bubble. "I suck."

Jesse punched her in the shoulder. "Don't say that about somebody I care about. You most certainly do not suck."

Mouse rubbed her shoulder and did a mock pout. "That hurt."

Jesse tousled her hair. "Ooh, you poor abused baby," she said, her accent several degrees more country. "Just trying to give you some of that home style lovin' you hill folk are so keen on."

Mouse spit her gum out into her hand and stuck it on the Batz Maru lunchbox that Jesse used as a purse. "Bitch monkey." She stuck out a pierced tongue.

"Put that thing up if you ain't gonna use it, Shirley Michelle," said Jesse, continuing her affected drawl.

Smiling nostalgically, Kelly glanced away, remembering dear dead days at Pepper's Pizza. Now why did the glowering bullethead lurching towards their table look familiar? "Heads up, guys," she said; "trouble's coming."

The kid she'd faced down on the street when she first arrived in town stopped and stood in front of them glaring, his golden-fuzzed upper lip quivering. Kelly idly wondered if the cigarettes in the rolled-up left sleeve of his sweat-stained T-shirt were Camels or Kools. Probably the former; he looked like the type who'd be negatively influenced by the number of black kids who smoked Kools.

"Time to go home, Michelle," he said, his voice more even than Kelly expected.

Mouse made a big display of holding Jesse's hand. "Says who?"

The kid looked almost uncomfortable doing this. "Says Daddy. He's in the truck and wants to talk to you. You know it's better if I send you out than if he has to come in and do it himself."

She appeared to think it over as nonchalantly as if she were deciding which pair of jeans to wear. "You're right," she said lightly, standing. "Nice meeting." This last was directed at Kelly. Meanwhile, she kneaded Jesse's shoulder. "Later, babe," she said, bending to kiss her neck.

"Christ on a stick," muttered Jake, turning away.

"On a crutch, you mean," said Jesse, sneering around Mouse's nuzzling head. "Christ on a stick sounds like something you'd buy at a Catholic snack food stand at the county fair."

"This doesn't concern you," said Jake with the same forced calm.

Mouse put a finger to her purple lips. "Don't fret." Then, to Jake, "You coming?"

His voice remained toneless. "No. Dad's dropping me off here."

"Toodles," said Mouse, wagging a finger as she departed.

"I'm going to ask this nicely . . ." said Jake as soon as she was out of earshot.

"That must be a strain," snorted Jesse.

Jake took a deep breath and began again. "I'm going to ask this nicely. Hell, I'm even sorry I hit you; I don't have respect for guys who hit girls. And I'm sorry I called you a muff diver and a carpet muncher—my guys were giving me shit on account of you and Michelle, and I didn't want to look bad in front of them. You gonna listen to me now?"

Jesse scraped off the gum that Mouse had stuck on her lunchbox and stuck it idly inside the heavy napkin dispenser, which Kelly had previously been eyeing, thinking it might make a useful weapon. "Should I?"

Kelly nodded. "It can't hurt to hear him out."

"Okay, shoot."

Jake sighed and cracked his callused knuckles. "Here's the deal. You can't imagine how bad it will get for Michelle at home once Daddy finds out about you and her, and you know how this town is, and that he *will* find out. Never mind how I feel about it, never mind what other people say. If you, uh, care about her, you don't want her to go through that. You really don't. Do the right thing and break up with her."

Jesse rested her chin on her fist and looked him straight in the eye. "No. I'm not going to do that. And if your daddy touches her, I'll kill him."

Jake flushed. "Don't threaten my daddy."

"That wasn't a threat."

This could get bad, though Kelly. She might need to bounce the napkin dispenser off his head after all. Idly, she rested her right hand on it.

He took a deep breath, and some dispassionate part of herself actually admired his restraint. "Okay, I've been nice but it didn't work, so here's how it is. You know I've got kin in the Klan. I don't much hold with them, and there's some black guys on the team would kick my ass for having anything to do with 'em, but family is family and keeping this mess from getting worse comes first. You understand what I'm saying? I got to look after my sister. By any means necessary, like that Malcolm X dude said."

Kelly didn't admire him now. "You better leave, Jake," she said, giving him the full-force no-holds-barred look.

He nodded. "Yes, Ma'am. I've said my piece, and your cousin is either gonna follow my advice or she won't. There's nothing else to say."

"Yes, there is," said Jesse through gritted teeth.

Kelly gently touched her shoulder. "Let him go. There's no point in extending this."

Jesse continued to glare at Jake's departing back. "Fuck. You."

Then she let out a big breath and gave Kelly what seemed like a forced smile. "As Mouse would say."

Kelly had a sudden impractical wish that she still had an apartment in Atlanta, and could spirit Jesse, and if need be Mouse, away from this nonsense. Or that she could just throw them into her car and drive. But no, she'd had to sell the Starfire to a gullible college student, probably mere days before the entire transmission fell out of it. "Anything I can do?"

Jesse's smile became less forced. "Nothing's necessary. He won't do anything. You don't sic the Klan on family, no matter how pissed you are at some dyke for seducing your sister. He's bluffing."

Que sera sera, though Kelly. *Best be ready for trouble, though.* Too bad she couldn't quite summon the old Fuck It If It's Not Happening Right Now attitude.

Two nights later, she was sitting up in bed in a T-shirt and boxer shorts with her Powerbook in her lap, trying to draft a letter to her publisher asking when the next royalty statement was due and mentally kicking herself yet again for having parted company so unpleasantly with Greg, her former agent. He may have wanted her to write fucking vampire novels for fucking ever, but at least he made the bastards cough up on time.

There was a gentle rap on the French doors. She looked up to see Jesse standing on the other side of them, haloed by porchlight and june bugs. She got up and padded to the door and opened it. Jesse stepped in quickly, so as few bugs as possible would come in with her.

"What's up?"

She held up a six-pack of Rolling Rock longnecks. "Me and Mouse are looking at the stars and drinking beer. You want to join us? We've got marshmallows and were thinking about roasting some."

Kelly laughed, wondering where Jesse had gotten the beer but glad she hadn't been asked to buy it for her. "Yum-yum, beer and marshmallows, two great tastes that taste great together! Where's your father?" She looked over at her clock radio. It was a weeknight and he wouldn't still be tending bar, as it closed at eleven, as ridiculously early as that hour seemed.

"He fell asleep watching Leno, like usual. I e-mailed Mouse after I mopped up his spilled drink and told her to come over. You don't have to hang out with us if you don't want to, but it felt rude, walking right by your place without asking."

Kelly was bemused to think of the little guest house as "her place." She walked over to the battered dresser, one leg of which was propped up by a moldering *Reader's Digest*, and took out a pair of black jeans, which she pulled on. Now where were her boots? "Sure, Jesse, I'll come hang out with you guys for a bit. I get cabin fever sometimes at night—I guess I'm just too used to having places to go." Not to mention a car to drive to them in.

Mouse was standing at the edge of the clearing, bag of marshmallows under one arm, twirling what turned out to be a buzzing june bug on a string around her head. "Hey there," she said to Kelly.

Once they stepped off the guest house deck and into the dark clearing, the bowl of sky overhead became a blaze of stars. A gentle breeze rustled the sunflower stalks and hissed in the Indian grass, and somewhere close frogs sang their baritone madrigals, accompanied by the higher pitched chorus of crickets and the electric whine of cicadas. "Man, this is *noisy*," said Kelly in bemused surprise. "I mean, compared to sitting on your front porch at night in town, at least when there's no one on the street and no cars are going by. Of course, a town like Chapel Hill or Greensboro isn't the same thing as a big loud city; a New Yorker might find this oppressively quiet."

Mouse had finally let her poor june bug go free. "I wish I lived in a big loud city," she said wistfully, apparently feeling talkative tonight.

Jesse lit some kindling with her Zippo, sending several large toads hopping away from a patch of bare earth where charred logs indicated previous fires. It took her a while to get the flames going, but eventually they were crackling away, drawing moths, which sometimes fell singed and popping into the embers. Mouse had skewered a marshmallow on a sunflower stalk and was happily roasting it, but Kelly decided her own beer didn't need sweet and gooey chasers.

"Isn't this kind of dangerous?" she asked. "I mean, if the past somehow sticks to this little patch of land, aren't we right now sitting in the middle of a vast wilderness, one in which there are animals that might not like us very much?" She didn't know when cave lions and saber-toothed tigers had gone extinct, but there'd certainly been bears and panthers here when the settlers came, and maybe wolves. And of course elk and buffalo could be dangerous.

"I don't think so," said Jesse, licking marshmallow off Mouse's fingers. "My family's always looked after this land, except when Granddaddy sold some to the neighbors and let them plow it under, which Dad still feels shitty about. We've taken care of it and I think it will look after us."

The sky flashed above their heads, although there was no accompanying thunder. "Cool beans," said Mouse, pointing.

More flashes came, lightning illuminating the clouds. Or rather, a rough oval of cloud directly above them, almost as if a spotlight was being shown there.

"Prairie lightning," said Jesse. "It used to cause the fires that kept the grasslands alive. It's probably lighting up the whole sky, hundreds of years ago, but we can only see a small patch."

"Fucking weird," said Mouse, who'd somehow managed to get a marshmallow stuffed down into her beer, where it floated like a pale and vaguely fetal specimen in formaldehyde.

Sounds from behind them distracted them from the sky. Somewhere beyond the main house, an engine gunned and there was a rattle of gravel from the driveway. Headlights flashed through the trees around the guest house. "Just who the *fuck* is driving right into my backyard?" Jesse snapped.

The two highbeams lanced through the night in a haze of dust and bugs, with a third shaft of illumination swiveling above them. *That must be a jacklight,* thought Kelly with undue calm. *Que sera fucking sera indeed.* She knew all too well who it had to be.

They were all standing now, and Kelly was tempted to tell the girls to run, but sensed that Jesse wouldn't flee her own property. "*Stop,* you fuckers!" yelled Jesse, her voice almost drowned out by the truck's encroaching roar. "Don't you dare drive into this field!"

Dare they did, though, with the pickup barreling over the silhouetted shafts of *Helianthus schweinitzii* and grinding the unseen clumps of ray-headed coneflower and prairie rosinweed under its wheels, coming to a halt only a few yards away from them. Recklessly, Jesse strode forward. "*Get the goddam hell off my property!*"

The first man out of the cabin was huge. He wore a sweatshirt with the hood pulled up like a gangbanger. The second, smaller man carried a rifle or shotgun and was dressed in a sheet and a different kind of hood, the top of it crumpled from his cramped ride. They left the engine running. Two more big forms jumped out of the truck bed. One was making a braying sound that must have been laughter. The other, coming to the front a bit hesitantly, turned out to be Jake. "You best be going with us," he said to Mouse.

Mouse shrunk behind Jesse, her eyes wide as a lemur's, her usual nonchalance completely gone. *I'd be pretty shaken if my own brother called the Klan on me, too,* thought Kelly. *They'd have to pull me off him, though.*

"Fuck you," said Jesse. "She's not going anywhere with these assholes!"

"Little lady's got a mouth on her," said the big man in the hooded sweatshirt, chuckling.

"Shut the fuck up, you goddam dyke cunt!" snarled the man in the sheet.

"Nah, L.W., you shut up," said the big man. "Just 'cuz some screwed-up high school kid has a gutter mouth is no reason for to be talking the same way. And take off that damn hood, so you can see what you're doing." Apparently dissatisfied by his companion's lack of compliance, he reached over and pulled off the hood, tossing it over his shoulder and onto the truck's rumbling hood. "L.W. dearly does love his uniform," he said easily, stepping up beside Jake. "I wouldn't be surprised if he sleeps in it. Done the same thing with his hall monitor belt back when we was kids at country elementary."

"Godammit, Elton, don't you be embarassin' me in front of strangers," said L.W. in a tone of injured petulance.

Jesse held Mouse tightly, perhaps not the best thing to do under these circumstances. Kelly got in front of them, cursing herself for believing Jesse's assurances that Jake wouldn't *really* call in his country relations. "You really need to be pointing a gun at three women, two of them just kids?"

The big man, whose age she could only guess at in the backlit gloom, shrugged amiably. "L.W. just gets excitable. Pay him no never-mind. Heck, you ladies could probably take that gun away from him if you really tried."

The idea had occurred to her. She thought of goodhearted, distant, drunken, useless Bob Gooch and wondered if he was still asleep on the couch with the TV blaring. *Please let him be awake and have called the cops, and now be coming up behind these bastards with a shotgun of his own.* L.W.'s balding head gleamed under a halo of gnats. She pictured herself stepping nonchalantly up to him and bending towards his shadowed face as if she was going to kiss it, then sinking her teeth hard into his cheek. Biting somebody in the face was always a good tactic if you wanted to keep your hands free to grab something away from them. The bastard would probably taste like the fatback sandwich she once ate on a dare.

Unfortunately, Elton seemed to have some idea of her intentions. "Give me that thing," he said, reaching out and easily prying the shotgun from L.W.'s grip, then resting it on his shoulder like a baseball bat. "It's empty," he said in the same friendly drawl. "No way was we gonna trust L.W. with a loaded one. I just done him a favor, and you, too, Missy. I expect you would have hurt him when you grabbed it away from him like you was just fixing to do, and then you would have been in a world of pain."

"Still will be, Elton," said the third Klansman, who Kelly now saw was wearing a baseball cap with a big X on it. "Damn straight," agreed L.W., licking his lips.

"Hey," said Jake, "we're only going to take Michelle out of here. You guys are just along to show the Gooch women how serious this has gotten, and to remind them that they'd best stay away from my sister."

Elton spit and rubbed his hands together. "Well, Jacob, we never really decided on that, did we?"

"You and Mouse get out of here, Jesse," said Kelly, not looking back. "These guys can't run as fast as you, and they won't hurt me with you out there to be witnesses." She thought that Jake probably could run as fast as them, actually, but he looked to be having second thoughts.

Balancing the empty shotgun on his shoulder with one hand, Elton reached into his sweatshirt and brought out a damn big pistol. "Sorry, but there won't be no running. Now you ladies get in the back of the truck, and be quiet. There's no need to be waking up Miss Gooch's poor hardworking daddy. Man's got enough problems, worrying about the way his daughter likes girls."

"Goddamit, Elton," said Jake.

"Don't be turning chicken on us, coz, not after getting us involved in the first place," said Elton, his voice less mild now. "We ain't gonna hurt your sister none. We may not even hurt these other two, not if they play along right."

Kelly was suddenly aware of a thousand different things: her heartbeat, the chill touch of sweat down the back of her neck, the truck's uneven idle, the muted nightsong of crickets and frogs, her own breathing and that of Jesse and Mouse behind her, the smell of truck exhaust and something else, the trembling grass beneath her feet.

More than trembling. The grass hissed and rustled, the ground itself seemed to vibrate and the still-standing sunflower stalks shook as if in a high wind. But there was only the faintest of breezes, carrying a scent that reminded her of the livestock tents at the state fair.

"What the hell?" said Elton.

The odor was stronger now, overpowering the engine fumes, and the air became more turbulent, washing over them in a pungent wave that reeked of wet burnt hay and musk and farts and sour milk and something like moldy bread. From behind them came a rumbling noise, no longer a distant tremor, and Kelly thought of the sound that precedes a subway train from a darkened tunnel.

"Shit, is a tornado coming or something?" asked L.W.

"Can't be that, dumbass," said Elton, "not on a clear right." He had to shout to be heard. The men were all looking past her. This was their chance to escape. Kelly turned back towards the girls.

A rushing wall of shaggy horned heads, as huge and awesome as gods from some bovine pantheon, was illuminated by the truck's headlights, golfball-sized eyes reflecting back the beams, a threshing line of hooves churning the earth and throwing up an advance wave of loamy dirt.

Knowing what they were seeing, the three women were less

transfixed than the men bracing them. "Run!" mouthed Jesse, hauling Mouse after her.

Kelly didn't need the cue. The edge of the clearing was only a dozen yards away, but she doubted they could make it. Shoving between Elton and L.W., who just stood there empty-eyed and open-mouthed as crappies on a stringer, she leapt up into the bed of the truck rather than running past it. "Up here!" she shouted, waving her arms. The words couldn't have carried, but Jesse and Mouse saw and followed her example. Reaching out with both hands, Kelly hauled them up after her.

The sight of his sister running past had gotten Jake moving more quickly than his companions. He was alongside the truck bed, reaching into it, a huge horned head bigger than the one mounted above Bob Gooch's bar right behind him. Mouse grabbed for his outstretched hand, screaming something that was probably his name. Acting instinctively, never minding that he'd started this, Kelly gripped his sweaty thick forearm in both hands, put her feet against the sideguard and *hauled* with more strength than she thought she had. The next moment she and Jake were lying on their sides in the truck bed, her gasping and him shaking like a man having an epileptic fit, as the shaggy hillocks thundered past, buffeting the vehicle as they brushed against it. Kelly had a glimpse of a pale sheeted shape borne aloft, bouncing atop the sea of horns and humps, the robe turning dark before it vanished underneath the ruminant flow. There was no sign of the other men. Her eyes burned with dirt and dander, her lungs choked on musk.

Jake lay on his side, his hands clasped in what looked like prayer, his mouth moving and his eyes empty. Mouse squatted beside him, stroking his brow, not even looking at the bison pounding past. Jesse stood over her, one hand on her shoulder, watching the stampede with triumphant eyes. Rising unsteadily and looking over the cabin, Kelly saw the animals were continuing to break to either side, parting like water just before crashing into them, and she thanked God that the truck's owners had left the headlights on, for without those beams spooking them, the beasts might have charged directly into it. They continued to brush against it in passing, those glancing blows causing the bed to shake and rattle and groan on its springs, and with one particularly sharp impact, Jesse lost her balance and sat down hard behind Mouse and Jake. Fearing the same might happen to her, Kelly squatted too. Above the barnyard smell, there was a sharp acrid tang, the stench of raw animal panic, and a distant sweeter odor of burning grass. Kelly guessed that the lightning they'd seen earlier had ignited a prairie fire, perhaps miles and certainly hundreds of years away.

The herd continued to roar past, a sea of heaving hairy humps and tossing horns. And then they were simply gone, like the passenger pigeons had been three days before. Their tumult echoed for a few moments longer, then ceased rather than faded. No grass or flower stalk rustled to mark their passing, all having been beaten down.

"Jesus jesus jesus jesus jesus jesus," mumbled Jake.

"It's okay," said Mouse, patting his shoulder. "They're gone." She reached out to Jesse, who pulled her to her feet. "They're all gone." The smile on her face suggested she wasn't talking about the buffalo.

Kelly stood on the side of the truck and looked out at the hoof-churned earth and the flattened manshapes beaten into it. *Not quite gone*, she thought, but they certainly weren't a threat to anyone.

Jesse stroked Mouse's spiky hair. "I told you it would look after us," she said softly.

Overhead the stars burned cold and quiet, emerging from their shroud of settling dust.

Brian Stableford received the 1999 Pilgrim Award for his lifetime contribution to SF scholarship. His most recent novel is *Architects of Emortality*, the second volume in a future history series begun with *Inherit the Earth* (1998) and to be continued in *Living In the Future*. *Vampire City*, his translation of Paul Féval's *La Ville-Vampire* (1867), was published by Sarob Press in December 1999, and he hopes to follow it with translations of Féval's other vampire novels, *La Vampire* (1865) and *Le Chevalier Ténèbre* (1875). It was while trying to figure out how best to render Ténèbre (the chevalier's name) into English without the troublesome accents that he first looked up *Tenebrio* in the dictionary, thus setting off the train of thought that produced "Tenebrio."

TENEBRIO

BRIAN STABLEFORD

John Hazard had just started on the pile of first-year essays when there was a rap on the lab door. He didn't get the chance to say, "Come in." Steve Pearlman wasn't the type to wait for an invitation. Instead, Hazard said: "No. Absolutely not. I told you last time—never again."

"Hi, Doc," Pearlman said, breezily. "Got something here that might interest you." The young man reached into the leather pouch attached to his belt and pulled out a map, which he threw on the desk while he rummaged around for something more deeply buried.

Pearlman was in full ecowarrior regalia: faded blue jeans that hadn't been washed for a month, a fawn sweater so thick and lumpy it might have been knitted with chopsticks, and mud-spattered Doc Martens. His blond hair was no longer in dreadlocks, but it looked less tidy than ever. Pearlman had been Hazard's tutee during the three years he had spent at the university, notionally studying ecology. Hazard hadn't seen a lot of him in the lab or the lecture theater but had been forced to spend time with him at the beginning and end of every term to discuss the various complaints that invariably accumulated. It had been a great relief to Hazard when Pearlman had actually contrived to get a third-class degree; he hadn't expected to see or hear from him again after the post-graduation piss-up—Pearlman wasn't the kind of student who required his teachers to produce references for dozens of different jobs—but he hadn't been so lucky.

Although Steve Pearlman had never shown much interest in entomology while he'd been studying, the veterans of Crookham Heath had taught him that academics had their uses, and the battle of Egypt Mill had sent him scurrying back to his alma mater in search of an expert on the habits of hawk-moths. Hazard was more a beetle man, but he'd been so flattered that he'd agreed to appear at the press conference set up to argue that the area between Egypt Mill and Cramborne Barrow ought to be designated a Site of Special Scientific Interest and that the railway line north of Sutton station ought not to be diverted across it in order to allow the road to be widened. Unfortunately, the tabloid press had decided to take the other side, and Hazard's name had been an open invitation to pun-hungry headline-mongers. By the time the bulldozers had actually moved in, Hazard felt as if he'd done a stint on the Somme in 1914, and the Dean of the Faculty had been seriously displeased by the damage supposedly done to his department's reputation for objectivity and scientific seriousness.

A full thirty seconds had passed by the time Pearlman found what he was searching for in the bottom of his bag. He hauled out a plastic specimen-bottle a little longer and a little thicker than a tube of Smarties, which he passed to Hazard. It was full of small

beetles—hundreds of them. They'd probably been alive when
Pearlman had scooped them into the tube, but crowding and lack of
air had done for most of them by now. Hazard released the cap in
order to provide belated relief for the survivors, but he was careful
not to spill any onto his desk. They weren't all the same species,
but the vast majority were very similar. Hazard didn't require a
magnifying glass to identify the dominant genus, although he suspected that he'd need a microscope to figure out exactly how many
species were represented.

"Tenebrio, except for three or four undersized carabids and a
couple of others," he said. "Common as muck. Thanks to agriculture, Tenebrio species are the most cosmopolitan of all beetles,
although most of their immediate cousins prefer a warmer and
drier climate. They're farmed in their own right because their larvae are used as fishing-bait—mealworms, they're called."

"I knew they weren't woodworm beetles," Pearlman replied,
cheerfully. "I wish I could say that you taught me that, but I had
plenty of opportunity to get acquainted with that kind of critter
when I was at the squat in Curzon Street."

"Some Tenebrionidae are wood-borers," Hazard told him,
holding the specimen-tube up to the light and peering at the interior, trying to find something more interesting than he'd seen so
far, "but none of these guys have the jaws for it. Look, Steve, I can't
see the point. They're perfectly ordinary species—pests, even—
and even if they weren't, they'd be no help to the cause. The hawk-
moth fiasco must have taught you that no self-respecting tabloid
will ever go out on a limb for an insect. Newts maybe—but even
that colony of snails on Twyford Down was simply relocated.
There's not a single instance on record of a road development
being stopped, even at the pie-in-the-sky stage, for the sake of an
insect—and this one has to be way past the pie-in-the-sky stage if
the Friends have mobilized the Last-Ditch Brigade."

"It's not actually a brigade at present," Pearlman confessed.
"Hardly a platoon, so far. Even the Friends don't think this one is

worth fighting, but that's because they don't have any domino players on the steering committee. Tenebrio is what they call a darkling beetle, no?"

Hazard's eyebrows went up in response to the revelation that Steve Pearlman actually knew what a darkling beetle was. "You've already shown these to someone else, haven't you?" he said.

"I can use a library," Pearlman retorted, as he took up the map again and unfolded it. It was just a road map, not an ordnance survey map—but that made a sort of sense, given that Steve Pearlman's vocation was trying to make sure that today's road maps didn't go out of date as fast as earlier editions. The army he'd joined had been so successful back in the nineties, in the wake of the Newbury bypass fiasco, that no brand-new road had been built for a decade within a hundred miles—but that had only served to shift the war into a new phase. Road widening was all the rage now, and it was very difficult for the protesters to defend sites that already sat alongside significant traffic arteries. The tide of public opinion that had briefly got behind them was dead against them now. Everybody but the Friends' Last-Ditch Brigade figured that the inevitable cost of not building any new roads was making the most of the ones that already existed.

"There," said Pearlman, passing him the map.

Hazard looked at the place where the younger man's finger was pointing and frowned. "That's the A303," he said. "I didn't know they had any plans to widen the A303 this year."

"They don't," said Pearlman. "They're widening this one here."

Hazard had to squint to see it. The "road" Pearlman was indicating was so small that it didn't even have a B-number. "But it doesn't go anywhere," he said.

"Yes it does," said Pearlman. "It goes to Tenebrion Farm. Tenebrion Farm's in the Domesday Book—I checked on-line. So far as I can tell, it was a thriving enterprise from the eleventh century all the way through to the nineteenth—then it began to fade because its owners couldn't or wouldn't fall in with new fashions. It must have been losing money for two generations before the Common Agricultural Policy gave it a new lease on life. If the owner had switched entirely into cereals and rape-seed he'd probably be okay, but he didn't. He built up his dairy herds instead—then BSE and the supermarket price-lock came along and the whole operation crashed. He tried a few desperation measures—even planted potatoes at one stage—but nothing could stem the cash-hemorrhage and he had to sell out to a developer. All the developer could do to begin with was revamp the actual farm buildings—but there were three big barns as well as a row of workmen's cottages. He converted the lot into dwellings, with the encouragement of a local council that had been ordered by Central Government to make room for six hundred extra homes in the next five years, and Tenebrion Farm was suddenly a village ripe for expansion. The only problem with that is this stupid cart-track connecting it to the A303. It's not even wide enough for two cars to pass one another. That didn't matter while the farmer was driving his tractors back and forth, but once you've got eight separate family dwellings with two cars apiece, you've got what your bog-standard planning application calls a 'pressing need for improvement.'"

While Pearlman was talking Hazard had worked out how his ex-student had found out that Tenebrio was a darkling beetle. He must have taken the name of the farm to the dictionary and the Britannica. The name of a farm recorded in the Domesday Book couldn't possibly have anything to do with the name assigned to a beetle in the Linnaean classification, but Tenebrio was so cosmopolitan that you could probably find specimens on every farm in England if you could be bothered to look. Pearlman had obviously bothered to look—but Hazard still couldn't see what good it was going to do him.

"Well," the entomologist said, carefully, as he put the cap back on the specimen-tube, "it seems to me that the developer has a good case. Presumably, you're worried about the possibility that once the road is there, he'll start angling to build more houses on either side of it."

"That's the least of it," Pearlman said. "The real point is that the A303 offers an easy connection to the M3. Look to the north, at that cluster of newish villages west of Hurstbourne Priors. At present, their access roads all connect to the A343, which means that the local yuppies have to make their way over to the M4, with Newbury sprawling right across their path. The bypass was supposed to make that access easier, of course, but that was fifteen years ago. It's Nightmare Junction now—but once the cart-track connecting Tenebrion to the A303 is a real road, the temptation to extend it northwards to give the villagers a new way out will become enormous. The new Tenebrionites won't like it, of course— all they want is to be a nice coy cul-de-sac—but you can bet your pension that the developer always had it in mind. He understands the domino principle, if no one else does. Once he's got the go- ahead to expand Tenebrion Village he's going to send his bulldoz- ers northwards to plant the spine of a whole bloody town. That's why the battle's worth fighting and why it's worth fighting here and now, between the farm and the A-road. The strip either side of the road's mostly hedgerow, but there's a little patch of woodland here that must have been there from the very beginning, untouched by the hand of cultivation since the Norman invasion. The Domesday Book identifies it as Tenebrion Wood—my bet is that the farm was named after it."

"It's not entirely untouched," Hazard said, raising the speci- men-tube. "No matter how long Tenebrion Wood's been there, this Tenebrio's an invader, carried into the British Isles with European grains. These may have adapted to local produce, but they're no more native to the wood than you are. I suppose you've considered the argument that setting up tree-houses, digging tunnels and get- ting set to fight a pitched battle against the developer's security men will completely wreck the fragile ecology of your precious wood. Even if you did save it from the bulldozers—which you won't—you'd destroy it in the process. Anyway, I already told you I'm not getting involved. I can't afford the hassle."

"That's what they'll put on the ecosphere's tombstone," Pearlman said, predictably. "We might have saved it, but we couldn't afford the hassle. I just want you to take a look, Doc. I just want you to stroll around the site, and tell me whether there's anything better than darkling beetles there—anything we can actually use in an all-out propaganda war. It's an exceptional site in more ways than one, and the leaf-litter seems to be beetle heaven. I scooped that lot up in two minutes flat, in daylight. You don't have to lead the charge—just give us the benefit of your expertise. One day, the front line will reach your backyard, and you'll be screaming for my help."

"My backyard is a cemetery," Hazard pointed out.

"You think that makes a difference? You think that because you're living in a redundant vicarage next to a derelict church you're safe? Come on, Doc, even you aren't that naive. It won't be nearly so much fun living next to that folly once they've connected your little lane to the A303—and they'll do it. Inch by inch, wood by wood, they'll do it. Just take a look. That's all I'm asking."

"It's pointless," said Hazard.

"It's better than marking first-year essays," Pearlman retorted. "It's coming on summertime, and I'll bet you haven't been out in the field since September last, even if you do live in the darkest heart of the green belt."

Hazard could feel himself weakening. Summer was coming on, and he hadn't been in the field since the start of the Autumn term. Even if there was nothing to see but darkling beetles, it would be a day out.

"Tomorrow's Friday," he said, finally. "I'm teaching till three, but I can wrap up after that. Probably reach you by five, traffic permitting."

"Tonight would be a lot better," the ecowarrior retorted, unable to suppress a wide grin of self-satisfaction. "The beetles mostly come out at night. That way, you could give me a lift."

"Tomorrow," Hazard said, flatly. He figured that he'd made enough compromises.

"I'll leave you the map," said Pearlman, who was prepared to be generous now that he'd got what he wanted. "Leave your car in the lay-by west of the turn-off—it's a good three-quarters of a mile, but the walk'll do you good. Bring your wellies."

Because it was Friday the traffic was dire, so Hazard didn't get to the relevant stretch of the A303 until five-thirty. What Pearlman had described as a "lay-by" was just a gap in the hawthorn hedge which already had one car parked in it: a red Citroen Saxo. Having received no attention for at least two years, the hedge was so over-grown that it was difficult to maneuver his Daewoo in beside the Saxo, but Hazard managed. He pulled his Wellington boots out of the front seat and put them on. He threw his loafers on the seat and put his mobile phone out of sight in the glove compartment before locking the vehicle and setting forth.

Although the gate guarding the "cart-track" had been tied open—presumably by the new residents of Tenebrion Farm—it still bore a notice saying PRIVATE ROAD: NO RIGHT OF WAY. It hadn't occurred to Hazard until he saw it that Pearlman's Last-Ditchers would be trespassing, thus requiring him to break the law even to look at the site, but he had come too far to turn around. Cursing himself for allowing himself to be sucked in, he began to walk up the narrow lane.

The unkempt hedges were seething with small birds and the fields beyond hadn't been ploughed or planted for as long as the hedges hadn't been trimmed. Spring had been warm and wet, as spring usually was nowadays, and grasses had run riot in the fallow fields. To the uneducated eye, it might have seemed that the land to either side was already halfway returned to wilderness, but Hazard's eye was not uneducated. He knew that the patchwork of hedges and square fields which even country folk tended to think of as "natural" was entirely the product of technical artifice. If Tenebrion Farm really had been a thriving operation when the Domesday Book took account of its productivity, the artifice in question might go back a thousand years—but it was no more "natural" for that.

For the first half-mile, during which the track curved gently to the left, there was little or no change in the surroundings. Then Hazard came to the border of what Pearlman had called Tenebrion Wood—although his earlier description of it as "a little patch of woodland" seemed far more accurate. The hedges dissolved into a chaotic mess of thin-boled trees and thick-leaved undergrowth, which crowded more closely upon the track than the hedges. The foliage loomed over the pathway with dismal effect, although the arching branches hadn't quite contrived to form a tunnel roof.

Hazard observed, wryly, that this really could pass for "natural" woodland. It was crammed with sickly and diseased specimens, having nothing of the airy spaciousness of a well-managed and carefully coppiced wood. It was certainly plausible that the site of Tenebrion Wood had never been brought under cultivation since the Norman invasion—although, as he'd pointed out to his former student, that was a far cry from being "untouched." If Steve Pearlman could scoop up Tenebrio beetles by the dozen, even by day, Hazard was prepared to bet his last sixpence that other invaders would be equally at home here: grey squirrels, brown rats, black-and-white magpies as well as hundreds of invertebrate species. Supermarket supply-chains, cross-channel trains, and global warming were combining forces to import alien species into southeast England on a massive scale. Whatever Pearlman's Last-Ditch Brigade was striving to defend, it wasn't the native ecosystems of ancient Britain; those were currently in the process of being shot to hell for the fourth or fifth time since the Celts allegedly imported agriculture to this not-very-green and not-very-pleasant land during the last-little-Ice-Age-but-one.

It wasn't difficult for Hazard to find Steve and his half-dozen friends, although they were discreet enough not to reveal the extent and nature of their operation to passing cars until they had established a defendable coign of vantage. The wood was so dense that there weren't many places within spitting distance of the road where any sane person would try to pitch a camp. As he approached the Last-Ditchers' base, Hazard could see that the canopy squad were having some difficulty getting their tree-houses and rope bridges into shape, and the diggers had only managed to sink a single shaft. By the time he came into the camp the sentry had whistled a warning, and a mud-caked head had bobbed up out of the shaft.

"Oh, hi, John!" said the muddy head. "Steve said you were expected." He raised his voice to shout "Okay, boys, he's on our side!" before lowering it again to say: "You remember me, don't you?"

Hazard would never have recognized the face of the boy beneath the mask of mud, but the voice finally clicked. "Um . . . Adrian," he said. Hazard knew perfectly well that because he was a digger named Adrian his compatriots inevitably called the boy Moley, but that would have seemed an intimacy too far, in spite of the fact that Moley had used his first name. "Where is Steve?" he asked.

Moley pulled himself out of the hole, revealing a body that was every bit as filthy as his head. "He's showing the skirt round. He'll have heard the signal—won't be long." Hazard knew that the digger's use of the word "skirt" wasn't a symptom of thoughtless sexism. In road-protest parlance "skirt" referred specifically to a female outsider—female ecowarriors never wore skirts.

"I take it that the developer doesn't know you're here yet," Hazard observed.

"I think the residents might have caught on," Moley told him.

"We're not expecting the opening salvo of blustery threats any time soon, though. You're a scientist, right? You know about soil structure. We're having a hell of a job digging this tunnel—stuff's like black treacle, keeps seeping between the boards no matter how tightly we place 'em. Need more wood underground than up top at this rate. Appreciate it if you could take a look and give us an expert opinion."

"I'm a beetle man," Hazard said, unable to think of anything more foolhardy than taking a look at a tunnel whose walls had communicated so much filth to the young man's body. "I sift leaf-litter when I have to, but everything below the surface is out of my jurisdiction. Sorry."

"Well, there's plenty of dead leaves," Moley replied, unresentfully. "Never seen so many creepy-crawlies before either. I figured out that all woods aren't the same when we were at Egypt Mill, but this baby is seriously yukky."

"That's how things go when they're left to themselves," Hazard said, patronizingly. "If the woodcutters don't keep coming in to clear out the old growth and thin out the saplings, none of the acorns ever grow into mighty oaks. Mother Nature's a real slut when it comes to housekeeping. As for the creepy-crawlies, every frostless winter we have sets off a new population explosion—just one damn plague after another. Tenebrio came to raid our granaries, but it's as versatile as any other vermin. Rats, people, even cockroaches—you name it and Tenebrio will give it a run for its money."

Steve Pearlman had now become visible between the densely-packed and crooked tree trunks now, so Moley must have figured that he had done his bit for the cause of courtesy. With a casual wave of a black hand he disappeared back into his shaft.

The woman with Steve was indeed wearing a skirt, but she'd had the sense to bring Wellingtons. Her hair was cut short, but not as severely as the general run of Steve's female friends. She was older, too—more Hazard's age.

"Hi, Doc," said Steve. "Glad you made it." To his companion he added: "This is the entomologist I mentioned—taught me at Uni, or tried. John Hazard. John, this is Claire Croly."

Claire Croly was clean enough for Hazard not to mind taking the hand she extended. His slight hesitation was caused by the thought that she might be a reporter. "What pretext did he use to drag you out here?" was the politest way he could think of to ask.

"He says the place gets lively after dark," the woman said.

"I'll bet it does," Hazard countered. "But it's not the kind of party you wear your best clothes to—and the gatecrashers some-times get ugly."

"We're not expecting the opposition yet," Steve Pearlman said, sharply. "And we won't be doing any partying. We're under-manned and way behind schedule. Claire's here for the same rea-son you are: to see how weird the site is."

"You're a biologist?" Hazard said, looking quizzically into the woman's clear brown eyes.

"Not exactly," she said, wryly. "I'm on the staff of the *Fortean Times*."

Hazard felt as if his face had been slapped. The worst suspicion he'd so far entertained was that she might be from the local rag; this was far worse. He rounded angrily on Steve Pearlman, who was wearing the same infuriating grin that had possessed his face when he'd initially closed the trap on his old tutor. "You little shit!" he said. "I can't believe you'd set me up for this! Jesus, it's bad enough being fucked over by the *Sun*. Plastering my name all over the *Fortean Times* will just about kill my career."

"I told you yesterday would be better," Pearlman replied, unrepentantly. "You insisted on double-booking yourself."

"I can assure you that I've no intention of plastering your name anywhere, Dr. Hazard," Claire Croly was quick to add. "Your presence here is of no relevance to me. Even if something were to happen—and I see no reason, as yet, to think that it will—I'm perfectly prepared to leave your name out of any report I might make, if that's your wish."

Hazard gulped air as he fought to control his outburst of temper. He didn't want to make a worse fool of himself by blustering. His gaze flickered back and forth between Pearlman and the woman. "So I'm an afterthought, am I?" he said, trying to speak lightly. "I'm your last hope, if the Fortean Society can't give you any ammunition to fight with."

"If you'd come when I asked," Pearlman pointed out, again, "you'd have been in and out before Claire arrived. Short notice, I admit, but still—for you, I took the trouble to collect the beetles. All I offered Claire was a cupful of unease—and the name, of course."

"What name?" Hazard asked, although he knew as soon as he said it that he'd been cleverly wrong-footed.

"Tenebrion Wood. You didn't think it was named after the beetles, did you?"

"Of course not," Hazard said, knowing that it wouldn't sound convincing in spite of the fact that it was the truth.

"According to my admittedly brief research," Pearlman said, "the beetle genus was probably named after the same thing as the farm."

"Tenebra is Latin for darkness," Hazard said, trying to regain the intellectual high ground. "Hence darkling beetles."

"Yes," said Pearlman, "but Tenebrion, with an n, is Old French for goblin, and there's even an obsolete English word tenebrio, referring to a kind of night-spirit."

"Are you telling me that you brought me out to hunt for ghosts and fairies?" Hazard said, coldly.

"No," said Pearlman, patiently, "I brought you out here to look at insects. I brought Claire out here to hunt for ghosts and fairies. It's called not putting all your eggs in one basket. We are the Last-Ditch Brigade, remember? Even the Friends aren't wholly behind us on this one. Do you know how the circulation of the *Fortean Times* compares with that of *The British Journal of Entomology*—or *New Scientist*, come to that?"

Hazard did know; he had always thought it a sad comment on the times in which he was living. "I should never have come," he said.

"Yeah," said Steve Pearlman, "well, you knew that yesterday, and you came anyway. Now you're here, you might as well take a look around, mightn't you? Then you can go back to your ivory-tower and your graveyard, protect your reputation as a scrupulous bore, and pray that urban blight won't come marching over your own personal horizon for a few years yet."

Hazard clenched his jaw, but decided against striking back. He knew that the young man had a point. He'd over-reacted. On the other hand, he did have to hope that this reporter's promise was worth more than the average. He could really do without a mention in the *Fortean Times*—a mention which one of his students was, alas, guaranteed to spot. "Okay," he said, eventually. "Show me what you've got."

What Pearlman had, it transpired, was little more than Hazard had already guessed from his first sight of the little wood. The ecowarrior had elected to defend a little corner of nature that had already been more than half-choked by nature's own fecundity. The wood had been unhealthy for centuries. Far from bringing it back from the brink, the recent string of mild winters and benign springtimes had given a tremendous boost to its parasites. More than three in every five of the standing trees were dying, and the leaf-litter that had accumulated with undue rapidity had begun to rot down with almost-tropical alacrity.

Pearlman had called the wood "beetle heaven" but that had just been a come-on. Moley had been spot-on when he'd described it as "seriously yukky." All kinds of insects were having a high old

time here, including the mealworms that were the larvae of darkling beetles, but the only message implicit in their unusual activity
was that this thousand-year-old stand of trees was doomed,
regardless of whether or not bulldozers were allowed to pulverize
it in the interests of transforming a farmer's access-track into two
lanes of neatly laid tarmac.

Hazard did, however, play his part. He let Steve Pearlman
show him a couple of muddy hollows six or seven feet in diameter,
which would allegedly become seething pools of insectile flesh
when darkness fell. They were not exactly "clearings," because the
emaciated tree-branches clustered just as densely above them as
they did everywhere else, but they were the only patches of
almost-bare ground to be seen except where Moley and his fellow
excavators were at work.

"Odd, no?" said Pearlman, as Hazard tested the second concav-
ity with his fingertips.

"Maybe," said Hazard, cursing the sticky mud which clung to
his fingertips. He borrowed a few leaves from a nearby tree to wipe
it off. The leaves seemed dry and peculiarly autumnal, considering
that the saps of spring ought to be rising lustily.

As Pearlman beckoned Hazard on, a host of slender branches
drew their tips across his face, but they didn't get tangled in his
hair and they didn't leave scratches. They too seemed oddly limp
and effete. It was almost as if the wood knew that it was doomed,
and had become listless in the face of adversity.

"Don't worry about the stroking," Pearlman said. "The spirit
of the wood's just trying to get acquainted. No thorns. It'll like
you, with you being a biologist and all. It doesn't seem to like me
much, even though I've come to help it out. The tips are always
catching in my hair."

"You should get it cut occasionally," Hazard suggested. "Anyhow, if trees were capable of forming relationships at all, I expect
these would want to keep a polite distance until they'd been properly introduced. They're English, after all. They can't take kindly to

having shanties connected by ropy rat-lines erected in their canopy."

Pearlman laughed at that—but then he got called away by one of his fellow climbers. Hazard continued his investigations solo, shoving his way through the seemingly amorous undergrowth with as much delicacy as he could, pausing now and again in order to inspect all kinds of chewed and pock-marked leaves. If nothing else, pottering around in Tenebrion Wood gave his spotting skills a thorough and much-needed work-out. There were Silvanidae as well as Tenebrionidae left over from the days when cereals had been grown on the adjacent fields, numerous Rhizophagidae and— perhaps most interestingly, a couple of Acanthoceridae that were a very long way from their normal subtropical habitat. There was a possibility that these might be the first ever sighted north of Southampton, but who would care?

He took the trouble to collect a few of the more interesting specimens, but even after two hours of assiduous study he couldn't believe that he'd found anything that might be of the slightest relevance to Pearlman's frail hope of mustering public sympathy behind the wood. The simple truth was that it wasn't a Site of Special Scientific Interest. The old cemetery behind Hazard's house was much more interesting, in an objective sense, although it wasn't nearly as well-populated with beetles.

When Hazard eventually found himself, rather unexpectedly, on the fringe of the wood, he figured that it was time to give up and go home. Then everything changed again.

Having caught sight of something tiny and black-and-yellow out of the corner of his eye, he took three paces towards it, and knelt down. He hadn't even stabilized his crouching position when a groan of despair escaped his lips.

For a moment, Hazard wondered again whether Pearlman might have set him up, and whether he'd been brought in merely to find something that the ex-ecology student had already found. But that didn't make sense. If Pearlman really had seen and identified what Hazard had just found, he'd have known full well that his

petty crusade was futile, and that the technologically assisted exe-
cution of the wood was a mere formality waiting to be recognized.

On the other hand, Hazard thought, even if Pearlman hadn't
set him up, he had exposed him to the attention of a reporter from
the *Fortean Times*, and made him a hostile witness to the front end
of a ghost-and fairy-hunt. He had enough resentment left in him
not to spell out what he'd found, or what its consequences would
be, when he made his way back to the encampment.

All he said to Pearlman was: "Give it up. It's hopeless. There's
nothing here worth defending—quite the contrary, in fact."

"Even if it were hopeless," Pearlman told him, "I couldn't give
it up. Come on, Doc—this is your life's work, for Heaven's sake.
Insect Utopia. Give me something I can make a fuss about. I'll keep
your name out of it—all I want is ammunition."

"I can assure you that it is hopeless," Hazard insisted. "Even if
you trapped a whole bloody family of Norman goblins and stuck
them in a cage at Whipsnade, you couldn't save this wood. You
have my solemn word on that."

"That's not enough for me," said Pearlman, unwisely. "You
can't be a conscientious objector in this war, Doc. If you're not part
of the solution, you're part of the problem."

"You don't know how true that is," said Hazard, with a sigh.
"I'm sorry, Steve. If you'd paid more attention to my lectures,
you'd be able to see how badly you'd misjudged this battleground—but all you brought to show me was darkling beetles and
carabids. I hope you're a better judge of goblins."

Pearlman protested that he would see far more when darkness fell, but Hazard had already seen enough. He walked back to
the Daewoo as fast as he could and he took his mobile phone out
of the glove compartment. Then he called the Department of
Agriculture to notify them of the bad news, as he was bound by
law to do.

·   ·   ·

The next day was Saturday, which was Hazard's shopping day. He still followed the same ritual he and Jenny had adopted when they first moved into their little haven of peace, before Jenny had decided that she was a city girl after all and couldn't stand the isolation. Mercifully, they'd never actually tied the knot, so there was no divorce to fight—and no threat to Hazard's tenure in the Old Vicarage. He drove into town, stopping at the baker's for fresh bread before going on to Savacentre and stocking up for the week. He filled up the Daewoo on the way out, collecting double reward points in the process.

After lunch, he went out into the cemetery, to reassure himself that it really was more deserving of the title of Site of Special Scientific Interest than Steve Pearlman's disgustingly fecund wood. It was man-made, of course, but that wasn't the point at issue; the simple fact was that it was a unique environment: a special habitat with precious few parallels. There had, of course, been a village here in the days when the church had been functional and the vicarage had been occupied by a resident clergyman, but when the great migration to the towns had begun in the early nineteenth century the forward-looking landowner had seized the opportunity to modernize his methods. He'd concentrated his declining labor-force in the hamlets on the north side of the estate and he'd taken down the houses north and west of the church brick by brick, so that he could extend his oblong fields into greatly elongated rectangles. He'd been the first man in the county to use a steam traction-engine to pull a plough, and one of the consequences of his revolutionary spirit had been that he'd been able to obliterate an entire village and put the land under cultivation. He'd obviously taken his freethinking ways very seriously, because he'd elected to destroy the village rather than the smaller hamlets, isolating the church. The church commissioners had refused to sell their own parcel of land but they hadn't been able to maintain the living. They'd closed the church and the cemetery and sold the vicarage with the proviso that its exterior aspect was preserved. When he'd bought it, Hazard had become the official keyholder of the church, although he had no more than a couple of inquiries a year from tourists wanting to look inside—mostly American Mormons hunting down scraps of evidence relating to the lives of their more remote ancestors.

The abandonment of the cemetery more than a hundred years before had allowed the graves to develop their own peculiar ecosystems, in which alien flowers still vied for space with grasses and the old headstones supported extraordinary tapestries of lichen and moss. The flowers attracted butterflies and wild bees, but Hazard's favorite neighbors were the Lampyridae which lit the cemetery by night and the death-watch beetles that were slowly clicking their way through the timbers of the dead church.

Hazard was still immersed in his desultory contemplation of the peculiar ecology of the derelict graveyard when a police car pulled up in the lane and a uniformed man got out. Hazard made his way back to the narrow gap in the wall on the opposite side of the cemetery to the more imposing lich-gate.

"Can I help you?" he said.

"Dr. Hazard?" the policeman enquired, for form's sake. "I'm Constable Potts, Sherfield. I'm making enquiries about an incident at Tenebrion Wood last evening. I believe you were there."

"It's hardly a police matter," Hazard said. "I reported the infestation to the Department of Agriculture. They'll take care of it."

The constable frowned, quizzically. "I'm sorry, sir," he said, uncertainly. He obviously didn't have the faintest idea what Hazard meant.

"My fault," said Hazard. "I reported a infestation of Colorado beetle in some potatoes growing on the edge of a field where they'd once been cultivated. You must be referring to some incident that occurred after I left. I take it that the residents had found out about the fledgling demonstration and notified the developer."

"No sir," the policeman said. "I'm afraid there was an accident.

A young man named Adrian Stimpson was killed when a tunnel collapsed."

There was a moment of shock, when Hazard's mind refused to recognize that Adrian Stimpson was Moley, but then the pressure of reality asserted itself. "Oh," he said, finally. "I'm sorry."

"Did you speak to the young man?" the policeman asked, his words falling with appalling weight on Hazard's stunned consciousness.

"Yes," Hazard said, numbly remembering the seemingly trivial conversation whose ominous quality now stood fully revealed. "He asked me if I knew anything about soil structure. He said that he was having difficulty shoring the tunnel up. He asked me to take a look but I said that I wasn't a soil scientist and couldn't help him. I really couldn't. I'm an entomologist. He knew more about soil than I ever did—he spent days underground at Crookham Heath and Egypt Mill. What could I have done?"

"It was an accident," the constable said. "No one was at fault, except for the boy. The coroner might call it misadventure, but it was just one of those things. There'll have to be a inquest, I'm afraid, but I doubt that you'll be called. A statement will probably be sufficient—but your testimony is relevant."

"Yes," said Hazard, still dazed. "Wasn't there anything they could do? I mean, there were a half a dozen people there." And they all had mobile phones, he added, silently. My going didn't make any real difference. I'd only have been one more pair of hands. "Nothing," said the policeman. "He didn't have a chance to call for help, but they were checking on him at regular intervals. As soon as they became aware of the collapse they started digging, in case there was an air pocket, but he must have asphyxiated very quickly. He was long dead when the Fire Brigade finally got the body out." The policeman turned as he spoke, having heard the sound of another vehicle drawing up behind his own. It was a red Citroen Saxo. "If you could drop into the station at Sherfield some time soon, Dr. Hazard," Potts added. "We'll take a formal statement. Shouldn't take long."

"Of course," Hazard said. The entomologist stood where he was while the policeman went back to his car, nodding politely to Claire Croly and Steve Pearlman as he passed them.

Pearlman had obviously changed his clothes within the last couple of hours, and the *Fortean Times* reporter was no longer clad in the skirt she'd been wearing the previous evening. They had both showered recently, presumably separately. Hazard hoped that he knew Pearlman well enough to be reasonably sure that the only reason the woman from the *Fortean Times* was with him was that he'd been desperate for a lift. The ecowarrior didn't own a car, and Hazard's house wasn't on a bus route.

"You could have told me about the Colorado beetle," Pearlman said, accusingly.

"Would it have made a difference?" Hazard countered, fearing the possibility that it might have. "Would you have told Moley to fill in the tunnel and pack up if I had?"

"No," said Pearlman. "Even if you'd spelled out exactly what the ecopolice would do, we'd have stayed. We're still determined to defend as much of the wood as possible. We think we still have a chance to save something."

Steve Pearlman was far too young to remember the days when they'd had posters in post offices identifying Colorado beetle as a significant public enemy. They'd still been on show when Hazard was a toddler in the mid-sixties: a stubborn hangover from the late forties, when potatoes had been just about the only significant foodstuff that wasn't on ration. If Hitler had only had an entomologist on his General Staff to advise him to equip the Luftwaffe with jars full of Colorado beetles—plundered by his Japanese allies from occupied China if his American spies couldn't oblige at

source—he might never have had to suffer D-Day. Instead, he'd
stuck to incendiary bombs and had generated the spirit of the Blitz.

"They aren't going to stint on the pesticides, Steve," Hazard
said. "They have to make sure the infestation doesn't spread to
fields where potatoes are still being grown for market. Colorado
beetle may not be rabies, but it could do a hell of a lot of economic
damage if it became endemic. The wood's already nine parts
dead—the sprayers will kill it off completely."

"It'll regenerate, if it's given the chance." Pearlman said.

"True—but you can't defend a dead wood on the grounds that
it will probably resurrect itself in twenty or thirty years time.
Anyway, that's not the issue anymore, and you know it. You got
someone killed, Steve. It's time to give it up."

"We all knew the risks," Pearlman retorted, obstinately.

"Oh, sure. You all knew the risk of falling out of a tree when
the cherry-pickers moved in. Poor Moley probably thought he
knew the risk of being caught in a collapse if the JCBs came on site
before it was completely clear—and probably thought of it as a
heroic risk to run—but what killed him was his own inability to
cope with the sloppy soil. He was just a boy, Steve! He didn't have
a clue what he was doing!"

"Yes he did," said Steve. The determination in his voice was
tangible.

"Oh, shit!" said Hazard, finally catching on to the reason why
Pearlman was here. "You're going to try and use it, aren't you? You
don't give a damn about the Department of Agriculture's clean-up
squad. You're going to try to build Moley's death into some kind of
martyrdom. Worse than that—you're going to claim that the goblins did it, aren't you? You're going to splash the whole sorry incident over the front page of the *Fortean Times* and make a fucking
circus of it. What about the poor kid's parents, for Christ's sake?
What are they going to make of it? Do you really imagine that you
can stop the developer widening the access road by establishing the
wood as a Site of Special Pseudoscientific Interest? You're off your

fucking head—and you can leave me out of it, you hear. No more. Ever."

"You're in it," Steve Pearlman said, ominously. "You were there. He asked you to take a look, and you refused."

Hazard had already turned to look at Claire Croly. "Aren't Forteans supposed to be agnostics?" he said. "Aren't you supposed to pretend to be objective, or at least not to be completely bonkers? You can't be willing to go along with this!"

"It's not as simple as that," the woman replied. "Steve's got it backwards, actually. The problem isn't that you were there, but that you left so soon."

Hazard was beyond shock by now. His blood was no longer capable of running cold. The realization that the woman was in on Pearlman's new master plan was just one more faint rap on his tired skull. "You actually think the goblins did it," he said, slowly. "You spent the night in the dark and deathly wood, and you saw exactly what you'd been primed to see. Every shadow a tenebrio, every rustle a night-spirit. Then someone shouts out that the tunnel's collapsed and Moley's trapped, and bang—the goblins did it. Are you absolutely sure that it wasn't a giant Colorado beetle, resentful of the fact that I'd discovered their invasion force before they could run riot?"

She didn't flinch. "You weren't there, Dr. Hazard," she reminded him. "You left, as soon as you'd found something that satisfied your spirit of enquiry."

"That's right," Hazard said, softly. "I was long gone. Be sure to mention that in your report, won't you? I spotted the infestation, and I left. I am not part of your crazy stunt. Now, I'd like you both to leave. It's very kind of you to warn me that the shit will be hitting the fan, but now you've done it I don't think I ever want to see either of you again."

"It's not as simple as that," Pearlman said, deliberately echoing Claire Croly's formula. "We've got something to show you. It won't take a minute. It's in the boot of the car."

"Fuck off," said, Hazard.

"You have to look," said Pearlman, doggedly. "Afterwards, you can tell us to fuck off—but first you have to look. We've come a long way."

Hazard let loose an almighty sigh, but he followed Pearlman when the youth led the way back to the Citroen. He waited patiently while Claire Croly unlocked the boot and raised the hatch.

Inside, sitting between a toolbox and a petrol can, there was a huge glass jar with a capacity of at least three gallons. It had a narrow neck and a rubber stopper, so it was sealed as tightly as the specimen-tube Pearlman had brought to Hazard's office, with much the same result. Most of the insects enclosed in the jar were dead—but that still left thousands, perhaps tens of thousands, that were not yet motionless.

Hazard had no idea how many Tenebrio beetles would be required to fill a three gallon jar, but he knew that it was a lot—perhaps a million. He could see, too, that there were more than a few carabids mixed in with this lot, and maybe forty or fifty other species. He could even see a couple of brightly colored burying-beetles. For the most part, though, the beetles were Tenebrionidae, genus *Tenebrio*, in a profusion which had surely never been seen outside a mealworm farm.

Now, at last, Hazard admitted to himself what he hadn't quite admitted before. Tenebrio was basically a grain beetle, a granary pest. It had no business being in a dying wood in any considerable numbers, certainly not in such awful profusion as this. Not even a dying wood called Tenebrion Wood, which had Colorado beetle in the margin that had once marked the edge of a potato-field. The hot weather was causing all kinds of unexpected outbreaks—plague after plague after plague—but global warming wasn't scapegoat enough to explain why Tenebrion Wood was full of darkling beetles. That was odd—damnably odd, in fact.

"Twenty minutes," said Steve Pearlman. "I wasn't entirely

sure that you weren't coming back, so I thought I'd better make provision to get you back. I certainly didn't know Moley was going to die. All I knew was that something was happening that shouldn't be, and maybe couldn't be. It was as if they just came up out of the ground, like oil from a well."

"That's ridiculous," Hazard said.

"Yes, it is," said Pearlman. "Where do you think Moley started to dig? Where else but in one of those funny hollows—the biggest of the three. Maybe the worst place he could have chosen."

"You have to make up your mind," Hazard said, tight-lipped. "Either the goblins did it, or the beetles did it. They're both impossible, so it really doesn't matter, but it really has to be one or the other."

"No it doesn't," said Claire Croly. "The forms this thing takes are probably arbitrary. The point is that the wood's not as nearly dead as it seems, and that the life it has is a strange kind. You left before it came into its own, Dr. Hazard. You really ought to give us a second chance to convince you."

"It'll be just the three of us," Pearlman put in. "When the Dep of Ag's hit squad turned up we made a tactical withdrawal—but it'll take them all weekend to figure out exactly how much ground they have to spray. There are a lot of stray potatoes on the farm. They won't start spraying until Monday. No one will disturb us if we go back tonight—no one except whatever's kept that wood free of cultivation for a millennium and more."

"You're quite mad, you know," said Hazard.

"The only way you'll be able to say that with authority," Pearlman retorted, "is to come and meet the goblins yourself. Until you've faced them, you can't say for sure that they don't exist."

Hazard disagreed. He knew perfectly well that the goblins didn't exist, and that a million beetles and one dead boy couldn't possibly prove that they did. But Steve Pearlman had been able to push his buttons ever since he'd found out where Hazard lived. One day, the bulldozers really would put in an appearance on his

own doorstep—and when that day came, Hazard would be screaming for help from the Friends and anyone else who would conde-
scend to listen. Come that day, he'd be perfectly prepared to
populate his private cemetery with imaginary ghosts, and pretend
that the empty church had once played host to the Holy Grail.
Anything to hold back the tide. Tenebrion Wood wasn't his backyard, and the people whose backyard it was wanted it gone, but
that wasn't really the point.

"I'm not going out to bat on page one of the *Fortean Times*,"
Hazard insisted. "Whatever you talk me into seeing, I'm not putting my own head on the public chopping-block. Not for the Angel
of Death with a flaming sword, let alone a night-spirit that takes
the form of a horde of beetles."

"For your eyes only, Doc," said Steve Pearlman. "I just want
you to know that I'm not as mad as you think I am."

"I'll be there," Hazard said. "Eleven o'clock suit you? If your
goblins haven't come out by midnight, though, I'm done with it,
once and for all."

"That's fine," Pearlman replied. "Eleven till midnight it is. I'll
let the wood-spirit know. It might not like me as much as it likes
you, but good news is always welcome."

"Quite mad," Hazard repeated, determined to have the last
word, at least for the time being. Pearlman had won enough to give
it to him. Claire Croly shut the boot, then the two of them got into
the car and drove away.

Hazard went indoors; he had had enough of the cemetery for
one day.

This time, thanks to the thin Saturday night traffic, Hazard was
bang on time. He pulled into the lay-by on the stroke of eleven,
sliding the Daewoo in alongside Claire Croly's Citroen.

He slipped on his Wellington boots before getting out of the
car. He had taken the precaution of changing the battery in his

flashlight before setting forth, and he pocketed a spare just in case. Unlike Jenny, he wasn't in the least afraid of the dark, but he didn't have a cat's eyes and was just as likely as any common-or-garden coward to get himself filthy or hurt while blundering blindly around.

A few stars were visible amid the clouds, but the light-pollution from Newbury collaborated with the usual oxides and micro-particles to impart a curious salmon-pink stain to the strip of sky visible above the lane. The hedgerows seemed taller and closer by night than they had by day, and the impression was enhanced by a background susurrus that owed more to the stirring of slender branches in the breeze than to the movement of rodents and birds. He heard an owl hoot once, but it didn't come from the direction of the wood, whose branches were far too dense to allow fliers to hunt therein.

It was just as easy to find the way to the Last-Ditchers' campsite by night as it had been by day—easier, given the number of booted feet which had tramped back and forth since Adrian's accident and Hazard's report of the presence of Colorado beetle on the wood's further fringe. As Hazard moved away from the lane he played his light over the ground expectantly, but the only beetles he saw were glossy carabids out hunting. The beam reflected back more than once from tiny pairs of eyes, but they were only mice.

The track he was following was now a well-worn path and there was no need to fight his way through tangled branches. A few trailing tips brushed his arms, but he was wearing a protective track-suit top over his shirt and there didn't seem to be anything intimate in the way the leaves slid across its synthetic surface.

Steve Pearlman and Claire Croly had torches of their own, but they'd turned them down low in order to conserve power. Hazard switched his own light off when he joined them, knowing that his eyes were already half-adjusted to the gloom. By the light of Pearlman's torch he could see where the hole that Adrian Stimpson had dug had been filled in again, leaving a convex mound like an oversized molehill. Hazard knew that one always took more dirt out of a hole than was required to fill it again; it was a matter of compaction.

"Well?" said Hazard.

"It feels strange," Pearlman said.

"That's why I'm here," Hazard said. "It's supposed to feel strange. Goblins to the right of us, kobolds to the left . . ."

"It's not like that," Claire Croly said. "It wasn't like that last night—but it wasn't like this either. Something's changed."

"Sure," said Hazard. "You're down half a dozen ecowarriors— one of whom is lying in a mortuary—and you're up one skeptic, who can't feel a damn thing. Maybe it's the breeze. Last night was still, and that must have made a big difference to the background noise. Ears adjust their sensitivity in much the same way that eyes do, and they can play peculiar tricks on the town-bred. Your brain gets used to screening out familiar noises, but unfamiliar ones can seem very eerie when they become newly obtrusive. That was what spooked Jenny when we moved into the vicarage. I kept telling her that it was just a matter of adaptation, but she couldn't wait."

"Jesus, Doc, you really are full of bullshit sometimes," Pearlman told him. "I've spent a hell of a lot of time sitting in trees at night, and Claire's no novice. Did it ever occur to you that the fact that your girlfriend had already been living with you for ten years without ever pushing you to marry her might be a symptom of a deep-lying unease that had nothing whatsoever to do with the silence of the countryside?"

That speech was followed by an uncomfortable silence. The crowns of the trees quivered in the breeze, as if in the grip of a sudden chill. "Show me your beetle Heaven, Steve," Hazard said, quietly. "Let's see what kind of plague it is that afflicts your goblin wood."

Pearlman led him to the smaller of the two hollows that he'd shown Hazard by daylight. It was just as empty and dull now as it had been then.

"Douse your light, Claire," Pearlman said. "If we all stand still and keep quiet for a few minutes, and give what passes for normality around here a chance to reassert itself, we might see something. Let me judge the wait. I'll switch on when the time is right."

Claire Croly obeyed, and Pearlman switched off his own torch.

In order to play the game—and Hazard still felt that it was a game and nothing more—they all had to stand perfectly still and not make a sound, so that was what Hazard did, knowing that the darkness and the strain of keeping still would be bound to exaggerate the perceptions of his ears. In such circumstances it would only be natural to sense communicative effort in the whispering of the branches, and he was on guard against it. The darkness was profound; there were no fireflies here. The crowns continued to shiver and quake. If the wood really did have a spirit, Hazard thought, it was obviously coming down with something: vegetable meningitis.

Thirty heartbeats passed while Hazard savored the quality of the feverish whisper. It wasn't quite as clamorous as he had expected—the density of the branches stifled the slight wind more effectively than he had anticipated. There were no birds moving in the crowns of the sickly trees, and it seemed that even the rats and mice preferred the hedgerows, because he could clearly hear a faint cacophony of scratching sounds which he knew from experience to be the sound of carabid beetles scurrying across the dried-out surface of the leaf litter. There might have been thousands of Tenebrio beetles following their own courses—or even taking line-dancing lessons—without their being able to add much to that slight symphony, because the discrepancy in size between the two kinds was so very considerable.

Thanks to the patchy cloud cover the night wasn't particularly cold, especially within the canopy-blanketed wood. Hazard felt quite comfortable, although he kept his hands flat upon his track-suit top so that the fingers wouldn't begin to go numb. There wasn't the remotest suggestion of goblin presence, unless one were prepared to count the inflammation of the metaphorical sore spot that Steve Pearlman's last gibe had touched. It had occurred to Hazard that the business about not being able to stand the quietness and isolation of the Old Vicarage had been an excuse, and that what had really sent Jenny scurrying back to London was the awareness—brought out by closer confinement and the suspension of customary support-systems—that she really didn't want to spend the rest of her life with John Hazard. That possibility still rankled, and it didn't need one of Pearlman's random darts to suggest that there might be more symbolic weight than ecological fascination in Hazard's fondness for the cemetery that lay between his home and the corpse of the church.

When Pearlman's torch came back on there were indeed beetles in the saucer-shaped depression, including Tenebrionidae, but they were not present in anything remotely like the abundance that would have been required to allow Pearlman to fill the jar he'd loaded into Claire Croly's car as entomologist-bait.

"Shit!" said Pearlman. "She's not cooperating, is she?"

Hazard remembered that the wood had been "it" when it was allegedly attempting to get to know him on Friday afternoon, and had still been "it" earlier that day. The further personalization seemed to him to be in rather bad taste, given that its motherly earth had taken poor Moley in an embrace that was far too cloying.

"It happens," Hazard said. "Miss Croly can probably tell you about hundreds of occasions when the presence of a single skeptic was enough to banish all manner of paranormal phenomena that had been running riot while there were only true believers to bear witness."

"That's uncalled for," the reporter objected.

"So is all this," said Hazard. "It's over, Steve. Sometimes, you just have to settle for fighting on a different battleground."

"Maybe so," said Pearlman, his tone retaining an obstinacy

that belied the words. "Let's take a look at the other one." He set off in the direction of the larger hollow.

Hazard followed him meekly, not bothering to switch on his flashlight even though there was not the slightest glimmer overhead; the canopy was quite opaque. The branches clutched at him more insistently now, but the man-made fibers of his seamless top repelled them effectively enough. He didn't feel that the wood was trying to take him prisoner.

The second hollow was as bare as the first, but Hazard was prepared to be patient. He was committed until the witching hour; after that, he could go home. He even knelt down to inspect the saucer-shaped depression, and condescended to touch it even though he knew from glutinous experience what it might do to his fingertips. This time, however, the surface didn't seem in the least gluey. Indeed, it felt strangely soft, as if he were touching skin rather than soil. After a moment's pause he laid his palm flat upon the ground, wondering why it didn't feel cold.

The ground made no attempt to grip him. It was the power of his own muscles that forced the hand down, pressing harder than he had consciously intended. He gasped in surprise, although he tried to strangle the sound lest Steve Pearlman and Claire Croly derive too much satisfaction from it. The hand didn't sink into the compacted earth, but he did have the impression that the contact subtly changed its nature—and that it was he, not some external force, which had imported some perverse shadow of meaning into the meeting.

He knew that something was amiss, and that it was not the kind of thing he was on guard against.

Steve Pearlman was waiting for Hazard to get up again before switching off his torch, so there was still light enough to see by. Indeed, the beam of the torch played directly upon Hazard's splayed fingers, confirming to the sense of sight that there was nothing unusual in the manner in which it rested there. There had been no visible change in the texture of the soil—nor in the texture of Hazard's flesh, although Hazard felt a curious sensation within his own being. It did not flow from the ground; rather, it seemed to begin deep in his own abdomen before reaching out into his limbs and through his extremities—not just the naked resting hand, but his rubber-booted feet.

It's in me, Hazard thought. So far, it's just in me.

Nothing was visible, even in the light, and nothing was audible, even in the silence, but Hazard could not deny that something was happening: that he was reaching out, in a way that he had never reached out before and had never thought to be possible.

Then the earth, or the wood, or the resident spirits of the wood, responded.

Oh shit, Hazard thought, realizing that intelligence was not enough, that rationality was not enough, and that even sheer bloody-mindedness would not protect him.

The soil in the depression was abruptly transformed, visibly and quite impossibly, into a seething mass of beetles: a plague of beetles that, for all Hazard knew, might have extended down to the very center of the earth. Instead of black soil that felt like skin, there were adult insects by the million: darkling beetles, every one. Tenebrion beetles, cursed by a coincidence of nomenclature to embody the spirit of Tenebrion Wood, at least in the impious mind and sinful eyes of a fallen entomologist.

An entomologist ought to have snatched back his hand in response to such a miracle, even if his very next response was to run for a specimen-jar the size of a beer-barrel, but Hazard was no longer in possession of any such reflex or intention. He left his hand where it was and the beetles swarmed over it in line-dancing legions, as if to seal a bargain by clasping it.

"I fucking told you so!" was Steve Pearlman's reaction. Claire Croly could only gasp, in spite of the fact that she must have seen it before.

It went on and on, regardless of the light. Adrian Stimpson's death, Hazard realized, must indeed have been an accident. Just one

of those things, as the constable had said. Not murder and not sacrifice: just a breakdown of communication, a misunderstanding. He
realized, too, that as soon as the men from the ministry had
decided how much ground their spraying had to cover, every beetle
in the wood would be living on borrowed time. To be harmless was
no defense in that kind of war. To be as common as muck was no
defense either. Come hell or high water, the path through the wood
was destined to become a real road. The wood had avoided cultivation for more than a thousand years, but tarmac was too ultimate a
weapon—and in law there was no such thing as a Site of Special
Supernatural Interest.

Hazard waited a full five minutes before standing up. He didn't
have to wipe his hands—the remaining beetles fell away like dripping darkling water. They took nothing with them; they had
already achieved their purpose, if they were indeed representative
of some kind of purposeful being. If not . . . well, they had had
their effect.

"You told me so," Hazard admitted to Pearlman. "And I listened. In spite of everything, I listened. I came, I saw, I played my
part—and now I'm out of it. I'd prefer it if my name wasn't mentioned in the *Fortean Times* account of derring-do in Goblin
Wood."

"You have to give me something," Pearlman said. "Now
you've seen, you have to give me something I can use."

"Don't be stupid," Hazard said. "You've known from day one
that there isn't anything here that you can use. Something worth
protecting, granted—but not something you can use. Whatever
Claire writes in the *Fortean Times* will be more damned data. I
really can't help you, Steve. No one can. Sometimes, you just have
to settle for fighting the war on a different battleground."

"But you saw it," Pearlman protested. "You saw."

"I saw beetles," Hazard told him. "Not Bigfoot or the Loch
Ness Monster. Just lots and lots of beetles. It's not enough."

That wasn't the end of the argument, of course—and Hazard

kept to his promise to stay till midnight—but it was the end of the story, so far as Steve Pearlman's last-ditch defense of Tenebrion Wood was concerned. The next chapter required a different approach, and a different hero.

Hazard wasn't unduly surprised when Claire Croly's red Saxo made its way up the lane to the Old Vicarage two weeks later. She could have posted his complimentary copy of the issue that contained her name-free account of the exotic haunting of Goblin Wood and the mysterious death of Adrian Stimpson, ecomartyr—but she was never going to do that now that she knew the way to where he lived. Hazard didn't invite her in, though. He was in the cemetery when she arrived, and it was among the tapestried gravestones, observed by wild bees, that he received his gift.

It was summer by now, and the day was glorious. The overgrown graves were beautifully green, and the wild flowers that grew in profusion were as colorful a flock of alien species as any painter in Bedlam could have imagined.

"I can see why you like this place so much," the reporter said. "It must be at its best now."

"Pretty much," Hazard agreed.

"Interesting, too—to an entomologist."

"As the man said when asked what a lifetime of study had taught him about the mind of the Creator, He has an inordinate fondness for beetles. He was talking about the Christian God, of course, but the implication of Nature remains the same no matter how you animate it behind the scenes. Think of the Egyptians and their scarabs. I like it here."

"Pity your girlfriend didn't feel the same."

"Yeah," said Hazard. "Well, as I told Steve, the mind can play tricks when the senses move into a new environment. All the things we've subconsciously ceased to notice are suddenly conspicuous by their absence, and vice versa. Jenny thought living out in the country, next to an old church, would be romantic. She hadn't expected it to be scary, and she couldn't quite get her head around the notion that its seeming scariness was all in the eyes and ears of the beholder. She thought the place was haunted—the cemetery, not the house. She couldn't accept that the lights were just Lampyridae—to her, they were lost souls. She just couldn't shake the notion loose. But maybe Steve was right too—maybe, at an even deeper level, she just couldn't stand living with me any longer."

"He's right more often than one might think," Claire Croly told him. "He's right about your not being safe, even here. The day might come when the bulldozers appear even on this remote horizon."

"No way," Hazard said. "There are no dominoes hereabouts. Even if the farmer weren't descended from a long line of agricultural geniuses, he'd never let go the way the owner of Tenebrion did. When it comes to stubbornness, he'd even make Steve look like a quivering mass of querulous capitulation. I've got the one and only hole in the patchwork. If there's a single safe spot within a hundred miles, this is it. The landscape's not natural, of course—everything the eye can see in every direction is the product of human artifice and the spirit of technological endeavor—but it's green, and it's alive. Every year it dies, and every year it comes back to life, always changing, adapting, evolving. Especially the cemetery, where there really is life after death."

The reporter smiled. "But it really wasn't haunted, back in the days when your girlfriend ran away, was it?"

"No," he replied, knowing exactly what she was going to say next, "it wasn't."

"But it is now," she said, fulfilling his private prophecy to the letter. "Isn't it?"

"Oh yes," he said, serenely. "It is now."

William Shunn holds a degree in computer science from
the University of Utah and works as a programmer for the
Children's Television Workshop. His short fiction has been
published in *F&SF, Science Fiction Age*, and *Realms of Fantasy*.
He recently completed his first novel and is at work on a
memoir of his two years as a Mormon missionary. Born in
Los Angeles and raised in Utah, he now lives in New York
City. He welcomes e-mail at bill@shunn.net.

"Dance of the Yellow-Breasted Luddites" is set in the
same future as an earlier story, "The Practical Ramifications
of Interstellar Packet Loss" (*SF Age*, September 1998).

DANCE OF THE YELLOW-
BREASTED LUDDITES

WILLIAM SHUNN

Hannah Specter crouched in the blind with a flutter in her stomach, waiting for Deacon's signal. It was always like this for her,
introducing a new species into the preserve. Watching strange
breath and blood and behavior mesh with the chaotic dance of life
in this harsh land filled her with a joy she'd never known before
coming to Sutter's Mill—a joy almost great enough to drown the
ache that was the rest of her life.

But anxiety tempered the joy. As usual, the decision of what
species to send next had been reached with no semblance of common sense. Hannah was not the most experienced Rescue Star
operative, but even she knew that randomly jumbling species from
disparate ecosystems was a recipe for disaster. Case studies on that

subject dated clear back to Earth, and there the natives had only had access to species from their own planet.

But more immediately worrisome was the sketchy data on the *hrkleshira* themselves. Deacon, the new xenobiologist, had recorded his observations during transit, but little other source material existed. Equally deficient was the literature on the *hrkleshira*'s original habitat. Dry geological briefs summarized data gleaned from space, while the accompanying survey maps offered nothing but blurry images of shale-covered hills and scraggly forests. Though the lack of data was frustrating, it wasn't unexpected; the *hrkleshira* came from a world deep in Exclaimer space.

Choking down a dry cough, Hannah raised her peepers and peered out at the distant spot where Deacon would release the *hrkleshira*. Their blind was constructed of limbs broken from indigenous shrubs, and the creosote stink of their sap clogged her lungs with a taste like crumbled asphalt.

Beneath her faux-cotton shirt, a runnel of sweat tickled her spine. Scalp prickling, she retracted her hair to one millimeter, its shortest length. The hair net, seamlessly integrated with her scalp, was one of the many frivolities that had landed her on Sutter's Mill, working off her debts in service of Rescue Star. Her accelerated training in xenoecology was not entirely adequate to the tasks at hand, but at least it was cheap, and it might even be useful when her term was up and she could return home to Netherheim. To Fatima.

Stubbly hair made the dust-clotted heat only somewhat more bearable. She imagined the *hrkleshira* broiling in their enclosures. "I hope they can take this climate," she said. "It's not exactly as temperate here as Cretacea."

"*Cretacea is scarcely temperate,*" said the spindly Exclaimer beside her, its voice startlingly loud.

Hannah sighed. "It's called hyperbole, Jack," she said. She hadn't bothered to learn the alien's actual name. To her it was so many unpronounceable consonants.

The alien snorted, but Hannah didn't know what that meant.

"The hrkleshira *will do better in this climate than either you or I, with suitable supervision."*

Hannah winced at the loudness. The *ykslamera*—or Exclaimers, as humans called them—came from a world with a thin, tenuous atmosphere, and had evolved capacious lungs and powerful voices. Those assigned to posts in human space were bio-engineered to cope with the greater atmospheric pressure, but their voices usually remained unchanged.

"Can't you keep it down?" Hannah said, lowering the peepers. "They can probably hear you clear out there."

The Exclaimer snorted again. Its gray skin reminded Hannah of a mushroom, and its face was wide and lumpy like a frog's. When standing, it towered over her by half a meter; sitting, the alien's stalklike legs caused its knees to stick higher than its head. It breathed in gasps and seemed uncomfortable in the heat, and a scent like dry mildew rose from its skin. *"The* hrkleshira *are gifted with excellent vision,"* it said, *"but they hear well only in a narrow range."*

"Perfect," muttered Hannah. "They'll be able to see me strangling you, but they won't hear you scream."

"Excuse me?"

"Oh, wipe it." Hannah raised her peepers. A recent treaty revision meant that Exclaimer observers would now accompany every endangered species resettled from their worlds, and one of Hannah's jobs was to pump this one for all the intelligence possible. But the damn thing didn't volunteer much, and their few exchanges left her feeling like she'd given away more than she gleaned. She was too keyed up to play the spy game now, even for the sake of the *hrkleshira.*

She flexed her throat mike. "How're things at ground zero?"

"The *hrkleshira* downsettle, most," said Deacon. His voice was a gentle bass rumble, and she envied his easy mastery of the alien phonemes even as she struggled to parse his dialect. "The outride distress eases, it seems."

"Wait," said Hannah, "they're settling down?"

"That corrects."

"And . . . their distress from the ride out is easing off."

"As I said." Deacon sounded impatient.

"Sorry," she said peevishly. Deacon came from Friarhesse, a religious colony whose founder had constructed an artificial dialect meant to help its speakers achieve a mental state more in harmony with the thoughts of God. For Hannah, all it achieved was a headache. "I just want to be sure I understand what you're saying."

"I unknow why it problems."

"Uh . . . right," said Hannah.

"Anywise, the time soon readies. Spy my position?"

Hannah sighed and scanned the horizon. A landscape of rocky ground and scrub brush leapt into focus as she switched diopters. She panned across low hills and dry washes, but the only sign of human encroachment was a drone ore prospector, huge and red and bulbous, about three klicks away. She smiled at the sight of a clutch of zori deer grazing happily on saw grass in the middle distance, then continued her sweep.

When she was sure she'd looked past Deacon's position several times, she relented and switched to autospot. Immediately the scene in the viewfinder jumped to a copse of gnarled old trees, beyond which glinted the perspex windscreen of Deacon's groundrover. Deacon himself crouched in the saw grass at the base of the trees, his red beard brown in the shade. Beside him sat the wheeled dovecote with two dozen *hrkleshira* inside.

"I have you, Deacon," Hannah said. "Got an estimate on time?"

"Five minutes, moreless—sofar as concerns the *hrkleshira*."

"What do you mean?"

"The *hrkleshira* calm in sufficiency." Deacon hesitated. "But I fear the environment unwelcomes, herenow."

"The banshee here says the climate's fine. And you've got the feed and water troughs set up, right?"

"Unmeant."

"What *did* you mean, then?"

"You spied the machineworks, a kilometer thence?"

"The prospector?"

"Must be."

"What about it?"

"It can reposition?"

Hannah shook her head. "I'm afraid not. Why?"

"An observation from shiptime. Certain machineworks outstress the *hrkleshira*. They insanify nearwise."

Hannah shook her head. "What are you saying? That machines make them crazy?"

"That corrects. Some machineworks, anywise."

"Well, the prospectors are out of our jurisdiction. We couldn't move them if we tried."

"Try you have?"

Hannah took a calming breath. With Jongnic Bontemps's recent reassignment, she was the acting senior operative on Sutter's Mill. Deacon might have more experience overall—and he was definitely in competition for her job—but she knew this outpost. "The prospectors are property of the Natural Resources Ministry, and we have no control over where they go. They're not dangerous. Every other species does fine around them. The *hr—hrkleshira* will have to do the same."

"Yes, but repositioning has attempted? You have asked?"

Hannah ran a hand over her sweaty scalp, sighing. "We're here at NaRM's sufferance, Deacon. One of our directives is not to be a nuisance and jeopardize our operation."

"Pardon begged, but it legals every habitable planet to home a wildlife preserve. How can NaRM jeopardy us?"

"Goddammit," Hannah said, so angrily that even the Exclaimer turned its head, "the preserve doesn't have to be *here*. If we piss off the wrong people, they might pack us up and move us to one of the ice caps. We have to worry about the welfare of *all* the animals, not just the flavor of the month."

"Blasphemy unnecessaries." Deacon sounded more rankled than chastised. "I merewise—"

Hannah rolled her eyes. "Miles, have you been listening to this?"

"Of course, Hannah," said Miles$_{70}$ from the base, his voice eager and amused and eerily childlike.

"Will you assess for Deacon the chances of getting an ore prospector moved off the preserve?"

"Sure thing." Hannah could picture the little big-brain steepling his fingers in thought. "See, Deacon ol' buddy, Sutter's Mill is a veritable treasure-trove of heavy metals, from gold on up, but the ore's scattered in traces all over the surface. NaRM spends a shitload here on satellite surveys and AI cycles, calculating the most cost-effective routes for these roving ore prospectors. The prospectors themselves have limited intelligence—they're able to stray a bit if they encounter obstacles or surprisingly rich ore deposits, but for the most part these survey paths are programmed as much as a year in advance, and they're crucial to the Ministry's projections for metal production. Any change costs mucho dinero and makes NaRM a distinctly unhappy little brat, so we leave his messes alone, no matter how bad they stink." He emitted a spine-tingling chuckle. "And when you're in the crapper long enough, it stops smelling so bad."

"Thanks, Miles. Hear that, Deacon?"

"Heard." The mellow voice smoldered underneath.

"I've been here almost two years," Hannah said. "I know the territory like you don't." The Exclaimer regarded her with its wide, unblinking eyes, and she fought the urge to snap at it too. Her hands shook. As poor a job as she did at avoiding them, she hated confrontations. "Are the, uh, the damn birds ready to release?"

"*The* hrkleshira *are not birds*," said the Exclaimer.

Hannah waved it to silence.

For a moment, she thought Deacon was not going to respond. "Cooing audibles," he answered at last. "The *hrkleshira* wellseem.

Respiration and pulse are low and even crossboard, say the monitors."

"That's good, right?"

"Pardon?"

"I'm joking," said Hannah, raising the peepers again. She raised her elbows to unstick her shirt from her underarms. "So let's do it."

As she watched, Deacon touched a control in his hand. A crack appeared down the center of the dovecote, and a pair of two-paneled doors folded back from the matrix of pigeonholes within. One, two, four, then more than a dozen pebbled red heads peeked out into the sunlight, blinking oversized blue eyes.

Hannah held her breath. The *hrkleshira* had been hunted nearly to extinction by the Exclaimers, who, rumor claimed, prized the small creatures for the euphoric properties of a secretion from their brains. Whether or not that were true, a small population had been rescued, and this, after a journey of many light-years, was their first exposure to their new home.

The boldest of the *hrkleshira* stretched its body to its full length of twenty centimeters. It unfurled delicate leathery wings, flapping them for balance, and flexed its neck to reveal the supple yellow skin of its breast and underbelly. The little creature danced back and forth on its wiry hind legs, then bounded into the air.

It fell several centimeters before its wings caught the breeze. It flew a rapid loop before the dovecote, and the other *hrkleshira* darted out to join it. A toroid cloud of small red-and-yellow bodies formed—curiously chaotic, but conveying a definite sense of pattern and intent.

She realized she was holding her breath. "That's beautiful," she said softly. "It's like an electron cloud."

"*They are certainly . . . challenging creatures,*" said the Exclaimer, and this time Hannah scarcely noticed the loudness of its voice.

As the cloud of *hrkleshira* drifted higher, a tendril broke off and dipped toward the water trough. A handful of the creatures skimmed the water, making strange motions with their mouths. Hannah tightened the focus of her peepers, but she saw only one *hrkleshira* taste the water as they streaked past.

"Are they making any sounds?" she asked.

"Squeaking evidences," Deacon said. "But it whelms the norm in volume and frequency."

"Can you put it on?"

Deacon patched two external mikes into his audio feed while Hannah watched the breakoffs rejoin the main group. By the time any sound came through, the entire flock was wheeling higher into the sky. Hannah heard a few moments of rodentlike chattering before the creatures had flown so high and far that the mikes could no longer pick up their calls.

"Unforget to write," said Deacon, with a trace of bitterness.

"I've got them, don't worry." Hannah had switched her peepers to tracking mode; if she kept them pointed in the right general direction, the visuals would stay locked on the tracers implanted beneath the creatures' wings. A broad grin spread across her face as she watched the *hrkleshira* rise higher and higher, describing an ever-widening spiral through the warm air. "Mommy's watching."

The *hrkleshira* flew intricate and almost hypnotic patterns for several minutes. About two and a half kilometers from Hannah's position, however, the flock suddenly fanned out into a broad V and flew north, as unswerving as an aircraft following a guidance beam.

"The prospector," said Deacon. "They pinpoint and arrow."

"What? Are you sure?" Hannah asked.

"As warned," Deacon said with exaggerated patience. "The *hrkleshira* unlike certain machineworks."

Hannah glanced at the Exclaimer, but it only stared back with its huge froggy eyes. Raising the peepers again, she focused forward to the prospector, unwilling yet to admit that this really was the *hrkleshira*'s goal. The prospector towered six meters above the desert floor, its red dome capping an undercarriage of trundling tank treads, robotic arms, and sensors of every type imaginable. Though the treads remained motionless, several of the arms were extended, taking samples from the ground.

As Hannah watched, the *hrkleshira* dive-bombed into view in single file. Sensor extensions on the prospector swayed like fronds in an ocean current, tracking their approach. Just when it appeared they would smash into it, the *hrkleshira* curved sharply around the red dome. Time after time, the line circled the machine, rising and falling in waves, like thread winding itself around a bobbin.

Then suddenly, as one, the *hrkleshira* began to dash themselves against the smooth hull of the dome, scrabbling at the curved surface with their broad, clawed forefeet before darting out for another go. Hannah sat frozen, unable to speak, as the surreal scene played out before her in stark silence. One creature battered itself so hard against the dome that it left behind a smear of blood—no more than a small shiny patch on the red metal, but one that made Hannah's heart race and shocked her out of her stupor.

"Oh, jack me!" she exclaimed, bursting from the blind and running for her groundrover. "Do you see that?"

"Seen," said Deacon's grim voice in her ear.

"Miles! Get NaRM on the horn! If that thing's got defensive systems, see if they'll turn them off!"

"Roger," said Miles$_{70}$. "I'll try."

"Deacon, get out there and start collecting those birds. I'll be as close behind you as I can."

"Underway already."

Hannah leapt into the driver's seat. She pounded her forehead on the steering column, then sat for a moment in despair. When she straightened up, she felt the Exclaimer's alien gaze upon her, devoid of any recognizable emotion. It hadn't moved from the blind, but simply sat watching her.

Hannah made an obscene gesture. "*And* the ship you rode in on," she hissed, throwing the rover in gear.

The base was white and ovoid, like a giant egg planted in the ground, its long axis thirty meters end to end. Gentle hills rolled away to the east of the structure, rising in rumpled ridges toward the distant brown mountains. Trailing a plume of tawny dust, Hannah braked to a violent stop beside Deacon's rover, which was parked out front. He and the *hrkleshira* were nowhere in evidence.

By the time Hannah had reached the prospector, Deacon had already managed to collect more than half the little creatures. Hannah had retrieved her net from the backseat of the rover and joined him. The nets had been provided by the Exclaimer; nearly two meters in length, each ended in a wide hoop that rimmed a bag of thin, sticky plastic. A beeper on the rim of the hoop attracted the *hrkleshira*, making it relatively easy to scoop them out of the air.

"Your hunters use these?" Hannah had asked the alien earlier that day. "That had hardly seems sporting."

"*Committed sportsmen, no,*" the Exclaimer had answered. "*The slothful—perhaps.*"

And which would you be? Hannah had wondered in silence.

When the *hrkleshira* were gathered and deposited in the back of Deacon's rover, he had driven directly back to the base, a trip of about ten kilometers. Hannah had returned to the blind to pick up the Exclaimer.

The alien now unfolded itself awkwardly from the passenger seat. Hannah stalked to the entry portal without waiting for it to catch up. Three blue-furred picholeins—sleek, ferretlike scavengers from Serendipity which could mimic human speech—burst out of the weeds nearby, chattering *shoo! shoo! shoo!* as they scampered away. From around the near curve of the base came the answering whoops of the urks in their pen. Hannah smiled despite herself as she pushed her way inside. It wasn't as if the picholeins would respond to the urks' mating calls with anything but abject terror.

The central passageway, narrow and poorly lit, smelled of machine oil and plastic, but at least it was cool. The upsloping ceiling and random piles of boxes gave the place an air of impermanence. In a storeroom on the right, feed for a score of different species was kept, including a year's supply of unperishables for the humans. White hexagonal containers covered with indecipherable chicken-scratches—the Exclaimers' written language—were stacked outside the door, waiting to be stowed. Hannah didn't care to examine the nutrients inside.

Soft bleating issued from the infirmary on the left. Inside, a young zori deer recuperated from two crushed rear legs and a broken pelvis. Jongnic had been tending to the deer, which he had named Ujamaa, for six weeks before his reassignment. He had left her in Hannah's care upon his departure. "Good Ujamaa, good girl," she murmured as she passed. "Mommy'll be back soon."

At the end of the corridor, she emerged into Central Command, a high, broad room littered with a mélange of computer equipment, feed sacks, flimsy maps, rover parts, and empty crates. "All hail," she said.

"Hannah!" said Miles$_{70}$, pushing his wheeled chair back from the control console. He hopped down from the chair while it was still rolling, an impish figure one meter tall, and bowed so low that Hannah could see the serial number tattooed on the back of his bulbous head. "I've got to hand it to you. That was one hell of a show. When those birdies started doing the kamikaze thing, I was laughing so hard I thought I'd piss myself." He looked down. "Uh-oh. I think I did!"

Hannah's mouth twitched as she tried not to laugh. Deacon was at a console across the room, studying video from the afternoon's fiasco, and though he didn't look up, his brow was deeply furrowed. "Better stow it, Miles," she said, indicating Deacon with a flick of her eyes.

Miles$_{70}$ winked broadly and pushed his chair back to the console. "Oh, by the way," he said, "you got an ansiblegram while you were out. From your poppa bear."

Hannah's stomach tightened. "Thanks," she said, heading for the door to the team's quarters.

Deacon looked up. "The Exclaimer unevidences," he said, masking his unhappiness rather ineffectively.

She glanced around, only now realizing that the alien had not followed her inside. "Oh, damn. Miles, can you spot him out there?"

"*It*," said Miles, clambering up into his chair. His small hands flew over the console, and in a few moments the view from an outside camera spot winked into life on the flat surface of the console. "Looks like our favorite stick figure's paying the Zero squadron a social call."

Hannah and Deacon came together to watch the high-angle shot over Miles$_{70}$'s shoulders. The Exclaimer was just latching the door to one of the mesh cages in which *hrkleshira* were housed. It folded itself to the ground and sat, knees jutting above its head, staring into the cages.

"What did he just do?" Hannah demanded.

Miles$_{70}$ shrugged. "It was just taking its arms out of the cage when I tuned in."

"Did he extract aught?" Deacon asked. "Insert aught?"

"It did *naught* as far as I saw," Miles$_{70}$ said with a grin.

Deacon nodded, as if expecting that answer, but a horrible notion had occurred to Hannah. "There's no blood on him, is there?" she asked.

Miles$_{70}$ looked at her skeptically. "Do *you* see any blood? I don't see any blood."

"No, um, apparatus lying around?"

"Hannah," said Deacon, "what on earth implies?"

"Count them, Miles."

"Huh?"

"I want to know how many there are. Count them."

$Miles_{70}$ sighed dramatically. "You da massah, massah."

The *hrkleshira* were housed in six cages, piled three high in two adjacent stacks against an exterior wall of the base. $Miles_{70}$ brought up two additional views of the cages, one from either side.

"Hannah," said Deacon, "what thoughts—"

She shushed him brusquely.

$Miles_{70}$'s eyes flicked rapidly across the three screens. "One hundred thirty-seven," he said.

"Shit," said Hannah. "Are you sure?"

"I counted eleven times, just to be safe."

"That's seven missing. God*damn* that alien bastard. He's eating their brains."

As Hannah whirled toward the door, $Miles_{70}$ burst out laughing. "What?" she snapped.

Deacon rolled his eyes. "The missing *hrkleshira* we tended infield—the injured. I infirmaried the seven. They saferest."

Hannah's cheeks burned. Seeing her flush, $Miles_{70}$ fell out of his chair, rolling on the floor and holding his stomach as his high-pitched cackles filled the air.

She took a deep breath. "Miles, I want you to keep an eye on that thing. I want to know *anything* he does not out of the ordinary."

$Miles_{70}$ sat up. "That'll be just about everything," he said, wiping his eyes. "But you got it, boss."

Deacon had returned to his seat, shaking his head. "*Brthklashikort* planetsides to help us," he said, "not to selfgratify."

His flawless pronunciation only made Hannah angrier. "What's that gibberish—his name? And what are you, his girlfriend? What makes you think you know why he's here?"

"No." Deacon pursed his lips, his dark eyes burning. "I solewise . . . intuit."

"Oh, great, you *intuit*," said $Miles_{70}$, climbing into his chair and chuckling all the while. "You two are a real pair—Paranoid and Freakazoid."

"Shut up, munchkin," said Hannah. "Deacon, this *observer* comes from a species that's been known to wipe out whole human colonies for no better reason than target practice."

"Eighty years have truced us," said Deacon.

Miles$_{70}$ shook his head. "Cease-fired, not truced."

"Exactly," said Hannah. "So what makes you think we can trust him about *anything*, let alone not to shoot up on birdie extract?"

"Our shiptime ampled, if that he intended," Deacon said. "I mosttime cryoslept. Prevention unabled."

"Maybe Exclaimers can go years between fixes. We really don't know anything about them, or their physiology."

Miles$_{70}$ raised his hand. "Oooh, teacher, teacher. Yeah, um, I read that we don't even know if they're subject to addiction in the same sense that we understand it."

"Thanks, Miles," said Hannah. "You're a big whelp. Help. The bottom line is, I don't trust him, and I don't want him screwing up this project."

Miles$_{70}$ nodded. "Let alone the cease-fire."

Both Deacon and Hannah looked at him curiously.

"What?" said Miles$_{70}$, putting on an innocent expression. "It's just some idle speculation I picked up on the nets. Wirehead chatter from NaRM."

"Spill," Hannah said.

Miles$_{70}$ shrugged. "There's some talk from the xenopsychologists that maybe the reason the *ykslamera* agreed to this animal-rescue program in the first place is to demonstrate to themselves what a bunch of hopeless incompetents we humans are. And if they decide *that*—well, maybe they'll have no compunction about attacking us again."

"Great," said Hannah. "Glad to hear there's no added pressure."

Deacon turned back to his console. "Ridiculity."

"Okay, whatever," said Hannah, though her stomach was beginning to hurt. "This doesn't change the most important thing, which is that we have a job to do, and that job is to figure out how to introduce the *her—herk—her-klesh-eera* into the wild here without endangering them or letting them endanger themselves to too great an extent."

"The Exclaimer can help," said Deacon.

"Maybe, maybe not," said Hannah. "It's a roll of the dice I don't care to make, so here's what we'll do. I want to go over exactly what happened out there, review the tapes and everything, right here in fifteen minutes. Humans only. I want theories from both of you, and suggestions as to what to try next. Until then, I'll be in my quarters."

Deacon stood to intercept her as she headed for the far door. "Hannah, may I word with you, pardon?"

"When I get back," Hannah said.

He indicated Miles$_{70}$ with a jerk of his bristly chin. "Private-wise?"

Hannah sighed. "All right. Ten minutes, my quarters."

"You gratify," said Deacon.

"You wish," Miles$_{70}$ muttered.

Filled with increasing disquiet, Hannah left Central Command and shut the door firmly behind her.

Hannah read the ansiblegram four times, then closed the message window on her desktop and sat thinking.

TO:	Hannah Specter, Rescue Star, Sutter's Mill
FROM:	Derek Koepp, Eigencity, Netherheim
DATE:	67.08.14.13.37.25 NLST
PREPD:	<=256char
SUBJ:	Big killing!

Sweet H! Sold nu novel 4 2× ask. Can cover yr debts EZ w/yr bless.
Just say word. /Met Fatima @ last. Keep this I! Nuts 4U & Mrs U2.
Approval!/Say word&come home soon!/L, D

She shoved herself back from her console and stood. Her quarters were too small to pace effectively, so she drummed her heel impatiently on the floor. I travel four light-years from Netherheim, she thought, and serve nearly two years of my pledge, and they've still only just managed to meet. God.

To be fair, Fatima had spent the first three years after Hannah's departure in coldsleep—as long a sabbatical as she could afford to take from her job, and a career risk even at that. That wasn't what was really bothering Hannah, though, as she well recognized. The real issue was her father's continuing attempts to manipulate and subordinate her. Much as he thought he could still apply a salve to her wounds and make everything right for her, he couldn't, and he simply refused to accept that fact. Her debts were her debts. She would take care of them herself.

Instantaneous faster-than-light communication had been around for less than a decade; pioneered by the megaconglomerate Celestial Messengers, the process was so expensive that most private citizens could afford to send only brief text messages, if they could afford to send anything at all. According to this message header, her father had paid for Hannah to send a response of up to 256 characters. So how to refuse Derek's offer in that short a space without having to dip into her savings?

She wished she could do it in just two short keystrokes— NO—but she couldn't bring herself to be that mean-spirited. She loved Derek, and she knew he meant well. That was the problem.

She was still lost in thought several minutes later, compulsively extending and retracting her hair, when Deacon knocked. When she entered her quarters, she had removed her safari vest, which bore her insignia as acting senior operative. She slipped it back on and said, "Come in."

Deacon entered. Hannah's quarters were closer to the outer rim of the dome than his; she was pleased to see that the low ceiling forced him to stoop slightly. Hannah could move about comfortably, but once she had greeted him with a nod she sat back down in her chair and waited for him to speak.

For a moment Deacon seemed at a loss. His eyes swung left to right, settling briefly on the twenty-first-century painting displayed on the east wall. The work of E. Riley, it depicted a blasted orange landscape, perhaps Mars, diagonally traversed by an endless line of power transmission towers. A naked Christ figure hung bloody and crucified on the foremost tower, his skin charred black at the wrists and ankles by crackling electricity. As Deacon stiffened, Hannah recalled that the Stewardship of Friarhesse were gnostic Christians. She suppressed a grin. She was an atheist herself, though one of her mothers had tried to inflict neo-Catholic doctrine upon her as a child.

Turning away from the discomfiting painting, Deacon's eyes fell on the 3D snapshow of Hannah and Fatima that sat atop Hannah's footlocker, which had been taken in a holobooth at the Himmelburg Municipal Zoo on Netherheim. "Fineseen couple," he said. "You espouse him?"

"Her," said Hannah, perversely pleased.

Deacon recoiled. "Pardon?"

Hannah normally preferred not to discuss her relationship, letting images like the snapshow project a half-truth that discouraged unwanted male attention. But with Deacon Greenleaf, Hannah felt a contrary urge to shove her preferences in his face.

"Fatima's my unbonded partner," said Hannah. She ran a hand through her hair, which was now about ten centimeters long. "That image was taken in her male phase, but she's female far more often."

"Christbless," Deacon murmured, almost too low to hear.

"She's got extensive biomods, and she rates F_6M_1. She works as a cop, so it's useful for her to be able to shift genders at will. And since I've got a low but definite bisexual orientation, it works out for me, too."

Deacon's hands opened and closed, as if he were physically grasping for a change of subject. "Your, ah, father messaged. All wells with you homeside?"

"Actually, he's only one of my fathers, but he's fine. Thanks for asking." Hannah viewed the color rising in Deacon's cheeks with satisfaction. "I was raised in a fivehand. They all contributed DNA, but Derek's the only one who really maintained an interest past adolescence."

"A hazard ofttime with parents of the unwombed," said Deacon coldly. "Childperil contraindicates the practice. But pardon—businessward."

Hannah's calm smile froze. "Yes . . . of course," she said, feeling sand suddenly shifting beneath her feet. "Businessward. What is it you wanted to talk about?"

Deacon clasped his hands behind his back. "I comprehend your seniorstatus, respect your planetside experience."

Hannah nodded. "Thank you."

"But it unnecessaried to downdress me so infield. Professional embarrassment."

Hannah considered her response. "I was maybe a little too forceful," she said, "and I shouldn't have sicced Miles on you like I did. He can be—well, 'gleefully cruel' would be putting it mildly. I apologize." She drummed her fingers on the desktop, frowning. "But two minutes before release is hardly the time to raise an objection of the magnitude you did."

"Better than never."

"Better to have shared your observation a lot earlier."

"But I righted. The test should have aborted."

"You think you were right?" Hannah shook her head. "I don't agree."

"Why? The *hrkleshira* insanified. They sillybeat themselves, bloodied themselves. We could have prevented."

"Yes," said Hannah. "And then what?"

"Elsewhere release. Away from machineworks."

Hannah rose. "Two problems with that, Deacon," she said. "First, the birds don't respond that way with *all* machines, right? They didn't go nuts around the rovers."

Deacon was holding himself very still, but his beard bristled and his brow was tightly clenched. "Correct."

"Can you predict exactly what kinds of machinery *are* going to set them off like that?"

He hesitated. "No."

"Can you even state with certainty that only machines are capable of setting off this reaction, and that it's not, say, a natural behavior that evolved in response to something from their home environment? Something that might also exist or be mimicked on this planet?"

His eyes slid back and forth, focused on some shifting point above Hannah's head. "No."

"Okay, so there's *something* out there that makes the *hurr— klesh—eera* go kamikaze, as Miles put it." She felt her voice sliding toward harshness, but kept it under control. "We're not doing them any favors if we just release them somewhere else and hope the problem never manifests again. We could wander out someday and find the ground littered with a hundred bruised little bodies and never understand why it happened."

"Which is solewise why—"

Hannah held her hand up. "Which is why we do field tests like this. Your instinct to protect the *her—kleshira* from injury is very noble—and believe me, I don't like seeing hurt animals any more than you do—but if we don't give them the opportunity to show us what their vulnerabilities are, then we put them at greater risk later."

"Fine, granted," Deacon said, low in his throat, looking over her head and not directly at her. "Point two?"

Hannah sighed. "The second point is that there really isn't a place we could release the *hrkleshira* where the prospectors might not eventually show up."

"*Brthklashikort* knows the needed answers," Deacon said after a few moments of silence. "I certain."

"Not this again," Hannah said. "I'm sure he has the answers, too. I just don't think we can trust him to share."

"I differ."

"I know."

They stared at each other for several seconds.

"Let's try to figure this out on our own," Hannah said. "Pump him for what information we can, but not consider it reliable. If we're still stuck in a few days, we can reevaluate. How's that?"

"Earplay timebeing, glean what possibles slywise?"

"That's the plan."

Deacon considered. "It suits—timebeing."

"Yes, for now."

"For now." With a course of action agreed upon, Deacon seemed to relax a little. "Brainpicked him on your trips fieldward and baseward, you did?"

"I—I tried," Hannah lied. "It's not easy to pin him down. To be fair, he offers a lot of information, but it never seems to be anything really applicable."

"Agreed!" said Deacon, a sudden brightness filling his eyes. "I theory he advises us maxpossible within raceloyalty boundaries, no more."

"Could be. But if that's true, it's an awfully small boundary."

Deacon was nodding, almost smiling. "Small, yes. But he wellmeans, I certain. It possibles even that he cryptics us help."

"Cryptics? Like giving us coded messages?"

"Clues, hints—subtlewise."

"I don't know," said Hannah. "He hasn't said anything really cryptic to me."

"To me mayhap he did, shipboard. I spoke him Christwise, of

our Gospels and Apocrypha. Scripture fascinated him, and post-study he dubbed the *hrkleshira* Christianlike."

"You were trying to convert an Exclaimer?"

"Not convert. Jointshare, comprehend botheach."

Hannah couldn't resist a poke. "Onward Christian birdies, huh? Well, I can't imagine what he meant by that. Can you?"

"Not at all." Still, Deacon seemed quite excited by the puzzle.

Which probably meant she should quit while she was ahead. "Well, if you have any brainstorms about it, be sure to let me know. Maybe we can get Miles thinking, too."

"Bigbrains," said Deacon, his expression clouding. "More abomination." He turned, almost abstractedly, to examine the snapshow of Hannah and Fatima again.

"Yeah, well, you might want to avoid expressing that opinion in front of him. He can be a vindictive little cuss, and you *know* someone like him has powerful friends."

"Highfriends? What manner of—"

A chime sounded. "Receive," said Hannah loudly. "Over?"

$Miles_{70}$'s voice emerged from Hannah's console. "I hate to interrupt your little tryst there, boss, but I think I just earned myself a bonus. You have to see this."

"Whose brilliant idea was this again?" came $Miles_{70}$'s exasperated voice.

"It was *your* extraordinarily brilliant idea," Hannah said brightly from behind the wheel of her rover, "and I love you for it."

"Yeah, sure. Not that it's going to get me anywhere," $Miles_{70}$ muttered. "Jesus, I'm broiling alive out here. What is it, slow-roasted bigbrain julienne on the menu tonight and no one bothered to tell me? I swear to God, air-conditioning was not a creature that evolved by mere chance."

"You can cope. You're a big boy."

"How would *you* know?"

"You'd be amazed how much information there is in your personnel file."

"Oh, it *constantly* amazes me."

Sort of a silly joke for her to have made, since Miles$_{70}$ probably did know more about the contents of all their files than she ever would. Hannah didn't know how she felt about that.

As she approached the top of a long rise, the rover bounced roughly over a rock she failed to spot in time. The *hrkleshira* complained with loud squeakings from the dovecote in the back. She worried for a moment that they would go crazy on her, but after a moment they quieted down again.

"Have you spotted it yet?" asked Miles$_{70}$. "I'm guessing you should almost be there by now, but it's hard for me to be sure with nothing but these damn peepers for input."

"Oh, come on. You probably have it figured out down to the centimeter and the second."

As the rover crested the ridge, a long vista opened up to view, low scrubby bushes peppering an inclined plain of yellow dust and shattered rock. Vagrant breezes tossed sheer veils of dust into the air. Less than half a kilometer away, at the bottom of the slope, a twisting confluence of shallow dry washes thrashed across the landscape. A cluster of the knobby trees known as hagfists curled their knuckled roots into the earth on an island between the washes; jutting from among them like an upthrust red finger was the broken-down prospector she sought.

Hannah shook her head with a grin. "Like I was saying . . ."

Prowling through what were supposed to be restricted NaRM records, Miles$_{70}$ had managed to track down the location of a broken-down prospector that had not been judged worthy of salvage. The site lay nearly 140 kilometers northwest of the base, and the drive across the uneven terrain had taken Hannah most of the morning. She had dropped off Miles$_{70}$ and his telemetry gear at the halfway point, and even then the mountains to the east had been no more than a smudge on the horizon. Her aloneness in these vast surroundings exhilarated her. Several times she had felt a tightness in her throat and a stinging in her eyes as she drank in the stark beauty all around her.

Downslope, Hannah spotted an outcropping of rock large enough to cast a shadow even this close to noon. She angled the rover toward it and pulled up just short of the shade. She tied a bandanna around the lower half of her face, slung the peepers around her neck, settled the radio stud tightly in her ear, and climbed out into the dry heat.

It took half an hour of lugging, tinkering, and heavy-duty sweating to get things set up the way they had been at the release site the day before. As she hauled the dovecote into position, snapped together the water trough, and filled it from the tank in the back of the rover, she stopped thinking so much about the landscape, stopped hearing the occasional complaints of the *hrkleshira,* and spent the time brooding over how she would respond to her father's financial offer.

When all was ready, Hannah flopped down beside the dovecote in the shade of the boulder and radioed Miles$_{70}$. "I think I'm all set here," she said. "The birds are quiet, and we've got a straight line of sight to the prospector."

"It's about goddamn time," said Miles$_{70}$. "I've been ready here for a couple of hours. Shit, I must have sweated off five kilos in this heat."

"The only place you could afford to lose five kilos is your head. Miles. Now, how about Deacon and the Exclaimer?"

"Yeah, they could stand to be separated from their heads, too."

"You know what I meant."

"Oh, *that.* They're fine, they're ready." Because of the distances and terrain separating them all, Miles$_{70}$ was not only monitoring both halves of the test from his location but also manning the communications link. "And from what I can hear, they've been just chattin' up a storm all morning. Want me to patch the Jesus freak in?"

Hannah's stomach clenched. Was Deacon ignoring their agreement? "Wait. Chatting about what?"

"Jesus. *About* Jesus, I mean. What else does the Apostle Paul Bunyan ever discuss?"

Whew. "Okay, yeah, patch him in."

"Here we go," said $Miles_{70}$. "Okay, listeners, we have Hannah from Himmelburg, Netherheim, on the line with us. You had a question for our religious expert, Hannah?"

"Shut up, Miles. Deacon, what's the situation there?"

"All readies," came Deacon's gentle voice. She could hear the faint rumble of machinery in the background. "*Brthklashikort* wards the dovecote. I ward the prospector, outsight. Should the *hrkleshira* oncemore attack, I can prevent injury themward."

"That's a good idea," Hannah said, wishing she'd thought of it. "Miles, you're picking up all twenty-four birds on your channels?"

"Twelve of yours, a dozen of the other," said $Miles_{70}$. "Oh, but wait a second. I'm only seeing eleven of Deacon's."

Hannah caught her breath. *"What?"*

$Miles_{70}$ cackled. "Just kidding. I've got all twelve."

"Monsterling," Deacon muttered.

"One of these days I'm going to thrash you good, Miles," said Hannah.

"Is that a promise?"

"No." She pushed herself to her feet and withdrew a remote control from a pocket of her vest. The smell of hot dust was thick in her lungs. "So I guess there's no reason to keep waiting. Deacon, can the Exclaimer hear me?"

"No, but I handsign."

"Okay, then signal on my mark. Three . . . two . . . one . . . mark."

"Mark," Deacon repeated.

Hannah touched a pad on the remote, and the doors of her dovecote folded open.

Only half the pigeonholes were occupied. She and Deacon had decided to put only as many *hrkleshira* at risk as they had on the first trial, and that number had been split between the two of them. They had also selected only *hrkleshira* that had not been part of the original experiment.

Again the sauroids stretched their sinewy red necks, spread their wings, exposed their yellow breasts and bellies. Again they bounded into the air, by ones and by twos, their wings laboring to grasp the wind. Again they gathered in a loose torus, drifting this way and that as they rose further from the ground. Squeaks and rustles sounded in faint counterpoint to the soothing sough of the wind.

Hannah smiled at the glimpses of yellow that flashed like sun-fire from within the busy red formation. "The way they flock," she said, shaking her head in wonder. "It's remarkable. More like insects than like terrestrial birds. God."

"Yeah, very stirring," said Miles$_{70}$. "This week on *Wild Universe*, the dance of the yellow-breasted Luddites."

Unexpectedly, Deacon laughed. "Yellow-breasted Luddites. I like."

"Anything going on where you are?" Hannah asked.

"The *hrkleshira* flock, drift," said Deacon. "Wait . . ." His voice fell. "They arrow. Meward."

"Well, get ready to scoop them up." She watched her group float uncertainly through the air, maybe twenty meters away. "My guys aren't doing much, just sort of drifting back and forth, like they don't know where they want to go."

"So!" Deacon said. "Machinesounds indeed insanify."

The *hrkleshira* seemed to make up their minds as Hannah watched. They drifted back toward her, descending, then settled to the rim of the water trough. Three or four of them craned their necks down to taste the water, flapping their wings for balance. A few more hopped down to the ground to investigate the rocks and the dust.

"Well," said Hannah, "at the very least we can agree that it's probably not the size, color, or shape of the prospector that's setting them off."

"No, I think it's Deacon's personal hygiene," said Miles$_{70}$.

But Deacon wasn't responding. Hannah could hear him grunt and strain as the *hrkleshira* dove in toward the prospector and he tried to catch them in his sticky net.

She sat down again in the diminishing shade of the outcropping, content for the moment simply to watch her small flock and to soak up the sound of their contented chirping.

"What's the deal, guys?" she asked softly. "What are you crazy birds thinking?"

That evening, Hannah went to the infirmary to check on Ujamaa. She closed the door behind her. The zori deer, a delicate, tan-skinned quadruped about the size of a Great Dane, stumbled to her feet and bleated plaintively. "Shh, girl, shh," Hannah said. "Mommy's here."

The sharp scent of antiseptic filled the air. Ujamaa's cage sat on the floor at the back of the infirmary, beneath the incubator with five lavender skingko eggs inside. As Hannah undid the latch, the recuperating *hrkleshira* cooed and squeaked from their enclosure. Hannah knelt as Ujamaa limped forward to crane her head cautiously through the cage door.

"It's okay," said Hannah. "Come on, girl."

With shaky steps, the animal crossed the floor and licked Hannah's face with its snakelike tongue. Hannah wrapped her arms around Ujamaa's neck. "Good girl! Good Ujamaa! Mommy loves you, yes."

Ujamaa had appeared on their doorstep near death one day, out of the blue. Whoever had brought her there—most likely someone from NaRM—hadn't stuck around to answer questions. The deer had probably crossed paths with a large vehicle, maybe a prospector, but Jongnic had decided it was best not to probe too hard. Nanodocs had knitted Ujamaa's bones about as well as could be expected; it remained to be seen if she would ever walk well enough to return to the wild.

Hannah leaned back against the examining table, and the deer curled up with her head and forelegs in Hannah's lap, softly bleating. The cooing of the *hrkleshira* soothed Hannah's overstressed nerves, and a bittersweet smile touched her lips as she stroked the tufts on Ujamaa's head. It was so like a child's daydream that she half expected the skingkos to burst out of their eggs and break into song.

She laughed at the image, but then without warning tears were streaming down her face. Ujamaa bleated in confusion and licked Hannah's cheeks. Despite the deer's presence, she had never felt more lonely in her life.

She was still sitting there half an hour later when $Miles_{70}$ came looking for her. "Hannah?" he said, cautiously poking his oversized head around the corner of the table. "Hannah, hey, are you okay?"

Ujamaa had fallen asleep in Hannah's arms, but now she bleated in alarm and tried to struggle to her feet. "Shh, it's okay," said Hannah, stroking the deer's head as she hastily tried to wipe her tacky face. "Yeah, yeah, Miles, I'm fine, I was just . . . you know."

"Right, okay." $Miles_{70}$ nodded his head solicitously. "I just stopped by to let you know you got another ansiblegram."

"Oh, you're kidding. Not my father again?"

"No, it's from that, um—boyfriend of yours. Fatima."

Elation and alarm warred inside her. "Fatima?"

"I didn't stutter, did I?" He turned to leave. "So anyway, it's waiting for you whenever you're ready."

"Hang on there," Hannah called.

Miles$_{70}$'s head reappeared around the corner of the table.

"Come around here, Miles," she said. "I want to talk to you a minute."

Reluctantly, Miles$_{70}$ waddled around in front of her, her eyes not quite at his level, his eyes not quite meeting hers.

"Why did you come all the way down here?" she asked. "Why didn't you just signal me?"

"I wanted to see all the nice animals." Miles$_{70}$ reached a hand out toward Ujamaa, who drew her head back warily against Hannah's chest.

"I didn't think you even liked animals," said Hannah.

Miles$_{70}$ tucked his hands into the pockets of his child-sized jumpsuit. "Hey," he said brightly, "I'll bet you didn't know something else about me. My namesake, Miles Covio, was one of the guys who originated the theories that led to the development of the ansible."

"You're right," said Hannah, "I didn't know that. And I didn't care."

"Yeah, well, the whole Miles series is based partially on his DNA, so you *should* care. And did you know that the term 'ansible' itself actually originated on Earth, in the twentieth century, in the writings of—"

"Miles, I don't think I've ever mentioned Fatima to you by name."

"Well, you know us bigbrains," he said, shifting on his feet, "the way we pick things up, piece things together . . ."

Hannah shook her head. "You were listening in yesterday while I talked to Deacon."

Miles$_{70}$ gaped in mock umbrage. "Hey, can I help it if the walls are thin?"

"No, but you can help it if the walls are *bugged*." Hannah ran a hand through her hair, which she was wearing only a couple of centimeters long. "Jesus, Miles, how long has this been going on? Ever since I've been here?"

He was silent.

"God, is this just for your own amusement, or are you working for someone? Miles?"

He looked her in the eyes, more soberly and directly than he ever had. "Don't make me answer that, Hannah," he said. "You suspect enough about me already."

Hannah's mouth opened slowly. "Oh, jack me. You broke into that conversation yesterday when you did because it was right when I was telling Deacon . . . shit. You don't think he's . . ."

"No, not really. I just don't like him. And I only distrust him as a matter of habit, not because he's a threat."

Hannah looked down in thought, stroking Ujamaa's head. "And what about me?"

Miles$_{70}$ feigned great interest in the *hrkleshira*. He studied them closely, hands clasped behind his back. "Let's just say that it hasn't hurt your career any to have a friend filing positive reports on you. Positive and *accurate* reports, by the way."

"Miles, I . . ." Hannah took a deep breath, feeling disconnected from reality. "Whoever you work for, that's your business. I can just compartmentalize you as our technical liaison and not worry about who or what you're actually liaising *with*. But Miles—who do *I* work for?"

He didn't look at her. "Rescue Star, of course. A volunteer organization allied closely with the human World Union. *Closely*, Hannah. And that's all I have to say."

Hannah nodded dumbly, and Miles$_{70}$ slipped out of the room. He closed the door carefully behind himself.

She was returning Ujamaa to her cage, still assimilating the conversation, when the door opened again. She turned. The Exclaimer, *Brthklashikort*, stood just inside the entrance, head and shoulders hunched below the ceiling, hands dangling far below its knees.

"Yes?" said Hannah neutrally.

"*Can you accompany me out back, please?*" it asked. "*Deacon Greenleaf has made an observation of some concern.*"

Ujamaa cowered at the far end of her cage, bleating in terror at the sound of the Exclaimer's voice.

Hannah latched the cage. "I'll be right there," she said. "Can you just *please* try to keep it down?"

The Exclaimer nodded once, silently.

"They undrink," said Deacon, pointing to the mesh cages.

Hannah squatted on her heels, peering at the *hrkleshira*. "Do you mean they're *not* drinking, or that they're drinking and then vomiting it back up?"

The Exclaimer folded itself to the ground beside her. "*It means they're drinking almost nothing.*"

The sun was setting over the mountains in the east; shadows lengthened, and a cooling creosote scent blew in on the evening breezes. Nearby, the urks stamped, lowed, and snorted in their pen.

Hannah opened the nearest cage and picked up a *hrkleshira*. Heavy and dry, like a bag of sand in her hands, it did not try to get away, but only watched her from one eye with a lethargic distrust. "How long have they been like this?" she asked.

"They downsettled afternoonlong, singlewise," said Deacon. "Leastwise, solong as I observed postreturn. But I unperceived the problem until shortago."

"Damn." Hannah stroked the supple skin of the little creature's throat. "Have you tried changing their water? Maybe there's something bad in it."

"Tried, yes. They roused briefwise, sniffed the new water, then resullened." He shuffled in place. "I fear, themward."

"Yeah, me too," Hannah said. She set down the *hrkleshira* and turned to the Exclaimer. "How long can they survive like this, without drinking?"

"Without water they'll eventually slip into a hibernative state. Or perhaps 'comatose' is the more apt term." The alien regarded her levelly from its globular eyes. The dying sun reflected from them like a bloody portent. *"It can be very difficult to successfully rouse them again once that happens. Eventually they die."*

"So how long until they're . . . hibernating?"

The Exclaimer tapped its spindly fingers rapidly up and down its lower legs. *"Two days. Perhaps three, but I would not count on that."*

Hannah latched the cage, though there wasn't much danger of any *hrkleshira* escaping. "So what do we do? Is there any way to make them drink?"

"Likely."

"But you're not going to tell us, right?"

The Exclaimer only stared at her. The light of the setting sun vanished from its eyes, and cold shadows engulfed them all.

Hannah jerked herself to her feet. "Can you at least tell us this much? Does what they're doing now have anything to do with the way they reacted to the prospector?"

"Likely," said the Exclaimer.

"Likely. Christ." Hannah flung a hand out toward the cages. "Only three dozen birds have been out to that site, but nearly twelve dozen are here dehydrating. What the hell's the link?"

"Gentlewise, Hannah," said Deacon, touching her arm. "I rehearsed this himward already."

Hannah shrugged his hand away, but regretted it as soon as she saw the hurt look in his eyes. "Shit," she muttered. "Okay, gang, let's have a powwow in fifteen minutes. Central Command. I want ideas from *everyone* on what to try next. You too, Frogman."

She stamped off through the shadows like she meant to rip open the twilight itself.

.   .   .

In her quarters, Hannah brought up Fatima's ansiblegram:

> Yr pop tres charming. Insisted on pay 4 this. We want U back soon!
> Pls say Y to him. Only way we can afford bond./Miss U so^3 much!
> I take E=mc^2 cruz ASA I know yr ETA. Cant live w/o U./L^∞, F

She wiped her eyes. Fatima and Derek were teaming up to get her back to Netherheim, but despite the fact that their manipulations were so transparent, she was tempted, oh so tempted, to just give in. How could two people nearly forty trillion kilometers away—just specks in an unimaginably huge and empty vastness—exert such an influence on her?

Hannah knew how much Fatima must be hurting. What Fatima was offering would mean the end of her law-enforcement career in Himmelburg. To go for a relativistic cruise—the best way to kill time next to coldsleep, which was dangerous to repeat more than once a decade—would mean taking another long sabbatical, and Fatima didn't yet have the seniority. But if Hannah left Sutter's Mill without completing her pledge, her job prospects would hardly be brighter.

Not to mention how badly she would miss Ujamaa and all the other animals, *hrkleshira* included . . .

"Why did you have to bring this up *now*?" she asked the silent snapshow on her footlocker. "I've got work to do."

She blew her nose, straightened her clothing, and returned to Central Command.

Deacon shook Hannah gently by the shoulder. "All readies," he said. "Coffee included."

Hannah sat up abruptly, breathing the thick scent of coffee and blinking in slow motion. Deacon set a cup down on the console beside her. She had fallen asleep. "What time is it?"

"Ninth hour," said Deacon. "The audio processing completes, and Miles zombies. Testing time readies."

"Great, great. Give me a minute or two." Hannah tasted the inside of her mouth and winced. She blew on the coffee and tried a sip. "Not bad. Hey."

Deacon smiled. "I gratify."

The previous night, the three humans had tried everything they could think of to get the *hrkleshira* to drink and to solve the mystery of the prospector, while the Exclaimer offered the occasional elliptical comment. They had separated the *hrkleshira* into smaller cages, exposed them to various machines both inside and outside the base, added what *Brthklashikort* assured them were flavorful nutritional supplements to the water in different combinations in different cages, and more, but they were no closer to a solution by the wee morning hours than when they started.

Hannah's final idea had been to record the typical sounds the prospector made during operation, separate the various waveforms into their component elements, and expose the *hrkleshira* to each in turn to see if they could link any individual sound to the violent reactions. Deacon volunteered to drive out and make the recording, after which Miles$_{70}$ had worked through the rest of the night on the signal processing. Hannah tried to pass the time by studying the scant literature on Cretacea. She read and reread the source materials until she thought her eyes would bleed, but shale, shale, and more shale was all she could recall upon waking.

Haggard and red-eyed, Miles$_{70}$ wandered in from the forward passageway. "Morning, Sleeping Beauty," he said in a slurred voice. He scratched his armpit. "I managed to separate twenty-two different channels out of that recording for you. I got schematics from NaRM—that wasn't easy, you owe me big—and I managed to match most of the sounds to actual physical systems inside the prospector. You got your power cells, your servomechanisms, your scoopers, your sifters, your hydraulics, your cooling system, your

heating system, your sonar system, your bloody fucking basic
solar system worth of shit crammed in there, so have fun with
your little mix tape, babe. I've got a wet dream with my name on it
waiting for me. Good *night.*"

"Thanks, Miles," Hannah said as he shuffled off. "You're a
star."

"Yeah, a red dwarf."

After Hannah finished her coffee, she and Deacon wheeled a
rack of audio components out back to the cages. The Exclaimer was
there already, sitting on the ground like a strange origami construct. If it had suffered any ill effects from its long sleepless night,
she couldn't tell.

The Exclaimer moved aside, and a picholein which had been
sitting beside it scampered away. *"So the next experiment is ready
to begin,"* the alien said.

"Just about." Hannah peered into the cages as Deacon affixed a
trio of flatplate speakers to the side of the dome. The *hrkleshira*
seemed even more lethargic than before—and was it her imagination, or were they losing color? "So tell me, now that we've spent
so long preparing. Is this even worth trying?"

*"I believe there may be something to be learned from the
attempt, yes."*

Hannah rolled her eyes. "Fantastic. And what we'll probably
learn is that we've wasted an entire night, right? Okay, Deacon,
let's get started."

They cycled through each of Miles$_{70}$'s twenty-two audio channels, holding for a full minute on each. Hisses and splutters,
revving and grinding, humming and thrumming all played in
turn, but the *hrkleshira* did no more than stir. At the end of the
run, Deacon began trying the sounds in pairs, holding for only fifteen seconds on each.

Before the end of an hour, Hannah was ready to quit. It would
take far more time, by many orders of magnitude, than they could

afford to cycle through every possible combination of channels. The Exclaimer had already made itself scarce, probably to escape the crushing boredom.

Hannah wanted to rage at the *hrkleshira*, pick them up and shake them and beat some sense into their tiny heads. It's only water, for God's sake! All you have to do is drink it! If you don't, you're going to die! But there was no point in getting angry with them. It wasn't their fault they were dying—it was hers for not being a proper steward, for not having done everything in her power to help them.

But she was finally ready to take that next step.

"I give up," she said to Deacon. "It's time to try it your way. I'll go talk to the Exclaimer."

Deacon's very bones seemed to sag with relief. "Godthanks," he said, closing his eyes and nodding.

Hannah took a deep breath, straightened her safari vest, and knocked at the door to *Brthklashikort*'s quarters. "*Come in,*" it said from within, with perfect audibility.

Hannah opened the door. The Exclaimer rose from a flat mat at the far end of the room, removing a pair of opaque goggles from its face. This room was the closest to Central Command; its high ceilings permitted the Exclaimer to stand erect. "*Hello, Hannah,*" it said. "*I've been hoping you would seek an opportunity to speak to me one-on-one, though I didn't wish to push.*"

The alien's elaborate courtesy set Hannah's teeth on edge. "I didn't want to push either," she said. "But I don't have a choice at this point."

"*I wish I could offer you a chair, but I'm far more comfortable sitting on the floor, so I don't have any handy. Please accept my apologies.*"

"Don't sweat it," said Hannah. "There's plenty of floor." And not much else, she noted. Except for the mat and a couple of hexagonal crates, the Exclaimer's quarters were as barren of decoration as a monk's cell.

The alien folded itself down again, setting aside the goggles. It wore what she guessed were input gloves on its hands, though they were less substantial than the sort she was used to. "*I was just reviewing what material I have on the* hrkleshira *and their habits and environment,*" it said.

"Probably enough to fill a small library," said Hannah, sitting down with her back against one of the crates. "I don't suppose I could take a peek?"

"*Oh, you're welcome to, but you wouldn't understand any of it, and the presentation would probably induce illness.*"

"Maybe you can just digest it for me."

The Exclaimer drummed its fingers up and down its legs. "*Hannah, I will give you all the assistance that is within my compass,*" it said, "*but I think you have intuited the limit to which that extends.*"

Stomach clenching, Hannah shook her head. "We need more than that," she said. "I'll freely admit that I don't grasp the politics that have created the situation here. All I know is, there's a bunch of animals out there, completely apolitical, that are going to die unless we get more help from you than we've been getting."

"*Let me assure you, first,*" said the Exclaimer, "*that I have no wish to see the* hrkleshira *come to any harm. I'm rather more . . . shall we say, 'progressive' in this respect than are many of my fellows.*"

"Then *help* us," Hannah said.

The Exclaimer raised a hand. "*Please. I have no wish to see harm done, but I also have a High Commission to which I must answer, and no chance of concealing my actions from it even were I to overstep the bounds to which I have sworn myself. It is a precarious line I must walk, between the health of innocent creatures and the requirements of the government to which I owe fealty.*"

"Life is more important than any government."

"What life? The lives of a few animals, or the lives of my entire race? Or of yours?" The Exclaimer spread its arms in a surprisingly human gesture. "I have observed your game of chess. I know that your government understands the concept of sacrificial pawns as well as mine."

Hannah clenched her eyes. "Screw your government and mine both."

The alien stilled its hands. "Do you not see that government—mine, yours, any race's—is a phenomenon as natural as speciation? Is it less deserving of life than are the hrkleshira?"

"I don't see how the two can even be compared," she said, confused.

"If you cannot, and if you are a representative member of your race, then I don't see how humanity will survive much more expansion. Any race which lacks such self-awareness is certain to generate friction with those which do not."

Hannah's simmering anger began to boil. "How can you accuse us of a lack of self-awareness? How much do you even know about us? You've only been here a few days."

"I've been among humans since the beginning of my voyage here," said the alien, "and all the observations I have made only bear me out. Take your own group here. Miles, the small human with the large head, thinks to make up for his physical shortcomings by projecting a facade of cynicism and bravado, but doesn't perceive that he only puts up a wall between himself his fellows by doing so—and that's not even taking his obvious sexual attraction for you into account. Deacon Greenleaf sublimates his fear of openness and change and learning and growth into single-minded devotion to a god whose greatest accomplishment was getting himself gruesomely killed, and therefore denies himself any chance of achieving the apotheosis he seeks.

"And you, Hannah—you act as incomprehensibly as either of them, always finding the most difficult and laborious angle from *which to attack any problem. You do it so effectively, I can only imagine the behavior is deliberate."*

The Exclaimer stopped talking long enough to slip the goggles back over its eyes. *"In that respect, I find it impossible to understand why, yet at the same time perfectly comprehensible that you have not yet penetrated the mystery of the behavior of the hrkleshira. For they are, in that very peculiar, self-defeating way, your soulmates."*

Hannah was on her feet, nails pressed into the palms of her fists. "Where the hell do you get the nerve? You can sit there and make your pithy pronouncements all you like, but at the end of the day you're as lost and ineffectual as the rest of us! Look at you, stuck on Sutter's Mill with a bunch of humans you find beneath your contempt. If you're so much better than we are, then why aren't you somewhere more responsible in this vaunted government of yours? What does that say about you?"

The alien made curious gestures in the air with its gloved fingers, staring into an artificial realm Hannah could not begin to imagine. *"I hold neither you nor your colleagues in contempt. As I said, I differ from most of my race in that I am capable of mustering an unusual level of sympathy for members of other species. That is why I'm here."*

It turned its head to stare directly at Hannah; finding herself at the blind focus of those opaque goggles made her skin crawl. *"You really can have no concept of contempt until you've witnessed the reactions of many of my peers to your human talk of 'endangered species.' As some of your fellows so interestingly phrase it, this to us is a clear case of the pot calling the kettle black."*

"So that's it, huh?" said Hannah, planting her fists on her hips. Her pulse pounded behind her eyes. "That's all the help I'm going to get?"

"Hannah, my sympathy is not infinite, and your repetitiveness grows tiresome. You know everything you need to know, and

what you may not know, you have access to in the materials sup-
plied to you by your superiors. Now please, don't force me to
become as tiresome as you. Leave me to my studies."

She opened her mouth to fire one parting shot, but the alien
had already stopped paying her any attention.

Still, she made a firm point of slamming the door behind her
when she left.

Hannah lay tossing on her bed for an hour before her anger
began to ebb. She finally began to realize that despite its insults
the alien might really having been trying to tell her something
useful.

"Okay," she said to herself, swinging her legs off the bed,
"everything I need to know is in the stuff I've already read. And
the stupid birds do everything the hard way."

But what did that mean, that the *hrkleshira* did things the hard
way? Dying of thirst when there was water right in front of them
wasn't just doing things the hard way—it was suicide.

The hard way, the hard way. Just like her . . .

Nuts. That's what she was for paying any attention to the goddamn alien. Totally nuts. Grasping at straws.

Just like her.

The hard way.

"Shit," she said. Rubbing her eyes, she padded over to her
console and woke up the desktop. She sat down, hung her head. As
she idly rubbed the back of her neck, she tried to marshal her
thoughts.

Fact one: the *hrkleshira* went crazy around ore prospectors and
beat themselves bloody against them.

Fact two: the *hrkleshira* wouldn't drink water when it was
placed right in front of them.

Fact three: the *hrkleshira* did things the hard way.

Wait, she was confusing facts with opinions now. She sighed and rubbed her head vigorously with both hands. The hard way. She was digging for answers the hard way . . .

Hannah suddenly raised her head. "Jack me black and blue," she said, eyes wide.

She brought up the geological survey of Cretacea and paged through it rapidly. When she found the information she was looking for, she sat back in her chair, a smile playing at the corner of her mouth. A solution seemed within reach, but if she were wrong she might spend several hours testing an invalid theory—hours the *hrkleshira* didn't have . . .

Moments later she had several different translations of the Bible open on her desktop, including the King James 1611, the Douay-Rheims, the New English, the Mons Olympus, the New Alpha Centauri Prime, the Joseph Smith, and the weirdly poetic Friarhesse Low Synod version used by the Stewardship. The exact phrase she recalled from her childhood occurred in every version but the Alpha Centauri and the Friarhesse, and even in those it was strikingly similar.

Hannah bookmarked the passages and sent her desktop back to sleep.

She found Deacon out back near the cages. He was sitting in the Exclaimer's favorite position, arms wrapped around his knees, staring at the listless *hrkleshira*. "Ah, Hannah," he said, greeting her dully. The sun stood almost directly overhead. Sweat matted his hair and beard, and he looked pale and drawn. "Why sits *Brthklashikort* here soöft, suppose you?" He shook his head. "I unimagine."

"I don't know either," said Hannah, though she finally had a suspicion. "Listen, can I ask you something?"

Deacon shrugged, mirroring the lethargy of the *hrkleshira*. "Surewise."

Hannah sat down near him in the dust. "Remember you were telling me about something cryptic the Exclaimer said to you on the ship?"

It took Deacon a moment to focus, but then he nodded his head. "I recall."

"I think you told me it compared the *hrkleshira* to Christians. Is that right?"

"It corrects. Coursewise, I uncomprehend the why."

"That's okay, Deacon." She leaned forward. "Did it say anything else? Or do you remember what you were saying that prompted its comment?"

Deacon squinted, thinking, then shook his head. "No, I regret. I unrecall the antecedents."

Hannah licked her lower lip. "Deacon—had you perhaps said something about Jesus being the source of living water? Or 'quickwater,' maybe?"

For a long moment, Deacon said nothing, his eyes focused inwardly. "Mayhap," he said at last. His voice grew stronger, and he nodded, wonder dawning in his eyes. "Factwise, that corrects. I preached him Christ as quickwater's source, as lifesource eternal. How guessed you?"

Hannah shrugged. "Something that, uh, the Exclaimer said to me gave me the idea, that's all. I was just curious." She feigned a look of concern, but as she spoke she was surprised to realize that her concern was genuine. "You don't look well, Deacon, and you're not even wearing a hat to keep the sun off. Go inside. I'll watch the birds."

"But . . . I . . ."

"You've been awake I don't know how long now, and we need you sharp. Get some sleep. That's an order."

Deacon nodded, then slowly got to his feet. "Comprehend we must," he said. "Soon. Or the *hrkleshira* forever sleep."

"We'll figure it out, don't worry."

Hannah stood as he shuffled past. As soon as he was out of sight, she wiped a rivulet of sweat from her temple, opened the topmost cage, and reached inside.

Time to put her theory to the test.

The sun hung a hand's breadth above the eastern horizon as Hannah made the last adjustment to the recycler. "How does that look?" she radioed.

"It looks like a bunch of yellow dust and some rocks," came $Miles_{70}$'s exasperated voice. "You knocked the damn peepers over again, Hannah. I can't see shit."

"Oh, sorry." She scooted out from beneath the elevated water trough, setting aside the wrench in her hand, and righted the peepers. She propped a rock beneath the forward sights so $Miles_{70}$ would be able to see up to the crude apparatus she had attached to the bottom of the trough. "How's that?"

"Can you give me a little more elevation? Okay, now a couple of degrees to the right . . . there!"

Hannah stretched her arms. She was covered in dust and sweat and engine oil, and her back ached, but she felt good. "Well?"

"Looks good, as far as I can tell. Only thing to do is give it a try."

Hannah stood up. "Well, all right. Here goes."

She had propped up one end of the trough so it sat at a slight angle to the ground. She wrestled the water tank from the back of the rover and filled the trough halfway, keeping an eye on the prospector that rumbled slowly through the underbrush two hundred meters away. She was about four kilometers north of the original release site, which was how far the prospector had ranged in the time since.

"Well, no leaks," said Hannah. "That's a good sign." She flipped the switch on the recycler that $Miles_{70}$ had helped her scrounge together from odds and ends. There were coughing and gurgling sounds, and the water began to churn at the upper end of the trough. In a few moments there was a nice little flow running from the top end to the trough to the bottom.

"Well?" said Miles$_{70}$. "I can't see jack from ground level."

Hannah picked up the peepers and pointed them down into the trough. "How's that?"

"Excellent, Hannah! Looks perfect. Better get the rest set up now, because you've got visitors coming in about fifteen minutes."

"Roger," she said. "I couldn't have done this without you, you know. I already owe you two or three, but if this works I'm going to owe you . . . hell, a *lot*."

"If this works, you'll make senior field operative for sure, and then you can really start paying me back."

Hannah grinned. "Gladly, my friend. Gladly."

She went back to the rover and retrieved the solar collector that would keep the recycler running indefinitely. When that was deployed, she began gathering rocks, which she placed carefully in the bottom of the trough. She kept adding rocks until the water threatened to overflow the bottom end of the trough. The water turned cloudy and brown with dust, but after a few minutes the filters had rendered it clear again. She had created an artificial streambed two meters long, with clean water babbling cheerily over ore-veined rocks.

As Hannah stood back to admire her work, a rover appeared in the distance, trailing a clouds of dust like a bridal train. She went back to work.

She was just wrestling the dovecote into position when the rover drew near and stopped. Deacon and the Exclaimer emerged. The alien, with its long, loping stride, reached her first.

"*Interesting apparatus, Hannah,*" it said, bending over the trough with its hands propped on its bony knees. "*You've been hard at work.*"

Deacon caught up a few moments later. His hair stuck out every which way, but at least he seemed to have gotten some rest. "Miles said you experiment freshwise. He bade us come." He caught sight of the splashing water in the trough. "Hello. What evidences?"

Hannah smiled. "You're just in time to find out."

She raised her remote control and clicked. The doors of the dovecote folded open.

For thirty seconds, nothing happened. Hannah could see the listless *hrkleshira* mounded in their pigeonholes like lumps of dead clay. But then something seemed to penetrate their fog. First one, then another and another, began to stir. Quizzical squeaks and chatters emerged from the dovecote, and two *hrkleshira* poked their heads out into the twilight.

Hannah realized she was holding her breath, and she forced herself to exhale.

In another few moments, fully half the *hrkleshira* were alert and bobbing their heads at the ends of outstretched necks. Their yellow breasts caught the last fires of the dying sun. Then the chattering squeaks crescendoed, and the *hrkleshira* took to the air.

Hannah's breath hitched. The cloud of red-and-yellow bodies coalesced briefly into its familiar shape, drifting and spinning like an exotic flower unfolding in an airborne whirlpool—and then, one by one, the *hrkleshira* swooped down and away, out of formation.

They alighted in the trough's rushing streambed.

The first ones to land began vigorously scratching at the rocks with their clawed feet. As more and more *hrkleshira* joined them, they dipped their supple necks to the water and drank. In moments, the entire flock was splashing around in the trough, pawing the rocks, drinking, and squeaking loudly enough to drown out the sound of the recycler. They paid the distant prospector no attention whatsoever.

Hannah found herself swept into a broad hug by Deacon, who planted a bristly kiss on her cheek. "Quickwater!" he said, grinning broadly. "How the *hrkleshira* similars the Christian! You *genius*, Hannah!"

"*Insightfully done, indeed,*" said the Exclaimer, who stood a few meters away, bobbing slightly as he watched the *hrkleshira* cavort in the water.

"Yes," said Miles$_{70}$, for her benefit alone. "You done good, kiddo."

Surprised, she felt herself blush.

"How figured?" Deacon asked, holding her at arm's length and studying her with a rapt expression. With his crazy red hair, he resembled some ecstatic Biblical prophet rejoicing in the sunset.

"Well," she said with a glance at the Exclaimer, "I just started wondering if there was some kind of evolutionary reason why the *hrkleshira* should start refusing water, if it might be a survival trait in some way. I took another look at the geological surveys from Cretacea, and it turns out they come from a region of the planet where it's hilly and there's lots of groundwater. Hilly and *shaly*, I might add. Lots of flat loose rock everywhere."

Deacon cocked his head to one side. "They solewise take their water 'on the rocks'?"

"Deacon, was that an actual *joke*?" She smiled at the sight of his reddening face. "Not exactly, I don't think, and, uh, *Berth*-what's-your-name, you can correct me if I get the details wrong. It's standing water that turns them off, probably because it's more likely to get brackish and polluted. When I stirred up the water in their cages, that actually made some of them start drinking."

"Clever," said Deacon.

"But frequently on Cretacea, actual moving water, *living* water, is flowing just *under* the surface of all that loose shale. I think the *hrkleshira* use some kind of sonar—since they only hear well in their own vocal range—to locate trickles of living water below the surface of the rock. When they find it, they dig for it."

Deacon was nodding now. "Seen, seen. And prospectorward, what we mislabeled insanity was truewise . . ."

"It was really just them trying to dig through the skin of the dome. What they detected was the sound of coolant circulating beneath the surface. That's why they bypassed the standing water in the trough. They wouldn't let themselves drink it when living water seemed to be so close at hand."

The Exclaimer folded itself to the ground. *"Excellently reasoned, Hannah,"* it said, *"and all very correct. You've done well."*

Hannah turned again to watch the *hrkleshira* cavorting in the trough, yellow breasts bright in the last light of day, and she permitted herself to feel a moment of joy.

Hannah snapped on the headlights as the rover jounced across the twilit landscape. She flexed her throat mike, severing the radio link with Miles$_{70}$. "There's still one thing I'd like to know," she said.

After gathering the *hrkleshira*, she had sent Deacon back to the base alone in his rover. The Exclaimer *Brthklashikort* sat folded into the passenger seat beside her. *"Yes?"*

"Well, two things, really. First, how *all* the *hrkleshira* became affected when only a few of them were exposed to the prospector—and next, what you were doing out there with them so often."

"Watching, monitoring, no more," said the Exclaimer, turning its blank globular gaze on her.

Hannah nodded dubiously. "Overtly maybe," she said. "But are you sure there wasn't more to it than that?"

The Exclaimer straightened in its seat as much as it could. *"I'm intrigued. For instance?"*

"For instance, oh . . . communication of some sort? Something very subtle. Maybe even telepathy."

"Telepathy?" The Exclaimer drummed its long fingers on its legs. *"You're joking, surely."*

Hannah shrugged. "Some of the reports I saw, even some made by Deacon himself, noted how preternaturally coordinated some of the *hrkleshira*'s actions seemed to be. I've observed it myself. Maybe they actually do have some kind of crude group telepathy at work, sharing survival information, or maybe it's simple instinct that lets them pick up on behavioral cues from the rest of the group. But whatever it is, you must know a lot more about it than any of us do, and you may even know how to strengthen or weaken those signals." She paused to steer them around a large boulder. "Maybe even to the point where you could keep them out of hibernation for longer than they ordinarily would have stayed without water."

"*Or perhaps I might have been driving them to it prematurely.*"

"Perhaps," said Hannah. "But at this point I would tend to doubt it."

The Exclaimer stared straight ahead out the windshield. "*Not all your people would.*"

"But *telepathy*, man!" Hannah pounded the steering column in her excitement. "If it exists, do you realize what an amazing *miracle* that is? Come on, please, you have to tell me if I'm right."

For several moments, the alien sat in silence. "*Hannah,*" it said at last, "*you're rushing to conclusions again, as you so often tend to do. The true miracle lies not in telepathy or any other fanciful process, but in the mere fact that widely disparate species can communicate with one another at all, whatever the mechanism.*"

It turned its huge eyes toward her. "*Humans are easily startled creatures, as are my people. We wouldn't want to upset the balance of that delicate, fragile,* vital *mechanism with wild speculation in paranoid ears. Correct?*"

Chastened, Hannah watched the dusty ground churn through the cones of her headlights for nearly half a kilometer. Finally she said, "In that case, I'll just say thank you. Thank you for all the help you've given us. *All* of it."

"*You're very welcome,*" said the Exclaimer. "*And thank you. Thank you for listening beyond what was said. It was a braver act than I hope you will ever have cause to realize.*"

Hannah nodded without understanding, wanting to ask for

clarification but somehow afraid that to do so would be to betray some fundamental and tragic racial flaw that only an Exclaimer could see.

They finished the rest of the drive in silence.

In her quarters, Hannah extended her hair to its greatest length and lay on her bed with it pillowed around her head in a comforting nimbus. She stared at the dim ceiling, feeling pleased and proud and strong, but for some reason completely unable to sleep.

After a while, she realized what she needed to do. She rose, crossed the room, and woke up her desktop. She fussed over the wording of her two ansiblegrams for a very long time, though in the end she said much the same thing in each. Her message to Fatima, however, contained an extra invitation that Derek's didn't:

> Nixed da's offer. Hard way 2 go, but debts R mine alone, catharsis
> mine. No I can proxy./Bsides, love work & animals here 2 much.
> MayB promotion, more $, but still @ least 2 yrs pledge. Cant predict
> return date yet./MayB we find way U join me?/L^∞, H

With the messages queued for transmission, Hannah put her worries about the future aside and slept peacefully, at least for that one night.

David J. Schow is the author of two novels, *The Kill Rift* and *The Shaft*, as well as several collections of short stories, including *Seeing Red* and *Lost Angels* (both recently reprinted by Alexander Publishing), *Black Leather Required*, and, most recently, *Crypt Orchids*. He edited the landmark anthology of cinema horror, *Silver Scream*, and he's currently editing the second of two volumes of Robert Bloch's stories and *Hell on Earth, Volume 2*. The first volume, *The Lost Bloch, Volume 1: The Devil with You* was published in 1999. He's also at work on a collection of his columns from *Fangoria* and other sources, tentatively titled *Wild Hairs*.

Schow has written widely for television and film, scripting, as he puts it, "the unsavory activities of such social lions as Leatherface and Freddy Krueger," as well as *The Crow*. Most recently he's written for Showtime's *The Hunger* and completed a script for James Cameron's production company. Schow's original on-line fiction can be found at http://www.gothic.net. He lives in the Hollywood Hills with Christa Faust.

BLESSED EVENT

David J. Schow

It wasn't exactly an argument that drove Detective Lieutenant Dion Curson out of his house at one in the morning; it was more like a recurrent migraine no one had warned him about when he first said "I do" to his bride, Sondra, whom he loved without reserve.

Sometimes, *almost* without reserve. Like tonight.

They had flown through the discussion about having kids . . .
again. It struck like a sinus blockage about once very week to ten
days, that little talk. Both of them had said their lines so often they
sounded the way earnest high school drama students do when
required to mouth lengthy, knotted ropes of cliché.

She would ask, faking innocence, if he had thought any more
about it. He would say no he had not, and lie about being too busy
with work and stress and business and living.

She would remind him she was over thirty, that her "clock"
was ticking down faster and faster—

*And just where in hell had women gotten that idiotic expres-
sion about their biological countdown? Jesus! This was the point
where the caveman who lived in the darkness of Curson's occipital
began sharpening his adz.*

—and he would shoot himself in the foot by conceding the
future possibility of fatherhood (way *distant* future, to be sure),
which was always the beginning of his downfall, because . . .

She would exploit that foothold—foothole?—and strive to
steer him toward the admission that he had actually, realistically,
honestly, just once, maybe for an instant, considered spending the
remainder of what he called his "non-senile adult life" as a daddy.
To this attack he would harshly counter that they might as well
shove their life's savings onto one spin of a roulette wheel and win
a bundle of joy whose odds of curing AIDS or becoming a serial
murderer were equal in the cosmic scheme of things.

Sondra would play the emotion card, her eyes going wet and
leaky. Curson's jaw would lock and he would begin to use his
answers to hurt her. He did not wish to hurt his wife; he was
merely trying to drive her away from the "discussion" that unerr-
ingly hurt them both, left them weak and defensive, and eroded
every good thing about a marriage which was otherwise brimming
over with good things.

His beeper had gone off at 12:45. It was Janeway, his partner,
who frequently rang a chime late at night because he no longer

had Curson's kind of wife-strife. This page was from Division, which meant crime was afoot, and whether it was an excuse or not, Curson deployed it toward Sondra in order to slingshot his ass out the door by 12:50. Saved by the razzing radio surrogate bell.

Like a leaky pipe, badly puttied, the "discussion" was neutralized for one more day. Curson felt supremely guilty about the sense of relief he experienced as he jammed his car out of the drive. Sondra had not moved to the window to forlornly witness his departure. That was a good sign.

He loved Sondra more than anything.

But he felt better fleeing, and he wanted to do something good to repay Janeway's rescue extraction. His partner needed him, so he went.

"Bad one." That was Janeway's answer to Curson's "What've we got?" on the cellular phone as Curson sped toward Division.

"Define bad."

"Guy mutilated his girlfriend with one of those knives that never needs sharpening. Biggest one in the set."

"And?"

"Guy says she was pregnant and he tried to cut the baby out of her."

"She dead, the girlfriend?"

Janeway almost chuckled. "What do *you* think?"

"I think you haven't defined *bad* yet; what are you leaving out?"

"Guy broke out of prison to do it, didn't fight back when he was caught, and doesn't want a lawyer."

"I'd call the last two things good, for us." Curson's phone frazzed out briefly. He took his other hand off the wheel for a second to rub his face, though he wasn't tired.

"You still there?"

"I'm five minutes away. Guy have a name?"

"Victor Quintelle Solos, twenty-five-year-old white male."

"Sounds like a serial killer name you hear on Court TV."

"His gig was fifteen years at Fordmill Pen."

"What, a dime and a half for butchering people?"

"No. Accessory to an armored car robbery in nineteen ninety-two."

Curson's face pinched. "Doesn't sound kosher, does it?" He tried to figure out the anomaly. "What'd his girl do wrong?"

"Zero. They were gonna get married. She had conjugals. No fights to speak of; no drug use."

"So . . . he killed her because she was pregnant."

"Yes and no." Janeway paused before continuing. Janeway only drew a dramatic breath when evidence didn't track, or thought he was confusing his partner. He spaced out the words carefully. "He claims she was not pregnant with, uh, a human being."

"Ah, *that's* the bad part." Curson felt a vast weight settle onto his shoulders.

"Just get here."

Curson thought of calling Sondra, to tell her he was in for an all-nighter, but hesitated. He wanted to see more before he actually had to confront her voice on the phone.

Victor Quintelle Solos looked like an out-of-work comedian— soft, round, blunt, slightly bug-eyed, and not at all the reptilian predator for which Curson had girded himself. It would have been an easier ride if Solos had come with satanic jailhouse tattoos and the usual hot-seat tough talk. His eyes did not shut out Janeway or Curson, but invited them in. He sought their approbation the way a child seeks to apologize to an adult. He smiled too much; not the smug leer of a guy who could take a beating (if that's what his captors and inquisitors had to offer), but a smile of hope that these cops might comprehend his essential innocence in tonight's drama.

He looked, Curson thought, like a fellow in one of those vampire movies who has staked his best friend in front of witnesses and trusts the authorities to buy a fantastic tale of supernatural bloodsuckers. He sat and smoked while Janeway and Curson watched him through the observation mirror.

"There's no smoking in this building anymore," Curson said.

"Please, daddy." Janeway mopped his head with a fast-food napkin imprinted with a jaunty logo. One of the desk drawers beneath the recording gear was a repository for take-out tools— plastic utensils, chopsticks, drinking straws—which testified that some cops ate too much crap. Curson noticed several fortune cookies which he knew had lived in the drawer for at least a year. He wondered whether the fortunes were still valid, or came with spoilage dates.

"He says he'll tell his story, but not to me," Janeway said. "So I called you."

"He's jacking you. Waiting for a lawyer."

"I told you, he waived."

"So why won't he talk to you?"

"That's where the weirdness starts."

"Goddammit, Leo, I hate this fucking game you always play."

The innocence spiking across Janeway's face was the most transparently bogus expression Curson had seen in weeks. "What?"

Curson mimed a fist. "You know exactly what. I always have to ask you the question directly; you won't just tell me, and if it's to drive me nuts, it's working, it's late and I am already getting pissed off. So what is the weirdness, Leo?"

Janeway shook his head, the way a dog does when it hears a space noise. "Sorry. I always think of you as my goofy little brother, and it's fun to egg you on. I'm just trying to wrap my brain around this guy and I can't. Know what the first thing he asked me was?"

"The first thing *he* asked *you*?"

"He asked if I had any kids, and when I said yes, he shriveled completely shut. Then all he would tell me was what I told you."

Curson looked at the floor, at the drawer, almost anywhere but Janeway's eyes. "So you called me."

"Looks like I tore you away from something really grim."

"No, it's just . . . the thing about kids. I had another fight with Sondra tonight, about kids."

"Fight?" Janeway put on his doubtful attorney face. "You and Sondra don't 'fight' in the conventional sense of the term as it applies to every other married couple in America, if I may be so bold."

"Okay, call it more a stiff debate with stomach acid poured all over it. She wants to get pregnant and I want to breathe, and there doesn't seem to be an accord."

"Didn't you ever hear about the three C's? Communication, cooperation, coordination?"

"I didn't change my mind, Leo. She did."

"I thought it was just smoking that had been banned; I didn't know changing your mind was against the law."

"You're a vast friggin' help."

"Why don't you just have a kid? One kid. One more kid won't topple the planet off its axis. It'll be as handsome as Sondra and as bilious as you."

"Please. I've suffered every variation of this speech that has existed since the dawn of mankind."

"Just doing my bit. I love my daughter. She is perhaps my greatest achievement."

"Yeah, but we don't get paid for reproducing, we get paid for prying reality out of Victor the Knife Man, in there."

"I live to serve. Meanwhile, I need you to see if you can pry anything out of Victor the Knife Man in there."

Janeway was peering at him sidewise, testing depths. "You up for this, partner?"

Actually, Curson preferred grilling a murderer to going home just now.

"He tried to cut a baby out of his wife?"

"Girlfriend, affirmative."

"How pregnant was she?"

"Seventh, eighth week."

"So it wasn't a baby, it was a fetus." In Curson's mind, the crime changed from *baby killer* to someone who had terminated a scrap of tissue and some chemicals, incidentally bumping off the host—the mother.

Janeway made a face. "Oh, you're gonna be a laugh riot, I can tell." He motioned toward the interlock door. "After you."

Victor Quintelle Solos lit his third cigarette since Curson had first seen him. "Detective Curson, do you have any kids? Any children?"

"No."

"You lying?"

"You wouldn't talk to my partner, and if you don't want to talk to me, then you're wasting everybody's time and I'll tank you in thirty seconds. My answer to your question is no, I do not. I also do not play good cop, bad cop, so if you're waiting for one of us to be mean to you, forget it. Now do you have a story to tell us, or do we say good-bye?"

"He wouldn't understand," Victor said, indicting Janeway. "He has reproduced, so his beliefs about them would cloud his judgment."

"I think I've just been insulted," Janeway said.

"Detective Janeway stays in the room with us. No negotiation."

"Sorry," said Victor. "No offense."

"That's a good one," said Janeway. "We've already got a two-inch stack of crime scene Polaroids that are pretty fucking offen-

220   DAVID J. SCHOW

sive." Janeway often ran coarse when he was fed up, and as a result Curson tried to avoid common cursing—another manifestation of the seesaw nature of most cop partnerships.

Curson had examined the pictures, which reminded him of a photo he'd once seen of Jack the Ripper's final victim, alleged to be one Mary Kelly, who had been eviscerated over the course of two long hours of butchery more than a century earlier. Victor's handiwork made Jack's look streamlined.

"I don't want to see them," said Victor. "I did what I had to do."

Janeway rolled his eyes. Curson could tell he was getting ready to shitcan Victor—prematurely—because so far Victor sounded as though he had nothing new to say beyond the standard-issue excuses and prattle of just another killer.

"Shit, Dion, if I have to listen to this fucker spew—"

"Hang on, Leo. *Tranquilo. Momentito.*" Settle down. Give me a moment. A *tiny* moment. Janeway's home life had been the dullest, most predictable standard family-issue Curson could imagine. Bland, even. Janeway could handle everything from body parts strewn across an intersection to the million child-sized catastrophes with which his little girl had gifted him every day while growing up . . . so why was he running redline, acting like he wanted to strangle Victor right here in the hot room?

Curson sat down close to Victor's corner of the table. *First fold your hands to demonstrate calm,* Curson thought, *then open them to show you're willing to listen, that you want to hear the tale. Maintain eye contact. Pay attention and don't look away while the subject is speaking. Make him feel protected in a hostile environment.*

"You want coffee, water, a soda?" Curson cleared his throat. "I know I do, and you must be dry. Leo, do me a favor and snag us a couple of bubble waters from the fridge. Club soda okay?"

Victor looked slightly stunned, his gaze drifting. He answered automatically. "Yeah."

Curson waved off Janeway's protest with an A-OK. He wanted

to see how Victor acted when Janeway seemed to be out of the room—even though Janeway would linger right by the door, watch-dogging, and have his free hand on a fully charged shockstick.

Victor lit another cigarette. "I know you saw the photos. I know what it looks like. Guy goes berserk and carves up his lady; if you expect me to say I'm possessed or something, I'm going to disappoint you."

"I just want to know what's going on, Victor. What did you mean when you said Leo's beliefs about his children would bias him against you?"

"How many times have you heard that rap about children being the most precious commodity in the world?" Victor was focused now. "Everything we do has gotta be oriented around making children, protecting children, accommodating fucking *children*. Doesn't it seem a bit *disproportionate* to you? Allowing one segment to dominate the entire society?"

"I don't think you're going to get a lot of support for not protecting children."

"That's just it—that's the way everybody is programmed, by our society, by our media, by our goddamn parents and families and relatives. Children have become sacred in this culture even though their mean worth to the culture has diminished to practically zero."

This was kind of creepy. Victor was suddenly using big words and speaking like a man with an education.

"I mean, it's one thing if we're tribes squabbling over a water-hole, and every birth means another soldier, which is good because nine out of ten babies die and there's only a couple thousand apemen on the whole planet. It's another thing if we're still pre-Industrial Revolution and most of the kids die of consumption or crib death, and we're agrarians who need all the hands on the farm we can get. But we've got how many *billion* people overrunning the planet, now? Double that in fewer than thirty years? Reproducing irresponsibly is a sick, atavistic notion."

"You're not going to talk people out of having kids, Victor." Once the words were out of Curson's mouth, he was mildly shocked to hear himself saying *those* words in particular.

"I know. It's an imperative logged right into our DNA alongside fight-or-flight. We've evolved a little bit—our wisdom teeth are being bred out, the hair is disappearing from our bodies as a species, the field of focus of our eyes is changing and fingernails and toenails will be completely gone in the next few thousand years. But in order to survive long enough to really evolve, we've got to evolve mentally, intellectually, to the point where we stop breeding like fucking bacillae, because the world can't use more people right now, no matter how wonderful they are."

"It's an individual choice," said Curson.

"No, it's a species choice. Everybody says, *fine, you choose not to have kids, but I'm having all the kids I want and when you die, my kids will be running things and you'll be forgotten.* And I say, no, moron, because when the planet finally chokes to death on an overdose of people, thanks to your untethered spawning, we'll all go down together."

"I take it your girlfriend was pregnant and you didn't want her to have the baby." Curson was trying to keep his eye on the target.

"Her name is Marisole. Was Marisole."

Janeway delivered a pair of bottled club sodas. "Would you two like to hear about our specials for this evening? No?"

Curson said, "Was Marisole seeing someone while you were in prison, Victor?"

"Oh, *man* . . ." Victor vised his temples as though trying to exorcise some toxin from his forehead. "Simple infidelity is not what it's about. I'm being completely straight with you, and you have to pay attention. I'm sterile, okay? The plumbing all works fine but reproductively speaking, I'm shooting blanks, okay? That's not what this is all about."

Solos was playing the same claw-the-wallpaper game Janeway

used to joshingly irritate Curson. He had to ask. "You tell me what it's about, Victor."

"It's about this guy, Johnson Howard."

"Like the hotel?"

"Only backwards."

"He was the baker who put the bun in Marisole's oven?" said Janeway.

"*No*." Victor was getting angry, and Curson wished he could just command Janeway outright to clamp. "Johnson Howard was this guy in Fordmill. I was working as a trustee—you know, delivering meals and library books and shit to C Wing."

"Death row." Janeway raked up a seat at the far end of the table.

"Johnson told me this story about his wife, when she got pregnant. He killed her. He killed her because of what he saw *after* she got pregnant."

Curson sipped. Janeway had thoughtfully brought plastic bottles without twist-caps, which had serrated edges and could therefore be classified as a potential weaponry.

"Detective Janeway there has a child, so he'll know what I mean when I say once women get pregnant, they smell different."

Janeway shrugged. *Sure, I guess.*

"It's more fundamental than that. Pregnant women exude a radically altered grade of pheromone. All most people know about pheromones is that their purpose is to attract potential mates, which you don't need if you're pregnant."

"I think this guy just said my wife stank," said Janeway. Curson could see the constant spousal references were stoking his partner's boiler, almost as if Solos somehow knew that Mrs. Janeway—Michelina—was dead.

"No. I said that once she's pregnant, she sends out signals that are never transmitted at any other time."

"Signals. That's a pleasant way to say it," said Janeway.

Curson saw, in Janeway's expression, the face he once used when complaining about his wife's bizarre behavior and wild mood swings when she was carrying their daughter, Alicia. The crying jags, the flash-fire rages, the quasi-suicidal dips. It had been a World War of a pregnancy. Everything was diagnosed as "normal" . . . and blamed on hormones.

Normalcy was relative. Victor was proof.

"This guy Johnson thought his wife was going to kill herself, so he kept watch on her. He spied on her, without her knowing it. And that's when he saw it happen. He says it was during the first full moon after his wife was diagnosed as pregnant."

"That's another intriguing turn of phrase," Janeway put in, snidely.

"Like she was sick," said Curson, "and the baby was the sickness?"

"Babies are parasites. They suck the mother's blood, drain nutrients, and toxify the host metabolism with their waste. They self-eject in a shower of blood and afterbirth, and they continue to feed off *both* parents even when outside the womb. We drape the whole horror show in a socially approved blanket of warmth and nurturing, and we spend millions of dollars and people-hours reinforcing the idea that *this* is what human beings are supposed to do. Our media, our culture all present this enslavement as freedom, and people embrace it because they are incapable of grasping any other freedoms beyond their choice of beer or car or what's on cable—the choices themselves being no real choices at all. Nobody has the *right* to pump out children unchecked anymore; it's reckless endangerment of humanity. Even the Chinese have realized that. When most people have kids their excuse is that the children 'just sort of happened'—as though they're completely unaware of what *caused* the child. Or they have some religious dogma to fall back on that conveniently prohibits termination, and—what else?—encourages the idea of producing even *more* kids. It's no blessed event, no miracle—it's a fucking nightmare."

"Maybe we should get you a podium to whack with your shoe," said Janeway flatly. Before Curson could intercede, he leaned closer. "I'm an atheist. My kid was *not* an accident. And you're one baby step away from a rant. Does any of this have a point?"

"What about Johnson, what about the signals his girlfriend sent out?" Curson's interest in Victor's apparently bottomless polemic was waning. He thought about calling Sondra. He wondered if Sondra had already called him, at the message station in the outer office.

"She went out one night about two in the morning. He followed her to a house with a FOR SALE sign in front. The fence was half-wrecked, the yard overgrown with weeds, all the windows were dark or shaded. He thought, *here it comes, man. Some dude is banging my pregnant wife.* He got to a window. He was very good at stealth. He saw his wife lay on a dining room table, hike up her skirt, and pull her own panties off like she was drugged. She lay there with her legs spread for half an hour. Johnson told me, he wanted to charge in and drag her away, all stiff and erect like a hero, but another part of him wanted to hang back and see what was up."

"Or he was a coward, or he was just making all this shit up," said Janeway. "Get to the gangbang, already."

Curson, on the other hand, was listening raptly.

"Three men came in. At least, Johnson thought they were men at first. Very pale-skinned. Their faces were indistinct, as though seen through steam or heat shimmer. One minute, they had normal hands. The next, the hands elongated. You ever see an iguana's foot—the super-long digits, four or five joints each, really slender? The hands were like that.

"Then Johnson said the faces changed too. All three men were utterly bland-looking. Crowd pedestrians. Pattern baldness, sandy hair, light eyes, the type you brush past a thousand times a week and never notice. The eyes went yellow around oblong black pupils like punctures. Their features blurred like hot wax running and re-formed into what Johnson said were long, narrow, needle-like beaks, ebony-colored. No teeth, but ridged gums of mottled brown-black. 'You just knew those gums could cut like sharpened obsidian,' Johnson told me.

"Two of the things held her arms while the third reached up inside her with its long fingers. Then it pierced her stomach with its beak like a hypodermic right where—you know, where the fetus was. After a minute it withdrew one little gob of meat. It swallowed it the way a gull swallows a fish. Then it inserted a different gob of meat."

"Like a changeling, but in the womb?" said Curson.

"Yes, essentially."

"And the beaks were long and thin, like a . . . a humming-bird's?"

"Yes, like a green hermit or a sicklebill."

Neither Curson nor Janeway could appreciate the distinctions. Both refixed their vision on Victor as if he'd just grown multiple heads.

"They have a library at Fordmill," he offered. "I looked it up."

Victor might even have supplied Johnson Howard with bird books, thought Curson. If there was such a convict at all. Now he and Janeway regarded each other, dourly.

"I'm telling you what you asked me to tell you. The things you came to hear."

"You're asking us to buy that this guy Johnson just stood there while all this was going on, while his wife was being—" Janeway was trying to find the words in mid-air. He failed.

"Violated?" said Curson.

"He said he was paralyzed, that he couldn't move. Once he started watching, he was frozen to the spot."

"That's touchingly convenient." Janeway snorted.

"He said he couldn't even make a sound with his voice."

"Fucking *enough*." Janeway's voice cut through the acoustics of the room; even the distant hum of the air unit seemed to shut up. "Enough. I've heard as much of this horseshit as my brain can tolerate." He spaced his words like hammer blows. "What the *fuck* do big fucking *storks* from outer *space* have to do with *you* hacking your *girlfriend* into a *casserole*?" When he finished, he was almost yelling, so abrim with pent-up anger and the need to lash out that his hand sideswiped the stack of crime scene photos, which fanned like dropped playing cards toward Victor.

"I didn't say they were from outer space," Victor said contritely. His eyes locked on to one of the photos and did not stray.

"Not to mention this bullshit doesn't hold an ounce of water! Even a dummy like me knows about X rays and ultrasound! You think a doctor wouldn't be able to tell it was a bird or an alien or a mutant or whatever the fuck you claim it is through even the most incompetent examination?!"

"They're like chameleons," said Victor. "They can change. It's automatic, a protective reaction. Even the fetuses can do it."

"Oh, thank you very much!" Janeway had had his limit, and that usually signaled the end of any exchange—hostile, interrogative, or otherwise.

Curson spoke very softly. "I think we're almost done, Victor, if you could tell me a little bit about Marisole."

Curson was relieved when the demon of burden leapt from him to Victor; the prisoner's shoulders visibly sagged. *Gotcha.*

"She told me on the phone she was pregnant."

"So you weren't so sterile after all."

"No way. I had myself checked out by the doctor the minute I heard. Double zeros."

"And you concluded that Marisole was stepping out on you."

"Yeah, basically. Like I said—I was shooting blanks."

"How'd you bust out?"

"Johnson told me about how erosion had screwed up the west fence. He heard it from a convict who dug post holes on the work crew until he got into a fight with another prisoner and split his skull with a shovel. Guy wound up in the cell next to Johnson's."

"So you wormed out and went after Marisole?"

"I told myself the whole time that she was just cheating on me, you know? Good pure, clean, macho rage. Some free man had tried to make my woman a *puta* and me a cuckold. I said that to myself all the way in. But I was thinking about what Johnson had told me. And further back in my mind, I was hoping that I could be in time to prevent something if Johnson was even a little bit right."

"What'd Marisole have to say about it?" Curson's voice was down to a whisper.

Victor was still staring at one of the photos as his expression finally broke. Tears began to stream freely from his hollow and haunted eyes. "She tried to lie. She fucked someone else and tried to lie. Because her pheromones changed. Because I was too late. I saw the puncture scar on her stomach—"

"Well, there sure as hell's no scar there *now*," Janeway said, more or less closing the case for all of them.

It had been a sleepless few hours for Sondra, and when Curson went to phone her there was already a message waiting for him. In a sense, they would fall in love all over again tonight . . . only to have that love jeopardized the next time they restaged the argument. The difference now was that Curson felt stronger. He and Sondra would fight a lot during their coming years together, but the bottom line was that they loved each other.

"I fished up the data on Victor's Death Row buddy," said Janeway, chugging half a styro cup of cold coffee. "There really is a guy named Johnson Howard in Fordmill, and as far as I can tell, he did kill his wife almost the same way as Victor did his lady. Ready for the big punchline of the night?"

Curson was ready for almost anything.

"Guess what Johnson Howard got arrested for prior to turning pro murderer?"

"Thrill me."

"Fraud and forgery. He forged autographs. Celebrity signatures. You know those documents signed by old presidents or dead astronauts or pop stars or movie people? Johnson was the Monet of his particular form of Impressionism. When he was nailed, a fake John Lennon was grabbing five to six grand, blind. He also helped forge those so-called "vintage" movie posters in a year where a big King Kong sheet could snare sixty thousand dollars at a perfectly reputable auction at Christie's."

"Point being?"

"A guy like that could make up anything in the world and a suggestable nutcase like Victor would buy it—at least so far as using it as an excuse."

Curson shook his head. "Jeez. Would you prefer to just execute him in the cell right now?"

"That would be illegal. Like smoking in the building."

"You don't think your feelings about Michelina helped, uh, contour your attack in there?"

"Sure it did. I'll admit that to you because I love you, and you're my partner, and I don't want you to eat two fights in one night. I'm entitled to be angry when fucksticks desecrate the memory of my dead wife. Now he just gets flushed into the system that'll ultimately execute him for murder. So I don't *have* to kill him right now, because he'll suffer more this way."

Curson tried to imagine Victor telling his tale to another convict, infecting someone new with the fiction. "Why did you say to Victor that his little monsters were from outer space?"

Janeway shrugged. "I was pissed off. It just jumped into my mouth. It was no less reasonable than the sewage Victor was excreting." He collected the crime scene photos, noticing that Victor's cigarettes had been left behind. But for two mangled smokes, the killer had pretty much killed the pack, which was headed for the personal effects box. "Why are you hanging around, Dion? Isn't it safe for you to go home yet?"

"It's okay. New day and all that." Curson slung his jacket.

"See if you can knock up Sondra when you two make up."

"Is that your way of wrapping on a lighter note? I still have one more question."

"I am gravid with expectation." Janeway's "deadpan face" was truly a hoot.

"Leo, do you have any idea what getting a vasectomy involves?"

Janeway cracked a smile. "Whoa—don't tell me that fucker's got *you* going, now."

"No, I was thinking maybe Victor had one, it didn't take, and maybe he concocted this whole thing to set himself up for an insanity plea for murdering his girlfriend in a crime of passion."

"Works for me. Want me to check it out?"

"No. I will."

"Kiss Sondra and tell her I'll see her soon."

Curson bid his partner good night and left, feeling bad about lying to Leo. He wanted to know about the vasectomy for himself.

Oddly, Janeway also felt bad, about lying. But it was late, and no one was watching, and a sniff of curiosity could safely be indulged right now. With much the same queer thrill he had experienced upon tasting Marisole's unborn child, Janeway retrieved Victor's smokes, and with long, multi-jointed, black-taloned fingers, lit up his very first cigarette.

Karen Joy Fowler is the author of the novels *Sarah Canary* and *The Sweetheart Season* and the World Fantasy Award–winning collection of short fiction *Black Glass*. "Faded Roses" was first published in the November 1989 *Omni*, commissioned for a group of short-shorts on the theme of "Man's Best Friends."

FADED ROSES

KAREN JOY FOWLER

Thirty-two sixth graders from Holmes Elementary lined the rails that protected the glass of the Gorilla Room from fingerprints. Two of them were eating their lunches. Sixteen had removed some item from their lunch bags and were throwing them instead of eating them: their teacher paid no attention. Five were whispering about a sixth who fiddled with the locked knob on the workroom as if she didn't hear. Five were discussing the fabulous Michael K.'s eighty-two-point game last night, and three were looking at the gorillas. Anders approached one of these three. It was part of his job. He was better at the other parts.

"We have a mixture of lowland and mountain gorillas," he told the boy in the baseball cap. The boy did not respond. That suited Anders fine. "I know which is which," he continued, "because they're my gorillas. Now, some experts argue the noses are differ-ent or the mountain gorilla's hair is longer, but I've studied the matter and never seen that."

There were thirteen gorillas inside the exhibit. Five sat on rocks at the back. One baby played with a tire swing, batting it with her feet and turning an occasional somersault through the center. One stared in contemplative concentration at nothing. Four

alternated through a variety of grooming arrangements. One nib-
bled on the peeled end of a stick. One surveyed all the others. It
was a dignified scene. *Sullen. Reserved. Moody. Shy.* These were
some of the words commonly applied over the years to gorillas.
They had none of the joie de vivre of chimps. Gorillas were not
clowns. It took a dignified, reserved person to appreciate them. Perhaps it took a little loneliness. And Anders had that.

The boy pointed over the rail. "That one looks really mean."
Anders did not have to follow the finger to know which gorilla the
boy meant.

A lowland gorilla. Gargantua the Great. "Paul du Chaillu was
probably the first white man to see gorillas," Anders told the boy.
"He tracked them and shot them and came back to France and told
stories about their ferocity. Made him look brave. Made his books
sell. Barnum did the same thing with his circus gorillas. He knew
people would pay more to be scared than to be moved." Beyond the
glass, Gargantua swiveled his huge head. The teeth were permanently exposed, but the eyes, directed obliquely left, said something else. Anders was proud of those eyes.

"That gorilla there, well, an angry sailor poured nitric acid on
him. The sailor'd lost his job and wanted to get even with the
importer. The acid damaged the muscles on the gorilla's face, so he
always looks like he's snarling. It's the only expression he can
make."

A storm of peanut shells hit the glass. Anders identified the
culprit and took him by the arm. Anders did not raise his voice. "I
was telling a story about the big gorilla in the corner," he said to
the second boy. "This will interest you. He was raised by Mrs.
Lintz, an Englishwoman, and he lived in her house in Brooklyn
until he got too big. He may look fierce, but he was always terrified
of thunder. One night there was a thunderstorm. Mrs. Lintz woke
up to find a four-hundred-pound gorilla huddled on the foot of her
bed, sobbing."

There were perhaps six children paying attention to Anders

now. Somewhere an elephant trumpeted. "They don't look at us," one boy complained, and a girl in a plaid shirt asked if they had names.

"Actually we have three gorillas who were raised as pets by Englishwomen," Anders said. "John Daniel. And Toto, too, the fat one there looking for fleas. And Gargantua, whose real name is Buddy. Gorillas don't look at anyone directly and they don't like to be stared at themselves. Very unsuited to zoo life. The first gorillas brought to this country died within weeks. The gorillas who lived in private homes with mothers instead of keepers did better."

Toto yawned. Her eyes closed as her mouth opened. She smacked her lips when the yawn was over. She was the newest of the gorillas. Anders had added her last year. It was harder to love Toto, but Anders did. Anders had learned everything he could about his gorillas and he knew that Toto was used to being loved. Spoiled and prone to five-hundred-pound tantrums, Toto had terrorized her way out of her first home. When her mother, a Mrs. Hoyt, saw that she could no longer control Toto, Toto was sold to a zoo, but Mrs. Hoyt came along also. "Toto was bought as a bride for Buddy," Anders said. "She was raised in Cuba, where she had her own pet. A cat."

Anders had ten children listening now. Did any of them have cats? Anders doubted it. And there were other indulgences. "When Toto came to the U.S. she brought along a trousseau. Sweaters, dresses, and socks," Anders said, "all with the name *Totito* in embroidery. The papers loved it. *The future Mrs. Gargantua.* But Toto threw her bed at Buddy when they first met, and her attitude never softened."

The prospective mother-in-law had done much to sabotage the union. "She's only a nine-year-old child," Mrs. Hoyt had said. "What do you expect?"

John Daniel moved along the back of the exhibit. His steps were slow and fluid; muscles rippled on his back. He was Anders's favorite. "John Daniel was purchased from Harrod's by Major

Rupert Penny of the Royal Air Force as a present for his aunt. John Daniel had a variety of ailments, including rickets, but the aunt, a Mrs. Cunningham, fixed that. She raised him as she would have raised a small boy. A certain amount of indulgence. A certain amount of no nonsense. He ate at the table with them and was expected to get his own glass of water and to clear his own dishes. He was taught to use the toilet and, since he cried when he slept alone, was given a room next to the major's. Mrs. Cunningham consulted no experts but used her own judgment in devising his diet, which included fruit, vegetables, and raw hamburger. And roses. He loved to eat roses, but only if they were fresh. He wouldn't eat a faded rose."

When he became too big to keep, Mrs. Cunningham sold him to a private park she believed would be ideal. Tragically, he ended up in the circus instead. Anders had lost his own indulgent mother at the age of eight. He thought he had some insight into John Daniel. He knew what it was like to suddenly, inexplicably, exchange one home for another far less happy one. John Daniel's expression was intelligent but bewildered and bereaved.

Too subtle for sixth graders. Anders was down to an audience of four. "So interesting," the teacher said brightly, although Anders did not think he had been listening. Probably he had been there with a different class last year and perhaps the year before that. Probably he had heard it before. Probably he had never listened. "Can you all thank Mr. Anders for showing us his gorillas?" the teacher suggested, and then, without pausing for thanks, "We won't see the giraffes if we don't press on."

No one else was scheduled until three. Anders opened the workroom to get his own lunch and a book. He was studying Koko now, a gorilla raised by a Stanford graduate student and taught to sign. He planned to eat inside with his gorillas, but Miss Elliot arrived instead. "Have lunch with me," she said. "I made cookies. It's a beautiful day."

Miss Elliot often came at lunchtime. She had no real interest in

Anders, or so Anders thought. Her own upbringing as the baby of a large, loving family had left her with a certain amount of affection to spare. She regarded Anders as a project. No healthy young man could be allowed to molder among the exhibits. Get him out. Give him a bit of medicinal companionship. Miss Elliot wore a uniform with an elephant on the sleeve and below that the black circle. Miss Elliot showed the elephants, but they weren't her elephants and Anders doubted she even understood the distinction.

If he refused her offer, he would face her brand of implacable, perky determination. He found it unendurable. So he nodded instead and put the book back beside his tools and his sketches. He joined her at the exit, opening the door.

Miss Elliot shook her head. "You always forget," she said. Her tone was indulgent but firm. She reached back past him, brushing across the black circle on his sleeve, and threw the switch that turned the gorillas off. They ate lunch on the grass outside the Hall of Extinction. The cookies were stale. The flowers were in bloom.

Mark W. Tiedemann has over forty stories and articles to his credit and a novel scheduled from Byron Preiss's new ibooks. More of both are in the works. He has a photograph in the permanent collection of the St. Louis Art Museum.

The idea for "Links" came to Tiedemann during a discussion on the "what-ifs" of evolution and after reading a biography of Darwin. The combination of local English folklore with paleontological speculation grew naturally—"evolved" one could say—from the fact that previously unknown and unverified species are found all the time. Many such creatures are only known to us through folklore.

LINKS

MARK W. TIEDEMANN

Reverend William Fox wandered among the cages of pigeons. The tents flapped in a light breeze; everywhere the sound of muffled coos mingled with ardent conversation. Men in tall hats with badges pinned to their lapels moved from display to display, occasionally asking to have a particular bird taken out for inspection. A brilliant June sun burned across Cheshire.

Breeders greeted Reverend Fox with broad smiles and cordial bows. He had been buying birds all during the show, especially young ones, and he had not seemed too particular. Some fanciers doubtless thought him eccentric, or at best a novice who had yet to learn the finer points of the fancy. Still, none of them had really cheated him. If any of them knew what it was all about they might charge more.

" 'Morning, sir." A short man with broad features and heavy hands lightly clasping the lapels of his worn coat came up to him. His right hand was bandaged.

"Good morning," Fox returned. "I don't believe I've had the pleasure . . . ?"

"Well, sir, no, you wouldn't. My name is Humphrey Paley. I've got a place a few miles south o' here."

"Do you breed pigeons, Mr. Paley?"

"Aye, sir, I do. One o' the few pleasures I've got, if you take my meaning." He turned partway and waved toward a stack of cages. "My birds are there." He smiled briefly, showing uneven teeth. "I understand that you've been buying, sir."

"Reverend Fox. Yes, as a matter of fact. Young birds mainly. I'm acquiring them for a friend in Kent. Do you have any to sell?"

"Aye, Reverend, I think I might, if you'd care to have a look."

Fox fell into step beside the man and crossed the grass to his modest collection of birds. He peered through the wooden bars. "Nice pair of turbit there . . ."

"Oh, I couldn't part with them, Reverend."

"Of course, they look well presented. Any chicks?"

"Aye, but I didn't bring them along."

Fox straightened. Besides the turbit, he saw the usual collection of magpie and swallow and one old fantail that looked past its prime. Nothing remarkable.

"Forgive me, Mr. Paley, but I thought I knew everyone in the parish."

The man blinked for a few moments, then looked surprised. "Oh, you're *that* Reverend Fox! Well, I had no idea. Well, we're not in your parish, Reverend. But I've heard many speak well of you." He laughed self-consciously and looked around. "I do have a good stock o' chicks you might be interested in. As I say, though, I didn't bring them here. If you'd care to, Reverend, I'd be pleased to have you out to my place to look them over. As a matter of fact, I'd be most grateful, as there's another matter upon which I'd be most appreciative of your opinion."

"Oh? This isn't something best left to your own deacon, is it?"

"Oh, no, sir, no. This has to do with birds and Reverend Gromley, if you don't mind my saying, isn't much about them. No, this is to do with birds. Or, I should say, with one bird. I have one that's most curious and—well, Reverend, I'd appreciate a man of your stature and associations having a look."

"My 'associations'?"

"Yes, sir, like Mr. Hooker and Mr. Owen and Mr. Darwin."

Fox felt his lips pucker in amusement. "You have more than a pressing familiarity with me, Mr. Paley. Is paleontology a hobby of yours?"

"We might have a good talk about that, if you'd be so good as to pay us a visit, Reverend. This bird, if I might call it that, is quite an odd example. I think you'd be quite interested."

"You intrigue me, Mr. Paley."

The man looked suddenly relieved. "Thank you, sir. Then may I tell my wife you'll be coming?"

"Yes, I shall be glad to, Mr. Paley."

"I am at a loss," Fox wrote later to Darwin, "to explain my decision to visit this contradiction of a man. He had clearly misrepresented himself to me, but he did it in so mawkish a manner that I found it impossible to be offended. Rather than wonder why he had approached me in such a way I immediately wondered what it was that made him believe he had to."

Paley's farm consisted of about one hundred and fifty acres. Fox smelled the barley before the carriage topped the last rise. The residence was an old stone structure with a thatch roof. Smoke curled from one of three chimneys. Beyond he saw a newer wooden barn and an extensive yard wherein chickens mingled thickly. There was a thatch-roofed warren and attached to this a shed containing a few cows and horses. Even over the thunder of the carriage, Fox could hear the complaining of chickens. As he dismounted, he could also hear pigeons, loudly cooing, and, distantly, crows.

The door opened and Paley stepped out, grinning. "Reverend, it is good of you to come!"

Fox glanced in the direction of the barnyard and Paley gave the clamor a dismissive wave.

"You get so you don't notice after awhile."

"I don't believe I've ever heard such a racket."

"Please, Reverend, come inside. It's much quieter."

As the heavy oak door closed the sound diminished significantly. Fox stood still while his eyes adjusted to the dim light. He handed his hat and cane to Paley and surveyed the large main room. Chairs gathered close to the big hearth. Just behind these stood an old, scarred table. An enormous cabinet contained china service and another held perhaps two score of books. Lanterns hung on support beams, unlit now with daylight flooding in through the squarish windows. Curtains blocked either end of the house. Fox smelled the aroma of stew cooking from one end. He assumed the other to be their bedroom.

"This appears quite old," he said appreciatively.

"Aye. It's been in my family for about five generations now, but it's older than that."

"You own it yourself then?"

"Aye, sir." Paley swept the room with a proud look. "Mind you, it's not easy. Not quite hand-to-mouth, but almost. Still, we make out all right. There's not many of us left anymore, you know. A family like us, no titles or any real background to speak of, owning its own place like this. Not for so many generations like this. Lot of places are selling out to local gentlemen, deacons, petty lords, businessmen, and the like. Not many of us left, but, God willing, the Paleys will hang on."

"You and your wife?"

"Aye. Annie! Come out and greet our guest."

A woman came out from behind the lefthand curtain. Her nearly white hair was tucked under a worn lace cap tied beneath a strong chin. She was half a head taller than her husband and barely spoke. She curtsied shyly to Fox and excused herself to get back to the kitchen.

"She's a good one, Annie is," Paley said. He gestured for Reverend Fox to come sit by the unlit fireplace.

"Do you smoke, Reverend?" Paley asked, taking a pipe from his pocket.

"No, thank you. You have children?"

"Two boys. Grown. Both of 'em are in the Crimea. Annie worries over them. They're good boys, I'll be proud to have 'em take over the place when they're old enough. Or when I'm tired enough." He laughed.

"It must be difficult with just your wife and yourself."

Paley nodded. "That's true enough. I sometimes wonder what would become of Annie were I to take sick. But we manage. Sometimes by the skin of our teeth, if you take my meaning, but we manage. It's a responsibility, though. My grandfather near lost the place, when the factories went up in the cities. All the sons went there to work for wages. Now it's the war." He shook his head. "If it weren't for Annie sometimes I'd just as soon throw in and walk away. Annie and my pigeons."

"Yes, your pigeons. About them, Mr. Paley—"

"You're collecting them for Mr. Darwin, aren't you? I've heard talk around the other fanciers. I'm a member of the Borough Club, though you might not know to look at me."

"As a matter of fact, I am."

"Hmm. Thought so. I've read Mr. Darwin."

"Indeed?"

"Aye." He aimed the stem of his pipe toward the books. "I own a copy of his *Journal of Researches* from the *Beagle*."

Fox blinked. "Well, if you don't mind my saying, sir, that surprises me."

"Oh, I read, Reverend. 'Course lately there hasn't been much time or money for books. But I quite admired that book. I don't mind that it's Mr. Darwin, but I would like to know what he intends with 'em."

"I'm afraid I can't say with any authority myself. He may be my cousin, but sometimes the workings of the man's mind . . . if you take my meaning."

"An acquaintance o' mine from Monmouth told me he's been collecting barnacles for some time. Packages from all over the world, he said."

"That's true."

"Now it's pigeons. Hm. Can't say I see the relation myself, but Mr. Darwin's a smarter man than me."

"You indicated yesterday that you had something out of the ordinary."

"That I did." Paley leaned forward and stared for a time into the dead hearth. "I've got problems with foxes."

"Foxes."

"Eggs are a good portion of my livelihood. I keep on average about two hundred hens. Foxes get to be a problem for poultry farmers. I hunt them, of course, but there's not always time for that. So I lay traps. Of course, I don't always catch foxes in my traps. The occasional rabbit, now and then a hedgehog. I caught me a hawk once. It had pounced on a mouse and just happened to do so in one o' my traps. Still had it clutched in its claws. Poor thing had a broken leg, but it flew off anyway. Don't know what became of it."

"I take it you snared this out of the ordinary something in one of your fox snares?"

"Indeed I did. Knowing Mr. Darwin's interest in the unusual it seemed reasonable he might be of a mind to see this."

"You say it's a bird?"

Paley's face compressed as if in pain and he gave a slight shake of his head. "Mr. Darwin's a smarter man than me. I'd say so, but only at first look. Matter of fact, Reverend, I can't say honestly what it is. Of course, you hear stories, especially out here among us rustics." He laughed dryly. "If feathers make a thing a bird, then I guess it is."

"You certainly have my interest, Mr. Paley. I would very much like to see this creature."

Paley looked at him then and Fox felt uneasy. The man's eyes locked on him, an ember of fear wavering within them.

"Don't torment the Reverend," Annie broke in suddenly. She stood by the part in the curtains, glaring across at her husband. "Show him. If he wants it, make a price and finish it."

Paley returned a bitter look, then nodded. "Come with me, if you will, Reverend. It's in the barn."

The moment they stepped out of the house the clamor of the barn-yard struck Fox again. He winced as he followed Paley quickly to the barn. The chicken coops extended from its left rear corner out along the length of the fenced yard in which the hens milled. To Fox's eyes they seemed unusually agitated. They pressed as a group away from the wall, toward the far end of their enclosure.

"I've had it a week now," Paley said as they stepped into the gloomy interior. "The nature of it is such that I kept it hid till I knew what to do with it. I'm sure you'll appreciate my position, Reverend."

Hay filled the air with a pleasant musky odor. Paley led Fox to the rear and climbed a ladder set against the edge of the loft. At the top Fox found himself in a cluttered space, piled with crates and canvas-covered objects stacked against the walls. It was darker still and he had to pick his way with care following Paley through the maze. From here the chickens sounded like a roomful of people chattering excitedly.

Paley stopped within a small cleared area near the back wall.

Fox could only see Paley's back as he bent over, searching for things. But he heard a faint rustling and a delicate clicking like fingernails on glass.

Suddenly Paley struck a lucifer and lit the wick of a lantern. Paley dropped the glass in place and a soft glow filled the space. He turned and motioned Fox closer. Then, with a nod, he indicated a cage on top of an old barrel.

For a moment Fox thought he was looking at a falcon of some kind. But as he looked closer he grew puzzled. It was the size of a small goose, but the proportions were all wrong. It crouched on legs much too thick. Its chest puffed out above a slim waist and its neck was short. What struck Fox most odd, though, was the head. Too large for a duck or goose, more the size and proportion of an owl, but shaped wrong. The skull looked prominently domed. A thick crest of feathers rose along the center of the skull, framed by back-swept tufts on either side. Paley had a leather muzzle on its beak. Above this the eyes glared out, shifting between Fox and Paley.

The eyes were too large and vaguely wolf-like. It blinked once, slowly and deliberately. The irises looked oily black with only the yellow point of reflected lantern glow to give them any sense of surface.

"My God . . ."

"Look close at the feathering," Paley said. "Watch."

Paley raised the lantern and lowered it to let the light shift over the thing's body. The feathers that had appeared white now shimmered irridescently with a faint rainbow play of color. Fox moved forward. The creature stepped back, eyes now fixed on him. The crest on its head lifted slightly.

"Are those . . . ?"

"Feathers? You might well wonder. Here."

Paley handed him a shaft. Fox turned it over in his palm. "This isn't a feather," he said. "It's solid, more like . . ."

"Scales?"

"Yes . . . scales. Except for right here at the end it starts to separate. Still, it's terribly stiff even there. My God, man, what have you found here?"

"Do you think p'haps Mr. Darwin would be interested?"

"Yes, surely. If not him I know a dozen zoologists offhand who'd like to see it."

"What do you think he'd be willing to give for such a find? Not meaning to be blunt about it, Reverend, but—"

"Oh, quite. Well . . . why don't you tell me your price?"

"Well. I've gotten as much as two hundred pounds for one o' my prize fantails . . . I couldn't part with it for less than three hundred."

Fox blinked at him. "That's a considerable sum."

Paley rubbed his face briefly. "It's a considerable find." He nodded curtly. "Let me show you the rest."

"Rest?"

Paley handed him the lantern. "Step back, Reverend."

Paley pulled a thick glove over his left hand. The creature stared at him, seeming to crouch even further down on its stout, overmuscled legs. Paley stood over the cage, hands held up. He drew a few deep breaths and licked his lips, then, quickly, jerked open the top of the cage with his right hand and plunged his gloved left down over the thing.

Fox started at the sudden fury. The creature moved swiftly, but there was no room to maneuver. Paley closed his gloved fingers on it just below its neck. The creature bucked and Paley strained to hold it. Deftly he reached in with his free hand and undid the muzzle. He jerked it out and slammed the lid.

The creature leapt from place to place until it seemed convinced that the door was once more locked. Then it stood in the center, chest heaving, head crest fully erect, eyes dancing from side to side hatefully.

Paley took the glove off and found a long slice of dried beef.

"Watch," he said and dangled the strip before the cage.

The creature's posture changed the moment it saw the beef. The head crest lowered and it straightened on its legs. Fox saw then that it was elegantly shaped. Though still birdlike, it seemed closer to some mammalian ideal. It moved to the bars. Paley brought the strip within inches.

Very deliberately, then, it reached forward. What Fox had taken for wings folded back now proved to be articulated limbs ending in long-fingered hands. The fingers of its left hand curled delicately around a wooden bar—sharp claws glinted darkly in the soft light—and the other reached out for the beef. Paley let the strip go and the creature drew it back inside the cage, stepped away from the bars, and squatted to eat.

Fox saw the "beak" then. It looked oddly fleshy and seemed too flexible, more like the under beak of a pelican than the hard chitin of a hawk's. And as it ripped at the tough beef he saw rows of sharp teeth.

They watched it till it finished. It licked its claws, then looked up expectantly. Paley nodded again. "Last item," he said and picked up a long iron poker.

He thrust it between the bars and prodded the creature roughly in the chest. Fox almost protested, but stared, fascinated at the response. The thing jumped aside, dodging the poker, until Paley had it cornered. He thumped it on the chest a few times while the creature's beak opened wide and high pitched keening came out. Then Paley pulled back.

The creature jumped forward in an unmistakable posture, arms akimbo, ready for combat. From its back unfurled a wide, many-hued pair of brilliant wings.

Fox stared, stunned.

"I don't know if it can fly," Paley said. "Not much better than a chicken, if it can. But—" He pointed with the poker, nodding.

"Yes, indeed." Fox forced himself to turn away. His scalp tingled coldly. "My God. I've never . . . where?"

"You hear stories all the time, Reverend. Folklore and such.

But when you grow older you put less and less stock in them. At least, I did. But what would you make of it?"

"Indeed. Three hundred pounds, you say?"

"To be honest with you, Reverend, it's what I need. Since I brought it here my chickens have stopped laying. Annie, bless her, thinks it's the devil's spawn, if you take my meaning. I'd put it on show, but frankly, the effect it has on other birds—well, you hear 'em. I'd like to contribute to science if I can, but I don't really want to go to the zoos. I thought this might be the best use of it. Annie wants it out. Frankly, she'd give it away, but times are hard—"

"I quite understand, Mr. Paley. It's just that such a sum requires that I contact Mr. Darwin and clear it. You understand, of course."

Paley nodded. "Of course. But you think perhaps he'd do so?"

"I'm quite sure. And, as I say, I know several others who would." Fox looked at the creature again. The wings were now folded back, hidden, and its forelimbs tucked in. As it watched the two men, Fox could not escape the feeling that it hated them, as a human being might hate, coldly and intelligently. "I shall return home and write to Mr. Darwin. A few days at most, I assure you, Mr. Paley."

"Very good, then, Reverend. I can wait."

"And . . . thank you, sir. Thank you very much for showing me this."

Three days later Fox received his cousin's confirmation to spend the sum. "Your enthusiasm prompts both my eagerness to see this marvel and my skepticism as to its authenticity," Darwin wrote.

Fox had seen a pouter pigeon with exquisite toe feathers go for seven hundred pounds at auction to a member of the Philoperisteron Club during a show at the Freemason's Tavern, but such sums remained rare. He felt a bit heady contemplating spending three hundred pounds even for such a creature as Mr. Paley's. He took his carriage directly to the Paley farm, a bank draught in his pocket.

As he pulled up to the old stone house he paused, disturbed, until he realized how quiet the place was. He listened for a few moments. He heard pigeons and chickens, but faintly, at a level expected on such a farm.

He knocked on the door, uneasy. After knocking twice more without answer, he wandered toward the barn. The chickens were scattered about their yard, serenely pecking and strutting. Fox called out for Mr. Paley, but heard no response. He entered the barn.

From the loft he saw a faint glow. He climbed the ladder and made his way to the small space where he now found Paley sitting on a box in the lantern light.

"Mr. Paley . . . ? It's Reverend Fox . . ."

The cage was empty.

"Mr. Paley . . . ?"

Paley looked up at him then. "Ah. Reverend. Sorry, I didn't hear you."

"No need to apologize." He looked anxiously at the cage, then back to Paley. He noticed then that the man held a letter in his left hand.

Paley shook his head. "I must apologize, Reverend. Things haven't gone well the last couple days."

"Uh . . . where is—?"

"Dead. I don't know how, but it got out. I woke up in the middle of the night, day before yesterday, to a sound like the hinges o' hell creakin' open. I got my piece and ran outside. It was my chickens. I thought, God, a fox is in the yard! I lit a lantern and hurried over. They were all gathered in the center, pushing and shoving each other, all converged on one spot. I couldn't see what it was, so I waded in. Some of 'em even pecked at my legs. When I got to the center, though, I saw what it was."

He gestured at the cage. "It got out. It must've tried to escape through the coop. My chickens killed it. Pecked it to death. Oh, it killed a few o' my birds, sure enough, but it didn't have a chance. I'm sorry, Reverend. I don't know how it happened. But I never saw chickens act like that before, except maybe with a dog or a cat, some old hen chasing them out. But all of 'em, like they couldn't wait to get a peck at it, and screaming!"

Fox closed his eyes. "Was anything left of it?"

"Some. I saved what I could. Annie wanted me to take it out into the woods and bury it, but . . . well, it wouldn't be right to just bury a find like that, would it, Reverend?"

"No, I dare say it wouldn't. May I see the remains?"

Paley pointed listlessly to the floor beneath the cage. Fox drew a shallow box forward into the lantern light.

"I'm not young anymore, Reverend. Me or Annie. She's been through a lot and given her best." He shook his head. "Not many of us left, you know."

"No, quite . . ."

The ruined mass in the box resembled little the creature he had seen a few days earlier. The legs seemed fairly intact, though the right one bent at an angle indicating a break. The torso, though, had been ripped open and the internal organs pecked out and destroyed. The arms had been separated at the shoulders and only one, badly mangled, lay in the box. The face was caved in, both eyes gone, which saddened Fox the most. He recalled the intelligence in those eyes. Blood had soiled and darkened the scaly feathers. He lifted it slightly to see the brilliant wings, but all he found were spiny shafts extending from between the shoulders. A few of the colorful plumes were gathered to one side.

"You hear stories," Paley said, "but when you get older you pay less and less attention. Nowadays you don't hear much about them anymore, but when I was boy . . ."

"This is most unfortunate, Mr. Paley."

"I do understand, Reverend. I can't ask for anything for this."

"Not at all, Mr. Paley. It has a skeleton . . . hmm . . ." He prodded in the chest cavity. "Well, it's not a bird . . ."

"No?"

"No, look. No wishbone. All birds have wishbones." Fox stood. "I shall still be glad to take the remains. Of course, there must be some adjustment to the price."

Paley nodded, not rising. "I understand."

"No need to be so forlorn, Mr. Paley. There may still be considerable scientific value in it."

"I'm sorry, Reverend. I'm not myself." He glanced at the box and shook his head. "It's not that. Not *only* that, you see." He waved the letter. "My boys. I just learned that they've both been killed."

"Oh, my. I am sorry, Mr. Paley. Forgive me, I had no idea."

"Don't bother yourself, Reverend. It's just—well, there's not many of us left anymore. I s'ppose I'll have to sell the place now. No one really to leave it to." He looked down again at the box. "What do you s'ppose it was, Reverend?"

"I don't know, Mr. Paley."

Paley stood there for a few seconds, then sat back down. He opened the letter on his lap and started to read it. Fox noted a tear tracing its way down his cheek. He took the cheque from his pocket and laid it beside Paley. Then he picked up the box, bid the farmer good day, and made his way down the ladder one handed.

Daniel Abraham grew up in the southwest desert. A recent attendee of Clarion West, he is presently putting the final touches on a novel, working full time as a computer technician, and considering the spiritual advantages of adding a B.A. in art history to his present B.S. in biology.

Although "Chimera 8" was his first sale, two other stories have been published in *Asimov's Science Fiction*. About his story, Abraham notes that "humans are presently facing an age in which massive extinctions are coming at the same time as the creation and even patenting of new species. As we take over the job of designing life, the idea of 'endangered species' becomes much more ambiguous."

CHIMERA 8

DANIEL ABRAHAM

Mack leaned toward the screen, the remote tight in his hand, and watched the end of the tape. The field team had forty seconds, but they didn't know it.

"No, I'm serious," the white boy on the tape said. The flimsy cloth of the tent fluttered behind him. "The blacks have to be part of things, too. I mean you can't solve a problem with only half the people involved."

An Asian woman appeared on the screen and mouthed the word *American*. The man holding the camera laughed deep and low. Mack didn't know anything more than that laugh, but he liked the man.

The sound came sudden and sharp. Like a giant, coughing. The laughter died.

"What the hell was that?" the Asian woman demanded and the tape cut out. Mack thumbed the rewind. The three returned to life, speeding backwards a few seconds. He let the tape play.

". . . half the people involved."

Mack closed his eyes. The beautiful laugh. The cough. He touched the rewind. Laughter. The cough. *What the hell was that?*

"What are you doing, sweet thing?" Erin asked.

Mack sat back and thumbed off the tape so she wouldn't see exactly what he was looking at, wouldn't hear the cough.

"Watching the Walker Island tape," he said. "Trying to find . . . something. I don't know."

Erin nodded as she walked past the desk. Her hair was down from its usual tight braid. Her robe—blue silk—flowed back from her shoulders, caressing air. She was much more casual about nudity than he was. Her body was strong and efficient. Mack had always thought of himself as athletic, but she could make him feel soft.

As regional security chief, she had larger quarters and more comfortable furniture than all but the most illustrious scientist. There was room for her to stretch as she walked to the small kitchen and turned off the light. Mack found he'd been spending very little time in his own four small rooms adjoining the labs.

"Don't stay up too late," she said, closing the window against the sounds of the rain forest night. "The transport trucks leave for the coast at seven."

"Seems early," Mack said.

"You don't have to go, you know," she said. "If you don't want to."

"What? And miss the case of the missing anteaters?"

"It's the case of the missing field scientists now," Erin said.

"I'm in. I need a break," Mack said. "Tracking poachers might be fun. Besides, you'll be there."

Erin chuckled as she walked over to him.

"You say the nicest shit."

She kissed him on the precise spot where his close-cut, sand-colored hair was growing thin and went upstairs to the bedroom. Mack ejected the tape, handling it gently as he put it back in its case. As if the black plastic were poison.

The half second of rough noise before the tape went blank could have been anything, he told himself. Walker Island was hundreds of miles away from Peru and the Manu rain forest. But in his mind, the tape still played. The sound grew clearer to him each time, and more familiar.

He put the tape case on the table with the rest of the briefing materials—schedules, maps of the island, transport manifests—and turned out the lights. At the foot of the stairs, he paused. The bedroom was already dark. Silently, he opened the front door and slipped out into the darkness.

He walked, gravel crunching under his feet, rather than risk her hearing the car. Rain still dripped steadily from the forest canopy though the clouds had cleared away. Birds cried out in the darkness, and insects buzzed close to his head. If he paid attention, he could tell the chimeras from their natural cousins. Chimeric insects were quieter, and the calls of the modified birds were harsher. He walked through the cool night air, and in ten minutes he saw the light from the lab's windows glimmering through the trees.

The Manu Reservation labs were the same as all the genetic laboratories at all the reconstruction sites in the world. Arabian desert, toxic Mississippi swamp, or rebuilt Peruvian rain forest; they all had the same cream and sand paint and the same layout—a global scientific suburb. Only nature changed them. Tiny vines pressed up from the ground and trailed up the walls, black in the dim night. Moss grew like a bruise on the south side where the sun rarely burned it clean.

He keyed himself in and walked down the sterile corridors to the cream-colored lab door with his name beside it. Fluorescent lights still flickered to life as he closed the door behind him.

The chimera in the cage was about the same size and metabolism as the jaguars whose niche it filled, a predator as near to perfect as Mack could design. Its coat was brindled black and brown, short hair as coarse as thin wire. A blunt jaw covered sharp, ripping teeth—a carnivore's mouth. Its head was larger and rounder than a hunting cat's, and the forward-set eyes glowed golden in dim light. It blinked in the sudden light and sat up, smiling almost like a dog, though Mack had hardly used any canine DNA. Rotating ears tracked Mack as he crossed the lab.

"Hey, kiddo," Mack said. "You ready for dinner?"

The chimera huffed and stood, its thin tail rigidly out at attention. Mack could feel the gold eyes following him as he took a slab of meat from the refrigerator. The chimera skittered in excitement, and Mack could hear it sniffing the air.

"I've got a new spice for you tonight," Mack said as he dropped the meat onto a steel tray. "Just a little something to help you sleep. We're going on a trip tomorrow, and I don't want anyone to know I took you."

The chimera huffed again. Mack took an oral sedative capsule out of the supply closet, broke the gel capsule, and sprinkled the powder over the meat.

"All right," Mack said. "One steak, very rare."

He walked over to the cage and carefully placed the tray outside it, just too far for the chimera's raccoon-like fingers to reach.

The animal sniffed and looked up at him, confused. And a little hurt, Mack thought. It reached out, its fingertips brushing the tray, its shoulder straining against the bars.

"What's the matter, kiddo? Can't reach?" Mack asked.

The chimera looked up, then reached out again. It was getting frustrated. Mack stepped forward and squatted, his eyes on a level with the animal's. Again the doglike smile. Mack pushed the tray a little closer, then, as it reached out, he pulled the tray out of reach again.

The chimera's smile vanished, frustration on its features. It leaned forward, weight shifting over its forelegs, back legs cocked to spring. It bared its teeth.

"Come on," Mack said quietly. "Talk to me."

The chimera barked, a sudden, rough sound.

Like a giant, coughing.

Mack's stomach turned to lead. He pressed his lips thinner as he pushed the tray up against the bars.

"I'm sorry," he said. "I was just testing a theory. No harm meant."

The chimera pulled the meat through the bars and wolfed it down in four violent chewing motions, its jaw working the flesh, crushing blood out of it. Mack watched, fascinated, as the animal licked its muzzle and lay down, starting to groom itself with long, agile digits.

"Good boy," Mack said. "You're a good boy. Go to sleep. We've got a big day tomorrow."

The chimera smiled again, and Mack leaned forward, reaching through the bars to stroke its dark head. The animal pressed into the caress.

Mack found Erin at the rail of the transport ship, looking out at the water. Her eyes flickered across the horizon. Mack read the tension in her shoulders and her restless stance. At times like this, she made him uneasy.

He cleared his throat. She glanced over to him and smiled.

"Hey, darling," she said over the rush of wind and water. "Find anything in the notes?"

"Nothing new," he said. "You?"

"Still nothing," she said. "The insectivores started disappearing two months ago, but the satellites don't show heat trails for any poaching ships in the area for three months. I've got them searching back for six, but I don't think we're going to find anything. I don't know how they're getting to the island."

"Planes?"

"Nope, thought of that," Erin said. "Either someone got dropped off on the island a long damn time ago and is lying low or . . ."

She looked away.

"There's a rumor," she said. "Some people say that Earth First got a submarine."

"You're still thinking sabotage, then?"

"There's no other motive," Erin said, shrugging. "We'll see. The new batch of insectivores all have tracking implants. The kind you use in migration studies. Nothing much. If they leave the island or someone starts rounding them up in one place, we'll know."

"Maybe the animals are disappearing for a natural reason," Mack ventured.

Erin laughed.

"You're an optimist, sweetie," she said. "There's no nature out there we didn't build. It's barren. There's nothing to eat these little fuckers within two hundred miles. Unless they've all of a sudden started swimming and the sharks got them. And disease . . . well, I'd been hoping for disease until we lost the field team."

"Still no sign of them?"

"Nothing," Erin said.

Mack leaned against the rail, his hands pushed deep into his pockets, and tried not to think about the people on the tape. The wind smelled good—salty and fresh—and the sun flashed on the water. He tried to make his voice sound natural when he spoke.

"I've been thinking about disease a lot, recently," he said. "I'm a little worried about the eight series."

"Your carnivores?" Erin asked. "Are they getting sick?"

"No, nothing yet," Mack said. "I just . . . may have overlooked something. I'm going to run some tests when we get back home."

Erin put a hand to his shoulder. The concern in her eyes surprised him. He touched her hand and smiled, but he couldn't keep looking at her. He kissed her cheek and went back in. He walked toward the stateroom, but only paused at the door. Holding himself carefully, he went to the barn-sized animal hold.

There among the cages filled with chimeric anteaters, he sat on the deck and cradled his head in his hands. Lying to her was harder than he'd expected. But if he'd told her his suspicious, he'd have to tell her everything. As well as he knew her, he wasn't sure what she would do.

And there was still a chance that he was wrong.

The Walker Island site was simple—almost cartoonish—compared to their work at the rain forest sites in Peru. But in Peru, they'd still had an ecosystem to work from—a shuddering, failing one broken into disconnected patches by misuse, but it had been something to start with. It had been a question of shoring up what was there, filling niches where critical animals had gone extinct.

With Walker Island, like Easter Island to the west and Ducie and Henderson to the east, they were starting from scratch. The islands were deserts in the ocean. A few highly salt-tolerant grasses and shrubs with low soil requirements made the whole of the plant life. Then a mixture of chimeric and natural insects living off the plants, and at the top of the brief food chain, a single species of chimeric, slow-metabolism, low-representative rate insectivores built from a *Myrmecophaga jubata* base and altered so slightly it still looked like an anteater. It was the simplest artificial ecosystem that could be held stable.

Until the anteaters began to vanish. And then the people.

The field base was a rough group of buildings on the southern

shore, a town whose population hovered around forty, and that
nobody called home. There were barracks for the field teams that
rotated through, and separate quarters for visiting dignitaries and
permanent field staff. A shack housed the generator, and storage
sheds held a three month supply of food and fresh water, in case of
emergency.

The place was spare and smelled of dust and machine oil. A
six-foot chain link fence divided the camp from the bare island.
Mack didn't understand that—there should have been nothing to
guard against, nothing to keep out—but he was grateful.

Erin and the base manager, a harried Korean man with an
American accent, went out in a Jeep as soon as the transport
arrived. Erin wanted to resurvey the site where the field team had
vanished, hoping for evidence. Hauling the cage and the still-
sedated chimera to one of the emergency rations storerooms was
hard to do by himself. Mack's status as a scientist and Erin's lover
was such that none of the support staff questioned his activities,
but he didn't dare ask for their help.

He made dinner on the propane stove in her quarters, pesto
fettucini with a loaf of bread he'd taken from the lab commissary
in Peru and a chilled bottle of white wine. It was almost sundown
when Erin stalked in with dusty clothes and a dark expression,
dropped into her seat, and started eating without comment.

"No luck, then," Mack said. "Nothing new?"

"Not shit," she agreed. "No tracks, no spent shells, no bodies,
no ransom demands. Just a ripped tent, a little blood, and no people.
They didn't even take the Jeep. No hint who took them or why. I
mean, maybe terrorism—detain a few field crews, and get everyone nervous. But how did they get off the island? Or if they're still
here, where are they hiding?"

"You're thinking the submarine," Mack said.

"Yeah, I am. Nothing else makes sense."

"I'm sorry."

"But then, why Walker?" Erin went on, more than half to herself. "What we're doing here doesn't displace any native species. There's no existing ecology to screw up. It's too far from any viable habitats to risk contamination. It's completely inoffensive. It doesn't make sense, Mack. I don't get it."

"I don't know," he said.

"And what did they do with the insectivores? Ship them out? Kill them? And if they killed them, where are the bodies?"

"Buried, maybe," Mack said. Some predators do that, he added to himself. Bury their wastes when they've finished eating.

"I don't know," Erin said. "Something's . . . something isn't fitting together on this one. I'm missing something. Something obvious."

Mack poured her wine. She had a lovely face, lips he had kissed how many hundred times, and eyes that shone with a sharp intelligence. He could watch her stalking the problem, and it made him nervous and admiring at the same time.

"Do you ever wonder if they're right?" he asked, breaking her train of thought.

Erin looked up at him, confused.

"Who?"

"Earth First. The anti-transgenics lobby. All of them."

"No," she said, a trace of annoyance in her voice. "Why? Do you?"

"I mean, you could say they have a point," Mack said, looking out at the night sky. "We're building new organisms all the time, trying to fill niches. We don't really have time to see what's going to happen before we put them out there. And even if we ran everything through a strong statistical model, we'd probably be wrong. We *might* be doing more damage than good."

"So what's the option? Let the system collapse?" Erin said. "We do what we have to. The die-off is our fault. We're the only ones who can fix it."

"But there are limits. There are some things we just don't do, even if it would help."

Erin made an impatient sound in the back of her throat and shook her head.

"We don't use human genome sources, for example," he said and cleared his throat.

"No, but why would we want to?" Erin said dismissively. "It'd be the worst thing we could do."

"Intelligence is a good trait," Mack said, a defensive tone slipping into his voice. "Think about the jaguars. If they'd been smarter, they might not have died off. We select from other species for the traits we want. Humans are the smartest animal. It would make sense."

"It's different."

"Is it? I wonder why we draw the line one place and not another. Don't you?"

"We draw the line there because if we were messing with human DNA, we'd be crucified," Erin said.

"It's just a political decision," Mack said. "There's no *real* reason for it."

"There's a real reason for it. Political reasons are real," Erin said. "Besides, working with animals isn't like working with people. We're people. They're animals. You just don't mix the two."

"I don't see why not."

"There's a thousand reasons. Number one is that you'll hurt the project, and none of the other ones matter."

Mack looked down. He knew that she was right. And more important, he knew what her priorities would be, if she found out. There was nothing he could say.

"Sorry," Erin said. "Didn't mean to snap at you. I'm a little tense, is all."

Mack forced a smile.

"No offense taken," he said. "You've got a lot on your mind."

"Look, sweetie, I've got to go arrange tomorrow's schedule with the site manager," Erin said. Her voice was stern, but he could hear the hint of concern in it, afraid to hurt his feelings "Afterwards, I'm going to need a little down time. I don't want you to feel like . . ."

Mack raised a hand.

"I knew I was just coming as a hanger-on," he said. "I had them put all my things in different quarters. I don't want to be in the way."

"Thanks," she said. "You're one of the good ones, Mack."

She wiped her mouth with the napkin, a sharp, almost percussive motion, and stood up. Mack turned to watch her go. She paused at the door with the air of remembering something and turned back.

"Hey," she said. "Thanks for dinner."

"De nada," Mack said, and waved her on.

Alone, he cleaned the place carefully. He wasn't hungry, though he hadn't eaten anything. He threw the remains of her meal away.

Night on the island was warmer than the rain forest. It was the first time in months he'd been out from under the canopy of trees, and the sky seemed unbearably wide. Stars glittered and shone, and a near-full moon lit the flat island in monochrome.

He changed into field gear. The maps and notes on his computer showed the patterns of the ocean current around the island and the roads and tracks, such as they were, that the field crews used. If he hurried, he could cover several of the most promising sites before morning. The Jeep he'd set aside had everything he could think of—a winch, a spare can of gasoline, an axe, a rifle. He drove out of the encampment calmly, as if he knew exactly what he was doing.

The rough track to the water was hardly more than two long bare patches in the low grass a Jeep's width apart and a tire wide. Mack hummed to himself over the engine noise as he drove. His eyes flickered across the empty landscape, looking for the shore.

The first likely site was a small cove ten minutes out from the base. The smells of dust and ocean mixed in the air, and the surf made a constant background hush. He looked through the dry, twiggy clumps of bushes, but none of the undergrowth was large enough to provide cover, to hide the evidence he still only half-believed was there. He drove on, holding near the coast.

When dawn approached, he hadn't covered half of his most likely sites. His eyes were gritty, and the sterile land of grasses and scrub had lost its beauty hours before. No birds sang as the first light touched the eastern skyline, and the silence was eerie.

Halfway back to the camp, he stopped the Jeep at the shore and watched the lazy swell of the water against the sand. He pushed his mind hundreds of miles across the ocean to the rain forest that he had helped remake and the series eight carnivores that perched near the top of its food chain. His carnivores. His children.

He started up the Jeep and headed back to the encampment before Erin and the others woke up and found that he had gone.

"Insomnia," Mack said, pouring himself another cup of coffee. "Happens sometimes. I'll take a nap later. I'm fine."

Erin touched his shoulder, reassured, and turned back to the manager.

"We can deliver the insectivores to the spot you want, but it's going to take a couple days," he said. "We've only got two pickup trucks, and releasing the animals takes a while."

"Can we use the Jeeps?" Erin asked.

"We can, but you can only fit a couple cages into a Jeep. Doesn't seem like it'd be worth it."

"Okay," Erin said. "Two days. Then we'll start tracking them."

"I'm sorry," Mack said. "What's the plan?"

"We'll see where they're disappearing," Erin said, "and when. With any luck, that'll lead us to the poachers."

"And what then?"

"It depends," Erin said.

"They killed three of my people," the manager said, crossing his arms.

There was a slight pause, half a beat, before Erin said. "We don't know that yet. Not for sure." Mack could tell from her voice that she was sure. The manager looked down.

"I'll go make sure the animals are loaded," he said. Erin nodded, and he left, closing the door hard behind him. Erin let out a long, controlled breath. Mack raised an eyebrow.

"He wants military action now," she said. "Full sweep of the island. And a constant patrol looking for ships. He even talked about putting anti-sub mines around the coast."

"Seems like a lot for a few anteaters," Mack said.

"It's not about the animals. It's about the field team. I'd do it, too. If I had the resources. There are still no ransom demands, Mack. These aren't poachers or saboteurs we're dealing with. They're killers." Erin downed the last of her coffee. "I want you out of here with the transport."

"But . . ."

"I misjudged this situation. I thought there would be ransom demands by the time we got here. Tracking poachers is one thing. Murder makes it something else. If you're here, I'm going to be worried about you, and I can't afford the distraction."

"Then why did you let me come out in the first place?" he snapped.

"It was a mistake," Erin admitted. "I wanted you here for personal reasons, and it was a bad decision. I'm sorry. The transport's out of here tomorrow morning."

Mack frowned into his coffee. Leave with the transport? That didn't leave him enough time.

"I don't like this," he said.

"I know. I'm sorry. Look, we can talk about it tonight, when I get back, if you want."

Mack shook his head. Erin softened for a moment, just a shift in the way she held herself, then her professional veneer fell back into place. She stood, pulling on her holster and her field jacket, and left without speaking. Mack ate silently at the empty table. Eggs, fruit, coffee. He had until tomorrow morning. He wiped his mouth and went to his room.

The amphetamines in his kit were meant for the chimeras, but they'd work just as well on a human. He sat on the edge of the bed as the fatigue flowed out of him. When he was feeling awake and sober, he took a slab of meat sealed in a plastic bag and went out to the storage shed.

The golden eyes glowed in the dimness, following him as he opened the food bag with his pocket knife. The chimera huffed and held the bars of its cage in thin, strong fingers. Mack walked over and held out the flesh.

Sniffing excitedly, the animal reached out and took the meat. Its hand brushed his, and a shiver passed down his spine. The chimera ate quickly, then began to groom itself, its fingers running over its muzzle and ears like a cat's paws.

"Good boy," Mack said. "You're a very good boy. I'm going out to look one more time, and if I don't find anything, we'll go home, okay? We'll just go home."

The chimera huffed contentedly and rocked back on its haunches. Mack reached through the bars and stroked the short, wiry hair, feeling the bunched muscle beneath the skin.

The chimera smiled and took his hand in its own. Mack sat there for a moment, his fingers wrapped by the long, black hand. Then, trembling, he went out into the light.

He waited until the trucks were gone, filled the tank of his Jeep, and went out. It was a little after three in the afternoon when, stumbling through a thick patch of bushes on the north end of the island, he found the raft in a relatively dense clump of bushes.

It was crude, but solid. A deck of thin branches and the trunks of small trees lashed between two wooden pontoons—tree trunks that had been hollowed out by strong, raccoon-like fingers. He recognized the wood as a modified balsa, grown at the edges of the Peruvian cloud forests and light enough to carry through the passes to the sea. It was dry enough that it could have been out of the water for weeks. Mack sat beside the raft and wept.

The vines and strips of bark that held the wood together were tough. It took Mack an hour with his ax to pull the raft apart and drag it down to the sea. He watched the pieces float out on the receding tide, driftwood.

He waited in his quarters until it was past midnight. Then, as quietly as he could manage, he went out to storage. The chimera poked its nose through the bars, sniffing the night air as Mack struggled to load it into the back of the Jeep. The night's drive was short, now that he knew where he was going.

The moon was beautiful, and the smell of the sea was thick and somehow comforting.

When he reached the clump of bushes that had hidden the raft, he killed the motor and sat for a while. The chimera huffed in its cage, curious and impatient. Mack watched the moonlight on the water, listened to the surf and the wind. Slowly, took out the vial and flicked it hard with his finger until the concentrated virus at the bottom was suspended in the broth. When he opened the bag of meat, the chimera started to skitter excitedly. Mack poured the viral culture onto the flesh and dropped the meat to the sandy beach. It only took a second to open the cage.

The chimera blinked at him, then carefully stepped out, looking at Mack with its ears forward in disbelief.

"Go ahead, kiddo," Mack said. "You're going to be better at finding them than any of us will. Go on."

The chimera, still unsure, went over to the meat, snapping it down and swallowing. Three days, Mack thought. Three days of freedom—a whole lifetime. He closed the cage.

"Good boy," Mack said. "Go on, now. Go find them."

The chimera smiled and butted gently against Mack's leg. He scratched its head for the last time, and then it was gone, bounding across the sand, fast as a cat. Just the way he'd designed it.

And in three days, it would be dead. Any others it had found would die soon after. No more insectivores would vanish, and even if they eventually found the bodies, they'd only ask who brought carnivores to Walker. Without the raft, there was no reason to think they'd brought themselves. The mystery would fade into the background. And when he got back to the mainland, he'd do it all again.

Mack sat in the moonlight with the ghosts of all the eight series that were going to have to die—that he was going to have to kill. He wondered how many there really were—five hundred, a thousand. All of them, however many there were, all of them would sicken and die.

He started the Jeep and headed back to camp. No lights were on when he arrived. He parked and put the suddenly light cage back into storage. In his mind, he saw the chimera bounding across the hills, taking the slow, stupid insectivores in its mouth and shaking them, smiling as it groomed its bloody snout.

Erin was asleep on his bed. She still wore her field clothes, and her holster and pistol were on the table. He sat beside her, and the shifting of the mattress woke her.

"Hey," she said. "Where were you?"

"Walking around," he said. "I was having trouble sleeping again."

"I wanted to talk to you," she said, taking his hand in hers. "I was afraid I pissed you off."

"No," he said. "No. I understand. This isn't really my place after all. I'll run on home like a good boy."

"Thanks, Mack. Something's bothering you, though."

"No, I'm fine."

She sat up. In the darkness, he couldn't see her eyes.

"It's your carnivores. The eight series. Isn't it?" she asked.

Mack's mouth tasted like a penny. "It's worse than you told me," she said.

"I . . . I don't know . . . Oh, Erin. Oh, hell."

Tears stung the corners of his eyes, and he pressed his face into his hands. She knew. She'd known all along. The relief was more painful than he'd imagined.

"It's all right," she whispered. "It'll be all right. It's okay. I thought you weren't telling me everything."

"I'm sorry," he whispered. "I'm sorry, Erin. I should have. I'm so sorry."

"It's all right. Just tell me how bad it is."

"It's bad," he said. "It's really bad."

"On the ship, you said you'd been thinking about disease," she said. "It's their immune system, isn't it?"

He was silent. A sickly smile pulled at his lips as the secret folded back over him.

"Yes," he said. The lie sounded wooden and forced in his ears. "I think there's a kind of distemper they may be particularly susceptible to. I've seen some in other animals at the Peruvian sites, and I'm afraid they'll carry it to the carnivores."

"Well, we'll do what we can to stop it," Erin said. "It'll be okay, Mack. I'll do anything I can just as soon as I get back from this. And you start when the transport gets back. Maybe we can trap them—inoculate them against it."

"Yes," Mack said. "Capture, inject, release. That was what I'd been thinking."

They were silent together for a long time. Erin's hand pressed against his back, rubbing slowly.

"I know you're proud of the eight series. You put a lot of time into them, but it's better to deal with things straight on. It takes a brave man to admit he screwed up," she said.

"Thank you, Erin," he whispered. "Thanks."

"You're one of the good ones, Mack. One of the best."

Michael Cadnum has published sixteen novels, including, most recently, *In a Dark Wood, The Book of the Lion*, and *Rundown*. Cadnum's short fiction has been published in various volumes of the Datlow-Windling adult–fairy tale anthology series and in their children's–fairy tale anthology *A Wolf at the Door*. His short fiction has also been chosen for reprint in *The Year's Best Fantasy and Horror*.

The creature in "Bite the Hand" is a centaur (this is not giving anything away), and myths about centaurs date back to pre-Homeric times. While Chiron was a famously wise centaur who could practice medicine, most centaurs were thought to be wild and over-fond of wine, and prone to rape and generally impulsive behavior.

BITE THE HAND

MICHAEL CADNUM

The customs declaration read: *mummified specimen.*

What are our border officials doing, allowing such shriveled nightmares into the land of the free, I wanted to ask. Raymond had heard the delivery truck, and was dashing down the stairs.

"Weren't you afraid, living with such strange relics?" my current gentleman friend inquires, and I smile, in my special way, and allow that I'm afraid of nothing.

"It's here at last!" Raymond cried, reading the shipping label.

Professors have a good deal of idle time on their hands, and they get paid well, plenty of time for expensive and pointless behavior. Raymond scurried and got his pocket knife, and then ran to get his claw hammer and his screwdriver, and at last had to get the crowbar from the garage. "I've always dreamed of owning one of these!" he exclaimed. "Oh, this is a wonder indeed!"

He even talked like a book.

It was half horse, half man, no question. A centaur, found by one of the curiosity merchants Raymond e-mails, "the last one of its kind."

Raymond had to see the desiccated mannikin mounted in a bell jar, so the department chairperson and visiting scholars could peer at it and say, "I thought they were mythical" during brunch the following Sunday.

Both man-front and horse-rear were midget. The medical school sent its department vice-director over to look for sutures and tell-tale joiner's glue, but this was real, a man's upper body and a stallion's nether, and all I could keep murmuring was, "Isn't it a marvel?"

After the caterer's minions cleaned up the quiche and bubbly, I put the thing back onto the shelf with the plaster cast of Bigfoot's private parts, found in a mud wallow near Mount Shasta, always a distress to me whenever I happen upon it. But Raymond got that stubborn little Mount Rushmore expression on his face, and said, "Leave it where we can see it."

It was in the local newspaper that week, *English Prof Bags Horse-man,* and there was Raymond's face, looking very much the Andrew Marvell scholar, his smile gracing the Elm Hill *News Press* and proving that at least one member of the ivory tower set had world and time enough to add to his collection of "oddities from around the globe."

This was just one more, to go along with the balding unicorn, with that suspicious seam twixt horn and head, and that mummi-fied elf, looking very much like the permanent unborn human. Raymond was a man who fed his pet lorikeets pistachio nuts, handfuls of them while the yellow and lime-green charmers hopped all over him, imitating his gentle voice, "Sweet little darlings," a hopeless fool through and through. Women found him endlessly forgivable, regardless of his gaffes and whimsies.

I know how to survive married life: you keep your mouth shut, smile, and bide your time. My plan was to fake a burglary, snap up some insurance money, and eventually have a nice three-story Victorian a woman could live in without listening to English department gossip every night.

The afternoon the housekeeper complained it took me awhile to understand the enormity, as my mom used to say. "It moved!" Dora said, all hips and breasts, and I wondered if Raymond had dropped home early and slipped back into one of his old regrettable habits, like the sort that caused all that misunderstanding outside the ladies' room in the city park.

"It moved!" said Dora, a tireless woman of Norwegian descent, always reporting to me what she watched on TV the night before. "The centaur wiggled!" she exclaimed.

Raymond had once commented that Dora smelled of marijuana, and I took note that Raymond had gotten close enough to scent Dora's personal odor, whatever it might be.

Furthermore, it sounded as though Dora had said that the *center* wiggled, and I put down my tea cup in a mood of confused despair. "At me!" she added, and I took a moment to consider my life, how my late mother had warned me against marrying a nervous academic. "His head is in the clouds," she had opined, a woman who had run a shipping company after a load of kapok fell out of the boxcar, suffocating Dad.

Raymond is handsome in a careless way, nice eyebrows, broad shoulders. He had not wanted children, and neither had I, but he had his birds and his stuffed were-pig and his satyr's hoof instead. I had nothing but Raymond, a man who got excited reading bone catalogs.

"What has he done?" I asked, meaning: I would divorce the neurasthenic freak at last.

"I was dusting it with the duster," Dora said, hand to breast. "And it bit me!"

I marched down the hall, and there was the centaur, half-human, half-pony, looking stiff and still. "What happened to the glass covering?" I asked. The bell jar had vanished, and Dora explained that the "little guy" had looked in need of a whisk with the ostrich feathers.

I gave the withered horror a closer examination, and he did look a little dusty in the crevices, especially down around his private regions. So I borrowed a dust cloth from Dora, gave the little fellow's face and other areas a gentle wipe, and he bit me. A nip, right on my knuckle.

I was stunned.

And before I knew what I was doing, I hit back.

"It was suspended animation," Dora was saying as I realized what I had done. She has tapes of *Nova* going back ten years. She knows all about galaxies at the edge of the universe, cloned goats, psychic experiments. "It wasn't really dead!" she said. "Only suspended!"

Red blood on my hands, I fired Dora, and then when Dora insisted that she would sue me for violating a verbal contract, I hired her back again, on condition that she would resuscitate the bloody man-half on the floor.

Dora gave the gory little grotesque the kiss of life, but it didn't work. She kept looking up with a small smear of blood on her mouth, saying "You killed him! It's murder, Mrs. Quince."

"Self-defense," I said.

"He was just coming back to life after an eon," said Dora.

I considered my position.

"He was warmed by human contact," Dora was saying, "and you—"

I know how to survive married life, and I know how to manage a reversal. I crumpled up my face, and wept.

Dora put her arm around me, walked me down the stairs, saying that she had spoken too abruptly. "We should always count to ten when we are mad," she said.

Raymond popped home from his graduate seminar on the cavalier poets just then, brim full of the latest news on metaphor. He caught one look at my tear-stained face, and Dora's near-swoon of consolation, and dropped his backpack full of quarterlies.

"Dora wrecked the centaur," I said, talking fast. "She broke its neck—we mustn't fire Dora because she has two kids in junior high but we should insist she have treatment for her problem."

Dora took in a sharp breath, but her words stuck.

Raymond took one look at the remains of the centaur, and he was speechless with anguish. I failed to see the point of all his sorrow. It was dead now, and it had been dead when he ordered it from Brussels, except that it had not been absolutely deceased in the strictest sense.

"Blood," he said at last. "Like a living thing."

No ordeal is so crushing that it cannot be finessed. Even the load of kapok that fell upon my dad could have been survived by a man less afraid of closed-in places.

"It was imperfectly mummified," I said. "Send it back."

"It moved its head and looked at me," Dora insisted.

I raised one eyebrow, in my special way.

Dora fell into heavier and heavier dependencies on whatever drugs are in fashion. She took to accusing me of cruelty in letters to the Elm Hill *News Press*, the editor of which has become a kind and well-spoken gentleman friend of mine. She took to writing long declarations of love to Raymond, portions of which he quotes to his graduate seminar as examples of hyperbole. And when Dora gets out of the medical center she will move to Florida with her two foster-home-addled teens.

Raymond has agreed to an amicable divorce, and has moved to a double-wide trailer at the edge of the reservoir. He has even sworn off his fondness for collecting, after the *News Press* ran an article describing each and every one of his curiosities as frauds.

"How could they know?" Raymond was moaning, the last time he dropped by. "Where did they obtain all their information?"

He has sold off his treasures, each collectible grotesque.

All but one—which he could not find.

This house is lovely, and I enjoy the quiet. I stay in bed late, and take tea by the bay window, watching the sun through the elms and the sycamores. If only I could sleep better at night, and did not have dreams.

I wake alone, and sit bolt upright in the broad, cold bed. I do not utter a word, knowing how futile speech can often be, and every night I wake to a sound down the corridors through the dark, the undying music of hooves.

M. Shayne Bell has had short fiction and poetry published in *Amazing Stories, Asimov's SF Magazine, Fantasy and Science Fiction, Tomorrow SF, Gothic.Net, Realms of Fantasy,* and in ten anthologies, including *Starlight 2, Future Earths: Under African Skies, Simulations: Fifteen Tales of Virtual Reality,* and *War of the Worlds: Global Dispatches.* He published one novel, *Nicoji,* and edited the anthology *Washed by a Wave of Wind: Science Fiction from the Corridor,* for which he received the Association of Mormon Letters Award for editorial excellence. In 1991, he received a Creative Writing Fellowship from the National Endowment for the Arts. Bell was poetry editor of *Sunstone* magazine for six years.

He and his partner live in Salt Lake City, but Bell grew up on a ranch on the Snake River in Idaho, a place with hundreds of acres of forest, islands in the river, wildlife everywhere.

About the genesis of his story he says, "A few years back, I visited the Conservatory in San Francisco's Golden Gate Park. The rooms in this glittering glass-and-steel Victorian, modeled after Kew Gardens in London, are one tropical garden after another: each hotter and more humid—and more fragrant. And there, in planters and displays and climate-controlled glass boxes are ferns and flowering trees and orchids alive nowhere else in the world: They are extinct in the lands where they evolved. All that's left are these few. The rooms are hushed as if, though everything in them is alive, they are mausoleums. The latest estimate is that over one thousand plants go extinct each year now because of human activities (the natural rate is one to ten). Did we lose the cure for cancer yesterday? The cure for AIDS today around noon? We'll never know. The people who run places like the Conservatory will manage to save a few species. But I hope maybe some plants will be saved in other odd places besides."

THE THING ABOUT BENNY

M. Shayne Bell

Abba, Fältskog Listing 47: "Dancing Queen," day 3. En route from the airport.

Benny said, apropos of nothing, "The bridge is the most important part of a song, don't you think?"

"Oh, yeah," I said, me trying to drive in all that traffic and us late, as usual. "That's all I think about when I'm hearing music—those important bridges."

"No, really." Benny looked at me, earphones firmly covering his ears, eyes dark and kind of surprised. It was a weird look. Benny never has much to say, but when he does the company higher-ups told me I was supposed to take notice, try to figure out how he does what he does.

The light turned green. I drove us onto North Temple, downtown Salt Lake not so far off now. "Bridges in songs have something to do with extinct plants?" I asked.

"It's all in the music," he said, looking back at the street and sitting very, very still.

"Messages about plants are in the music?" I asked.

But he was gone, back in that trance he'd been in since LA. Besides, we were minutes from our first stop. He always gets so nervous just before we start work. "What if we find something?" he'd asked me once, and I'd said, "Isn't that the point?"

He started rubbing his sweaty hands up and down his pant legs. I could hear the tinny melody out of his earphones. It was "Dancing Queen" week. Benny'd set his player on endless repeat, and he listened to "Dancing Queen" over and over again on the plane, in the car, in the offices we went to, during meals, in bed with the earphones on his head. That's all he'd listen to for one week. Then he'd change to a different Abba song on Sunday. When he'd gone through every Abba song ever recorded, he'd start over.

"Check in," Benny said.

"What?"

"The Marriott."

I slammed brakes, did a U-turn, did like he'd asked. That was my job, even if we were late. Benny had to use the toilet, and he would not use toilets in the offices we visited.

I carried the bags up to our rooms—no bellhop needed, thank you. What's a personal assistant for if not to lug your luggage around? I called Utah Power and Light to tell them we were still coming. Then I waited for Benny in the lobby. My mind kept playing "Dancing Queen" over and over. "It's all in the music," Benny'd said, but I failed to understand how anybody, Benny included, could find directions in fifty-year-old Abba songs to the whereabouts of plants extinct in the wild.

Benny tapped me on the shoulder. "It's close enough that we can walk," he said. "Take these."

He handed me his briefcase and a stack of World Botanics pamphlets and motioned to the door. I always had to lead the way. Benny wouldn't walk with me. He walked behind me, four or five steps back, Abba blasting in his ears. It was no use trying to get him to do differently. I gave the car keys to the hotel car people so they could park the rental, and off we went.

Utah Power and Light was a first visit. We'd do a get-acquainted sweep of the cubicles and offices, then come back the next day for a detailed study. Oh sure, after Benny'd found the *Rhapis excelsa* in a technical writer's cubicle in the Transamerica Pyramid, everybody with a plant in a pot had hoped to be the one with the cancer cure. But most African violets are just African violets. They aren't going to cure anything. Still, the hopeful had driven college botany professors around the world nuts with their pots of begonias and canary ivy and sword ferns.

But they were out there. Plants extinct in the wild had been kept alive in the oddest places, including cubicles in office buildings. Benny'd found more than his share. Even I take "Extract of *Rhapis excelsa*" treatment one week each year like everybody else. Who wants a heart attack? Who doesn't feel better with his arteries unclogged? People used to go jogging just to feel that good.

The people at UP&L were thrilled to see us—hey, Benny was their chance at millions. A lady from HR led us around office after cubicle after break room. Benny walked along behind the lady and me. It was *Dieffenbachia maculata* after *Ficus benjamina* after *Cycus revoluta*. Even I could tell nobody was getting rich here. But up on the sixth floor, I turned around and Benny wasn't behind us. He was back staring at a *Nemanthus gregarius* on a bookshelf in a cubicle just inside the door.

I walked up to him. "It's just goldfish vine," I said.

The girl in the cubicle looked like she wanted to pick up her keyboard and kill me with it.

"Benny," I said, "we got a bunch more territory to cover. Let's move it."

He put his hands in his pockets and followed along behind me, but after about five minutes he was gone again. We found him back at the *Nemanthus gregarius*. I took a second look at the plant. It looked like nothing more than *Nemanthus gregarius* to me. Polly, the girl in the cubicle, was doing a little dance in her chair in time to the muffled "Dancing Queen" out of Benny's earphones. Mama mia, she felt like money, money, money.

I made arrangements with HR for us to come back the next day and start our detailed study. The company CEO came down to shake our hands when we left. Last we saw of Polly that day was her watering the *Nemanthus gregarius*.

Abba, Fältskog Listing 47: "Dancing Queen," day 3. Dinner.

The thing about Benny is, he never moves around in time to the music. I mean, he can sit there listening to "Dancing Queen" over and over again and stare straight ahead, hands folded in his lap. He never moves his shoulders. He never taps his toes. He never sways his hips. Watching him, you'd think "Dancing Queen" was some Bach cantata.

I ordered dinner for us in the hotel coffee shop. Benny always makes me order for him, but god forbid it's not a medium-rare hamburger and fries. We sat there eating in silence, the only sound between us the muffled dancing queen having the time of her life. I thought maybe I'd try a little conversation. "Hamburger OK?" I asked.

Benny nodded.

"Want a refill on the Coke?"

He picked up his glass and sucked up the last of the Coke, but shook his head no.

I took a bite of my burger, chewed it, looked at Benny. "You got any goals?" I asked him.

Benny looked at me then. He didn't say a word. He stopped chewing and just stared.

"I mean, what do you want to do with your life? You want a wife? Kids? A trip to the moon? We fly around together, city after city, studying all these plants, and I don't think I even know you."

He swallowed and wiped his mouth with his napkin. "I have goals," he said.

"Well, like what?"

"I haven't told anybody. I'll need some time to think about it before I answer you. I'm not sure I want to tell anybody, no offense."

Jeez, Benny, take a chance on me why don't you, I thought. We went back to eating our burgers. I knew the higher-ups would want me to follow the lead Benny had dropped when we were driving in from the airport, so I tried. "Tell me about bridges," I said. "Why are they important in songs?"

Benny wouldn't say another word. We finished eating, and I carried Benny's things up to his room for him. At the door he turned around and looked at me. "Bridges take you to a new place," he said. "But they also show you the way back to where you once were."

He closed the door.

I didn't turn on any music in my room. It was nice to have it a little quiet for a change. I wrote my reports and e-mailed them off, then went out for a drink. I nursed it along, wondering where we stood on the bridges.

Abba, Fältskog Listing 47: "Dancing Queen," day 4. UP&L offices.

World Botanics sends Benny only to companies that meet its criteria. First, they have to have occupied the same building for fifty years or more. You'd be surprised how few companies in America have done that. But if a company has moved around a lot, chances are its plants have not gone with it. Second, it's nice if the company has had international ties, but even that isn't necessary. Lots of people somehow failed to tell customs about the cuttings or the little packets of seeds in their pockets after vacations abroad. If a company's employees had traveled around a lot, or if they had family ties with other countries, they sometimes ended up with the kind of plants we were looking for. UP&L has stayed put for a good long time, plus its employees include former Mormon missionaries who've poked around obscure corners of the planet. World Botanics hoped to find something in Utah.

The UP&L CEO and the HR staff and Polly were all waiting for us. You'd think Benny'd want to go straight up to the sixth floor to settle the *Nemanthus gregarius* question, but he didn't.

Benny always starts on the first floor and works his way to the top, so we started on floor one.

The lobby was a new install, and I was glad Benny didn't waste even half an hour there. Not much hope of curing cancer with flame nettle or cantea palms. The cafeteria on the second floor had some interesting *Cleistocactus strausii*. Like all cactus, it's endangered but not yet extinct in the wild—there are still reports of *Cleistocactus strausii* growiing here and there in the tops of the Andes. As far as anybody can tell, it can't cure a thing.

We didn't make it to the sixth floor till after four o'clock, and you could tell that Polly was a nervous wreck.

But Benny walked right past her *Nemanthus gregarius*.

"Hey, Benny," I said in a low voice. "What about the goldfish vine?"

Benny turned around and stared at it. Polly moved back into her cubicle so she wouldn't block the view, but after a minute Benny put his hands in his pockets and walked off. Well, poor Polly, I thought.

But just before five, I turned around and Benny wasn't behind me. I found him at the *Nemanthus gregarius*. Jeez Benny, I thought, we need to know the name of the game here. Declare extract of *Nemanthus gregarius* the fountain of youth or tell Polly she has a nice plant but nothing special. I steered him out of the building and back to the Marriott.

Abba, Fältskog Listing 47: "Dancing Queen," day 4. Dinner.

I ordered Benny's burger and a steak for me. We sat there eating, the only sound between us a muffled "Dancing Queen." After last night, I was not attempting conversation.

I'd taken time before dinner to look up *Nemanthus gregarius* on the Net. It is not endangered. It grows like weeds in cubicles. It can't cure a thing.

I didn't know what Benny was doing.

He sucked up the last of his glass of Coke and put the glass down a little hard on the table. I looked up at him.

"I want to find a new plant and name it for Agnetha," he said.

"What?"

"My goal in life," he said. "If you tell anyone, I'll see that you're fired."

"You're looking for a new plant species in office buildings?"

"I'd actually like to find one for each of the four members of Abba, but Agnetha's first."

And I'd thought finding *one* completely new species was too much to ask.

"When Abba sang, the world was so lush," Benny said. "You can hear it in their music. It resonates with what's left of the natural world. It helps me save it."

It was my turn to be quiet. All I could think was, it works for Benny. He's had plenty of success, after all, and who hasn't heard of crazier things than the music of dead pop stars leading some guy to new plant species?

When I wrote up my daily reports that night, I left out Benny's goals. Some things the higher-ups don't need to know.

Abba, Fältskog Listing 47: "Dancing Queen," day 5. UP&L offices.

We spent the day looking at more sorry specimens of *Cordyline terminalis, Columnea gloriosa,* and *Codiaeum variegatum* than I care to remember. By the end of the day, Benny started handing out the occasional watering tip, so I knew even he was giving up.

"*Nemanthus gregarius?*" I asked in the elevator on the way down.

Suddenly he punched 6. He walked straight to Polly's cubicle and stuck out his hand. "I owe you an apology," he said.

Polly just sat there. She was facing her own little Waterloo, and she did it bravely.

"I thought your *Nemanthus gregarius* might be a subspecies not before described, but it isn't. It's the common variety. A nice specimen, though."

We left quickly. At least he didn't give her any watering tips.

Abba, Fältskog Listing 47: "Dancing Queen," day 5. Wandering the streets.

The thing about Benny is, if it doesn't work out and we've studied every plant on thirty floors of an office tower without finding even a *Calathea lancifolia*, he can't stand it. He wanders up and down the streets, poking into every little shop. He never buys anything—he isn't shopping. I think he's hoping to spot some rare plant in the odd tobacconist or magazine shop and to do it fast. I have a hard time keeping up with him then, and heaven forbid I should decide to buy something on sale for a Mother's Day gift.

We rushed through two used bookstores, an oriental rug store, four art galleries, three fast food joints. "Benny," I said. "Let's get something to eat."

"It's here," he said.

"What's where?"

"There's something here, and we just haven't found it."

The Dancing Queen was resonating, I supposed. Shops were closing all around us.

"You check the Indian jewelry store while I check Mr. Q's Big and Tall," he told me. "We meet outside in five."

I did like I was told. I smiled at the Navajo woman in traditional dress, but she did not smile back. She wanted to lock up. I made a quick sweep of the store and noted the various species of endangered cacti and left. Benny was not on the sidewalk. I went into Mr. Q's after him.

He was standing perfectly still in front of a rack of shirts on sale, hands in his pockets.

"These are too big for you," I said.

"Window display, southeast corner."

Well, I walked over there. It was a lovely little display of *Rhipsalis salicornioides, Phalaenopsis lueddemanniana,* and *Streptocarpus saxorum.* Nothing unusual.

Then I looked closer at the *Streptocarpus saxorum.* The flowers weren't the typical powder blue or lilac. They were a light yellow.

The proprietor walked up to me. "I'm sorry," he said. "But we're closing. Could you bring your final purchases to the register?"

"I'm just admiring your cape primrose," I said. "Where do they come from?"

"My mother grows them," he said. "She gave me these plants when I opened the store."

"Did she travel in Africa or Madagascar?"

"Her brother was in the foreign service. She used to follow him around to his postings. I don't remember where she went—I'd have to ask her."

"Do you mind if I touch one of the plants?" I asked.

He said sure. The leaves were the typical hairy, gray-green ovals; the flowers floated above the leaves on wire-thin stems. It was definitely *Streptocarpus,* but I'd never seen anything like it described.

"I think you should call your mother," I said, and I explained who Benny and I were.

The store closed, but Mr. Proprietor and his staff waited with us for the mother to arrive. The whole time Benny just stood by the sale rack, eyes closed, hands in his pockets. "You've done it again," I whispered to him.

He didn't answer me. Just as I turned to walk back over to the cape primrose, he opened his eyes. "*Streptocarpus agnethum*," he whispered.

And he smiled.

Abba, Fältskog Listing 32: "I Have a Dream." day 2. Agnetha's grave.

The thing about Benny is, he's generous. He took me to Sweden with him, and we planted *Streptocarpus agnethum*, or "dancing queen," around Agnetha's gravestone. Turns out the flower wasn't a cure for anything, but it was a new species and Benny got to name it.

"Agnetha would have loved these flowers," I told Benny.

He just kept planting. We had a nice sound system on the ground beside us, playing her music—well, just one of her songs. It talks about believing in angels. I don't know if I believe in angels, but I can see the good in Benny's work. Nobody's bringing back the world we've lost, but little pieces of it have survived here and there. Benny was saving some of those pieces.

"These flowers are so pretty," I told him.

Of course he didn't say anything.

He didn't need to.

A. R. Morlan lives in Wisconsin. Her short fiction has been published in magazines such as *Night Cry*, *The Twilight Zone*, *Weird Tales*, *Worlds of Fantasy and Horror*, and *The Horror Show*, and in the anthologies *Cold Shocks*, *Obsessions*, *Women in the West*, *Lethal Kisses*, *Love in Vein*, *Deadly After Dark: The Hot Blood Series*, *Sinestre*, *Twists of the Tale*, and in several volumes of *The Year's Best Fantasy and Horror*. She has had two novels published: *The Amulet* and *Dark Journey*.

Morlan is better known for writing horror than science fiction. Here she combines her flair for giving unique voices to her characters, bits of scientific fact, and a hint of horror.

FAST GLACIERS

A. R. MORLAN

23-1-02

Dr. Ridley wasn't exaggerating when he called the differences between the Whistlers tribe and *Homo sapiens* "disturbing"—I'd seen Dr. Tanner's video of a live birth and photographs of the tribesmen, but to actually *see*-see them . . . the others attributed my over-reaction to my status as an undergraduate. Or so they insinuated over dinner, in the compound, far from the Whistlers themselves.

Dr. Winslow assured me that I'd "get used to" them, that I'd "embrace their uniqueness" and "appreciate the opportunity" to experience the Whistlers' truly primitive existence.

Oh yes, they're very primitive. Wearing neon flip-flops and baggy poly-cotton sack dresses and shorts that the missionaries have foisted off on them. To hide their tattooed nudity, to make their facial differences less obvious through the ludicrous juxtaposition of western clothing on decidedly non-western bodies.

And the sad part is, the Whistlers don't seem to mind. Their clumsy efforts to mimic our speech—the speech of those damned missionaries camped out on the other side of the village—grow less awkward daily. I believe even Dr. Winslow suspects that they understand far more Spanish and English than they've been able to let on . . . their seeming eagerness to adopt our sartorial ways, coupled with the increase in non-Whistler sounds among the tribesmen under forty years of age, has been the talk of the camp ever since I arrived last weekend.

That and the other, less certain change within the Whistler community, the physical transformation of the Whistlers—although that in itself is still considered a matter of speculation. . . .

> The Peruvian Amazon was called a Tower of Babel by early Spanish missionaries stunned by the number of languages they found among isolated communities separated by dense jungle.
>
> "Missionaries estimated that more than 500 languages were spoken in an area half the size of Alaska. Linguists now estimate there were probably 100–150 languages, but with a dizzying variety of dialects.
>
> "Today, only 57 survive, and 25 of them are on the road to extinction, said Mary Ruth Wise, a linguist with the Dallas-based Summer Institute of Linguistics.
>
> "The process of language extinction begins when children stop learning a language," Ms. Wise said. . . .
>
> "Cultural Loss Seen As Languages Fade"
> *The New York Times*, May 16, 1999

Field Notes, Dr. Peter Ridley, University of California, Stanford, Peru Expedition, November 1989, Subject: "Whistler tribe," Southern Ucayali Region:

"—aside from their extreme isolation, the people dubbed the 'Whistlers' by those few tribes with whom they'd previously made limited contact in the past, exhibit signs of either inter-breeding or true genetic uniqueness, i.e. the distinctive shape of the lower jaw, soft palate and mouth, especially in the elder (those over thirty years of age) members of the tribe. Their facial aberration had come to the attention of earlier visitors to the tribe's region; reports dating back to the mid-1960s include references to the natives' "tube-like" lower faces, and numerous missionaries reported that their efforts to teach the tribe Spanish (or even other Peruvian dialects from surrounding tribes) were virtually useless among the older villagers, and only minimally successful when it came to the children. Photographic archives confirm this; at the time of the initial contact with visiting non-Peruvians, the Whistlers' facial structure was radically different from that of peoples living only twenty or so miles away from them, not to mention wildly divergent from *Homo sapiens* as a whole.

"Initially it was thought that this unprecedented facial abnormality might be the result of physical intervention on the part of the tribe members themselves (akin to the Native American practice of altering cranial shape by lashing a baby's head to a cradle board, etc.) but further study disproved this theory. In 1986, Dr. Kaitlin Tanner managed to videotape the birth of a Whistler baby, and the characteristic facial "tube" was present (albeit less pronounced) as the child emerged from its mother's vagina.

"Upon her arrival back at Harvard the next year, Dr. Tanner presented the videotape to the Department of Medicine, and received a grant to take a team of specialists down to Peru a year later to study the Whistler tribe more thoroughly.

"My own contribution to said team—genetics—has been less than satisfactory, due to the Whistlers' reluctance to allow me to take blood/tissue samples for DNA testing. The influence of the missionaries who have infiltrated the area and spread their anti-Darwinian propaganda/anti-scientific doctrines among the natives has made my job (at least) more difficult, thanks to continued sermonizing against anything which contradicts *their* religious views . . . including any testing which might somehow prove a scientific basis for the differences between the Whistlers and our own species. I cannot help but think of the Mayans, and the Incas, and the havoc the Church managed to cause in those civilizations. While the Whistler tribe seems to have no written language (hence no texts for modern missionaries to burn!), their language is utterly unique, far more so than even the Taushiro Indians with their lack of labial consonants and accompanying lack of lip movement.

"The tongue of the Whistlers is closer to pure sound than speech per se; modulations in tone and pitch account for approximately 90 percent of the variations between 'words' and those sounds which do not mimic reptilian hissing come close to pure whistling. So far, it has been all but impossible to do much more than mimic (or attempt to mimic) those sounds which accompany specific tasks, or are associated with particular objects or individuals, but even those efforts meet with limited success. The physical variance in the tribesmen's lower facial region either prohibits or lessens the success of them mimicking Spanish, English or other jungle tongues, although it is clear that the younger members of the tribe have had more success in mastering the most basic sounds. A few of them can pronounce vowels, and a couple have mastered consonants, most successfully "s" and "z." Another team member, Dr. Carlos Fuente from São Paulo, has managed to gain the trust of one family, and is working closely with their toddler boy and infant daughter, attempting to immerse the children in Spanish on a daily basis.

"While I have my reservations about Dr. Fuente's efforts, due to the risk of cultural contamination beyond the already curious endeavors of the missionaries who have tagged along with our team into the village (clothing for both sexes, dissuading them from certain rites, like full body tattoos for all adolescent females, etc.), his relations with this particular family have helped my own work—he's somehow convinced the entire nuclear family to allow themselves to be X-rayed and examined (although not pricked with needles—yet).

"The results are . . . more disturbing than merely exciting. The malformation of the lower face seems to be genetic, along with other less noticable deviations from other jungle tribes—or *Homo sapiens*.

"The mandible is elongated, with accompanying differences in the upper and lower teeth (most specifically a lack of rear molars and front incisors; the Whistlers are vegetarians, who rely on certain bean-like plants for protein). The shape of the cranium is also uniformly elongated, with a narrowing that continues the entire front-to-back length of the skull. The bones in the neck are likewise unique; the vertebrae are thicker and less flexible. While there seem to be vocal cords present, they appear thicker than normal.

"I cannot help but be reminded of the differences between *Homo sapiens* and *Neanderthals*. . . ."

4-2-02

Another disappointing day among the Whistlers—thanks, again, to those damned missionaries. Back at the university, I'd studied Dr. Tanner's diary after viewing that videotape from '86, and I was hoping to see one of the Whistlers' "hammock-cradles" (as Dr. T. dubbed them)—her description of their "yo-yo" movement (including a variation on the "cat's cradle" etc.) between the trees intrigued me, so of course I brought along a video camera and a 35mm in my knapsack.

The missionaries brought in those horrid springy baby-bouncers with plastic seats, and standard cradles which their do-gooder friends back in the States contributed to the clothing and goods drives held by their individual churches—instead of chucking the crap in the dumpsters where it belonged.

Damn them, and damn all their ugly cast-off clothes that they packed into big cardboard boxes and shipped surface rate down here. And damn the Bible-toting do-gooders who opened up said big cardboard boxes . . . which the tribe's children are now playing "house" in, even though they actually live in open-air lean-to style leaf and stick huts. I suppose the missionaries taught the children about "real" houses, too.

In his field notes, Dr. Ridley often spoke of the Mayans, and what the Spanish Catholics did to them—their culture, their history. Strange equals inferior. Then and now. And now the Catholics have help; the Baptists and the Methodists are stomping around Peru's jungles, too, competing for souls, racking up holy brownie points with the Almighty. But not the All-caring—how could He be, if He lets something so insidiously wrong take place?

Dr. Winslow assured me that this sort of small change was inevitable, that it would have happened in its own given time—he claims that Dr. Tanner witnessed at least one baby falling out of the old style "hammock" so he assured me that the Whistlers would've eventually figured out a better way to suspend their babies from the trees. Definitely. As soon as they created plastics and smelted the ore for the coiled springs.

I suppose my anger over not getting to see the baby hammocks made me keep on lashing back at him long after the subject should've been closed; for the first time in over a week, I dared to bring up what has now been so delicately termed "the *supposition*" (italics tacitly supplied).

(Despite what I consider to be hard evidence via comparison of the photos from the 1960s and the ones taken just days ago.)

I knew he was pissed as soon as I brought it up; why is it men can be so blind to anything new as long as a woman points it out to them? Such a universal trait, and such a deserves-to-become-extinct one. So I pointed at one of the tribeswomen, the pregnant one the missionaries call Arcelia, who was holding her youngest toddler in her horizontally-pigmented arms, and asked Dr. W., "Can't you *see* it? Look at her jawline, now look at the kid's. Her husband doesn't have the abnormality, so why should the baby? Why do *all* the children look like her boy? There's no reason why a change like that should—"

And that's as far as he let me go before cutting in.

"Do you honestly think that the missionaries, or our colleagues before us, brought these people more than clothing? Their diet has improved greatly, thanks to the infant formula and protein supplements introduced in the sixties. I suppose you haven't noticed that they've also been growing taller? Their situation's improving—"

" 'Growing taller' isn't what I'm *talking* about. Look at their faces. Listen to their voices. You can't have changes in the quality of the sound with accompanying changes in the—"

Of course, Dr. W. shot that theory down, too. Just like everyone else in camp; what gets me is that I know that they see the same things I do, and hear the variations in the Whistlers' speech, yet they just won't admit the obvious.

The Whistlers are changing. *Within* a generation.

And I think we just might be helping them along. . . .

> "There are hundreds of languages that are
> down to a few elderly speakers and are for the most

part beyond hope of revival," said Doug Whalen, a
Yale University Linguist who is president of the
Endangered Language Fund.

"It's like seeing a glacier. You can tell it's coming even though it's kind of slow."

"Cultural Loss Seen As Languages Fade"
The New York Times, May 16, 1999

16-3-02

Dr. Winslow seems to be trying to make up for his harangues
against my stand about "the *supposition*"—he actually made good
on his promise to bring me along when the tribeswomen held a
maturation rite. It was worth getting up after midnight, although I
was so groggy I forgot to bring an extra roll of film for the camera,
and had to ration the few exposures left on the roll.

The rite was performed by firelight, just a pile of sputtering
ashes, really; I don't know if this was tradition, or if the women were
worried lest the do-gooder patrol get wind of what was about to happen, and hurry into the jungles, Bibles in hand, to stop the ceremony.

The rite was similar to those of other jungle peoples in South
America, the Pacific, and regions of Africa; a girl who has had her
first menses undergoes physical alterations to signify her passage
into adulthood. The girl was naked, even of that ubiquitous strappy
waistcloth previously worn by all Whistlers (and still worn by
those defiant enough to eschew the missionaries' second-hand
cast-offs), and prone on the bare soil, surrounded by women of the
tribe, who watched and crooned in that eerie whistling drone (now
marred by what *has* to be changes in the younger women's soft
palates and teeth—there's simply no other way to account for the
acoustical change in the very sound of their voices, regardless of
what Dr. W. says), while an elder wielded a broad tattooing stick
tipped with parallel rows of nettles, which was periodically dipped

in ebony plant-ink. Using a mallet striker, she pounded the inked needles into the girl's flesh, leaving a smeary swathe of blood and raised, inflamed flesh in its wake. Much like the tattooing rituals elsewhere, but—

The girl was making noises, wholly unlike those of her elders, through lips set in a jaw whose shape was tacitly more (I'm loath to use the word, but I'm too damned tired to be more politically correct right now) *human* than those of her elders. Not as elongated, nor as tube-like. God, why couldn't Winslow *see* that? Too busy looking at the rest of her, I suppose. And then she reached her own threshold of pain, the moans and whimpers were closer to Spanish than her own fluted tongue; I could have sworn I heard the word for "mercy" as if she was begging for release in *our* tongues, even as her body became night-dark with neat lines of demarcation where the inked stick skipped a few centimeters of brownish flesh in epidermal imitation of her elders.

She'd been born different, I'm sure of it; these changes in her facial structure are the result of at least one generation of spontaneous, outside-influenced evolution. Birth of the future fittest— those best able to cope with the inevitable changes in their surroundings?

Just as the rest of her generation is altered, to varying degrees. But there seems to be one constant I've observed during my months here—not all of the tribesmen and women attempt to produce Spanish or English sounds. Those living on the outskirts of the village have maintained both a basic lack of linguistic diversity and their traditional facial structure. Even as their children, who come into contact with my kind, with the missionaries, out of childish curiosity, have begun to exhibit the first subtle signs of change. Villagers like the pregnant woman Arcelia, who seems to be the youngest tribeswoman still immune to any efforts at attempting "our" speech. Or her husband, the ones the Bible-thumpers dubbed Inocencio. He's older than she is, at least fifty-something. The few teeth he has left are deeply stained by coca-leaves. Despite his having given them up, as most of the villagers have done, urged to do so by those well-meaning Bible-belters. I think the Methodists, or the Baptists, were responsible for *that* alteration in the Whistlers' lifestyle. God, why didn't they just stay *home*?

Not that any of my people—the scientists, the linguists, the undergrad hangers-on like me—are doing them any more good. But at least we're willing to let them chew their coca, and hang their babies in those woven grass hammocks no one seems to even know how to make anymore. And run around pigmented and nearly bare. Even if we're nonetheless tainting their very essence, their very *species*, word by word, utterance by utterance.

We're just trying to understand them. Not eradicate them, not alter them. Even as it keeps happening, person by person.

I wish we had some phones, or radios, or shortwave that worked in this geographic jungle pit, but virtually everything brought into this place either won't work, or produces signals which are hopelessly garbled. Something to do with this particular region's isolation; audio contact has been all but impossible from the 1960s to today—not unlike the situation with the Whistlers. . . . I'd give anything to contact Dr. Ridley up in Stanford. I know he'd understand what I'm seeing, what the others see-but-won't-admit-they-see.

He realized their differences went beyond their facial structure—perhaps he'd understand that what the others refuse to acknowledge is making the Whistlers even *more* different now. . . .

From" " 'Homo hwistlian'—Homo sapiens' New-Found Cousin," Dr. Peter Ridley, Ph.D, *JAMA (Journal of the American Medical Association)*, October, 2001:

"... comparison of DNA samples from a broad cross-section of the tribe's 1,500 known members indicate a uniformity of deviation from the DNA of virtually all *Homo sapien* races, including Caucasian, Negroid and Mongolian. This difference between the Whistler tribe extends to physical attributes including, but not limited to, cranio-facial, soft tissue and esophageal variances from multi-cultural norms throughout the world.

"Exacavations of Whistler burial mounds which have been carbon-dated to 1000 B.C. indicates the same skeletal variances between this tribe and other human peoples; these abnormalities were consistent, and appeared to in no way hinder the abilities of the tribesmen to communicate, eat or drink, and thus should be considered to be fully normal physical attributes within that particular group.

"Despite the presence of other *Homo sapien* tribes in the surrounding jungle, the Whistler tribe remained genetically pure; due in large part to an inability to communicate, this tribe did not engage in trade with its neighbors, nor did they intermarry with surrounding tribes, perhaps due to their extreme facial variance from other jungle peoples. The mitochondrial DNA was remarkably pure in that respect, indicating a continuous genetic inheritance among all the tribespeople quite different from the mitochondrial DNA present in other *Homo sapiens* which can be traced to a single female in Africa . . .

12-5-02

I heard the first real words spoken by a Whistler child. Dr. W. was there, too, but he still refuses to admit what is happening to these people. To this *species.*

The little girl was aping the missionaries, who figuratively go for the throat when it comes to getting into these people's lives— praying, reading scripture, talking *at* them, until the inevitable happened. A girl-child said "el Christos" . . . and I fear that the other children will follow her example. Not because children like to join in, have that *need* to follow the leader, but because they *can,*

now. Their jaws are looser, their lips more supple. And Dr. Crane—
the Dr. Bonita Crane, former head of the linguistics department at
Princeton—told me that she saw what appear to be incisor buds in
the mouth of one of Arcelia's toddlers. What hurts most is that the
child's elders don't seem to care about what she'd said. There was
no overt concern that one of their took the first step toward becoming one of *us*. Which is so terribly, terribly sad, sadder even than
them covering their smooth, clean bodies with dirt-catching
grungy clothes, or wearing those silly rubbery flip-flops which do
little more than make obscene smacking noises with each step they
take.

More foreign noises to pollute their world, poison their very
way of being.

I suppose I should reserve some of my own wrath for Dr.
Fuente, and Dr. Ridley himself, as well as Dr. Tanner, but they were
trying to use our language not as a poison, not as a form of linguistic genocide, but merely as a bridge. None of them wanted to
see the Whistlers become us, not consciously. Not like those holy-
holy bringers of The Word, and The Doctrine, and ultimately, The
Universal Conversion.

Less overt, say, than the Jehovah's hanging on one's door,
Watchtowers in a mesh bag by their sides, but no less insidious.

And I know that Dr. W. and the others know what this means,
what those two short words—"el Christos"—have done to the
Whistlers' world. Other tongues will supplement, then augment,
then replace their language. And God knows, every tongue He
allows to die, often in His name, is another voice stilled in the universal wilderness. Are prayers sweeter to His ears in Spanish or
English, rather than Cocoma-Cocamillia or Chamicuro? Is He
somehow less omnipotent, that He prefers to hear His people speak
in fewer tongues?

I think Dr. Crane's observation is all the more frightening
because it concerns a child belonging to the last of the women of
child-bearing age whose physiognomy has yet to be altered by her

changed environment. If only women like Arcelia could raise their
remaining babies someplace free of *us,* not just free of those
blasted missionaries, but of all speakers of *Homo sapien* tongues.

I hear Dr. Crane and Dr. Winslow arguing in the next tent; not
much more than the sound of anger, but I can catch a word or two,
enough to realize they're indulging in a little midnight *"supposition."*

But I have no way of realizing whose side either is on anymore. Dr. C. has physical proof to back up any theories she might
have, but she's older than Dr. W., and of Dr. Tanner's generation, so
I don't know if she'd be willing to side with a mere undergrad with
an open prejudice against the Bible-thumpers. . . .

Nature adapts so quickly, far faster than even Darwin dared
imagine, let alone people like Dr. Crane. No wonder the Neanderthals simply seemed to vanish; the discovery of that little boy's
bones, the hybrid boy who was neither *them* nor *us* (or the people
who were soon to become *us*) but a mixture on the way to becoming a nondescript *one,* came as a surprise to some because no one
had truly wanted to accept the inevitable—species, even "human"
ones, don't always just die out, like dodos or passenger pigeons.
Sometimes, they simply give up and join the dominant
invaders. . . .

29-7-02

The professors in NYC are very interested in my proposal; judging
by their response to my letter, they're all but salivating for the
chance to observe the last of a species.

Funny, how they were persuaded by the same photos and
videotape my academic fellows in the camp refused to acknowledge. But apparently it was the audio tapes which ultimately convinced them; they, too, heard the differences in the tribesmen and
women's voices which could not be attributed to linguistic differ-

ences alone. Oh God, they *believe* me. They listened, they looked, they compared, and they believed.

Dr. Ridley hasn't responded yet, but he might be out of the country. Last I heard, he was doing a lot of lecturing, touting his discovery of *Homo hwistlian*. While leaving them to the influences of others less scientific minded than himself . . . like the missionaries.

But I'm closer to the salvation of the Whistlers now. I suppose that's an odd choice of words, considering how I feel about those Bible-belters, but there's saving, and then there's *saving*, as in preserving. Maintaining. Just plain hanging on to what's vanishing syllable by syllable among these people.

People. Another word that could be construed as unusual, I suppose. So much talk of Whistlers, or of Dr. Ridley's name for them, the hideous appellation *Homo hwistlian*. Yet another example of English, or Old English, taking over their lives. Especially since they're nowhere as strange as that archaic name Ridley saddled them with. When all they are, really, is people. People fast becoming too much like all the rest of the people on this planet.

The professors in New York have arranged for an isolation chamber for Arcelia, the woman not yet affected; although her children show signs of facial alterations, Arcelia is still "pure" Whistler—she understands some of our speech, but she cannot speak it, even though her children are no doubt picking up the two tongues most frequently spoken among the invaders, the researchers and the missionaries. We hope that if she raises her unborn child in cultural isolation, exposing it only to her own culture, her *language* (of which *my* species is still infuriatingly ignorant, despite well over three decades of contact—of contamination), it will *remain* Whistler . . . even if she has to do it in what amounts to a cage, a sealed environment. Free from *us*.

If I knew when Arcelia was due, I'd feel much better about what I'm planning. Whistler gestation seems to be somewhat longer than *Homo sapien* gestation, at least nine and a half to ten months on average.

She was already showing when I met her six months ago, even under that saggy dress the missionaries gave her.

If only I could ask her when she conceived (if, indeed, she'd even know), but my words are poison . . .

Not that it matters. I've already made arrangements with men of a neighboring tribe, to escort us out of the camp come midnight. The others will assume that I'm taking her north, the short route, but there's an old train that runs through the Andes, down to Bolivia—it's seldom used anymore, and badly maintained, but taking it will be so non-obvious, I'm betting it will buy me time to get Arcelia out of here, and off where her baby won't have to worry about word-poisoning.

With time, Arcelia might forget having heard them herself. . . .

Field Notes, Dr. Wesley Winslow, University of Chicago, Peru Expedition, July, 2002, Subject: *Homo hwistlian*, Southern Ucayali Region:

"—her gone, along with one of the native women around daybreak. The absence of the tribeswoman, called Arcelia by the missionaries, was deeply felt among the females of the group, especially the older, ritually tattooed women; their hooting wails and low keening noises could be heard in the next village. Some of them beat themselves with vines and branches, while others attacked the younger females in the tribe, whipping and slashing them with pliant vines and cutting tools usually reserved for harvesting foodstuffs. Apparently no one had physically left the village before; unfortunately, the lack of communication between the 'Whistlers' and visitors has made any attempt to comfort the tribespeople impossible. Even the missionaries are at a lack to explain or prevent this violent reaction to the departure of Arcelia from the tribe.

"While there has been no evidence of the death-cult mentality once common among ancient Peruvian peoples (i.e. the dead were buried, not mummified/preserved, and no effort was made to include remains of ancestors in daily life) prior to this incident, the outburst among the tribe is similar to that behavior exhibited during the Spanish conquest of western Peru, during which the venerated remains of the natives' elders were symbolically 'killed' before their eyes by their invaders.

"Dr. Crane has videotaped several of these inter-tribal attacks; while no outsider has yet to be harmed, we are worried that this grief-reaction has not abated after three days. . . ."

Field Notes, Dr. Neda Crane, Peru Expedition, Southern Ucayali region, July 2002.

"—journal was left in her tent; I suppose her other clandestine plans took up so much of her attention, she simply forgot it in her haste to spirit Arcelia out of here. Perhaps I should be grateful for her oversight, despite my anger over what she's done. Not only to Arcelia, but to the other Whistlers.

"Trying to imagine what she was actually hoping to accomplish with this insane folly is beyond me, beyond Dr. Ridley, truly beyond the ken of anyone she so blithely left behind. Apart from the medical danger of taking a pregnant lowlands native up into the Andes, what in god's name was she *thinking*? Wanting to put Arcelia and her baby into something akin to a Skinner box is one thing, but how in the world did she expect to get Arcelia out of the country? Not one word in her journal about passports, or how other people might react to the sight of Arcelia . . . how could someone so educated, so otherwise insightful be so damned *stupid*?

"While there was no way she could have foreseen what would happen to the tribe once Arcelia was gone, couldn't she have at least considered what might happen to Arcelia herself?

And to think she thought the missionaries were bad . . . it pains me to even try to imagine what Arcelia might make of real civilization. Or what the outside world might make of her.

"Especially since she and her child are now the last known survivors of their tribe.

"And even if Arcelia and the baby somehow do make it to that glorified cage in New York, if that idiot colleague of mine does figure out a way to follow through on this imprudent whim of hers, what will be accomplished?

"A language spoken by two is still very much a dead end once the elder speaker dies off. And after that happens, what language can be used to tell the survivor that he or she is now truly alone, not only as a last survivor of a species, but as the last keeper of that species' native tongue?

"Can anyone be called upon to say those words, in any language?"

Avram Davidson was born in 1923 and wrote his earliest stories for Yiddish-language periodicals. His first stories in English appeared in 1954. He was the editor of *The Maga-zine of Fantasy and Science Fiction* from 1962–1965. He won the Hugo Award, the Edgar Award, and the World Fantasy Award for his fiction. *The Avram Davidson Treasury*, a collection of some of his best short fiction written over a period of thirty years and with introductions by many of the luminaries of the field, is a must-have.

I first discovered "Now Let Us Sleep" in *Time of Pas-sage*, a reprint anthology about death edited by Martin H. Greenberg and Joseph Olander about twenty years ago. But its original publication was in *Venture Science Fic-tion* in 1957. I found it incredibly moving and could never get it out of my head. I think it's one of those rare science fiction stories that will never date but instead becomes more appropriate and more powerful with time. So I'm especially delighted to be able to include it in *Vanishing Acts*.

NOW LET US SLEEP

Avram Davidson

A pink-skinned young cadet ran past Harper, laughing and shout-ing and firing his stungun. The wind veered about, throwing the thick scent of the Yahoos into the faces of the men, who whooped loudly to show their revulsion.

"I got three!" the chicken cadet yelped at Harper. "Did you see me pop those two together? Boy, what a stink they have!"

Harper looked at the sweating kid, muttered, "You don't smell so sweet yourself," but the cadet didn't wait to hear. All the men were running now, running in a ragged semi-circle with the intention of driving the Yahoos before them, to hold them at bay at the foot of the gaunt cliff a quarter-mile off.

The Yahoos loped awkwardly over the rough terrain, moaning and grunting grotesquely, their naked bodies bent low. A few hundred feet ahead one of them stumbled and fell, his arms and legs flying out as he hit the ground, twitched, and lay still.

A bald-headed passenger laughed triumphantly, paused to kick the Yahoo, and trotted on. Harper kneeled beside the fallen Primitive, felt for a pulse in the hairy wrist. It seemed slow and feeble, but then, no one actually knew what the normal pulse-beat should be. And—except for Harper—no one seemed to give a damn.

Maybe it was because he was the grandson of Barret Harper, the great naturalist—back on Earth, of course. It seemed as if man could be fond of nature only on the planet of man's origin, whose ways he knew so well. Elsewhere, it was too strange and alien— you subdued it, or you adjusted to it, or you were perhaps even content with it. But you almost never *cared* about the flora or fauna of the new planets. No one had the feeling for living things that an earth-born had.

The men were shouting more loudly now, but Harper didn't lift his head to see why. He put his hand to the shaggy gray chest. The heart was still beating, but very slowly and irregularly. Someone stood beside him.

"He'll come out of it in an hour or so," the voice of the purser said. "Come on—you'll miss all the fun—you should see how they act when they're cornered! They kick out and throw sand and—" he laughed at the thought—"they weep great big tears, and go, 'Oof! Oof!'"

Harper said, "An ordinary man *would* come out of it in an hour or so. But I think their metabolism is different . . . Look at all the bones lying around."

The purser spat. "Well, don't that prove they're not human, when they won't even bury their dead? . . . *Oh*, oh!—look at that!" He swore.

Harper got to his feet. Cries of dismay and disappointment went up from the men.

"What's wrong?" Harper asked.

The purser pointed. The men had stopped running, were gathering together and gesturing. "Who's the damn fool who planned this drive?" the purser asked, angrily. "He picked the wrong cliff! The damned Yahoos *nest* in that one! Look at them climb, will you—" He took aim, fired the stungun. A figure scrabbling up the side of the rock threw up its arms and fell, bounding from rock to rock until it hit the ground. "*That* one will never come off it!" the purser said, with satisfaction.

But this was the last casualty. The other Yahoos made their way to safety in the caves and crevices. No one followed them. In those narrow, stinking confines a Yahoo was as good as a man, there was no room to aim a stungun, and the Yahoos had rocks and clubs and their own sharp teeth. The men began straggling back.

"This one a she?" The purser pushed at the body with his foot, let it fall back with an annoyed grunt as soon as he determined its sex. "There'll be Hell to pay in the hold if there's more than two convicts to a she." He shook his head and swore.

Two lighters came skimming down from the big ship to load up.

"Coming back to the launch?" the purser asked. He had a red shiny face. Harper had always thought him a rather decent fellow—before. The purser had no way of knowing what was in Harper's mind; he smiled at him and said, "We might as well get on back, the fun's over now."

Harper came to a sudden decision. "What're the chances of my taking a souvenir back with me? This big fellow, here, for example?"

The purser seemed doubtful. "Well, I dunno, Mr. Harper. We're only supposed to take females aboard, and unload *them* as soon as the convicts are finished with their fun." He leered. Harper, suppressing a strong urge to hit him right in the middle of his apple-red face, put his hand in his pocket. The purser understood, looked away as Harper slipped a bill into the breast pocket of his uniform.

"I guess it can be arranged. See, the Commissioner-General on Selopé III wants one for his private zoo. Tell you what: We'll take one for him and one for you—I'll tell the super-cargo it's a spare. But if one croaks, the C-G has to get the other. Okay?"

At Harper's nod the purser took a tag out of his pocket, tied it around the Yahoo's wrist, waved his cap to the lighter as it came near. "Although why anybody'd *want* one of these beats me," he said cheerfully. "They're dirtier than animals. I mean, a pig or a horse'll use the same corner of the enclosure, but these things'll dirty anywhere. Still, if you *want* one—" He shrugged.

As soon as the lighter had picked up the limp form (the pulse was still fluttering feebly) Harper and the purser went back to the passenger launch. As they made a swift ascent to the big ship the purser gestured to the two lighters. "That's going to be a mighty slow trip *those* two craft will make back up," he remarked.

Harper innocently asked why. The purser chuckled. The coxswain laughed.

"The freight-crewmen want to make their points before the convicts. *That's* why."

The chicken cadet, his face flushed a deeper pink than usual, tried to sound knowing. "How about that, purser? Is it pretty good stuff?"

The other passengers wiped their perspiring faces, leaned forward eagerly. The purser said, "Well, rank has its privileges, but that's one I figure I can do without."

His listeners guffawed, but more than one looked down toward the lighters and then avoided other eyes when he looked back again.

.   .   .

Barnum's Planet (named, as was the custom then, after the skipper who'd first sighted it) was a total waste, economically speaking. It was almost all water and the water supported only a few repulsive-looking species of no discernible value. The only sizeable piece of land—known, inevitably, as Barnumland, since no one else coveted the honor—was gaunt and bleak, devoid alike of useful minerals or arable soil. Its ecology seemed dependent on a sort of fly: A creature rather like a lizard ate the flies and the Yahoos ate the lizards. If something died at sea and washed ashore, the Yahoos ate that, too. What the flies ate no one knew, but their larvae ate the Yahoos, dead.

They were small, hairy, stunted creatures whose speech—if speech it was—seemed confined to moans and clicks and grunts. They wore no clothing, made no artifacts, did not know the use of fire. Taken away captive, they soon languished and died. Of all the Primitives discovered by man, they were the most primitive. They might have been left alone on their useless planet to kill lizards with tree branches forever—except for one thing.

Barnum's Planet lay equidistant between Coulter's System and the Selopés, and it was a long, long voyage either way. Passengers grew restless, crews grew mutinous, convicts rebellious. Gradually the practice developed of stopping on Barnum's Planet "to let off steam"—archaic expression, but although the nature of the machinery man used had changed since it was coined, man's nature hadn't.

And, of course, no one *owned* Barnum's Planet, so no one cared what happened there.

Which was just too bad for the Yahoos.

It took some time for Harper to settle the paperwork concerning his "souvenir," but finally he was given a baggage check for "One Yahoo, male, live," and hurried down to the freight deck. He hoped it would be still alive.

Pandemonium met his ears as he stepped out of the elevator. A rhythmical chanting shout came from the convict hold. "Hear that?" one of the duty officers asked him, taking the cargo chit. Harper asked what the men were yelling. "I wouldn't care to use the words," the officer said. He was a paunchy, gray-haired man, one who probably loved to tell his grandchildren about his "adventures." This was one he wouldn't tell them.

"I don't like this part of the detail," the officer went on. "Never did, never will. Those creatures *seem human* to me—stupid as they are. And if they're *not* human," he asked, "then how can we sink low enough to bring their females up for the convicts?"

The lighters grated on the landing. The noise must have penetrated to the convict hold, because all semblance of words vanished from the shouting. It became a mad cry, louder and louder.

"Here's your pet," the gray-haired officer said. "Still out, I see . . . I'll let you have a baggage-carrier. Just give it to a steward when you're done with it." He had to raise his voice to be heard over the frenzied howling from the hold.

The ship's surgeon was out having tea at the captain's table. The duty medical officer was annoyed. "What, another one? We're not veterinarians, you know . . . Well, wheel him in. My intern is working on the other one . . . *whew!*" He held his nose and hastily left.

The intern, a pale young man with close-cropped dark hair, looked up from the pressure-spray he had just used to give an injection to the specimen Yahoo selected for the Commissioner-General of Selopé III. He smiled faintly.

"Junior will have company, I see . . . Any others?"

Harper shook his head. The intern went on, "This should be interesting. The young one seems to be in shock. I gave him two cc's of anthidar sulfate, and I see I'd better do the same for yours. Then . . . Well, I guess there's still nothing like serum albumen, is there? But you'd better help me strap them down. If they come to, there's a cell back aft we can put them in, until I can get some cages rigged up." He shot the stimulant into the flaccid arm of Harper's Yahoo.

"Whoever named these beasties knew his Swift," the young medico said. "You ever read that old book, 'Gulliver's Travels'?"

Harper nodded.

"Old Swift went mad, didn't he? He hated humanity, they all seemed like Yahoos to him . . . In a way I don't blame him. I think that's why everybody despises these Primitives: They seem like caricatures of ourselves. Personally, I look forward to finding out a lot about them, their metabolism and so on . . . What's *your* interest?"

He asked the question casually, but shot a keen look as he did so. Harper shrugged. "I hardly know, exactly. It's not a scientific one, because I'm a businessman." He hesitated. "You ever hear or read about the Tasmanians?"

The intern shook his head. He thrust a needle into a vein in the younger Yahoo's arm, prepared to let the serum flow in. "If they lived on Earth, I wouldn't know. Never was there. I'm a third generation Coulterboy, myself."

Harper said, "Tasmania is an island south of Australia. The natives were the most primitive people known on Earth. They were almost all wiped out by the settlers, but one of them succeeded in moving the survivors to a smaller island. And then a curious thing happened."

Looking up from the older Primitive, the intern asked what that was.

"The Tasmanians—the few that were left—decided that they'd had it. They refused to breed. And in a few more years they were all dead . . . I read about them when I was just a kid. Somehow, it moved me very much. Things like that *did*—the dodo, the great auk, the quagga, the Tasmanians. I've never been able to get it out of my mind. When I began hearing about the Yahoos, it seemed to me that they were like the old Tasmanians. Only there are no settlers on Barnumland."

The intern nodded. "But that won't help our hairy friends here a hell of a lot. Of course no one knows how many of them there are—or ever were. But I've been comparing the figures in the log as to how many females are caught and taken aboard." He looked directly at Harper. "And on every trip there are less by far."

Harper bowed his head. He nodded. The intern's voice went on: "The thing is, Barnum's Planet is no one's responsibility. If the Yahoos could be used for labor, they'd be exploited according to a careful system. But as it is, no one cares. If half of them die from being stungunned, no one cares. If the lighter crews don't bother to actually land the females—if any of the wretched creatures are still *alive* when the convicts are done—but just dump them out from twenty feet up, why, again: no one cares. Mr. Harper?"

Their eyes met. Harper said, "Yes?"

"Don't misunderstand me . . . I've got a career here. I'm not jeopardizing it to save the poor Yahoos—but if *you* are interested—if you think you've got any influence—and if you want to try to do anything—" He paused. "Why, now is the time to start. Because after another few stop-overs there aren't going to be any Yahoos. No more than there are any Tasmanians."

Selopé III was called "The Autumn Planet" by the poets. At least, the P.R. picture-tapes always referred to it as "Selopé III, The Autumn Planet of the poets," but no one knew who the poets were. It was true that the Commission Territory, at least, did have the climate of an almost-perpetual early New England November. Barnumland had been dry and warm. The Commissioner-General put the two Yahoos in a heated cage as large as the room Harper occupied at his company's Bachelor Executive Quarters.

"Here, boy," the C-G said, holding out a piece of fruit. He made a chirping noise. The two Yahoos huddled together in a far corner.

"They don't seem very bright," he said sadly. "All my *other* animals eat out of my hand." He was very proud of his private

zoo, the only one in the Territory. On Sundays he allowed the
public to visit it.

Sighing, Harper repeated that the Yahoos were Primitives, not
animals. But, seeing the C-G was still doubtful, he changed his tactics. He told the C-G about the great zoos on Earth, where the animals went loose in large enclosures rather than being caged up.
The C-G nodded thoughtfully. Harper told him of the English
dukes who—generation after ducal generation—preserved the last
herd of wild White Cattle in a park on their estate.

The C-G stroked his chin. "Yes, yes," he said. "I see your
point," he said. He sighed gustily. "Can't be done," he said.

"But why not, sir?" Harper cried.

It was simple. "No money. Who's to pay? The Exchequer-
Commissioner is weeping blood trying to get the budget through
council. If he adds a penny more— No, young fellow, I'll do what I
can: I'll feed these two, here. But that's all I can do."

Trying to pull all the strings he could reach, Harper
approached the Executive-Fiscal and the Procurator-General, the
President-in-Council, the Territorial Advocate, the Chairman of
the Board of Travel. But no one could do anything. Barnum's
Planet, it was carefully explained to him, remained No Man's Land
only because no man presumed to give any orders concerning it. If
any government did, this would be a Presumption of Authority.
And then every other government would feel obliged to deny that
presumption and issue a claim of its own.

There was a peace on now—a rather tense, uneasy one. And it
wasn't going to be disturbed for Harper's Yahoos. Human, were
they? Perhaps. But who cared? As for Morality, Harper didn't even
bother to mention the word. It would have meant as little as
Chivalry.

Meanwhile, he was learning something of the Yahoos' language. Slowly and arduously, he gained their confidence. They
would shyly take food from him. He persuaded the C-G to knock
down a wall and enlarge their quarters. The official was a kindly old

man, and he seemed to grow fond of the stooped, shaggy, splay-footed Primitives. And after a while he decided that they were smarter than animals.

"Put some clothes on 'em, Harper," he directed. "If they're people, let 'em start acting like people. They're too big to go around naked."

So, eventually, washed and dressed, Junior and Senior were introduced to Civilization via 3-D, and the program was taped and shown everywhere.

Would you like a cigarette, Junior? Here, let me light it for you. Give Junior a glass of water, Senior. Let's see you take off your slippers, fellows, and put them on again. And now do what I say in your own language . . .

But if Harper thought that might change the public opinion, he thought wrong. Seals perform, too, don't they? And so do monkeys. They talk? Parrots talk better. And anyway, who cared to be bothered about animals *or* Primitives? They were okay for fun, but that was all.

And the reports from Barnumland showed fewer and fewer Yahoos each time.

Then one night two drunken crewmen climbed over the fence and went carousing in the C-G's zoo. Before they left, they broke the vapor-light tubes, and in the morning Junior and Senior were found dead from the poisonous fumes.

That was Sunday morning. By Sunday afternoon Harper was drunk, and getting drunker. The men who knocked on his door got no answer. They went in anyway. He was slouched, red-eyed, over the table.

"People," he muttered. "Tell you they were *human!*" he shouted.

"Yes, Mr. Harper, we know that," said a young man, pale, with close-cropped dark hair.

Harper peered at him, boozily. "Know you," he said. "Thir' gen'ration Coulterboy. Go 'way. Spoi' your c'reer. Whaffor. Smelly ol' Yahoo?" The young medico nodded to his companion, who took a small flask from his pocket, opened it. They held it under Harper's nose by main force. He gasped and struggled, but they held on, and in a few minutes he was sober.

"That's rough stuff," he said, coughing and shaking his head. "But—thanks, Dr. Hill. Your ship in? Or are you stopping over?"

The former intern shrugged. "I've left the ships," he said. "I don't have to worry about spoiling my new career. This is my superior, Dr. Anscomb."

Anscomb was also young, and, like most men from Coulter's System, pale. He said, "I understand you can speak the Yahoos' language."

Harper winced. "What good's that now? They're dead, poor little bastards."

Anscomb nodded. "I'm sorry about that, believe me. Those fumes are so quick . . . But there are still a few alive on Barnum's Planet who can be saved. The Joint Board for Research is interested. Are you?"

It had taken Harper fifteen years to work up to a room of this size and quality in Bachelor Executives' Quarters. He looked around it. He picked up the letter which had come yesterday. ". . . neglected your work and become a joke . . . unless you accept a transfer and reduction in grade . . ." He nodded slowly, putting down the letter. "I guess I've already made my choice. What are your plans . . . ?"

Harper, Hill, and Anscomb sat on a hummock on the north coast of Barnumland, just out of rock-throwing range of the gaunt escarpment of the cliff which rose before them. Behind them a tall fence had been erected. The only Yahoos still alive were "nesting" in the caves of the cliff. Harper spoke into the amplifier again. His voice was hoarse as he forced it into the clicks and moans of the Primitives' tongue.

Hill stirred restlessly. "Are you sure that means, '*Here is food. Here is water*'—and not, '*Come down and let us eat you*'? I think I can almost say it myself by now."

Shifting and stretching, Anscomb said, "It's been two days. Unless they've determined to commit race suicide a bit more abruptly than your ancient Tasmanians—" He stopped as Harper's fingers closed tightly on his arm.

There was a movement on the cliff. A shadow. A pebble clattered. Then a wrinkled face peered fearfully over a ledge. Slowly, and with many stops and hesitations, a figure came down the face of the cliff. It was an old she. Her withered and pendulous dugs flapped against her sagging belly as she made the final jump to the ground, and—her back to the wall of rock—faced them.

"Here is food," Harper repeated softly. "Here is water." The old woman sighed. She plodded wearily across the ground, paused, shaking with fear, and then flung herself down at the food and the water.

"The Joint Board for Research has just won the first round," Hill said. Anscomb nodded. He jerked his thumb upward. Hill looked.

Another head appeared at the cliff. Then another. And another. They watched. The crone got up, water dripping from her dewlaps. She turned to the cliff. "Come down," she cried. "Here is food and water. Do not die. Come down and eat and drink." Slowly, her tribespeople did so. There were thirty of them.

Harper asked, "Where are the others?"

The crone held out her dried and leathery breasts to him. "Where are those who have sucked? Where are those your brothers took away?" She uttered a single shrill wail; then was silent.

But she wept—and Harper wept with her.

"I'll guess we'll swing it all right," Hill said. Anscomb nodded. "Pity there's so few of them. I was afraid we'd have to use gas to get at them. Might have lost several that way."

Neither of them wept.

.   .   .

For the first time since ships had come to their world, Yahoos *walked* aboard one. They came hesitantly and fearfully, but Harper had told them that they were going to a new home and they believed him. He told them that they were going to a place of much food and water, where no one would hunt them down. He continued to talk until the ship was on its way, and the last Primitive had fallen asleep under the dimmed-out vapor-tube lights. Then he staggered to his cabin and fell asleep himself. He slept for thirty hours.

He had something to eat when he awoke, then strolled down to the hold where the Primitives were. He grimaced, remembered his trip to the hold of the other ship to collect Senior, and the frenzied howling of the convicts awaiting the females. At the entrance to the hold he met Dr. Hill, greeted him.

"I'm afraid some of the Yahoos are sick," Hill said. "But Dr. Anscomb is treating them. The others have been moved to this compartment here."

Harper stared. "Sick? How can they be sick? What from? And how many?"

Dr. Hill said, "It appears to be Virulent Plague . . . Fifteen of them are down with it. You've *had* all six shots, haven't you? Good. Nothing to worry—"

Harper felt the cold steal over him. He stared at the pale young physician. "No one can enter or leave any system or planet without having had all six shots for Virulent Plague," he said, slowly. "So if we are all immune, how could the Primitives have gotten it? And how is it that only fifteen have it? Exactly half of them. What about the other fifteen, Dr. Hill? *Are they the control group for your experiment?*"

Dr. Hill looked at him calmly. "As a matter of fact, yes. I hope you'll be reasonable. Those were the only terms the Joint Board for

Research would agree to. After all, not even convicts will volunteer for experiments in Virulent Plague."

Harper nodded. He felt frozen. After a moment he asked, "Can Anscomb do anything to pull them through?"

Dr. Hill raised his eyebrows. "Perhaps. We've got something we wanted to try. And at any rate, the reports should provide additional data on the subject. We must take the long-range view."

Harper nodded. "I suppose you're right," he said.

By noon all fifteen were dead.

"Well, that means an uneven control group," Dr. Anscomb complained. "Seven against eight. Still, that's not *too* bad. And it can't be helped. We'll start tomorrow."

"Virulent Plague again?" Harper asked.

Anscomb and Hill shook their heads. "Dehydration," the latter said. "And after that, there's a new treatment for burns we're anxious to try . . . It's a shame, when you think of the Yahoos being killed off by the thousands, year after year, *uselessly*. Like the dodo. We came along just in time—thanks to you, Harper."

He gazed at them. "*Quis custodiet ipsos custodes?*" he asked. They looked at him, politely blank. "I'd forgotten. Doctors don't study Latin anymore, do they? An old proverb. It means: 'Who shall guard the guards themselves?'. . . . Will you excuse me, Doctors?"

Harper let himself into the compartment. "I come," he greeted the fifteen.

"We see you," they responded. The old woman asked how their brothers and sisters were "in the other cave."

"They are well . . . Have you eaten, have you drunk? Yes? Then let us sleep," Harper said.

The old woman seemed doubtful. "Is it time? The light still shines." She pointed to it. Harper looked at her. She had been so afraid. But she had trusted him. Suddenly he bent over and kissed her. She gasped.

"Now the light goes out," Harper said. He slipped off a shoe and shattered the vapor tube. He groped in the dark for the air-switch, turned it off. Then he sat down. He had brought them here, and if they had to die, it was only fitting that he should share their fate. There no longer seemed any place for the helpless, or for those who cared about them.

"Now let us sleep," he said.

Ted Chiang won the Nebula Award for his first published story. He has had fiction published in the original anthologies *Full Spectrum 3* and *Starlight 2* and was hoping that this anthology would have "I" in its title to continue the countdown.

Chiang longs for the days of the passenger pigeon, Steller's sea cow, and the CP/M operating system. Occasionally he wishes he were rich enough that the administration of his alma mater would personally woo him for a donation, just so he could refuse them.

SEVENTY-TWO LETTERS

Ted Chiang

When he was a child, Robert's favorite toy was a simple one, a clay doll that could do nothing but walk forward. While his parents entertained their guests in the garden outside, discussing Victoria's ascension to the throne or the Chartist reforms, Robert would follow the doll as it marched down the corridors of the family home, turning it around corners or back where it came from. The doll didn't obey commands or exhibit any sense at all; if it met a wall, the diminutive clay figure would keep marching until it gradually mashed its arms and legs into misshapen flippers. Sometimes Robert would let it do that, strictly for his own amusement. Once the doll's limbs were thoroughly distorted, he'd pick the toy up and pull the name out, stopping its motion in mid-stride. Then he'd knead the body back into a smooth lump, flatten it out into a plank, and cut out a different figure: a body with one leg crooked, or longer than the other. He would stick the name back into it, and the doll would promptly topple over and push itself around in a little circle.

It wasn't the sculpting that Robert enjoyed; it was mapping out the limits of the name. He liked to see how much variation he could impart to the body before the name could no longer animate it. To save time with the sculpting, he rarely added decorative details; he refined the bodies only as was needed to test the name.

Another of his dolls walked on four legs. The body was a nice one, a finely detailed porcelain horse, but Robert was more interested in experimenting with its name. This name obeyed commands to start and stop and knew enough to avoid obstacles, and Robert tried inserting it into bodies of his own making. But this name had more exacting body requirements, and he was never able to form a clay body it could animate. He formed the legs separately and then attached them to the body, but he wasn't able to blend the seams smooth enough; the name didn't recognize the body as a single continuous piece.

He scrutinized the names themselves, looking for some simple substitutions that might distinguish two-leggedness from four-leggedness, or make the body obey simple commands. But the names looked entirely different; on each scrap of parchment were inscribed seventy-two tiny Hebrew letters, arranged in twelve rows of six, and so far as he could tell, the order of the letters was utterly random.

Robert Stratton and his fourth form classmates sat quietly as Master Trevelyan paced between the rows of desks.

"Langdale, what is the doctrine of names?"

"All things are reflections of God, and, um, all—"

"Spare us your bumbling. Thorburn, can *you* tell us the doctrine of names?"

"As all things are reflections of God, so are all names reflections of the divine name."

"And what is an object's true name?"

"That name which reflects the divine name in the same manner as the object reflects God."

"And what is the action of a true name?"

"To endow its object with a reflection of divine power."

"Correct. Halliwell, what is the doctrine of signatures?"

The natural philosophy lesson continued until noon, but because it was a Saturday, there was no instruction for the rest of the day. Master Trevelyan dismissed the class, and the boys of Cheltenham school dispersed.

After stopping at the dormitory, Robert met his friend Lionel at the border of school grounds. "So the wait's over? Today's the day?" Robert asked.

"I said it was, didn't I?"

"Let's go, then." The pair set off to walk the mile and a half to Lionel's home.

During his first year at Cheltenham, Robert had known Lionel hardly at all; Lionel was one of the day-boys, and Robert, like all the boarders, regarded them with suspicion. Then, purely by chance, Robert ran into him while on holiday, during a visit to the British Museum. Robert loved the museum: the frail mummies and immense sarcophagi; the stuffed platypus and pickled mermaid; the wall bristling with elephant tusks and moose antlers and unicorn horns. That particular day he was at the display of elemental sprites: He was reading the card explaining the salamander's absence when he suddenly recognized Lionel, standing right next to him, peering at the undine in its jar. Conversation revealed their shared interest in the sciences, and the two became fast friends.

As they walked down the road, they kicked a large pebble back and forth between them. Lionel gave the pebble a kick, and laughed as it skittered between Robert's ankles. "I couldn't wait to get out of there," he said. "I think one more doctrine would have been more than I could bear."

"Why do they even bother calling it natural philosophy?" said Robert. "Just admit it's another theology lesson and be done with it." The two of them had recently purchased *A Boy's Guide to Nomenclature*, which informed them that nomenclators no longer spoke in terms of God or the divine name. Instead, current thinking held that there was a lexical universe as well as a physical one, and bringing an object together with a compatible name caused the latent potentialities of both to be realized. Nor was there a single "true name" for a given object: Depending on its precise shape, a body might be compatible with several names, known as its "euonyms," and conversely a simple name might tolerate significant variations in body shape, as his childhood marching doll had demonstrated.

When they reached Lionel's home, they promised the cook they would be in for dinner shortly and headed to the garden out back. Lionel had converted a tool shed in his family's garden into a laboratory, which he used to conduct experiments. Normally Robert came by on a regular basis, but recently Lionel had been working on an experiment that he was keeping secret. Only now was he ready to show Robert his results. Lionel had Robert wait outside while he entered first, and then let him enter.

A long shelf ran along every wall of the shed, crowded with racks of vials, stoppered bottles of green glass, and assorted rocks and mineral specimens. A table decorated with stains and scorch marks dominated the cramped space, and it supported the apparatus for Lionel's latest experiment: a cucurbit clamped in a stand so that its bottom rested in a basin full of water, which in turn sat on a tripod above a lit oil lamp. A mercury thermometer was also fixed in the basin.

"Take a look," said Lionel.

Robert leaned over to inspect the cucurbit's contents. At first it appeared to be nothing more than foam, a dollop of suds that might have dripped off a pint of stout. But as he looked closer, he realized that what he thought were bubbles were actually the interstices of a glistening latticework. The froth consisted of *homunculi*: tiny seminal foetuses. Their bodies were transparent individually, but collectively their bulbous heads and strand-like limbs adhered to form a pale, dense foam.

"So you wanked off into a jar and kept the spunk warm?" he asked, and Lionel shoved him. Robert laughed and raised his hands in a placating gesture. "No, honestly, it's a wonder. How'd you do it?"

Mollified, Lionel said, "It's a real balancing act. You have to keep the temperature just right, of course, but if you want them to grow, you also have to keep just the right mix of nutrients. Too thin a mix, and they starve. Too rich, and they get over-lively and start fighting with each other."

"You're having me on."

"It's the truth; look it up if you don't believe me. Battles amongst sperm are what cause monstrosities to be born. If an injured foetus is the one that makes it to the egg, the baby that's born is deformed."

"I thought that was because of a fright the mother had when she was carrying." Robert could just make out the minuscule squirmings of the individual foetuses. He realized that the froth was ever so slowly roiling as a result of their collective motions.

"That's only for some kinds, like ones that are all hairy or covered in blotches. Babies that don't have arms or legs, or have misshapen ones, they're the ones that got caught in a fight back when they were sperm. That's why you can't provide too rich a broth, especially if they haven't any place to go: They get in a frenzy. You can lose all of them pretty quick that way."

"How long can you keep them growing?"

"Probably not much longer," said Lionel. "It's hard to keep them alive if they haven't reached an egg. I read about one in France that was grown till it was the size of a fist, and they had the best equipment available. I just wanted to see if I could do it at all."

Robert stared at the foam, remembering the doctrine of pre-formation that Master Trevelyan had drilled into them: All living things had been created at the same time, long ago, and births today were merely enlargements of the previously imperceptible. Although they appeared newly created, these *homunculi* were countless years old; for all of human history they had lain nested within generations of their ancestors, waiting for their turn to be born.

In fact, it wasn't just them who had waited; he himself must have done the same thing prior to his birth. If his father were to do this experiment, the tiny figures Robert saw would be his unborn brothers and sisters. He knew they were insensible until reaching an egg, but he wondered what thoughts they'd have if they weren't. He imagined the sensation of his body, every bone and organ soft and clear as gelatin, sticking to those of myriad identical siblings. What would it be like, looking through transparent eye-lids, realizing the mountain in the distance was actually a person, recognizing it as his brother? What if he knew he'd become as massive and solid as that colossus, if only he could reach an egg? It was no wonder they fought.

Robert Stratton went on to read nomenclature at Cambridge's Trinity College. There he studied kabbalistic texts written cen-turies before, when nomenclators were still called *ba'alei shem* and automata were called *golem*, texts that laid the foundation for the science of names: the *Sefer Yezirah*, Eleazar of Worms' *Sodei Razayya*, Abulafia's *Hayyei ha-Olam ha-Ba*. Then he studied the alchemical treatises that placed the techniques of alphabetic manipulation in a broader philosophical and mathematical con-text: Llull's *Ars Magna*, Agrippa's *De Occulta Philosophia*, Dee's *Monas Hieroglyphica*.

He learned that every name was a combination of several epithets, each designating a specific trait or capability. Epithets were generated by compiling all the words that described the desired trait: cognates and etymons, from languages both living and extinct. By selectively substituting and permuting letters, one could distill from those words their common essence, which was the epithet for that trait. In certain instances, epithets could be used as the bases for triangulation, allowing one to derive epithets for traits undescribed in any language. The entire process relied on intuition as much as formulae; the ability to choose the best letter permutations was an unteachable skill.

He studied the modern techniques of nominal integration and factorization, the former being the means by which a set of epithets—pithy and evocative—were commingled into the seemingly random string of letters that made up a name, the latter by which a name was decomposed into its constituent epithets. Not every method of integration had a matching factorization technique: A powerful name might be refactored to yield a set of epithets different from those used to generate it, and those epithets were often useful for that reason. Some names resisted refactorization, and nomenclators strove to develop new techniques to penetrate their secrets.

Nomenclature was undergoing something of a revolution during this time. There had long been two classes of names: those for animating a body, and those functioning as amulets. Health amulets were worn as protection from injury or illness, while others rendered a house resistant to fire or a ship less likely to founder at sea. Of late, however, the distinction between these categories of names was becoming blurred, with exciting results.

The nascent science of thermodynamics, which established the interconvertibility of heat and work, had recently explained how automata gained their motive power by absorbing heat from their surroundings. Using this improved understanding of heat, a *Namenmeister* in Berlin had developed a new class of amulet that caused a body to absorb heat from one location and release it in another. Refrigeration employing such amulets was simpler and more efficient than that based on the evaporation of a volatile fluid, and had immense commercial application. Amulets were likewise facilitating the improvement of automata: An Edinburgh nomenclator's research into the amulets that prevented objects from becoming lost had led him to patent a household automaton able to return objects to their proper places.

Upon graduation, Stratton took up residence in London and secured a position as a nomenclator at Coade Manufactory, one of the leading makers of automata in England.

Stratton's most recent automaton, cast from plaster of paris, followed a few paces behind him as he entered the factory building. It was an immense brick structure with skylights for its roof; half of the building was devoted to casting metal, the other half to ceramics. In either section, a meandering path connected the various rooms, each one housing the next step in transforming raw materials into finished automata. Stratton and his automaton entered the ceramics portion.

They walked past a row of low vats in which the clay was mixed. Different vats contained different grades of clay, ranging from common red clay to fine white kaolin, resembling enormous mugs abrim with liquid chocolate or heavy cream; only the strong mineral smell broke the illusion. The paddles stirring the clay were connected by gears to a drive shaft, mounted just beneath the skylights, that ran the length of the room. At the end of the room stood an automatous engine: a cast-iron giant that cranked the drive wheel tirelessly. Walking past, Stratton could detect a faint coolness in the air as the engine drew heat from its surroundings.

The next room held the molds for casting. Chalky white shells bearing the inverted contours of various automata were stacked along the walls. In the central portion of the room, apron-clad journeymen sculptors worked singly and in pairs, tending the cocoons from which automata were hatched.

The sculptor nearest him was assembling the mold for a putter, a broad-headed quadruped employed in the mines for pushing trolleys of ore. The young man looked up from his work. "Were you looking for someone, sir?" he asked.

"I'm to meet Master Willoughby here," replied Stratton.

"Pardon, I didn't realize. I'm sure he'll be here shortly." The journeyman returned to his task. Harold Willoughby was a Master Sculptor First-Degree; Stratton was consulting him on the design of a reusable mold for casting his automaton. While he waited, Stratton strolled idly amongst the molds. His automaton stood motionless, ready for its next command.

Willoughby entered from the door to the metalworks, his face flushed from the heat of the foundry. "My apologies for being late, Mr. Stratton," he said. "We've been working toward a large bronze for some weeks now, and today was the pour. You don't want to leave the lads alone at a time like that."

"I understand completely," replied Stratton.

Wasting no time, Willoughby strode over to the new automaton. "Is this what you've had Moore doing all these months?" Moore was the journeyman assisting Stratton on his project.

Stratton nodded. "The boy does good work." Following Stratton's requests, Moore had fashioned countless bodies, all variations on a single basic theme, by applying modeling clay to an armature, and then used them to create plaster casts on which Stratton could test his names.

Willoughby inspected the body. "Some nice detail; looks straightforward enough—hold on now." He pointed to the automaton's hands: Rather than the traditional paddle or mitten design, with fingers suggested by grooves in the surface, these were fully formed, each one having a thumb and four distinct and separate fingers. "You don't mean to tell me those are functional?"

"That's correct."

Willoughby's skepticism was plain. "Show me."

Stratton addressed the automaton. "Flex your fingers." The automaton extended both hands, flexed and straightened each pair of fingers in turn, and then returned its arms to its sides.

"I congratulate you, Mr. Stratton," said the sculptor. He squatted to examine the automaton's fingers more closely. "The fingers need to be bent at each joint for the name to take?"

"That's right. Can you design a piece mold for such a form?"

Willoughby clicked his tongue several times. "That'll be a tricky bit of business," he said. "We might have to use a waste mold for each casting. Even with a piece mold, these'd be very expensive for ceramic."

"I think they will be worth the expense. Permit me to demonstrate." Stratton addressed to the automaton. "Cast a body; use that mold over there."

The automaton trudged over to a nearby wall and picked up the pieces of the mold Stratton had indicated: It was the mold for a small porcelain messenger. Several journeymen stopped what they were doing to watch the automaton carry the pieces over to a work area. There it fitted the various sections together and bound them tightly with twine. The sculptors' wonderment was apparent as they watched the automaton's fingers work, looping and threading the loose ends of the twine into a knot. Then the automaton stood the assembled mold upright and headed off to get a pitcher of clay slip.

"That's enough," said Willoughby. The automaton stopped its work and resumed its original standing posture. Examining the mold, Willoughby asked, "Did you train it yourself?"

"I did. I hope to have Moore train it in metal casting."

"Do you have names that can learn other tasks?"

"Not as yet. However, there's every reason to believe that an entire class of similar names exists, one for every sort of skill needing manual dexterity."

"Indeed?" Willoughby noticed the other sculptors watching, and called out, "If you've nothing to do, there's plenty I can assign to you." The journeymen promptly resumed their work, and Willoughby turned back to Stratton. "Let us go to your office to speak about this further."

"Very well." Stratton had the automaton follow the two of them back to the frontmost of the complex of connected buildings that was Coade Manufactory. They first entered Stratton's studio, which was situated behind his office proper. Once inside, Stratton addressed the sculptor. "Do you have an objection to my automaton?"

Willoughby looked over a pair of clay hands mounted on a work-table. On the wall behind the table were pinned a series of schematic drawings showing hands in a variety of positions. "You've done an admirable job of emulating the human hand. I am concerned, however, that the first skill in which you trained your new automaton is sculpture."

"If you're worried that I am trying to replace sculptors, you needn't be. That is absolutely not my goal."

"I'm relieved to hear it," said Willoughby. "Why did you choose sculpture, then?"

"It is the first step of a rather indirect path. My ultimate goal is to allow automatous engines to be manufactured inexpensively enough so that most families could purchase one."

Willoughby's confusion was apparent. "How, pray tell, would a family make use of an engine?"

"To drive a powered loom, for example."

"What are you going on about?"

"Have you ever seen children who are employed at a textile mill? They are worked to exhaustion; their lungs are clogged with cotton dust; they are so sickly that you can hardly conceive of their reaching adulthood. Cheap cloth is bought at the price of our workers' health; weavers were far better off when textile production was a cottage industry."

"Powered looms were what took weavers out of cottages. How could they put them back in?"

Stratton had not spoken of this before, and welcomed the opportunity to explain. "The cost of automatous engines has always been high, and so we have mills in which scores of looms are driven by an immense coal-heated Goliath. But an automaton like mine could cast engines very cheaply. If a small automatous engine, suitable for driving a few machines, becomes affordable to a weaver and his family, then they can produce cloth from their home as they did once before. People could earn a decent income without being subjected to the conditions of the factory."

"You forget the cost of the loom itself," said Willoughby gently, as if humoring him. "Powered looms are considerably more expensive than the hand looms of old."

"My automata could also assist in the production of cast-iron parts, which would reduce the price of powered looms and other machines. This is no panacea, I know, but I am nonetheless convinced that inexpensive engines offer the chance of a better life for the individual craftsman."

"Your desire for reform does you credit. Let me suggest, however, that there are simpler cures for the social ills you cite: a reduction in working hours, or the improvement of conditions. You do not need to disrupt our entire system of manufacturing."

"I think what I propose is more accurately described as a restoration than a disruption."

Now Willoughby became exasperated. "This talk of returning to a family economy is all well and good, but what would happen to sculptors? Your intentions notwithstanding, these automata of yours would put sculptors out of work. These are men who have undergone years of apprenticeship and training. How would they feed their families?"

Stratton was unprepared for the sharpness in his tone. "You overestimate my skills as a nomenclator," he said, trying to make light. The sculptor remained dour. He continued. "The learning capabilities of these automata are extremely limited. They can manipulate molds, but they could never design them; the real craft of sculpture can be performed only by sculptors. Before our meeting, you had just finished directing several journeymen in the pouring of a large bronze; automata could never work together in such a coordinated fashion. They will perform only rote tasks."

"What kind of sculptors would we produce if they spend their apprenticeship watching automata do their jobs for them? I will not have a venerable profession reduced to a performance by marionettes."

"That is not what would happen," said Stratton, becoming exasperated himself now. "But examine what you yourself are saying: The status that you wish your profession to retain is precisely that which weavers have been made to forfeit. I believe these automata can help restore dignity to other professions, and without great cost to yours."

Willoughby seemed not to hear him. "The very notion that automata would make automata! Not only is the suggestion insulting, it seems ripe for calamity. What of that ballad, the one where the broomsticks carry water buckets and run amuck?"

"You mean 'Der Zauberlehrling'?" said Stratton. "The comparison is absurd. These automata are so far removed from being in a position to reproduce themselves without human participation that I scarcely know where to begin listing the objections. A dancing bear would sooner perform in the London Ballet."

"If you'd care to develop an automaton that can dance the ballet, I would fully support such an enterprise. However, you cannot continue with these dexterous automata."

"Pardon me, sir, but I am not bound by your decisions."

"You'll find it difficult to work without sculptors' cooperation. I shall recall Moore and forbid all the other journeymen from assisting you in any way with this project."

Stratton was momentarily taken aback. "Your reaction is completely unwarranted."

"I think it entirely appropriate."

"In that case, I will work with sculptors at another manufactory."

Willoughby frowned. "I will speak with the head of the Brotherhood of Sculptors, and recommend that he forbid all of our members from casting your automata."

Stratton could feel his blood rising. "I will not be bullied," he said. "Do what you will, but you cannot prevent me from pursuing this."

"I think our discussion is at an end." Willoughby strode to the door. "Good day to you, Mr. Stratton."

"Good day to you," replied Stratton heatedly.

It was the following day, and Stratton was taking his midday stroll through the district of Lambeth, where Coade Manufactory was located. After a few blocks he stopped at a local market; sometimes among the baskets of writhing eels and blankets spread with cheap watches were automatous dolls, and Stratton retained his boyhood fondness for seeing the latest designs. Today he noticed a new pair of boxing dolls, painted to look like an explorer and a savage. As he looked them over, he could hear nostrum peddlers competing for the attention of a passerby with a runny nose.

"I see your health amulet failed you, sir," said one man whose table was arrayed with small square tins. "Your remedy lies in the curative powers of magnetism, concentrated in Doctor Sedgewick's Polarising Tablets!"

"Nonsense!" retorted an old woman. "What you need is tincture of mandrake, tried and true!" She held out a vial of clear liquid. "The dog wasn't cold yet when this extract was prepared! There's nothing more potent."

Seeing no other new dolls, Stratton left the market and walked on, his thoughts returning to what Willoughby had said yesterday. Without the cooperation of the sculptors' trade-union, he'd have to resort to hiring independent sculptors. He hadn't worked with such individuals before, and some investigation would be required: ostensibly they cast bodies only for use with public-domain names, but for certain individuals these activities disguised patent infringement and piracy, and any association with them could permanently blacken his reputation.

"Mr. Stratton."

Stratton looked up. A small, wiry man, plainly dressed, stood before him. "Yes; do I know you, sir?"

"No, sir. My name is Davies. I'm in the employ of Lord Fieldhurst." He handed Stratton a card bearing the Fieldhurst crest.

Edward Maitland, third earl of Fieldhurst and a noted zoologist and comparative anatomist, was President of the Royal Society. Stratton had heard him speak during sessions of the Royal Society, but they had never been introduced. "What can I do for you?"

"Lord Fieldhurst would like to speak with you, at your earliest convenience, regarding your recent work."

Stratton wondered how the earl had learned of his work. "Why did you not call on me at my office?"

"Lord Fieldhurst prefers privacy in this matter." Stratton raised his eyebrows, but Davies didn't explain further. "Are you available this evening?"

It was an unusual invitation, but an honor nonetheless. "Certainly. Please inform Lord Fieldhurst that I would be delighted."

"A carriage will be outside your building at eight tonight." Davies touched his hat and was off.

At the promised hour, Davies arrived with the carriage. It was a luxurious vehicle, with an interior of lacquered mahogany and polished brass and brushed velvet. The tractor that drew it was an expensive one as well, a steed cast of bronze and needing no driver for familiar destinations.

Davies politely declined to answer any questions while they rode. He was obviously not a man-servant, nor a secretary, but Stratton could not decide what sort of employee he was. The carriage carried them out of London into the countryside, until they reached Darrington Hall, one of the residences owned by the Fieldhurst lineage.

Once inside the home, Davies led Stratton through the foyer and then ushered him into an elegantly appointed study; he closed the doors without entering himself.

Seated at the desk within the study was a barrel-chested man wearing a silk coat and cravat; his broad, deeply creased cheeks were framed by woolly gray muttonchops. Stratton recognized him at once.

"Lord Fieldhurst, it is an honor."

"A pleasure to meet you, Mr. Stratton. You've been doing some excellent work recently."

"You are most kind. I did not realize that my work had become known."

"I make an effort to keep track of such things. Please, tell me what motivated you to develop such automata?"

Stratton explained his plans for manufacturing affordable engines. Fieldhurst listened with interest, occasionally offering cogent suggestions.

"It is an admirable goal," he said, nodding his approval. "I'm pleased to find that you have such philanthropic motives, because I would ask your assistance in a project I'm directing."

"It would be my privilege to help in any way I could."

"Thank you." Fieldhurst's expression became solemn. "This is a matter of grave import. Before I speak further, I must first have your word that you will retain everything I reveal to you in the utmost confidence."

Stratton met the earl's gaze directly. "Upon my honor as a gentleman, sir, I shall not divulge anything you relate to me."

"Thank you, Mr. Stratton. Please come this way." Fieldhurst opened a door in the rear wall of the study and they walked down a short hallway. At the end of the hallway was a laboratory; a long, scrupulously clean work-table held a number of stations, each consisting of a microscope and an articulated brass framework of some sort, equipped with three mutually perpendicular knurled wheels for performing fine adjustments. An elderly man was peering into the microscope at the furthest station; he looked up from his work as they entered.

"Mr. Stratton, I believe you know Dr. Ashbourne."

Stratton, caught off guard, was momentarily speechless. Nicholas Ashbourne had been a lecturer at Trinity when Stratton was studying there, but had left years ago to pursue studies of, it was said, an unorthodox nature. Stratton remembered him as one of his most enthusiastic instructors. Age had narrowed his face somewhat, making his high forehead seem even higher, but his eyes were as bright and alert as ever. He walked over with the help of a carved ivory walking stick.

"Stratton, good to see you again."

"And you, sir. I was truly not expecting to see you here."

"This will be an evening full of surprises, my boy. Prepare yourself." He turned to Fieldhurst. "Would you care to begin?"

They followed Fieldhurst to the far end of the laboratory, where he opened another door and led them down a flight of stairs. "Only a small number of individuals—either Fellows of the Royal Society or Members of Parliament, or both—are privy to this matter. Five years ago, I was contacted confidentially by the Académie des Sciences in Paris. They wished for English scientists to confirm certain experimental findings of theirs."

"Indeed?"

"You can imagine their reluctance. However, they felt the matter outweighed national rivalries, and once I understood the situation, I agreed."

The three of them descended to a cellar. Gas brackets along the walls provided illumination, revealing the cellar's considerable size; its interior was punctuated by an array of stone pillars that rose to form groined vaults. The long cellar contained row upon row of stout wooden tables, each one supporting a tank roughly the size of a bathtub. The tanks were made of zinc and fitted with plate glass windows on all four sides, revealing their contents as a clear, faintly straw-colored fluid.

Stratton looked at the nearest tank. There was a distortion floating in the center of the tank, as if some of the liquid had congealed into a mass of jelly. It was difficult to distinguish the mass's features from the mottled shadows cast on the bottom of the tank, so he moved to another side of the tank and squatted down low to view the mass directly against a flame of a gas lamp. It was then that the coagulum resolved itself into the ghostly figure of a man, clear as aspic, curled up in foetal position.

"Incredible," Stratton whispered.

"We call it a megafoetus," explained Fieldhurst.

"This was grown from a spermatozoon? This must have required decades."

"It did not, more's the wonder. Several years ago, two Parisian naturalists named Dubuisson and Gille developed a method of inducing hypertrophic growth in a seminal foetus. The rapid infusion of nutrients allows such a foetus to reach this size within a fortnight."

By shifting his head back and forth, he saw slight differences in the way the gas-light was refracted, indicating the boundaries of the megafoetus's internal organs. "Is this creature . . . alive?"

"Only in an insensate manner, like a spermatozoon. No artificial process can replace gestation; it is the vital principle within the ovum which quickens the foetus, and the maternal influence which transforms it into a person. All we've done is effect a maturation in size and scale." Fieldhurst gestured toward the megafoetus. "The maternal influence also provides a foetus with pigmentation and all distinguishing physical characteristics. Our megafoetuses have no features beyond their sex. Every male bears the generic appearance you see here, and all the females are likewise identical. Within each sex, it is impossible to distinguish one from another by physical examination, no matter how dissimilar the original fathers

might have been; only rigorous record-keeping allows us to identify each megafoetus."

Stratton stood up again. "So what was the intention of the
experiment if not to develop an artificial womb?"

"To test the notion of the fixity of species." Realizing that
Stratton was not a zoologist, the earl explained further. "Were
lens-grinders able to construct microscopes of unlimited magnifying power, biologists could examine the future generations nested
in the spermatozoa of any species and see whether their appearance remains fixed, or changes to give rise to a new species. In the
latter case, they could also determine if the transition occurs gradually or abruptly.

"However, chromatic aberration imposes an upper limit on the
magnifying power of any optical instrument. Messieurs Dubuisson and Gille hit upon the idea of artificially increasing the size of
the foetuses themselves. Once a foetus reaches its adult size, one
can extract a spermatozoon from it and enlarge a foetus from the
next generation in the same manner." Fieldhurst stepped over to
the next table in the row and indicated the tank it supported. "Repetition of the process lets us examine the unborn generations of
any given species."

Stratton looked around the room. The rows of tanks took on a
new significance. "So they compressed the intervals between
'births' to gain a preliminary view of our genealogical future."

"Precisely."

"Audacious! And what were the results?"

"They tested many animal species, but never observed any
changes in form. However, they obtained a peculiar result when
working with the seminal foetuses of humans. After no more than
five generations, the male foetuses held no more spermatozoa, and
the females held no more ova. The line terminated in a sterile
generation."

"I imagine that wasn't entirely unexpected," Stratton said,
glancing at the jellied form. "Each repetition must further attenu-

ate some essence in the organisms. It's only logical that at some point the offspring would be so feeble that the process would fail."

"That was Dubuisson and Gille's initial assumption as well," agreed Fieldhurst, "so they sought to improve their technique. However, they could find no difference between megafoetuses of succeeding generations in terms of size or vitality. Nor was there any decline in the number of spermatozoa or ova; the penultimate generation was fully as fertile as the first. The transition to sterility was an abrupt one.

"They found another anomaly as well: While some spermatozoa yielded only four or fewer generations, variation occurred only across samples, never within a single sample. They evaluated samples from father and son donors, and in such instances, the father's spermatozoa produced exactly one more generation than the son's. And from what I understand, some of the donors were aged individuals indeed. While their samples held very few spermatozoa, they nonetheless held one more generation than those from sons in the prime of their lives. The progenitive power of the sperm bore no correlation with the health or vigor of the donor; instead, it correlated with the generation to which the donor belonged."

Fieldhurst paused and looked at Stratton gravely. "It was at this point that the Académie contacted me to see if the Royal Society could duplicate their findings. Together we have obtained the same result using samples collected from peoples as varied as the Lapps and the Hottentots. We are in agreement as to the implication of these findings: that the human species has the potential to exist for only a fixed number of generations, and we are within five generations of the final one."

Stratton turned to Ashbourne, half expecting him to confess that it was all an elaborate hoax, but the elder nomenclator looked entirely solemn. Stratton looked at the megafoetus again and frowned, absorbing what he had heard. "If your interpretation is correct, other species must be subject to a similar limitation. Yet from what I know, the extinction of a species has never been observed."

Fieldhurst nodded. "That is true. However, we do have the evidence of the fossil record, which suggests that species remain unchanged for a period of time, and then are abruptly replaced by new forms. The Catastrophists hold that violent upheavals caused species to become extinct. Based on what we've discovered regarding preformation, it now appears that extinctions are merely the result of a species reaching the end of its lifetime. They are natural rather than accidental deaths, in a manner of speaking." He gestured to the doorway from which they had entered. "Shall we return upstairs?"

Following the two other men, Stratton asked, "And what of the origination of new species? If they're not born from existing species, do they arise spontaneously?"

"That is as yet uncertain. Normally only the simplest animals arise by spontaneous generation: maggots and other vermiform creatures, typically under the influence of heat. The events postulated by Catastrophists—floods, volcanic eruptions, cometary impacts—would entail the release of great energies. Perhaps such energies affect matter so profoundly as to cause the spontaneous generation of an entire race of organisms, nested within a few progenitors. If so, cataclysms are not responsible for mass extinctions, but rather generate new species in their wake."

Back in the laboratory, the two elder men seated themselves in the chairs present. Too agitated to follow suit, Stratton remained standing. "If any animal species were created by the same cataclysm as the human species, they should likewise be nearing the end of their lifespans. Have you found another species that evinces a final generation?"

Fieldhurst shook his head. "Not as yet. We believe that other species have different dates of extinction, correlated with the biological complexity of the animal; humans are presumably the most complex organism, and perhaps fewer generations of such complex organisms can be nested inside a spermatozoon."

"By the same token," countered Stratton, "perhaps the complexity of the human organism makes it unsuitable for the process of artificially accelerated growth. Perhaps it is the process whose limits have been discovered, not the species."

"An astute observation, Mr. Stratton. Experiments are continuing with species that more closely resemble humans, such as chimpanzees and ourang-outangs. However, the unequivocal answer to this question may require years, and if our current interpretation is correct, we can ill afford the time spent waiting for confirmation. We must ready a course of action immediately."

"But five generations could be over a century—" He caught himself, embarrassed at having overlooked the obvious: not all persons became parents at the same age.

Fieldhurst read his expression. "You realize why not all the sperm samples from donors of the same age produced the same number of generations: Some lineages are approaching their end faster than others. For a lineage in which the men consistently father children late in life, five generations might mean over two centuries of fertility, but there are undoubtedly lineages that have reached their end already."

Stratton imagined the consequences. "The loss of fertility will becomes increasingly apparent to the general populace as time passes. Panic may arise well before the end is reached."

"Precisely, and rioting could extinguish our species as effectively as the exhaustion of generations. That is why time is of the essence."

"What is the solution you propose?"

"I shall defer to Dr. Ashbourne to explain further," said the earl.

Ashbourne rose and instinctively adopted the stance of a lecturing professor. "Do you recall why it was that all attempts to make automata out of wood were abandoned?"

Stratton was caught off guard by the question. "It was believed that the natural grain of wood implies a form in conflict with whatever we try to carve upon it. Currently there are efforts to use rubber as a casting material, but none have met with success."

"Indeed. But if the native form of wood were the only obstacle, shouldn't it be possible to animate an animal's corpse with a name? There the form of the body should be ideal."

"It's a macabre notion; I couldn't guess at such an experiment's likelihood of success. Has it ever been attempted?"

"In fact it has: also unsuccessfully. So these two entirely different avenues of research proved fruitless. Does that mean there is no way to animate organic matter using names? This was the question I left Trinity in order to pursue."

"And what did you discover?"

Ashbourne deflected the question with a wave of his hand. "First let us discuss thermodynamics. Have you kept up with recent developments? Then you know the dissipation of heat reflects an increase in disorder at the thermal level. Conversely, when an automaton condenses heat from its environment to perform work, it increases order. This confirms a long-held belief of mine that lexical order induces thermodynamic order. The lexical order of an amulet reinforces the order a body already possesses, thus providing protection against damage. The lexical order of an animating name increases the order of a body, thus providing motive power for an automaton.

"The next question was, how would an increase in order be reflected in organic matter? Since names don't animate dead tissue, obviously organic matter doesn't respond at the thermal level; but perhaps it can be ordered at another level. Consider: a steer can be reduced to a vat of gelatinous broth. The broth comprises the same material as the steer, but which embodies a higher amount of order?"

"The steer, obviously," said Stratton, bewildered.

"Obviously. An organism, by virtue of its physical structure, embodies order; the more complex the organism, the greater the amount of order. It was my hypothesis that increasing the order in organic matter would be evidenced by imparting form to it. However, most living matter has already assumed its ideal form. The question is, what has life but not form?"

The elder nomenclator did not wait for a response. "The answer is, an unfertilized ovum. The ovum contains the vital principle that animates the creature it ultimately gives rise to, but it has no form itself. Ordinarily, the ovum incorporates the form of the foetus compressed within the spermatozoon that fertilizes it. The next step was obvious." Here Ashbourne waited, looking at Stratton expectantly.

Stratton was at a loss. Ashbourne seemed disappointed, and continued. "The next step was to artificially induce the growth of an embryo from an ovum, by application of a name."

"But if the ovum is unfertilized," objected Stratton, "there is no preexisting structure to enlarge."

"Precisely."

"You mean structure would arise out of a homogeneous medium? Impossible."

"Nonetheless, it was my goal for several years to confirm this hypothesis. My first experiments consisted of applying a name to unfertilized frog eggs."

"How did you embed the name into a frog's egg?"

"The name is not actually embedded, but rather impressed by means of a specially manufactured needle." Ashbourne opened a cabinet that sat on the work-table between two of the microscope stations. Inside was a wooden rack filled with small instruments arranged in pairs. Each was tipped with a long glass needle; in some pairs they were nearly as thick as those used for knitting, in others as slender as a hypodermic. He withdrew one from the largest pair and handed it to Stratton to examine. The glass needle was not clear, but instead seemed to contain some sort of dappled core.

Ashbourne explained. "While that may appear to be some sort

of medical implement, it is in fact a vehicle for a name, just as the more conventional slip of parchment is. Alas, it requires far more effort to make than taking pen to parchment. To create such a needle, one must first arrange fine strands of black glass within a bundle of clear glass strands so that the name is legible when they are viewed end-on. The strands are then fused into a solid rod, and the rod is drawn out into an ever thinner strand. A skilled glass-maker can retain every detail of the name no matter how thin the strand becomes. Eventually one obtains a needle containing the name in its cross section."

"How did you generate the name that you used?"

"We can discuss that at length later. For the purposes of our current discussion, the only relevant information is that I incorporated the sexual epithet. Are you familiar with it?"

"I know of it." It was one of the few epithets that was dimorphic, having male and female variants.

"I needed two versions of the name, obviously, to induce the generation of both males and females." He indicated the paired arrangement of needles in the cabinet.

Stratton saw that the needle could be clamped into the brass framework with its tip approaching the slide beneath the microscope; the knurled wheels presumably were used to bring the needle into contact with an ovum. He returned the instrument. "You said the name is not embedded, but impressed. Do you mean to tell me that touching the frog's egg with this needle is all that's needed? Removing the name doesn't end its influence?"

"Precisely. The name activates a process in the egg that cannot be reversed. Prolonged contact of the name had no different effect."

"And the egg hatched a tadpole?"

"Not with the names initially tried; the only result was that symmetrical involutions appeared in the surface of the egg. But by incorporating different epithets, I was able to induce the egg to adopt different forms, some of which had every appearance of

embryonic frogs. Eventually I found a name that caused the egg
not only to assume the form of a tadpole, but also to mature and
hatch. The tadpole thus hatched grew into a frog indistinguishable
from any other member of the species."

"You had found a euonym for that species of frog," said
Stratton.

Ashbourne smiled. "As this method of reproduction does not
involve sexual congress, I have termed it 'parthenogenesis.' "

Stratton looked at both him and Fieldhurst. "It's clear what
your proposed solution is. The logical conclusion of this research is
to discover a euonym for the human species. You wish for mankind
to perpetuate itself through nomenclature."

"You find the prospect troubling," said Fieldhurst. "That is to
be expected: Dr. Ashbourne and myself initially felt the same way,
as has everyone who has considered this. No one relishes the
prospect of humans being conceived artificially. But can you offer
an alternative?" Stratton was silent, and Fieldhurst went on. "All
who are aware of both Dr. Ashbourne's and Dubuisson and Gille's
work agree: There is no other solution."

Stratton reminded himself to maintain the dispassionate attitude of a scientist. "Precisely how do you envision this name being
used?" he asked.

Ashbourne answered. "When a husband is unable to impreg-
nate his wife, they will seek the services of a physician. The physician will collect the woman's menses, separate out the ovum,
impress the name upon it, and then reintroduce it into her womb."

"A child born of this method would have no biological father."

"True, but the father's biological contribution is of minimal
importance here. The mother will think of her husband as the
child's father, so her imagination will impart a combination of her
own and her husband's appearance and character to the foetus.
That will not change. And I hardly need mention that name
impression would not be made available to unmarried women."

"Are you confident this will result in well-formed children?"

asked Stratton. "I'm sure you know to what I refer." They all knew of the disastrous attempt in the previous century to create improved children by mesmerizing women during their pregnancies.

Ashbourne nodded. "We are fortunate in that the ovum is very specific in what it will accept. The set of euonyms for any species of organism is very small; if the lexical order of the impressed name does not closely match the structural order of that species, the resulting foetus does not quicken. This does not remove the need for the mother to maintain a tranquil mind during her pregnancy; name impression cannot guard against maternal agitation. But the ovum's selectivity provides us assurance that any foetus induced will be well-formed in every aspect, except the one anticipated."

Stratton was alarmed. "What aspect is that?"

"Can you not guess? The only incapacity of frogs created by name impression was in the males; they were sterile, for their spermatozoa bore no preformed foetuses inside. By comparison, the female frogs created were fertile: Their eggs could be fertilized in either the conventional manner, or by repeating the impression with the name."

Stratton's relief was considerable. "So the male variant of the name was imperfect. Presumably there needs to be further differences between the male and female variants than simply the sexual epithet."

"Only if one considers the male variant imperfect," said Ashbourne, "which I do not. Consider: While a fertile male and a fertile female might seem equivalent, they differ radically in the degree of complexity exemplified. A female with viable ova remains a single organism, while a male with viable spermatozoa is actually many organisms: a father and all his potential children. In this light, the two variants of the name are well-matched in their actions: Each induces a single organism, but only in the female sex can a single organism be fertile."

"I see what you mean." Stratton realized he would need practice in thinking about nomenclature in the organic domain. "Have you developed euonyms for other species?"

"Just over a score, of various types; our progress has been rapid. We have only just begun work on a name for the human species, and it has proved far more difficult than our previous names."

"How many nomenclators are engaged in this endeavor?"

"Only a handful," Fieldhurst replied. "We have asked a few Royal Society members, and the Académie has some of France's leading designateurs working on it. You will understand if I do not mention any names at this point, but be assured that we have some of the most distinguished nomenclators in England assisting us."

"Forgive me for asking, but why are you approaching me? I am hardly in that category."

"You have not yet had a long career," said Ashbourne, "but the genus of names you have developed is unique. Automata have always been specialized in form and function, rather like animals: Some are good at climbing, others at digging, but none at both. Yet yours can control human hands, which are uniquely versatile instruments: What else can manipulate everything from a wrench to a piano? The hand's dexterity is the physical manifestation of the mind's ingenuity, and these traits are essential to the name we seek."

"We have been discreetly surveying current nomenclatoral research for any names that demonstrate marked dexterity," said Fieldhurst. "When we learned of what you had accomplished, we sought you out immediately."

"In fact," Ashbourne continued, "the very reason your names are worrisome to sculptors is the reason we are interested in them: They endow automata with a more human-like manner than any before. So now we ask, will you join us?"

Stratton considered it. This was perhaps the most important task a nomenclator could undertake, and under ordinary circumstances he would have leapt at the opportunity to participate. But before he could embark upon this enterprise in good conscience, there was another matter he had to resolve.

"You honor me with your invitation, but what of my work with dexterous automata? I still firmly believe that inexpensive engines can improve the lives of the labouring class."

"It is a worthy goal," said Fieldhurst, "and I would not ask you to give it up. Indeed, the first thing we wish you to do is to perfect the epithets for dexterity. But your efforts at social reform would be for naught unless we first ensure the survival of our species."

"Obviously, but I do not want the potential for reform that is offered by dexterous names to be neglected. There may never be a better opportunity for restoring dignity to common workers. What kind of victory would we achieve if the continuation of life meant ignoring this opportunity?"

"Well said," acknowledged the earl. "Let me make a proposal. So that you can best make use of your time, the Royal Society will provide support for your development of dexterous automata as needed: securing investors and so forth. I trust you will divide your time between the two projects wisely. Your work on biological nomenclature must remain confidential, obviously. Is that satisfactory?"

"It is. Very well then, gentlemen: I accept." They shook hands.

Some weeks had passed since Stratton last spoke with Willoughby, beyond a chilly exchange of greetings in passing. In fact, he had little interaction with any of the union sculptors, instead spending his time working on letter permutations in his office, trying to refine his epithets for dexterity.

He entered the manufactory through the front gallery, where customers normally perused the catalogue. Today it was crowded with domestic automata, all the same model char-engine. Stratton saw the clerk ensuring they were properly tagged.

"Good morning, Pierce," he said. "What are all these doing here?"

"An improved name is just out for the 'Regent,'" said the clerk. "Everyone's eager to get the latest."

"You're going to be busy this afternoon." The keys for unlocking the automata's name-slots were themselves stored in a safe that required two of Coade's managers to open. The managers were reluctant to keep the safe open for more than a brief period each afternoon.

"I'm certain I can finish these in time."

"You couldn't bear to tell a pretty house-maid that her char-engine wouldn't be ready by tomorrow."

The clerk smiled. "Can you blame me, sir?"

"No, I cannot," said Stratton, chuckling. He turned toward the business offices behind the gallery, when he found himself confronted by Willoughby.

"Perhaps you ought to prop open the safe," said the sculptor, "so that house-maids might not be inconvenienced. Seeing how destroying our institutions seems to be your intent."

"Good morning, Master Willoughby," said Stratton, stiffly. He tried to walk past, but the other man stood in his way.

"I've been informed that Coade will be allowing non-union sculptors on to the premises to assist you."

"Yes, but I assure you, only the most reputable independent sculptors are involved."

"As if such persons exist," said Willoughby scornfully. "You should know that I recommended that our trade-union launch a strike against Coade in protest."

"Surely you're not serious." It had been decades since the last strike launched by the sculptors, and that one had ended in rioting.

"I am. Were the matter put to a vote of the membership, I'm certain it would pass: Other sculptors with whom I've discussed your work agree with me about the threat it poses. However, the union leadership will not put it to a vote."

"Ah, so they disagreed with your assessment."

Here Willoughby frowned. "Apparently the Royal Society intervened on your behalf and persuaded the Brotherhood to refrain for the time being. You've found yourself some powerful supporters, Mr. Stratton."

Uncomfortably, Stratton replied, "The Royal Society considers my research worthwhile."

"Perhaps, but do not believe that this matter is ended."

"Your animosity is unwarranted, I tell you," Stratton insisted. "Once you have seen how sculptors can use these automata, you will realize that there is no threat to your profession."

Willoughby merely glowered in response and left.

The next time he saw Lord Fieldhurst, Stratton asked him about the Royal Society's involvement. They were in Fieldhurst's study, and the earl was pouring himself a whiskey.

"Ah yes," he said. "While the Brotherhood of Sculptors as a whole is quite formidable, it is composed of individuals who individually are more amenable to persuasion."

"What manner of persuasion?"

"The Royal Society is aware that members of the trade-union's leadership were party to an as-yet unresolved case of name piracy to the continent. To avoid any scandal, they've agreed to postpone any decision about strikes until after you've given a demonstration of your system of manufacturing."

"I'm grateful for your assistance, Lord Fieldhurst," said Stratton, astonished. "I must admit, I had no idea that the Royal Society employed such tactics."

"Obviously, these are not proper topics for discussion at the general sessions." Lord Fieldhurst smiled in an avuncular manner. "The advancement of science is not always a straightforward affair, Mr. Stratton, and the Royal Society is sometimes required to use both official and unofficial channels."

"I'm beginning to appreciate that."

"Similarly, although the Brotherhood of Sculptors won't initiate a formal strike, they might employ more indirect tactics; for example, the anonymous distribution of pamphlets that arouse public opposition to your automata." He sipped at his whiskey. "Hmm. Perhaps I should have someone keep a watchful eye on Master Willoughby."

Stratton was given accommodations in the guest wing of Darrington Hall, as were the other nomenclators working under Lord Fieldhurst's direction. They were indeed some of the leading members of the profession, including Holcombe, Milburn, and Parker; Stratton felt honored to be working with them, although he could contribute little while he was still learning Ashbourne's techniques for biological nomenclature.

Names for the organic domain employed many of the same epithets as names for automata, but Ashbourne had developed an entirely different system of integration and factorization, which entailed many novel methods of permutation. For Stratton it was almost like returning to university and learning nomenclature all over again. However, it was apparent how these techniques allowed names for species to be developed rapidly; by exploiting similarities suggested by the Linnaean system of classification, one could work from one species to another.

Stratton also learned more about the sexual epithet, traditionally used to confer either male or female qualities to an automaton. He knew of only one such epithet, and was surprised to learn it was the simplest of many extant versions. The topic went undiscussed by nomenclatoral societies, but this epithet was one of the most fully researched in existence; in fact its earliest use was claimed to have occurred in biblical times, when Joseph's brothers created a female *golem* they could share sexually without violating the prohibition against such behavior with a woman. Development of the epithet had continued for centuries in secrecy, primarily in Constantinople, and now the current versions of automatous courtesans were offered by specialized brothels right here in London. Carved from soapstone and polished to a high gloss, heated to blood temperature and sprinkled with scented oils, the automata commanded prices exceeded only by those for incubi and succubi.

It was from such ignoble soil that their research grew. The names animating the courtesans incorporated powerful epithets for human sexuality in its male and female forms. By factoring out the carnality common to both versions, the nomenclators had isolated epithets for generic human masculinity and femininity, ones far more refined than those used when generating animals. Such epithets were the nuclei around which they formed, by accretion, the names they sought.

Gradually Stratton absorbed sufficient information to begin participating in the tests of prospective human names. He worked in collaboration with the other nomenclators in the group, and between them they divided up the vast tree of nominal possibilities, assigning branches for investigation, pruning away those that proved unfruitful, cultivating those that seemed most productive.

The nomenclators paid women—typically young housemaids in good health—for their menses as a source of human ova, which they then impressed with their experimental names and scrutinized under microscopes, looking for forms that resembled human foetuses. Stratton inquired about the possibility of harvesting ova from female megafoetuses, but Ashbourne reminded him that ova were viable only when taken from a living woman. It was a basic dictum of biology: Females were the source of the vital principle that gave the offspring life, while males provided the basic form. Because of this division, neither sex could reproduce by itself.

Of course, that restriction had been lifted by Ashbourne's discovery: The male's participation was no longer necessary since form could be induced lexically. Once a name was found that could generate human foetuses, women could reproduce purely by themselves. Stratton realized that such a discovery might be welcomed by women exhibiting sexual inversion, feeling love for persons of the same rather than the opposite sex. If the name were to become available to such women, they might establish a commune of some sort that reproduced via parthenogenesis. Would such a society flourish by magnifying the finer sensibilities of the gentle sex, or would it collapse under the unrestrained pathology of its membership? It was impossible to guess.

Before Stratton's enlistment, the nomenclators had developed names capable of generating vaguely homuncular forms in an ovum. Using Dubuisson and Gille's methods, they enlarged the forms to a size that allowed detailed examination; the forms resembled automata more than humans, their limbs ending in paddles of fused digits. By incorporating his epithets for dexterity, Stratton was able to separate the digits and refine the overall appearance of the forms. All the while, Ashbourne emphasized the need for an unconventional approach.

"Consider the thermodynamics of what most automata do," said Ashbourne during one of their frequent discussions. "The mining engines dig ore, the reaping engines harvest wheat, the wood-cutting engines fell timber; yet none of these tasks, no matter how useful we find them to be, can be said to create order. While all their names create order at the thermal level, by converting heat into motion, in the vast majority the resulting work is applied at the visible level to create disorder."

"This is an interesting perspective," said Stratton thoughtfully. "Many long-standing deficits in the capabilities of automata become intelligible in this light: the fact that automata are unable to stack crates more neatly than they find them; their inability to sort pieces of crushed ore based on their composition. You believe that the known classes of industrial names are not powerful enough in thermodynamic terms."

"Precisely!" Ashbourne displayed the excitement of a tutor finding an unexpectedly apt pupil. "This is another feature that distinguishes your class of dexterous names. By enabling an automation to perform skilled labor, your names not only create order at the thermal level, they use it to create order at the visible level as well."

"I see a commonality with Milburn's discoveries," said Stratton. Milburn had developed the household automata able to return objects to their proper places. "His work likewise involves the creation of order at the visible level."

"Indeed it does, and this commonality suggests a hypothesis." Ashbourne leaned forward. "Suppose we were able to factor out an epithet common to the names developed by you and Milburn: an epithet expressing the creation of two levels of order. Further suppose that we discover a euonym for the human species, and were able to incorporate this epithet into the name. What do you imagine would be generated by impressing the name? And if you say 'twins' I shall clout you on the head."

Stratton laughed. "I dare say I understand you better than that. You are suggesting that if an epithet is capable of inducing two levels of thermodynamic order in the inorganic domain, it might create two generations in the organic domain. Such a name might create males whose spermatozoa would contain preformed foetuses. Those males would be fertile, although any sons they produced would again be sterile."

His instructor clapped his hands together. "Precisely: order that begets order! An interesting speculation, wouldn't you agree? It would halve the number of medical interventions required for our race to sustain itself."

"And what about inducing the formation of more than two generations of foetuses? What kind of capabilities would an automaton have to possess, for its name to contain such an epithet?"

"The science of thermodynamics has not progressed enough to answer that question, I'm afraid. What would constitute a still higher level of order in the inorganic domain? Automata working cooperatively, perhaps? We do not yet know, but perhaps in time we will."

Stratton gave voice to a question that had posed itself to him some time ago. "Dr. Ashbourne, when I was initiated into our group, Lord Fieldhurst spoke of the possibility that species are born in the wake of catastrophic events. Is it possible that entire species were created by use of nomenclature?"

"Ah, now we tread in the realm of theology. A new species requires progenitors containing vast numbers of descendants nested within their reproductive organs; such forms embody the highest degree of order imaginable. Can a purely physical process create such vast amounts of order? No naturalist has suggested a mechanism by which this could occur. On the other hand, while we do know that a lexical process can create order, the creation of an entire new species would require a name of incalculable power. Such mastery of nomenclature could very well require the capabilities of God; perhaps it is even part of the definition.

"This is a question, Stratton, to which we may never know the answer, but we cannot allow that to affect our current actions. Whether or not a name was responsible for the creation of our species, I believe a name is the best chance for its continuation."

"Agreed," said Stratton. After a pause, he added, "I must confess, much of the time when I am working, I occupy myself solely with the details of permutation and combination, and lose sight of the sheer magnitude of our endeavor. It is sobering to think of what we will have achieved if we are successful."

"I can think of little else," replied Ashbourne.

Seated at his desk in the manufactory, Stratton squinted to read the pamphlet he'd been given on the street. The text was crudely printed, the letters blurred.

"Shall Men be the Masters of NAMES, or shall Names be the masters of MEN? For too long the Capitalists have hoarded Names within their coffers, guarded by Patent and Lock and Key, amassing fortunes by mere possession of LETTERS, while the Common Man must labour for every shilling. They will wring the ALPHABET until they have extracted every last penny from it, and only then discard it for us to use. How long will We allow this to continue?"

Stratton scanned the entire pamphlet, but found nothing new in it. For the past two months he'd been reading them, and encountered only the usual anarchist rants; there was as yet no evidence for Lord Fieldhurst's theory that the sculptors would use them to target Stratton's work. His public demonstration of the dexterous automata was scheduled for next week, and by now Willoughby had largely missed his opportunity to generate public opposition. In fact, it occurred to Stratton that he might distribute pamphlets himself to generate public support. He could explain his goal of bringing the advantages of automata to everyone, and his intention to keep close control over his names' patents, granting licenses only to manufacturers who would use them conscientiously. He could even have a slogan: "Autonomy through Automata," perhaps?

There was a knock at his office door. Stratton tossed the pamphlet into his wastebasket. "Yes?"

A man entered, somberly dressed, and with a long beard. "Mr. Stratton?" he asked. "Please allow me to introduce myself: My name is Benjamin Roth. I am a kabbalist."

Stratton was momentarily speechless. Typically such mystics were offended by the modern view of nomenclature as a science, considering it a secularization of a sacred ritual. He never expected one to visit the manufactory. "A pleasure to meet you. How may I be of assistance?"

"I've heard that you have achieved a great advance in the permutation of letters."

"Why, thank you. I didn't realize it would be of interest to a person like yourself."

Roth smiled awkwardly. "My interest is not in its practical applications. The goal of kabbalists is to better know God. The best means by which to do that is to study the art by which He creates. We meditate upon different names to enter an ecstatic state of consciousness; the more powerful the name, the more closely we approach the Divine."

"I see." Stratton wondered what the kabbalist's reaction would be if he learned about the creation being attempted in the biological nomenclature project. "Please continue."

"Your epithets for dexterity enable a *golem* to sculpt another, thereby reproducing itself. A name capable of creating a being that is, in turn, capable of creation would bring us closer to God than we have ever been before."

"I'm afraid you're mistaken about my work, although you aren't the first to fall under this misapprehension. The ability to manipulate molds does not render an automaton able to reproduce itself. There would be many other skills required."

The kabbalist nodded. "I am well aware of that. I myself, in the course of my studies, have developed an epithet designating certain other skills necessary."

Stratton leaned forward with sudden interest. After casting a body, the next step would be to animate the body with a name. "Your epithet endows an automaton with the ability to write?" His own automaton could grasp a pencil easily enough, but it couldn't inscribe even the simplest mark. "How is it that your automata possess the dexterity required for scrivening, but not that for manipulating molds?"

Roth shook his head modestly. "My epithet does not endow writing ability, or general manual dexterity. It simply enables a *golem* to write out the name that animates it, and nothing else."

"Ah, I see." So it didn't provide an aptitude for learning a category of skills; it granted a single innate skill. Stratton tried to imagine the nomenclatoral contortions needed to make an automaton instinctively write out a particular sequence of letters. "Very interesting, but I imagine it doesn't have broad application, does it?"

Roth gave a pained smile; Stratton realized he had committed a *faux pas*, and the man was trying to meet it with good humor. "That is one way to view it," admitted Roth, "but we have a different perspective. To us the value of this epithet, like any other, lies not in the usefulness it imparts to a *golem*, but in the ecstatic state it allows us to achieve."

"Of course, of course. And your interest in my epithets for dexterity is the same?"

"Yes. I am hoping that you will share your epithets with us."

Stratton had never heard of a kabbalist making such a request before, and clearly Roth did not relish being the first. He paused to consider. "Must a kabbalist reach a certain rank in order to meditate upon the most powerful ones?"

"Yes, very definitely."

"So you restrict the availability of the names."

"Oh no; my apologies for misunderstanding you. The ecstatic state offered by a name is achievable only after one has mastered the necessary meditative techniques, and it's these techniques that are closely guarded. Without the proper training, attempts to use these techniques could result in madness. But the names themselves, even the most powerful ones, have no ecstatic value to a novice; they can animate clay, nothing more."

"Nothing more," agreed Stratton, thinking how truly different their perspectives were. "In that case, I'm afraid I cannot grant you use of my names."

Roth nodded glumly, as if he'd been expecting that answer. "You desire payment of royalties."

Now it was Stratton who had to overlook the other man's faux pas. "Money is not my objective. However, I have specific intentions for my dexterous automata which require that I retain control over the patent. I cannot jeopardize those plans by releasing the names indiscriminately." Granted, he had shared them with the nomenclators working under Lord Fieldhurst, but they were all gentlemen sworn to an even greater secrecy. He was less confident about mystics.

"I can assure you that we would not use your name for anything other than ecstatic practices."

"I apologize; I believe you are sincere, but the risk is too great. The most I can do is remind you that the patent has a limited duration; once it has expired, you'll be free to use the name however you like."

"But that will take years!"

"Surely you appreciate that there are others whose interests must be taken into account."

"What I see is that commercial considerations are posing an obstacle to spiritual awakening. The error was mine in expecting anything different."

"You are hardly being fair," protested Stratton.

"Fair?" Roth made a visible effort to restrain his anger. "You 'nomenclators' steal techniques meant to honor God and use them to aggrandize yourselves. Your entire industry prostitutes the techniques of yezirah. You are in no position to speak of fairness."

"Now see here—"

"Thank you for speaking with me." With that, Roth took his leave.

Stratton sighed.

Peering through the eyepiece of the microscope, Stratton turned the manipulator's adjustment wheel until the needle pressed against the side of the ovum. There was a sudden enfolding, like the retraction of a mollusk's foot when prodded, transforming the sphere into a tiny foetus. Stratton withdrew the needle from the slide, unclamped it from the framework, and inserted a new one. Next he transferred the slide into the warmth of the incubator and placed another slide, bearing an untouched human ovum, beneath the microscope. Once again he leaned toward the microscope to repeat the process of impression.

Recently, the nomenclators had developed a name capable of inducing a form indistinguishable from a human foetus. The forms did not quicken, however: They remained immobile and unresponsive to stimuli. The consensus was that the name did not accurately describe the non-physical traits of a human being. Accordingly, Stratton and his colleagues had been diligently compiling descriptions of human uniqueness, trying to distill a set of epithets both expressive enough to denote these qualities, and succinct enough to be integrated with the physical epithets into a seventy-two-lettered name.

Stratton transferred the final slide to the incubator and made the appropriate notations in the logbook. At the moment he had no more names drawn in needle form, and it would be a day before the new foetuses were mature enough to test for quickening. He decided to pass the rest of the evening in the drawing room upstairs.

Upon entering the walnut paneled room, he found Fieldhurst and Ashbourne seated in its leather chairs, smoking cigars and sipping brandy. "Ah, Stratton," said Ashbourne. "Do join us."

"I believe I will," said Stratton, heading for the liquor cabinet. He poured himself some brandy from a crystal decanter and seated himself with the others.

"Just up from the laboratory, Stratton?" inquired Fieldhurst.

Stratton nodded. "A few minutes ago I made impressions with my most recent set of names. I feel that my latest permutations are leading in the right direction."

"You are not alone in feeling optimistic; Dr. Ashbourne and I were just discussing how much the outlook has improved since this endeavor began. It now appears that we will have a euonym comfortably in advance of the final generation." Fieldhurst puffed on his cigar and leaned back in his chair until his head rested against the antimacassar. "This disaster may ultimately turn out to be a boon."

"A boon? How so?"

"Why, once we have human reproduction under our control, we will have a means of preventing the poor from having such large families as so many of them persist in having right now."

Stratton was startled, but tried not to show it. "I had not considered that," he said carefully.

Ashbourne also seemed mildly surprised. "I wasn't aware that you intended such a policy."

"I considered it premature to mention it earlier," said Fieldhurst. "Counting one's chickens before they're hatched, as they say."

"Of course."

"You must agree that the potential is enormous. By exercising some judgment when choosing who may bear children or not, our government could preserve the nation's racial stock."

"Is our racial stock under some threat?" asked Stratton.

"Perhaps you have not noticed that the lower classes are reproducing at a rate exceeding that of the nobility and gentry. While commoners are not without virtues, they are lacking in refinement and intellect. These forms of mental impoverishment beget the same: A woman born into low circumstances cannot help but gestate a child destined for the same. Consequent to the great fecundity of the lower classes, our nation would eventually drown in coarse dullards."

"So name impressing will be withheld from the lower classes?"

"Not entirely, and certainly not initially: When the truth about declining fertility is known, it would be an invitation to riot if the lower classes were denied access to name impressing. And of course, the lower classes do have their role to play in our society, as long as their numbers are kept in check. I envision that the policy will go in effect only after some years have passed, by which time people will have grown accustomed to name impression as the method of fertilization. At that point, perhaps in conjunction with the census process, we can impose limits on the number of children a given couple would be permitted to have. The government would regulate the growth and composition of the population thereafter."

"Is this the most appropriate use of such a name?" asked Ashbourne. "Our goal was the survival of the species, not the implementation of partisan politics."

"On the contrary, this is purely scientific. Just as it's our duty to ensure the species survives, it's also our duty to guarantee its health by keeping a proper balance in its population. Politics doesn't enter into it; were the situation reversed and there existed a paucity of laborers, the opposite policy would be called for."

Stratton ventured a suggestion. "I wonder if improvement in conditions for the poor might eventually cause them to gestate more refined children?"

"You are thinking about changes brought about by your cheap engines, aren't you?" asked Fieldhurst with a smile, and Stratton nodded. "Your intended reforms and mine may reinforce each other. Moderating the numbers of the lower classes should make it easier for them to raise their living conditions. However, do not expect that a mere increase in economic comfort will improve the mentality of the lower classes."

"But why not?"

"You forget the self-perpetuating nature of culture," said Fieldhurst. "We have seen that all megafoetuses are identical, yet no one can deny the differences between the populaces of nations, in both physical appearance and temperament. This can only be the result of the maternal influence: The mother's womb is a vessel in which the social environment is incarnated. For example, a woman who has lived her life among Prussians naturally gives birth to a child with Prussian traits; in this manner the national character of that populace has sustained itself for centuries, despite many changes in fortune. It would be unrealistic to think the poor are any different."

"As a zoologist, you are undoubtedly wiser in these matters than we," said Ashbourne, silencing Stratton with a glance. "We will defer to your judgment."

For the remainder of the evening the conversation turned to other topics, and Stratton did his best to conceal his discomfort and maintain a facade of bonhomie. Finally, after Fieldhurst had retired for the evening, Stratton and Ashbourne descended to the laboratory to confer.

"What manner of man have we agreed to help?" exclaimed Stratton as soon as the door was closed. "One who would breed people like livestock?"

"Perhaps we should not be so shocked," said Ashbourne with a sigh. He seated himself upon one of the laboratory stools. "Our group's goal has been to duplicate for humans a procedure that was intended only for animals."

"But not at the expense of individual liberty! I cannot be a party to this."

"Do not be hasty. What would be accomplished by your resigning from the group? To the extent that your efforts contribute to our group's endeavor, your resignation would serve only to endanger the future of the human species. Conversely, if the group attains its goal without your assistance, Lord Fieldhurst's policies will be implemented anyway."

Stratton tried to regain his composure. Ashbourne was right; he could see that. After a moment, he said, "So what course of action should we take? Are there others whom we could contact, Members of Parliament who would oppose the policy that Lord Fieldhurst proposes?"

"I expect that most of the nobility and gentry would share Lord Fieldhurst's opinion on this matter." Ashbourne rested his forehead on the fingertips of one hand, suddenly looking very old. "I should have anticipated this. My error was in viewing humanity purely as a single species. Having seen England and France working toward a common goal, I forgot that nations are not the only factions that oppose one another."

"What if we surreptitiously distributed the name to the laboring classes? They could draw their own needles and impress the name themselves, in secret."

"They could, but the name impression is a delicate procedure best performed in a laboratory. I'm dubious that the operation could be carried out on the scale necessary without attracting governmental attention, and then falling under its control."

"Is there an alternative?"

There was silence for a long moment while they considered. Then Ashbourne said, "Do you recall our speculation about a name that would induce two generations of foetuses?"

"Certainly."

"Suppose we develop such a name but do not reveal this property when we present it to Lord Fieldhurst."

"That's a wily suggestion," said Stratton, surprised. "All the children born of such a name would be fertile, so they would be able to reproduce without governmental restriction."

Ashbourne nodded. "In the period before population control measures go into effect, such a name might be very widely distributed."

"But what of the following generation? Sterility would recur, and the laboring classes would again be dependent upon the government to reproduce."

"True," said Ashbourne, "it would be a short-lived victory. Perhaps the only permanent solution would be a more liberal Parliament, but it is beyond my expertise to suggest how we might bring that about."

Again Stratton thought about the changes that cheap engines might bring; if the situation of the working classes was improved in the manner he hoped, that might demonstrate to the nobility that poverty was not innate. But even if the most favorable sequence of events was obtained, it would require years to sway Parliament. "What if we could induce multiple generations with the initial name impression? A longer period before sterility recurs would increase the chances that more liberal social policies would take hold."

"You're indulging a fancy," replied Ashbourne. "The technical difficulty of inducing multiple generations is such that I'd sooner wager on our successfully sprouting wings and taking flight. Inducing two generations would be ambitious enough."

The two men discussed strategies late into the night. If they were to conceal the true name of any name they presented to Lord Fieldhurst, they would have to forge a lengthy trail of research results. Even without the additional burden of secrecy, they would be engaged in an unequal race, pursuing a highly sophisticated name while the other nomenclators sought a comparatively straightforward euonym. To make the odds less unfavorable, Ashbourne and Stratton would need to recruit others to their cause; with such assistance, it might even be possible to subtly impede the research of others.

"Who in the group do you think shares our political views?" asked Ashbourne.

"I feel confident that Milburn does. I'm not so certain about any of the others."

"Take no chances. We must employ even more caution when approaching prospective members than Lord Fieldhurst did when establishing this group originally."

"Agreed," said Stratton. Then he shook his head in disbelief. "Here we are forming a secret organization nested within a secret organization. If only foetuses were so easily induced."

It was the evening of the following day, the sun was setting, and Stratton was strolling across Westminster Bridge as the last remaining costermongers were wheeling their barrows of fruit away. He had just had supper at a club he favored, and was walking back to Coade Manufactory. The previous evening at Darrington Hall had disquieted him, and he had returned to London earlier today to minimize his interaction with Lord Fieldhurst until he was certain his face would not betray his true feelings.

He thought back to the conversation where he and Ashbourne

had first entertained the conjecture of factoring out an epithet for creating two levels of order. At the time he had made some efforts to find such an epithet, but they were casual attempts given the superfluous nature of the goal, and they hadn't borne fruit. Now their gauge of achievement had been revised upward: Their previous goal was inadequate, two generations seemed the minimum acceptable, and any additional ones would be invaluable.

He again pondered the thermodynamic behavior induced by his dexterous names: Order at the thermal level animated the automata, allowing them to create order at the visible level. Order begetting order. Ashbourne had suggested that the next level of order might be automata working together in a coordinated fashion. Was that possible? They would have to communicate in order to work together effectively, but automata were intrinsically mute. What other means were there by which automata could exchange in complex behavior?

He suddenly realized he had reached Coade Manufactory. By now it was dark, but he knew the way to his office well enough. Stratton unlocked the building's front door and proceeded through the gallery and past the business offices.

As he reached the hallway fronting the nomenclators' offices, he saw light emanating from the frosted glass window of his office door. Surely he hadn't left the gas on? He unlocked his door to enter, and was shocked by what he saw.

A man lay facedown on the floor in front of the desk, hands tied behind his back. Stratton immediately approached to check on the man. It was Benjamin Roth, the kabbalist, and he was dead. Stratton realized several of the man's fingers were broken; he'd been tortured before he was killed.

Pale and trembling, Stratton rose to his feet, and saw that his office was in utter disarray. The shelves of his bookcases were bare; his books lay strewn face-down across the oak floor. His desk had been swept clear; next to it was a stack of its brass-handled draw-

ers, emptied and overturned. A trail of stray papers led to the open
door to his studio; in a daze, Stratton stepped forward to see what
had been done there.

His dexterous automaton had been destroyed; the lower half
of it lay on the floor, the rest of it scattered as plaster fragments
and dust. On the work-table, the clay models of the hands were
pounded flat, and his sketches of their design torn from the walls.
The tubs for mixing plaster were overflowing with the papers from
his office. Stratton took a closer look, and saw that they had been
doused with lamp oil.

He heard a sound behind him and turned back to face the
office. The front door to the office swung closed and a broad-
shouldered man stepped out from behind it; he'd been standing
there ever since Stratton had entered. "Good of you to come," the
man said. He scrutinized Stratton with the predatory gaze of a
raptor, an assassin.

Stratton bolted out of the back door of the studio and down the
rear hallway. He could hear the man give chase.

He fled through the darkened building, crossing workrooms
filled with coke and iron bars, crucibles and molds, all illuminated
by the moonlight entering through skylights overhead; he had
entered the metalworks portion of the factory. In the next room he
paused for breath, and realized how loudly his footsteps had been
echoing; skulking would offer a better chance at escape than running. He distantly heard his pursuer's footsteps stop; the assassin
had likewise opted for stealth.

Stratton looked around for a promising hiding place. All
around him were cast-iron automata in various stages of near-
completion; he was in the finishing room, where the runners left
over from casting were sawed off and the surfaces chased. There
was no place to hide, and he was about to move on when he noticed
what looked like a bundle of rifles mounted on legs. He looked
more closely, and recognized it as a military engine.

These automata were built for the War Office: gun carriages

that aimed their own cannon, and rapid-fire rifles, like this one, that cranked their own barrel-clusters. Nasty things, but they'd proven invaluable in the Crimea; their inventor had been granted a peerage. Stratton didn't know any names to animate the weapon— they were military secrets—but only the body on which the rifle was mounted was automatous; the rifle's firing mechanism was strictly mechanical. If he could point the body in the right direction, he might be able to fire the rifle manually.

He cursed himself for his stupidity. There was no ammunition here. He stole into the next room.

It was the packing room, filled with pine crates and loose straw. Staying low between crates, he moved to the far wall. Through the windows he saw the courtyard behind the factory, where finished automata were carted away. He couldn't get out that way; the courtyard gates were locked at night. His only exit was through the factory's front door, but he risked encountering the assassin if he headed back the way he'd come. He needed to cross over to the ceramicworks and double back through that side of the factory.

From the front of the packing room came the sound of footsteps. Stratton ducked behind a row of crates, and then saw a side door only a few feet away. As stealthily as he could, he opened the door, entered, and closed the door behind him. Had his pursuer heard him? He peered through a small grille set in the door; he couldn't see the man, but felt he'd gone unnoticed. The assassin was probably searching the packing room.

Stratton turned around, and immediately realized his mistake. The door to the ceramicworks was in the opposite wall. He had entered a storeroom, filled with ranks of finished automata, but with no other exits. There was no way to lock the door. He had cornered himself.

Was there anything in the room he could use as a weapon? The menagerie of automata included some squat mining engines, whose forelimbs terminated in enormous pickaxes, but the ax-heads were bolted to their limbs. There was no way he could remove one.

Stratton could hear the assassin opening side doors and searching other storerooms. Then he noticed an automaton standing off to the side: a porter used for moving the inventory about. It was anthropomorphic in form, the only automaton in the room of that type. An idea came to him.

Stratton checked the back of the porter's head. Porters' names had entered the public domain long ago, so there were no locks protecting its name slot; a tab of parchment protruded from the horizontal slot in the iron. He reached into his coat pocket for the notebook and pencil he always carried and tore out a small portion of a blank leaf. In the darkness he quickly wrote seventy-two letters in a familiar combination, and then folded the paper into a tight square.

To the porter, he whispered, "Go stand as close to the door as you can." The cast iron figure stepped forward and headed for the door. Its gait was very smooth, but not rapid, and the assassin would reach this storeroom any moment now. "Faster," hissed Stratton, and the porter obeyed.

Just as it reached the door, Stratton saw through the grille that his pursuer had arrived on the other side. "Get out of the way," barked the man.

Ever obedient, the automaton shifted to take a step back when Stratton yanked out its name. The assassin began pushing against the door, but Stratton was able to insert the new name, cramming the square of paper into the slot as deeply as he could.

The porter resumed walking forward, this time with a fast, stiff gait: his childhood doll, now life-size. It immediately ran into the door and, unperturbed, kept it shut with the force of its marching, its iron hands leaving fresh dents in the door's oaken surface with every swing of its arms, its rubber-shod feet chafing heavily against the brick floor. Stratton retreated to the back of the storeroom.

"Stop," the assassin ordered. "Stop walking, you! Stop!"

The automaton continued marching, oblivious to all commands. The man pushed on the door, but to no avail. He then tried slamming into it with his shoulder, each impact causing the automaton to slide back slightly, but its rapid strides brought it forward again before the man could squeeze inside. There was a brief pause, and then something poked through the grille in the door; the man was prying it off with a crowbar. The grille abruptly popped free, leaving an open window. The man stretched his arm through and reached around to the back of the automaton's head, his fingers searching for the name each time its head bobbed forward, but there was nothing for them to grasp; the paper was wedged too deeply in the slot.

The arm withdrew. The assassin's face appeared in the window. "Fancy yourself clever, don't you?" he called out. Then he disappeared.

Stratton relaxed slightly. Had the man given up? A minute passed, and Stratton began to think about his next move. He could wait here until the factory opened; there would be too many people about for the assassin to remain.

Suddenly the man's arm came through the window again, this time carrying a jar of fluid. He poured it over the automaton's head, the liquid splattering and dripping down its back. The man's arm withdrew, and then Stratton heard the sound of a match being struck and then flaring alight. The man's arm reappeared bearing the match, and touched it to the automaton.

The room was flooded with light as the automaton's head and upper back burst into flames. The man had doused it with lamp oil. Stratton squinted at the spectacle: Light and shadow danced across the floor and walls, transforming the storeroom into the site of some druidic ceremony. The heat caused the automaton to hasten its vague assault on the door, like a salamandrine priest dancing with increasing frenzy, until it abruptly froze: Its name had caught fire, and the letters were being consumed.

The flames gradually died out, and to Stratton's newly light-adapted eyes the room seemed almost completely black. More by sound than by sight, he realized the man was pushing at the door again, this time forcing the automaton back enough for him to gain entrance.

"Enough of that, then."

Stratton tried to run past him, but the assassin easily grabbed him and knocked him down with a clout to the head.

His senses returned almost immediately, but by then the assassin had him face down on the floor, one knee pressed into his back. The man tore the health amulet from Stratton's wrist and then tied his hands together behind his back, drawing the rope tightly enough that the hemp fibers scraped the skin of his wrists.

"What kind of man are you, to do things like this?" Stratton gasped, his cheek flattened against the brick floor.

The assassin chuckled. "Men are no different from your automata; slip a bloke a piece of paper with the proper figures on it, and he'll do your bidding." The room grew light as the man lit an oil lamp.

"What if I paid you more to leave me alone?"

"Can't do it. Have to think about my reputation, haven't I? Now let's get to business." He grasped the smallest finger of Stratton's left hand and abruptly broke it.

The pain was shocking, so intense that for a moment Stratton was insensible to all else. He was distantly aware that he had cried out. Then he heard the man speaking again. "Answer my questions straight now. Do you keep copies of your work at home?"

"Yes." He could only get a few words out at a time. "At my desk. In the study."

"No other copies hidden anywhere? Under the floor, perhaps?"

"No."

"Your friend upstairs didn't have copies. But perhaps someone else does?"

He couldn't direct the man to Darrington Hall. "No one."

The man pulled the notebook out of Stratton's coat pocket. Stratton could hear him leisurely flipping through the pages. "Didn't post any letters? Corresponding with colleagues, that sort of thing?"

"Nothing that anyone could use to reconstruct my work."

"You're lying to me." The man grasped Stratton's ring finger.

"No! It's the truth!" He couldn't keep the hysteria from his voice.

Then Stratton heard a sharp thud, and the pressure in his back eased. Cautiously, he raised his head and looked around. His assailant lay unconscious on the floor next to him. Standing next to him was Davies, holding a leather blackjack.

Davies pocketed his weapon and crouched to unknot the rope that bound Stratton. "Are you badly hurt, sir?"

"He's broken one of my fingers. Davies, how did you—?"

"Lord Fieldhurst sent me the moment he learned whom Willoughby had contacted."

"Thank God you arrived when you did." Stratton saw the irony of the situation—his rescue ordered by the very man he was plotting against—but he was too grateful to care.

Davies helped Stratton to his feet and handed him his notebook. Then he used the rope to tie up the assassin. "I went to your office first. Who's the fellow there?"

"His name is—was Benjamin Roth." Stratton managed to recount his previous meeting with the kabbalist. "I don't know what he was doing there."

"Many religious types have a bit of the fanatic in them," said Davies, checking the assassin's bonds. "As you wouldn't give him your work, he likely felt justified in taking it himself. He came to your office to look for it, and had the bad luck to be there when this fellow arrived."

Stratton felt a flood of remorse. "I should have given Roth what he asked."

"You couldn't have known."

"It's an outrageous injustice that he was the one to die. He'd nothing to do with this affair."

"It's always that way, sir. Come on, let's tend to that hand of yours."

Davies bandaged Stratton's finger to a splint, assuring him that the Royal Society would discreetly handle any consequences of the night's events. They gathered the oil-stained papers from Stratton's office into a trunk so that Stratton could sift through them at his leisure, away from the manufactory. By the time they were finished, a carriage had arrived to take Stratton back to Darrington Hall; it had set out at the same time as Davies, who had ridden into London on a racing-engine. Stratton boarded the carriage with the trunk of papers, while Davies stayed behind to deal with the assassin and make arrangements for the kabbalist's body.

Stratton spent the carriage ride sipping from a flask of brandy, trying to steady his nerves. He felt a sense of relief when he arrived back at Darrington Hall; although it held its own variety of threats, Stratton knew he'd be safe from assassination there. By the time he reached his room, his panic had largely been converted into exhaustion, and he slept deeply.

He felt much more composed the next morning, and ready to begin sorting through his trunkful of papers. As he was arranging them into stacks approximating their original organization, Stratton found a notebook he didn't recognize. Its pages contained Hebrew letters arranged in the familiar patterns of nominal integration and factorization, but all the notes were in Hebrew as well. With a renewed pang of guilt, he realized it must have belonged to Roth; the assassin must have found it on his person and tossed it in with Stratton's papers to be burned.

He was about to set it aside, but his curiosity bested him: He'd never seen a kabbalist's notebook before. Much of the terminology was archaic, but he could understand it well enough; among the incantations and sephirotic diagrams, he found the epithet enabling an automaton to write its own name. As he read, Stratton realized that Roth's achievement was more elegant than he'd previously thought.

The epithet didn't describe a specific set of physical actions, but instead the general notion of reflexivity. A name incorporating the epithet became an autonym: a self-designating name. The notes indicated that such a name would express its lexical nature through whatever means the body allowed. The animated body wouldn't even need hands to write out its name; if the epithet were incorporated properly, a porcelain horse could likely accomplish the task by dragging a hoof in the dirt.

Combined with one of Stratton's epithets for dexterity, Roth's epithet would indeed let an automaton do most of what was needed to reproduce. An automaton could cast a body identical to its own, write out its own name, and insert it to animate the body. It couldn't train the new one in sculpture, though, since automata couldn't speak. An automaton that could truly reproduce itself without human assistance remained out of reach, but coming this close would undoubtedly have delighted the kabbalists.

It seemed unfair that automata were so much easier to reproduce than humans. It was as if the problem of reproducing automata need be solved only once, while that of reproducing humans was a Sisyphean task, with every additional generation increasing the complexity of the name required.

And abruptly Stratton realized that he didn't need a name that redoubled physical complexity, but one than enabled lexical duplication.

The solution was to impress the ovum with an autonym, and thus induce a foetus that bore its own name.

The name would have two versions, as originally proposed: one used to induce male foetuses, another for female foetuses. The women conceived this way would be fertile as always. The men conceived this way would also be fertile, but not in the typical manner: Their spermatozoa would not contain preformed foetuses, but would instead bear either of two names on their surfaces, the self-expression of the names originally borne by the glass needles. And when such a spermatozoon reached an ovum, the name would induce the creation of a new foetus. The species would be able to reproduce itself without medical intervention, because it would carry the name within itself.

He and Dr. Ashbourne had assumed that creating animals capable of reproducing meant giving them preformed foetuses, because that was the method employed by nature. As a result they had overlooked another possibility: that if a creature could be expressed in a name, reproducing that creature was equivalent to transcribing the name. An organism could contain, instead of a tiny analogue of its body, a lexical representation instead.

Humanity would become a vehicle for the name as well as a product of it. Each generation would be both content and vessel, an echo in a self-sustaining reverberation.

Stratton envisioned a day when the human species could survive as long as its own behavior allowed, when it could stand or fall based purely on its own actions, and not simply vanish once some predetermined life span had elapsed. Other species might bloom and wither like flowers over seasons of geologic time, but humans would endure for as long as they determined.

Nor would any group of people control the fecundity of another; in the procreative domain, at least, liberty would be restored to the individual. This was not the application Roth had intended for his epithet, but Stratton hoped the kabbalist would consider it worthwhile. By the time the autonym's true power became apparent, an entire generation consisting of millions of people worldwide would have been born of the name, and there would be no way any government could control their reproduction. Lord Fieldhurst—or his successors—would be outraged, and there would eventually be a price to be paid, but Stratton found he could accept that.

He hastened to his desk, where he opened his own notebook and Roth's side by side. On a blank page, he began writing down ideas on how Roth's epithet might be incorporated into a human euonym. Already in his mind Stratton was transposing the letters, searching for a permutation that denoted both the human body and itself, an ontogenic encoding for the species.

Joe Haldeman has been writing poetry since childhood (his first publication was in the *Washington Post* at the age of nine), but his first science fiction story didn't come out until 1969. His novel *The Forever War*, based on his experiences in Vietnam, won the Hugo and Nebula Awards for best novel of 1975. His most recent novel, *Forever Peace*, won the Hugo, Nebula, and John W. Campbell Awards for best science fiction novel of 1997.

   "Endangered Species" is the perfect encapsulation of the concerns he's exhibited throughout his writing career about war and its effect on the human race.

ENDANGERED SPECIES

JOE HALDEMAN

Men stop war to make gods
sometimes. Peace gods, who would make
Earth a haven. A place for men to
think and love and play. No war
to cloud their minds and hearts. Stop,
somehow, men from being men.

Gods make war to stop men
from becoming gods.
Without the beat of drums to stop
our ears, what heaven we could make
of Earth! The anchor that is war
left behind? Somehow free to

stop war? Gods make men to
be somewhat like them. So men
express their godliness in war.
To take life: this is what gods
do. Not the womanly urge to make
life. Nor the simple sense to stop.

War-men make gods. To stop
those gods from raging, we have to
find the heart and head to make
new gods, who don't take men
in human sacrifice. New gods,
who find disgust in war.

Gods stop, to make men war
for their amusement. We can stop
their fun. We can make new gods
in human guise. No need to
call to heaven. Just take plain men
and show to them the heaven they could make!

To stop God's wars! Men make
their own destiny. We don't need war
to prove to anyone that we are men.
But even that is not enough. To stop
war, we have to become more. To
stop war, we have to become gods.

To stop war, make men gods.

ABOUT THE EDITOR

ELLEN DATLOW is fiction editor of SCIFI.COM, the website of the Sci Fi Channel. She was fiction editor of *Omni* magazine and *Omni* Internet for over sixteen years, and edited *Event Horizon: Science Fiction•Fantasy•Horror*, a webzine. She has edited numerous anthologies and has won the World Fantasy Award five times. Datlow's most recent anthologies are *Lethal Kisses; Black Heart, Ivory Bones* (the sixth in the adult fairy tale anthology series she co-edits with Terri Windling); *A Wolf at the Door*, a young adult fairy tale anthology (with Windling); and *The Year's Best Fantasy and Horror: Twelfth Annual Collection* (also with Windling).